"It may shock you, Eloise, but your misery is not actually my goal. What I want is my child."

"Why?"

"Is it not the most natural thing in the world to want your child?"

She stared at him. "You and I both know that it is not."

"Eloise..."

"No. I know that I don't have a lot of power here, but I have had so little choice in my life, Vincenzo. Surely you must want more than to hide me away in this place. Surely I deserve more than that."

"What is it you want?" he asked.

It came to her in a moment, because the truth was, it would be...a wonderful thing for her child to know its father.

It was only her fears of that palace, of that life, that truly held her back.

"Make me a beautiful Christmas there at the palace. Show me that there's something there other than what I remember. Other than that dreadful...awful empty feeling that I always get in the palace. Show me that there can be more."

Pregnant Princesses

When passionate nights lead to unexpected heirs!

Vincenzo, Rafael, Zeus and Jahangir are princes bound for life by their ruthless quests to rebel against their tyrannical fathers. But their plans will be outrageously upended when forbidden nights with forbidden princesses leave them facing the most shocking of consequences...and convenient marriages that spark much more than scandal!

Read Vincenzo and Eloise's story in
Crowned for His Christmas Baby by Maisey Yates

Available now!

Read Rafael and Amalia's story in
Pregnant by the Wrong Prince
by Jackie Ashenden

Read Zeus and Nina's story in
The Scandal That Made Her His Queen
by Caitlin Crews

And look out for Jag and Rita's story
by Marcella Bell

Coming soon!

Maisey Yates

CROWNED FOR HIS CHRISTMAS BABY

HARLEQUIN

PRESENTS

HARLEQUIN®
PRESENTS®

Recycling programs
for this product may
not exist in your area.

ISBN-13: 978-1-335-56914-1

Crowned for His Christmas Baby

Copyright © 2021 by Maisey Yates

All rights reserved. No part of this book may be used or reproduced in
any manner whatsoever without written permission except in the case of
brief quotations embodied in critical articles and reviews.

This is a work of fiction. Names, characters, places and incidents
are either the product of the author's imagination or are used fictitiously.
Any resemblance to actual persons, living or dead, businesses,
companies, events or locales is entirely coincidental.

This edition published by arrangement with Harlequin Books S.A.

For questions and comments about the quality of this book,
please contact us at CustomerService@Harlequin.com.

Harlequin Enterprises ULC
22 Adelaide St. West, 40th Floor
Toronto, Ontario M5H 4E3, Canada
www.Harlequin.com

Printed in U.S.A.

Maisey Yates is a *New York Times* bestselling author of over one hundred romance novels. Whether she's writing strong, hardworking cowboys, dissolute princes or multigenerational family stories, she loves getting lost in fictional worlds. An avid knitter with a dangerous yarn addiction and an aversion to housework, Maisey lives with her husband and three kids in rural Oregon. Check out her website, maiseyyates.com.

Books by Maisey Yates

Harlequin Presents

Crowned for My Royal Baby

Once Upon a Seduction...

The Prince's Captive Virgin
The Prince's Stolen Virgin
The Italian's Pregnant Prisoner
The Queen's Baby Scandal
Crowning His Convenient Princess

The Heirs of Liri

His Majesty's Forbidden Temptation
A Bride for the Lost King

Visit the Author Profile page
at Harlequin.com for more titles.

To Megan, Jackie and Marcella—what's better than alpha heroes? Alpha heroes that you get to write with your friends.

PROLOGUE

THEY WERE THE most notorious, shocking, dissolute group of rakes to ever grace the hallowed halls of Oxford. And given the school's illustrious and rather lengthy history, that was truly saying something.

Of course neither Prince Vincenzo Moretti, heir to the throne of Arista, nor his friends, Sheikh Jahangir Hassan Umar Al Hayat, Prince Zeus and Rafael Navarro, bastard child of a king of Santa Castelia, would ever say it themselves.

There was no need.

Their reputations preceded them.

With great pomp and circumstance. From the mouths of men who envied them, wishing only to find themselves ensconced in the afterglow of their power, as if it might give them even the tiniest bit of access to the women that they enjoyed, or the excess that they acquired with the snap of a finger.

And of course, from the women.

The women who declared themselves ruined for all other men, who sighed wistfully about the pleasure they had experienced at their royal hands and would never experience again.

For surely, no man alive could match the prowess of these ruthless royals.

And they could not. Vincenzo himself had no qualms about basking in the benefits of such a reputation.

Of course, his father believed that he would put on the public face required of him for all the world to see. All the while, seeking his own pleasure and lining his own pockets, as their people lived in spartan circumstances.

Vincenzo had begun to combat that with the establishment of many charities, using covert networks he had created outside of his country to bring money in that his father could not touch. Money that appeared to be foreign aid that he would keep his hands off in the name of keeping relations strong between other nations.

But that was not Vincenzo's only plan. No.

He was playing a long game. He could not move, not now. His mother's health—mentally and physically—was fragile. Especially after the scandal three years ago that had rocked Arista. After...

Eloise.

He refused to dwell on her.

He would not.

The destruction of the monarchy would end his mother. And he could not bear that. He would protect his mother. No matter what.

His mother had loved the palace once—and Arista. And the one thing she enjoyed still in life was her role as Queen. He could not let her see what he would do to the royal family. The royal line.

For he would not produce an heir. Never. He refused. He would not carry on the royal line of Arista. He would allow his country to change hands. To go into the hands of the people. And he would make sure that his father knew this before his death. This legacy... It was the only thing his father cared for.

And Vincenzo would see it destroyed.

Yes, his reputation as a notorious, shocking, dissolute rake was truly one that would make even the hardest of harlots clutch their pearls. But if they knew what he really was, if they knew what he truly intended to do... They would expire from the shock.

"A toast," he said, looking around the room that served as their clubhouse, where they conducted their meetings—all of them already earning their own money hand over fist, carving their own place in the world apart from the legacies of their dubious fathers. "To being unexpected."

"It could be argued," Rafael said, "that your rebellion might be seen as deeply expected."

"It will never be expected by our fathers. Who are far too prideful to think that anyone could surprise them in the least. But I have no trouble playing a long game."

"No indeed," Zeus said, looking down into his glass of scotch. "But I think, my friend, that you will find I am not a patient man. I prefer the game short. Hard and brutal."

"I'm all for brutality. But I find brutality is much more effective when meted out strategically."

"I didn't say I wasn't strategic," Zeus said, grinning broadly. "I said I wasn't patient." He lifted a shoulder. "Brutality now. Brutality later. Brutality all around." He waved a laconic hand and settled more deeply into his resolute lounging position.

"I admire your thinking," Jag said, one leg thrown out in front of him, his arm slung over the back of the couch. He elevated casual disdain to high art.

"For my part, I intend to let my father's kingdom…" Vincenzo swirled the glass and watched the amber liquid spin, an aromatic tornado. He lifted the scotch to his lips. "I will not produce an heir. Ever."

"How nice for me that it is not expected," Rafael said. "As a bastard, it is my younger legitimate brother who will inherit control of the kingdom, and the concern of carrying on the line is his. Not mine."

"My father cares so greatly for the reputation of our country," Jag said. "My greatest delight would be to find a woman he would see as desperately unsuitable."

"Only *one* woman?" Zeus asked. "I myself intend to acquire an entire stable of them. But no heir. Never that."

"A toast to that," Vincenzo amended. "To unsuitable women, revenge served hot or cold and to never falling in line."

CHAPTER ONE

ELOISE ST. GEORGE did not feel merry or bright. The snow falling outside felt like an assault, as did the roaring fire, beautiful evergreen garland and cheery Christmas tunes. Yet she was responsible for it all—save the snow. A resolute rebellion against the depression that was threatening to swallow her whole.

Christmas Eve.

She was without a Christmas tree. Since it was still back in Arista. With him.

She had hung garlands, wreaths and other hallmarks of cheer. She had baked cookies and decorated them, had made herself a beautiful dinner. But she wasn't feeling… Any of it.

She had made Christmas a happy time for herself all these years, in defiance of her upbringing. She'd always been happy to celebrate it alone, in her historic stone house in Virginia, which could not be more picturesque.

But alone felt… Alone this year. Truly, deeply.

With all the snow piled outside, she'd managed to get Skerret, her foundling cat, to finally come inside from the cold.

The little gray creature was curled up by the red brick fireplace in a contented ball, purring.

It should be wonderful.

It wasn't.

She put her hand down on her rounded stomach.

It would have been wonderful. If not for Vincenzo Moretti.

And the fact she was currently carrying the heir he had vowed to never create.

Seven months earlier…

This was the address he had been given, but Prince Vincenzo Moretti could not reconcile the crumbling manor before him with the woman he knew Eloise St. George to be. He remembered her vividly.

She had lived at the palace from the time

she was six years old, and he had found her disruptive. He was four years her senior and at ten he had been deeply serious. He had also suspected that her presence was emblematic of something that was wrong in the palace. He had been correct.

Her mother had come to the palace to be his father's mistress. He didn't advertise that, of course. Not the Upright and Honorable King Giovanni Moretti. He gave her an official job title to conceal her real purpose. But even at ten, Vincenzo knew.

He could see it in the decline in his mother's health.

He had resented Eloise at first. Had seen her as the mascot of his father's perfidy and her mother's sins.

But reluctantly, slowly, over the years she had become his… Friend.

A shock for an arrogant princeling who had never befriended anyone in his life.

Then he'd gone off to university and met Rafael, Zeus and Jag. And when he'd returned home…

Eloise had been a woman. And things had taken a turn.

He'd found her beautiful. Captivating. She'd seemed fragile and still so innocent.

But when she'd… When she had told him she wanted him, he'd turned her away. Out of deference to her youth, her innocence.

Because she had not chosen life in the palace. Had not chosen a life where she was forced to know him and he'd felt that she should… Go and experience life and men she had chosen.

But her true colors had been revealed after. Not innocent. Not his friend.

Not…

It did not matter except in the way she might be useful to him now.

The way that she might enhance his plan.

His father had been involved in one scandal. Only ever one.

Eloise.

She had become the symbol of an old man's folly. A man who could never have resisted the wiles of an eighteen-year-old beauty hell-bent on seduction.

His father's only sin.

While publicly, Vincenzo committed many.

For all the world to see, Vincenzo was a disappointment. A man who glutted himself on every indulgence available, a man who engaged openly in the kinds of behavior his father engaged in privately.

But in secret, it was Vincenzo who was saving Arista, and they would never know it until after his father died.

But he would not save it in the manner his old man wished. For he would not produce an heir. He would let the monarchy burn.

And he would be all the gladder for it.

His father was an old man now. And it was time to begin dismantling his legacy. His facade. For he wished to do it where his father could still see. Exposing his financial malfeasance and his mistreatment of his wife. The beloved Queen of Arista.

His poor mother had been... Disgraced in the end.

His father had told the country she'd fallen into a depression and had blamed a weak spirit.

Not his own actions of course.

His father had damaged his mother's legacy, and Vincenzo would *destroy* the King's.

And it began here. Though he had not expected this ramshackle collection of stones with ivy climbing up the side of it. Nor had he expected the crooked wrought iron gate with honeysuckle wound through the spires.

Eloise St. George he would've expected to live in an ultramodern flat paid for by her latest conquest. Somewhere near clubs and shopping and all the other vices her kind enjoyed. But not this. This place out in the middle of nowhere. Clearly, he had seen that it was near nothing when he had looked it up on the map, but he had expected something grander.

Or that perhaps she had built her own row of shops that had not yet appeared in the mapping program. For he could hardly imagine the girl that he'd known moldering away in the countryside. Least of all in a place like this.

He pushed open the gate, which creaked and caught on a vine that grew out of the cobbled walk.

It was a hazard, this place. He slammed the gate shut, though it did not close all the way, and he strode up the walk, careful not to catch his foot on any of the uneven stones. Nature, it seemed, had taken over this place. There were hedges, large trees wrapped in creeping vines. Most of the garden was shaded, with sun, golden as it was in mid-May, breaking through each time the breeze twisted the leaves.

It was hot. Far too hot for the bespoke suit that he was wearing, but it was not in his nature to yield to the elements. He preferred to force them to bend to him.

Why she had chosen to make her escape here in this rather rural corner of the United States he did not know. It made no earthly sense to him. Which in and of itself was a mystery, because Eloise should be simple. Her mother certainly had been. And as far as he'd been able to tell, Eloise was the same.

Her mother, protected by her title of Personal Assistant had spent lavishly and lorded her position over the household staff.

And Eloise, he had been certain, was driven by much the same things. He might have believed she was different once.

But he'd learned.

Yes. Eloise was no different than her mother. Which was why he was confident that he could enlist her services. Either through blackmail or bribery. It did not matter to him which.

He stood at the front door, blue with a cheerful wreath hung at the center. He could not imagine Eloise taking the time to hang a wreath at the center of her door.

She must have staff to see to such things.

Perhaps that was the piece he was missing.

Perhaps this was where her protector had installed her. Within a close enough proximity for his pleasure, but far enough away perhaps that she would not interact with his wife and children.

Yes. Eloise was exactly the sort of woman who would play mistress to a wealthy married man.

It would suit her. She had the cheekbones for it. Among other things.

He rang the doorbell. And there was no response.

Perhaps she was out.

He took a step off the path and around to the side of the house, checking for signs of life.

It was not a terribly secure property, and if nothing else, perhaps he would let himself in and see what information he could gather about Eloise and her current situation.

When he went around the side of the house, he heard a small sound.

It was… Humming.

Tuneless, rather terrible humming.

He paused and listened. He could not make out what the tune was, as it was just so sporadic and tone-deaf.

But there was something strangely charming about the cheer that seemed injected into the sound. And that was deeply strange as he could not remember being charmed by much of anything, least of all something cheerful. Not in his entire life.

When he rounded the corner, he was shocked by what he saw. The back of the most luscious figure he had seen in… He could not remember how long. The woman was bent over, working on something in the garden, and the trousers that she was wearing conformed to her ass in an extremely pleasing way. She stood, and he saw that the woman had wide hips, a narrow waist, and he was terribly hungry to see the front of her.

His second thought was that he had the wrong house. Because the Eloise he knew had that sort of gaunt, haunted look that her mother had, the hungry look of a woman who cared more to be attractive in photographs than in person. More angles than curves.

This must be the gardener, but if there was a gardener for the house then what had they been doing all this time? The place was wild as far as he could tell. He preferred things manicured and tightly kept. And this… Well, it was not.

The humming suddenly stopped. And the woman jumped, startled as if she sensed that she was being watched, and she turned. Her blue eyes went round, and her mouth dropped open. She was holding a potted plant, with a cheerful red blossom on the top. And then she dropped it, and the pottery shattered on the stones below.

"Vincenzo."

CHAPTER TWO

ELOISE COULD NOT stop the flutter of her foolish, traitorous heart. This was like a dream. Like every shameful dream she prayed wouldn't be there waiting for her at night when she fell asleep, but always was.

For she had never forgotten him.

The man with the dark, compelling eyes, who made her feel things that no other man ever had. Who had awakened a desire inside of her when she was only fifteen years old and had held her in thrall ever since. Even though her seduction attempt had ended in a refusal, all these years later she could understand it in a way an eighteen-year-old hadn't, the memory of the one and only time she had ever been close enough to touch him still lingered in her mind and made her tremble in her sleep.

But that wasn't her worst memory of Vincenzo. Her most painful. No. It had been the way he'd sent her away. The way he'd believed… Everything.

Everything except what she'd told him.

She'd been so certain they'd been friends. That he'd cared for her.

But that final moment between them…

He'd made it clear he'd never really cared for her at all.

Did that stop her body from responding to the steamy visions of him that floated through her subconscious at night?

No. No, it did not.

He occupied her dreams. He occupied her fantasies…

He was currently occupying her garden.

"Eloise," he said.

And she could see that he… He had not known it was her.

She was vaguely embarrassed by that, but only for a moment. Because she was accepting of the shape that her body had taken in the years since she had left the palace. She liked the changes in herself. The changes that had occurred when she could finally control her own life. When she could decide what her priorities were. When she no longer had to live beneath the shadow of her mother and her impossible standards.

Still, it was always vaguely hurtful to realize that you were so different you were not even recognizable.

"Yes," she said. "Quite. But you… You cannot be here by accident. Because this house is not on the way to anything, least of all anything that you would be headed to."

"Indeed it is not," he said, sliding his dark jacket from his broad shoulders and casting it onto a white chair that boasted intricate iron scrollwork, with one careless finger. It seemed a metaphor for his existence here. The very masculine object covering the delicate, feminine one.

He turned his wrist and undid the button on his cuff, rolling his sleeve up and revealing a muscular forearm before doing the same to the right side. She blinked, watching with deep interest. Interest that she tried not to feel. And definitely tried not to convey.

"Why are you here?"

His dark eyes met with hers and her heart slammed against her breastbone. He was still the perfect image of masculine beauty. And she feared that for her he always would be. The way his tanned skin gleamed in the sunlight, that same light catching in his dark eyes and displaying a dangerous fire there. She had always thought his eyes so compelling. They were so dark they were nearly black, and she wanted to get lost in the depths of them.

She had embarrassed herself horribly as a teenager staring at him, or at least, she would've liked to embarrass herself horribly staring at him. But he had never noticed. He had practically acted as if she was invisible. Again, with hindsight, she was grateful for that, and had she not horrifically misstepped he would probably never have noticed her at all.

But she had.

And she felt covered in shame about it even all these years later. That she'd believed she loved him. That she'd believed he loved her.

No. Forgive yourself. Forgive her.

She did try.

She had tried to change her life entirely. Step away from the path her mother had wanted her to be on. To find out who Eloise St. George was all on her own. Not a girl living in the palace and the shadow of her mother's great and terrible beauty. Not a girl who had been taught that the only value she had was in her beauty. That girl who had believed, in spite of all that, she might really find a fairy tale. When she'd left Arista, it had been under a cloud of shame. Every newspaper in the world printing lies about her and touting them as verified truths.

It had hurt her. Profoundly. As had Vincenzo's belief in them. But when she'd gone, when she'd found life outside the palace... Away from her mother, his father and Vincenzo himself...

She'd gained perspective. She'd realized how many things had been built up in that palace that simply weren't real. Her mother's ideals had no bearing on the life she lived out here, in the sunshine, amongst the flowers. The King's gaze didn't follow her here, and while the press might have tried to ensure she had no real peace or opportunity to get work, enough time had passed—and she'd managed to make for herself a good reputation in her field and she'd never struggled to get work.

Reality was rich and deep and warm away from the cold stone of Arista.

It felt like an illusion now.

Parts of it.

One thing she was confident in was that her feelings for Vincenzo had been real. They had not been based in a desire to snare herself a rich protector. They had not been about anything other than the fact that he had captured her from the moment she had first laid eyes on him at six years old. As silly as that was. Of course, back when she had been a child, there had been nothing sexual about it; it was simply that she had found him… Wonderful. There was something about him that reminded her of a knight in shining armor.

He had been kind to her. One of her few experiences of kindness. And in her memory, in spite of how things had ended between them, he was still that mythological figure.

But the way he was looking at her now…

There was nothing heroic about it. And she was quite certain that he had not come to save her.

You don't need to be saved.

"I'm here to take you back with me, Eloise." He did not look away from her, his dark gaze unwavering. Her chest went tight, her throat. She could feel her insides trembling.

"To Arista?"

Thinking of Arista, of returning there made her feel cold inside. And why he would want her to come back when he'd paid her to go away in the first place...

"Yes," he said.

"Vincenzo... Has something happened to your father...? Or my mother...?"

"No," he said. "But I require you, for a very specific purpose. You will not be returning with me in whatever capacity you might imagine. You see, you are an important instrument in my revenge against my father."

She blinked. "I am?"

"Yes," he said. "And I think you will find that there is sufficient reason for you to return with me. Whether you wish to or not."

"Vincenzo," she said, trying to force a smile, because after all, they had been a part of each other's lives for a great number of years, and there was no reason to be grim. "If you need my help, you have only to ask."

And she couldn't say then what was driving her. She could tell herself it was that she cared for him, whatever had passed between them. She could tell herself it was because she wanted to do something to ease the darkness coming off him in waves.

But what she did not tell herself was that it had anything to do with the tendrils of pleasure that curled around her stomach when she thought of revenge.

He made a compelling picture. A dark avenging angel standing before her, asking her to indulge her basest self.

You don't own that pain. That rage, none of it is yours. You let it go.

She breathed in deep and smelled the lilacs.

And thought of vengeance still. If only a little.

"I have only to ask?"

She forced a smile. "Of course. I'm sure that we can discuss whatever it is you're planning. There's no reason for you to come here all dark and angry and threatening. No reason to threaten me at all. Can you go over there to the shed?"

"I'm sorry?"

"To the shed. My broom is in there. And you made me break my plant."

"*You* broke your plant," he said.

"Yes," she said, feeling slightly testy. "But it was because you startled me. So would you be so kind as to get my broom."

"Perhaps you have forgotten who I am?"

"I haven't. You're the one who didn't seem to know who I was. I said your name immediately. How could I fail to recognize you? I could not. Ever. And I think you know that. Please get my broom."

"And…"

"And then we will discuss your plot."

"It is not a plot."

"It sounds like a plot to me. Complete with intrigue. Vincenzo, I am no great fan of your father, neither am I particularly fond of my mother. There is a reason that I have not been back to Arista in all these years. Depending on what you have in mind… I will help you."

"Just like that?"

She hesitated "Of course."

"I will get your broom, and then you will explain to me what you've been doing this past decade and a half."

"Oh, a great many things," she said, trailing behind after him as he went to the shed.

He opened the door, and fished around inside until he grabbed a broom. "Why did you follow me if you sent me on the errand? You could've easily retrieved the thing yourself."

"Yes, I suppose," she said. "I didn't mean to follow you. It just sort of happened. But I am intrigued. What has happened? What are your plans?"

"Nothing more has happened than what

has been happening in my country ever since my father ascended to the throne. He is corrupt. He has kept your mother in secret as his mistress while masquerading for all the world as an overbearing, pious leader who has inflicted a false morality upon the entire country that he himself is not held to. I, as you know, am his great public shame, and yet what he's done to my mother over the years is unconscionable. I will expose it. And I will do so by making a public display that will destroy him."

Hearing him say those words, while omitting any mention of her made her breathless and a bit dizzy. "And what do I have to do with it?"

"I may not approve of you, Eloise, but the fact is my father's…dalliance with you is another example of why he must be dealt with. Only you were ever hurt by it, not him. Do you not find that unfair?"

Even more unfair, considering she'd never touched him. And never would.

But the truth hadn't mattered to the press.

Or to Vincenzo.

"Life is not fair, Vincenzo, or did no one ever tell you that?"

"I aim to balance the scales. By taking everything he has."

His dark eyes glittered with a black flame, and an answering heat smoldered in her stomach, but she did not allow that to show.

Instead, she scrunched up her nose, looking up at him, backlit as he was by the sun. "That does all sound a bit intense. I don't suppose you've ever tried therapy?"

"Therapy," he repeated, his voice flat, the broom still in his hand, which was an incongruous sight. She had to wonder if Vincenzo had ever held a broom before. She did not imagine he had.

"Yes. I have found it incredibly helpful. I no longer get angry. Now I garden."

"You garden."

"Yes," she said. "Of course, now I have one less flower." She took the broom from his hand and went back over to the scene of its destruction. "But that doesn't matter. I can always plant more. That is the wonderful thing about nature. It is incredibly resilient. It grows, and it thrives, often in spite of us. I find it quite cheering. Bettering myself is one of my pursuits since leaving Arista. But only one of them. I went to school for horticulture. I made a lot of friends. I traveled around. I…"

"With my money?"

Heat lashed at her. "You gave it to me."

"I paid you off."

"Did you want revenge on me? Or on your father."

"It is only that you speak of those accomplishments as if they are yours when we both know how you paid for them."

"Do not look at me like that," she said. "How is it that you've managed to finance your life?"

"I have made my own way."

"From the starting position of 'billionaire prince,'" she said. "Your father, your lineage, gave you your start in life. I had to… I had to make the best of what I was given. I will not apologize for it."

His appraisal of her was decisive and cold, and she felt as if it had cut her down to her bones. "I don't require your apology."

"And I don't require your approval, so now we have that out of the way, what is it you want from me?"

"It's simple," he said, and she did not like the way he said that. Simplicity for a man with the sort of power and bearing Vincenzo

Moretti possessed meant nothing to mere mortals such as herself.

Simple could mean flying a private jet to an equally private island, or rallying the whole of the media to listen to him speak. It could be climbing a ladder to collect stars from the sky.

Simple for Eloise was something else entirely. An evening at home with a cup of tea, or an afternoon in the garden.

Definitely without her mother in her vicinity.

He was looking at her. As if "it's simple" was all she needed to know.

"If 'simple' involves reading your mind, you have the wrong idea of 'simple.'"

"It's not a negotiation," he said. "Nor am I asking for your help, I'm demanding you come with me. I see no reason to continue to speak in your garden."

"I said I would help you. You can stop looming so menacingly." She turned on her heel and stalked toward the house, throwing the back door open and going inside.

It was warm.

There was no air conditioner, and by late afternoon not even the stones could keep the heat at bay. But she didn't mind it. It was hers. And, all right, Vincenzo might dispute that, because she had taken that horrible money he'd flung at her to run away and had used some to purchase this house. But it felt like hers. It felt like home. And she'd been the happiest here than she'd been anywhere.

And yet he made her feel like she had one foot back in that life again.

You agreed to help him...

But she knew him.

The threats were not empty, and she wouldn't win if she argued. And if she didn't choose to go with him, she would be forced to go.

One thing Eloise could not bear, not ever again, was to have her choice taken away. And in this instance she knew she could change it, retain her power.

She had shocked him with her easy offer to help.

She wanted to keep shocking him.

She had spent her life in the palace at Arista on the defense. She had been out of place in every way. Her mother had always been a hard woman, who saw Eloise as an accessory to play dress-up with when it suited her, and a doll to discard when it did not.

The King had not paid any attention to her, until he had.

And Vincenzo? He'd been her only ally.

Until he wasn't.

"I will have to pack. And I need to see if my neighbor can feed Skerret."

His brow creased. "What is...that?" he asked.

"My cat. Well, she's not my cat entirely. She looms around the garden—a lot like you, actually—and I feed her."

He arched one dark brow, his expression beautifully insolent. "You have not fed me. Should I be offended?"

"Likely." But she was busy texting her neighbor Paula to see if she could leave food for the poor little tabby while she was away.

Paula responded with a quick yes. And when she looked back up at Vincenzo, it was because she could feel the impatience radiating off him in palpable waves.

"There is a breathing exercise I learned," she said. "It helps with tension."

"You are not my therapist."

"You don't have a therapist," she said. "I think we already covered that."

"No, I do not. But when we get back to

Arista...you will be playing the part of my mistress."

Her mouth dropped open and she couldn't help it. She laughed.

"Your *what*?" She couldn't stop laughing. She laughed so hard tears streamed down her face, because he could not be serious.

To her great shame she had followed his... Trajectory, she would call it, for the last ten years. She had seen him in the news with an endless parade of women. All perfect. All gorgeous. All... Very not her.

"I do not believe I said anything that was difficult to comprehend."

"Oh, no, I comprehend, I just think you're way off. There is no way anyone would believe that I was your mistress."

"The world is unaware of *our* complicated history, *cara*."

Cara. He had never called her that. She had heard him call other women that, though. He used to bring them to the palace, after ostentatiously arriving in the country with them on his arm.

She could remember the fury of his father—always—when he had done so.

He is a disgrace.

Trying to humiliate me.

Trying to diminish the Crown.

She wondered now if he had been. All along. If Vincenzo had truly set out to tarnish the institution from day one.

But mostly the word *cara* echoed inside of her and made her feel light-headed.

She shook it off. "They are all too aware of…"

"Your affair with my father? That is why I want you. You were made to take all the scorn upon yourself. An eighteen-year-old temptation no man could resist." His dark eyes went blank, and she was glad. She'd defended herself already back then; she wouldn't keep doing it. But hearing him repeat the things the tabloids had said wasn't easy.

"Why bring me back?"

"A triumphant return, Eloise. On my arm. A reminder of when his mask slipped, and then we will tear it off together. We will force the reality of truth upon the masses. These are different times. Even I have changed in how I see things. A man of his age has a certain power. A man of his position more still. You were an eighteen-year-old girl and for all that I disapproved…you were given sole blame. I think if the world is forced to look at it in this new time they would see him for what he is. A predator with no morals."

He wasn't wrong. Things had changed. Too late for her, but they had.

"But why would anyone believe you're with me?"

"I'm a man of great debauchery—no one will find it hard to believe I've taken on my father's former... You."

"No, that's not what I mean."

She stared at him and waited for him to figure it out. He only stared back. Enigmatic and hard, like a sheer cliff face.

"Are you going to make me say it, Vincenzo? Because I knew you were a bastard, but I thought being deliberately cruel to me might be a bit beneath you."

"Explain to me how I am being cruel?"

"I am not beautiful. Not by the standards those people use to measure it. And sample sizes are hardly going to fit this figure."

He laughed. He dared laugh! That dark chuckle rolling through her like a lick of flame. "Sample sizes? *Cara*, I am not your mother. I do not need to debase myself bargain hunting. Whatever I provide for you will be fitted especially to your exquisite curves."

"Exquisite?" She had never been called

anything even adjacent to *exquisite*. "I am not your type," she said.

"Beautiful? Lush? Beddable? That is not my type?"

He said it as if he were reciting a shopping list.

Milk.

Bread.

Beddable.

Beddable. She couldn't get over *that*.

"I am round," she said, her voice flat.

"Lush," he said, his voice far too seductive. "The narrow view on beauty your mother fed you…"

"To be clear," she bit out. "I am not insecure. I like my life. I like my body. As much as I like cookies. But I do not want to subject myself to what will undoubtedly be a heap of criticism from the press. I have been there and I've done it all before. And this time I know exactly what they'll do. With glee. Don't you think they'll put photos of me side by side and speculate on my weight gain?"

"But you are not eighteen," he said, his voice fierce. "And you will not run this time."

"You mean I will not be banished?"

"Let us go."

"I should pack a bag."

"You will want for nothing. By the time we arrive at the plane, a seamstress and a rack of clothing will be there waiting. You will be fitted and the items altered en route to Arista. By the time we arrive, you will look every inch mine."

Mine.

She shivered.

Then she shook it off.

This was not a fantasy. He might be a prince, but in this case she had a feeling he was less knight in shining armor, and more the dragon who might eat her alive.

CHAPTER THREE

ELOISE SEEMED TO have a personal mission of being unexpected. He had expected her to do one of two things when he had demanded she go with him: to cry hysterically and call him a brute before ultimately capitulating to his blackmail. Or to flirt while succumbing to his bribery.

She did neither.

Instead she had looked up at him with round eyes and a seeming lack of artifice and had said she would help him.

She reminded him more of the girl he'd known than the woman he'd made her into in his mind when he'd discovered her association with his father.

But now he wondered if she'd changed in that moment, or if he had. And it was a discomfiting thought.

Even now as they boarded his private

plane, comfortably fitted with many rooms and all the amenities a person could ever want, she looked… She did not look *bored*, or as if she was stepping into her due. Rather she had an expression on her face of a woman who was surprised and delighted by her surroundings.

Perhaps *delighted* was an overstatement. But there was something fascinated in her gaze, and it was not the sort of bright avarice that he might've expected with a woman such as her. No. It seemed to be more interest.

Enjoyment.

There was a purity to her response that… Took him off guard. For he had never applied the concept of *purity* to Eloise St. George.

"Is there something you wish to say?" he asked as he settled onto the soft leather sofa in the main seating area of the aircraft.

"Only that it's quite grand," she responded. "The plane."

"It is to my advantage to have everything well in its place for when I travel. I must be able to function as if I were in my own home."

"Well naturally," she said. "It must be so horribly taxing for you to travel to and fro as you do. I myself have been quite stagnant for much of my life. Though, of course my mother enjoyed traveling with your father on occasion. And sometimes I went too. A testament to your father's great kindness," she said, the words biting. "That he would bring not only his assistant, but her child. But his plane is not quite so spectacular."

"Indeed not," Vincenzo said.

He could not quite figure out what game she was playing, and that caused him a hint of concern. Concern was a foreign feeling, as was the sense that he could not read another person.

He *knew* plenty enough about Eloise. A mere week after she'd come to *his* room—tried to seduce him. Told him she loved him, kissed him—the story had broken about her affair with his father.

And he'd... Well he'd considered himself a saint for sending her away. Desire had been a living, breathing beast inside of him and even then he'd known. She was far too young. And most importantly, she would barely remember life away from the palace. They had grown up together, and in some ways they'd grown up alone.

She'd thought she loved him because she was too innocent to know better.

And so he'd told her no. Told her they couldn't…

What a fool he'd been. An even bigger fool for the pain he'd felt when he'd discovered that she had never loved him—she only wanted to align herself with a crown.

And any would do.

He had learned. He had learned since then to harden himself.

"Have a drink," he said.

As soon as he said those words, his stewardess appeared and walked over to the bar. "What would the lady like?" she asked.

"Oh," Eloise said. "A club soda would be nice."

"A club soda," he said. "Please do not hesitate to put a larger dent in my bar than that."

"I don't often drink."

It surprised him. For he had imagined…

He had imagined a whole woman in his head that it seemed did not exist. And that was what he was finding here.

He had imagined Eloise sharp and pointed, like her mother. Had imagined her with heavy makeup and a daring taste in clothing. He had thought she would feign boredom at his plane, consume his entire bar and demand to know how she would be compensated for all of this time spent inconvenienced.

But she looked different. Spoke different. Acted different.

He was certain he was rarely wrong, and yet with her, it seemed he was.

"If you are saving it for a special occasion, then let us make this one. For we are rather triumphantly returning back to Arista, are we not?"

"I don't know that I find it triumphant to return to Arista."

He waved a hand and his stewardess poured two glasses of champagne. She brought them over on a tray and he took them both, before handing one to Eloise, who stared at the fizzing liquid blinking rapidly.

"You do not feel triumphant, Eloise? You are... A horticulturist with a... I suppose it is what passes for a home in some circles. Do you not feel pleased with yourself?"

He found himself waiting. Waiting for the truth of her to be revealed. And it was a strange thing, he acknowledged to himself, that he had not done exhaustive research on her before he had gone to look for her. For in most circumstances he would've walked into the situation already knowing all the answers. He would have made sure that he had them. But he had been so certain that Eloise St. George could not surprise him. That she was the exact same tawdry, sparkling bit of cloth that her own mother was, and cut right from it. Why should he do research?

"Nothing that I am is designed to make my mother proud," Eloise said, lifting the champagne to her lips. She looked somewhat surprised when the liquid touched her tongue, and he had to confess that either she was a very good actress, or she truly did not often drink.

He was leaning toward her being a very good actress.

"You know how I feel about her," she said softly.

"I thought I did," he said. "But then, I thought I knew you once."

"I never lied, Vincenzo," she said softly, "whatever you might think."

Her eyes were sincere, and this woman sitting in front of him was…

She was not a surprise.

He had created a fictional Eloise in his head because he had wanted to banish all images of the girl he'd once cared for. Had fashioned her into a mold that would make it easy for him to do that. The same mold as her mother.

But if…

If that night, when she'd kissed him. When he'd held her in his arms for a brief moment before sending her away. If he'd imagined who she might become then, he might have seen the person sitting before him.

He hardened himself. For that was a nice thought, but it was all it was. And he knew well how adept some people could be at fooling the masses, and while he had never fancied himself a member of said masses, he knew that Eloise had tricked him once.

He would not allow her to do it again.

"Lies. Truth. None of it matters now."

"It does to me. I don't enjoy sitting with a man who despises me."

"And yet you have agreed to help me. Why would you do that if you did not wish to return? Why would you do that if you hate me so?"

"I never said I hated you."

His gaze flickered over her, and her cheeks went pink. His blood warmed. "You should."

"Why? Because you hate me? It doesn't work that way."

"I don't hate you, Eloise. If I hated you, I

would have done this without you. What I want to know is the manner of your investment in this."

"I have always thought…" She did not look at him; rather she looked over the top of her champagne glass, straight ahead at the back wall of the plane. "We were not so different, Vincenzo. Your father does not care for you any more than my mother cares for me. We are simply caught in the middle of their games. That was why we were able to become friends. Me, a girl from America who didn't even know princes existed outside of fairy tales…and you, the heir to a country. I care for you. It was only that friendship that carried me through. And so I would happily act as your friend now."

The word cut him.

"*Friends*," he repeated.

"Please don't embarrass me," she said, her voice going tight. "Please do not bring it up."

It was anger that drove him now and he felt a sick shame with it. He was better than this. Better than the sort of man who was led around by emotion. Better than his father. And yet he couldn't help himself. "Are you speaking of our last encounter, when I sent you away, or of the night when you were eighteen and you…"

He looked up at his stewardess and gestured for her to leave the room. The woman stared for a moment, then caught herself before retreating to the staff's quarters.

He turned his eyes back on Eloise. "The night when you threw yourself at me with quite the brazen…"

"Oh, yes, I was so very brazen," she said, her tone tart. "Kissing you with all that experience of mine and crying and saying I loved you."

In some ways he was surprised that she even remembered it. And he had to wonder what the purpose of bringing it up now was. But he would've brought it up, she was correct. So perhaps using it against him before he could use it against her was the game.

"It is a vague memory for me," he lied. "Any number of women fling themselves at me, Eloise, and you were simply one more."

She looked wounded, and for a moment he regretted landing the blow. For the pain in her blue eyes did not seem to be manufactured. And if it was, she had manufactured it quite quickly and had managed to cover any sort of shock she might be experiencing.

"All for the best, then," Eloise said, taking another sip of champagne. She sat down on the couch, her feet—clad in white sneakers—pressed tightly together, along with her knees. Her shoulders seemed to be contracted, as if she was trying to shrink in on herself.

He took the moment to look at her. Really look at her. She had a red handkerchief tied around her head, her blond hair tucked into an old-fashioned-looking roll. She was wearing a bright blue button-up shirt knotted at the waist, trimmed to accentuate her full bust and small midsection. The pants she wore were red like her handkerchief and cuffed at the ankles. She looked like a 1950s pinup waiting to happen. All he would have to do was unfasten the top few buttons of her blouse. No doubt her cleavage was abundant. It was a shame that it was done up all the way so that he could not see it.

And it bothered him. Bothered him that he was sitting there counting buttons and trying to gauge how many it would take to reveal her glory.

She was subtle. She had no makeup on today, but her skin was bright and clear, her eyes that pale cornflower blue. Her lips a pale pink, full, the top lip rounded and slightly fuller than the bottom.

He remembered that.

The color of her eyes, the shape of her mouth. But her face had been much narrower then, while now it had rounded. Her cheekbones were high and elegant, but not razor-sharp, and he found the new arrangement of her features pleasing.

He could not think of any man who would not.

The truth was, she was an entirely lovely creature. He had been prepared to resist the creature he had made her into in his mind. He had not been prepared to confront the woman she was.

But it might be a ruse. "Tell me, what are your current entanglements?"

"My…entanglements?"

"Lovers. Employers."

"I'm a horticulturist. Though I am between jobs at the moment."

"Between jobs?" He could not work out if she was speaking euphemistically or not.

"I was working at a large estate up until last month. But the owner sold it, and…" She closed her eyes, as if the memory was painful. "The greenhouse that I was in charge of curating was done away with. It was quite a lot of work. Had some beautiful mature plants, all gone now so that someone can have a new pool area. I had enough money that it was not immediately necessary for me to get more work. So I've been considering starting my own nursery. I haven't gotten that far. But it is something that I'm in the early stages of planning."

He could not help himself. He wanted to know… Why? He kept trying to remember if she had particularly liked plants and flowers back when he'd known her and could not recall that she had. "And why horticulture? Why are you invested in that particular vocation?"

"I just like the idea of growing things. Of leaving the world a little bit more beautiful. I actually don't want to be notorious. And you know… It doesn't really matter if I am. For I will just fade back into obscurity. I will go back to the garden. It doesn't matter to me. I want to be able to live on my own terms. I know you might not believe that, but it's true. My mother controlled everything in my life. What I thought, what I did, what I ate, what I wore. And I like being myself. I like leav-

ing the world fuller, rather than simply taking from it."

She was not going to answer his question,
then. And he had to wonder if the person
who owned the manor house she had previously worked at had also been her paramour.
That would make sense. That she had not
simply lost her job, but been removed as his
mistress. Perhaps she was in between lovers then.

She seemed to have little concern for
money, and while he knew that she had been
given some money by his father, and she had
presumably been earning money at her job,
he could not credit that it was enough to truly
support her.

Especially not in the lifestyle she would…

But he was forced to look at her again and
ask himself what lifestyle she was truly paying for.

Well, he did not need to itemize the cost
of her clothing. She was in an outfit that she
had been gardening in. That was not a true
reflection of her life. And just because the
woman liked to dig in the dirt did not make
her truly unexpected.

"Are you finished with your champagne?"

"I suppose."

"Let us go for your fitting."

"My fitting?"

"I told you, that you would be fitted here on the plane."

"Oh, yes, but I…"

"All of the clothing is in my study. Along with the seamstress."

"I don't even know what to say to that. That feels a great amount of excess. Being fitted thirty thousand feet above ground."

"We have not reached cruising altitude yet."

She blinked. "Indeed."

He walked over to where she was and extended a hand. She looked up at him as though it were a shark.

"You must be comfortable with my touch."

Her eyes went round. "Must I?" He had the distinct feeling he was being mocked.

"You must *appear* to be," he amended.

She squinted, then took hold of his hand, and the contact of her soft skin against his was like a punch to the gut.

How he would like her hands to be wrapped around other parts of him.

It would be helpful if he could think of her as dowdy. But he was a man with far too much experience of the female form to look at that outfit and not understand exactly what she would look like naked. How she would appear when the layers of her clothing were stripped away.

She was not dowdy at all.

She was the embodiment of sex. Sex he would like to have. Quite a lot. And that outraged him.

He'd thought he would be immune to her now.

He was… He held on to his memories of that moment finding out she'd been with his father so that he would keep her at a distance. It should not be so easy for her to make him want her.

It should not be so easy for him to forget.

When they walked into the study, her eyes went even rounder than they'd been previously. "This is incredible," she said. "I had no idea that a private plane could be quite so… It is a palace unto itself."

"Yes. As I told you. I spend quite a bit of time flying."

There was a rack of gowns and a smooth, immaculate man ready to do his bidding.

He went to his desk and sat on the chair. "Begin," he said.

"You cannot possibly… You cannot possibly expect me to undress in front of you," she said.

Why was she so modest now? She had climbed into bed with him once, her thighs on either side of his as she'd kissed him earnestly, and now she didn't want to undress in front of him?

Do you want her to?

"You may lower your dander," he said. "There is a screen for you to step behind. But I will be approving each and every gown. So I will be here the entire time."

It turned out that the entire experience was an exercise in torture.

He had not intended to dress her subtly. And so the gowns that had been provided by Luciano were not subtle in the least. Gold and glittering, bright and tight. Creative shapes designed to accentuate curves, and cutouts that flirted dangerously with revealing parts of her body that only a lover should see.

"I…" She looked at herself in the mirror, and her face contorted with shock. She was currently in a gold gown with a deep V at the front, exposing the rounded curves of her breasts. The back was low, and the vision of the two dimples that he knew were just above her rounded ass was making him hard.

"This is far too revealing," she said.

"Are you uncomfortable?"

"I am."

"Do you think you look bad?" He felt the need to comfort her, and he could not untangle his feelings for her.

He was not a man who trafficked in uncertainty, and he hated this. Not enough to be cruel to her. Not now.

"Women of my shape do not wear dresses like this," she said.

"And why is that?"

"I am a strong breeze away from a wardrobe malfunction, and that's just the first issue. The second is that it's... Clearly made for a runway-ready sort of woman, and not..."

"Runways are changing, or have you not noticed?"

Her cheeks went pink and he wondered if he had said the wrong thing. In his opinion, the change was welcome. He was the sort of man who liked variety. To him, these changes were only good.

"It does not matter if they are changing," she said. "I would still be a novelty, not the accepted. I will be in the same room as my mother and I will look like..."

"You will look like what?" She had been confident and happy when he'd taken her from the garden, freely offering herself to his revenge, and he could see her changing before his eyes.

As if the closer they were to her mother, the further she was from her confidence.

When he'd decided she was a liar, he'd decided everything about her was a lie.

Their friendship. Her relationship with her mother. Her feelings for him.

What if some of it were true?

"I think it's fierce," Luciano said. "For what it's worth."

Eloise grimaced. "I… I appreciate that. But I do not feel fierce. I feel… Round."

"You say that as if it is a bad shape," Vincenzo said.

"Do not play dense," she said. "When I think you know that hip bones are much more de rigueur than hips."

"I understand that it is your mother's preference, but that has little bearing on the truth of actual beauty. It is not so narrow, I feel. And who are you trying to impress? Your mother? As you said yourself, she recognizes only a very specific thing. But I wish to show you to the world, and I guarantee you that your sex appeal will not be missed."

"People will compare. And they will comment."

"Perhaps. But I am your lover," he said, the words making his gut tight, increasing the flow of blood down south of his belt. "And I find you glorious. If Luciano were not here I would strip the gown off you and lay you down on the floor."

He intended it to be a performance. Establishing the connection between the two of them, but it felt all too real. It felt all too much like the truth.

He drew closer to her, and he had not meant to. She smelled…

The same.

And it took him back.

To the girl she'd been.

Worse still, to the boy he'd been.

He leaned in, as he traced a line from her neck down across her bare shoulder. And he whispered in her ear.

"And I would have you screaming my name inside of thirty seconds. That is what I see when I look at that dress."

And he forgot. Why they were here. And that it was now.

And that he was supposed to keep her at arm's length.

There was no distance between them now.

She turned scarlet. From the roots of her pale hair, down all the glorious curves of her body.

"I just… I just wonder if there is perhaps a more subtle way to accomplish this."

"I have an idea," Luciano said.

He took an emerald green gown off the rack and handed it to her.

She went behind the screen, and when she appeared, she was somehow all the more maddeningly beautiful. The gown was crushed velvet, off the shoulder and conformed itself to her curves, while not revealing overly much skin. It was tight all the way down to her knees, then flared out around her feet.

"This I like," she said.

"It will do," he said, keeping himself away from her this time. "But fit the gold one to her as well. And use the rest of the measurements to fit some casual clothes too."

"I like a retro style," she said.

"I have a good handle on your style based on the outfit you had on today," said Luciano. "The gowns will be ready by the time we land, and the rest of the items should be there within a day. I will call ahead to my studio and have my staff get to work."

"Thank you," he said. "You may get dressed," he said to Eloise.

"Oh, may I?"

"Yes."

"May I also use the bathroom?" she asked, disappearing behind the screen.

"You do not need a hall pass."

"It's only that I thought I might."

She appeared a moment later, dressed again, but still tying her shirt up at her waist, and he wanted to round the desk, step toward her, hook his finger through the knot and undo it. Then undo all the rest of the buttons. Sadly, Luciano was still in the room, and also, he was never going to touch her in that way. Not for purposes other than performance.

It is perverse, he thought. And in some ways... Expected. He was a royalty, and very little was forbidden to him. So of course the luscious apple he should not take a bite of was the one he craved most of all.

She scampered out of the room then, and he thanked Luciano before leaving. She had used the closest bathroom, and he waited outside the door for her to appear. When she did, she nearly ran into him, her cheeks going red.

"Let me show you to your room. Where I think you will find the lavatory much more to your liking."

"I don't see anything wrong with that one."

"You might like a bath," he said.

"Oh, might I?"

"Yes. Are you intent upon being angry about all that I offer? May I remind you that you did come of your own accord."

"Yes," she said. "I did. Because I could not stand the idea of someone controlling my life yet again. It is something I cannot bear. And so I made the decision to come back with you. It was easier. It was better. Better than… Better than the alternative."

Guilt, which was an emotion he was entirely unaccustomed to, lanced his gut. She was tearing him in pieces. With memories. Memories that challenged his certainty.

And with herself. All that she was, and no matter what he knew about her, it didn't seem to matter. Didn't seem to keep him from wanting her.

He gritted his teeth and gestured down the hall, toward a glossy mahogany door. "This is you," he said.

He opened the door to reveal an expansive suite with a large, plush bed. He knew for a fact that the bathroom was ornate and very comfortable. He also knew that if he stepped in there, he would be tempted to invite her to draw a bath that included him.

And he did not like this feeling of being off-kilter. He could not afford it. Not now.

"I shall perhaps need you to explain to me what it is you expect," she said.

She looked vulnerable. She looked young. She looked like everything he knew she was not. And she absolutely did not look like her mother's daughter.

Was this how it happened? Was this how a woman sank her claws deeply into a man?

No, that isn't fair and you know it. Her mother's claws were not sunk into his father any more than his fangs were not sunk into her. They were together of their own accord, toxic of their own accord, and while Cressida St George had played havoc with his mother, his father happily engaged in hurting both of them.

"Rest," he said. "It is five hours yet before we land in Arista. We will go to my apartment first. Before we go to the palace."

She nodded. "All right."

"And we will engage the press."

She looked frightened, and he had to wonder if it was genuine. It seemed so.

"You needn't worry about instructions," he said. "You need only to follow me, and do as I say. And look at me as if I am the sun, the moon and the stars." And then he could not help himself. "You did so once."

"Yes," she said, her eyes suddenly filling with tears. "But that night you barely remember knocked me out of the sky. And I have not tried to reach for the stars or the moon since."

Then she closed the door in his face and left him to wonder why his chest hurt.

CHAPTER FOUR

SHE HAD A BATH, but she did not rest—it was impossible to rest, knowing that she was landing in Arista. Impossible to relax after what had happened...

She had made a fool of herself. She had exposed all of her insecurities. She was far too honest. She had reminded him of that night between them, one he said he didn't remember. *He didn't remember.*

She had loved Vincenzo Moretti more than anything. And she had never thought she would ever want a man. She hated the way her mother was with her lovers, and even though she'd only been six when they'd moved to Arista and her mother had taken up with the King, she could remember the men before.

She had told herself she would never let herself fall apart over men. That she would

never depend on them. Vincenzo had always
felt different.

She'd seen him as a friend first. A protector. By the time she was fifteen, her heart felt
like it was going to pound out of her chest
when he was near. When he went away to
school, coming back so rarely, she'd thought
she would die.

She'd had no one, those lonely years, and
she had lived for the times he would come
home to visit. Which was why, when he grad-
uated and came to Arista for a visit, she had
decided to give herself to him.

To make sure he knew how much she
loved him.

She'd been eighteen and, in spite of everything, full of hope.

She'd borrowed one of her mother's dresses
that she'd never even worn. Tight and sexy
and hopefully something that would capture
his attention.

She'd sneaked into his room at midnight
and he'd been in bed, shirtless. He'd been so
beautiful her heart had caught in her throat.
She'd nearly wept.

"What are you doing here, Eloise?"

"I had to see you."

"You could have waited until breakfast."

"No. No, I couldn't."

She'd crossed the room and, with trembling limbs, climbed onto the bed, positioning her body over his. "I... I want you, Vincenzo. I love you."

She leaned down and kissed him. Her first kiss, and it was everything she'd ever wanted. Because it was him.

And for a moment, his hand went around to cradle the back of her head, and he kissed her back. She could feel him growing hard between her legs, and it sent a thrill through her body.

But then suddenly, he was pushing her away.

"Eloise, no. You are too young. You can't know what you want."

"I do know," she said, running her hands down his chest. "You. I want you. I love you."

"You don't know any other men. Go. Go away to school. Go away from here. Kiss other men. And if when you come back you think you love me still... You will always be my Eloise."

But she wasn't. She hadn't been.

He'd been so quick to believe the lies his mother had told about her, that the press had told about her.

"Go away from here, Eloise."

His face was like stone. "Vincenzo, I didn't... I would never."

"Take this." He held a check out in front of her. "Go and do not return."

In the end, she thought perhaps she wasn't lovable.

Now of course she realized that was not the case. And she could not define herself by what the people around her could not or would not give. It was not her responsibility. She could only be true to herself. She could not take on the baggage of others; she could not make it about her. She'd had therapy. She knew that. But something about being around him made her feel eighteen again. Desperate to perform and do the right thing, and she hated it.

And the way he had looked at her...

Like he thought she was beautiful now. But she couldn't understand that. She didn't understand any of this.

When she went back into the bedroom, she was sure she was going to have to dress in the outfit she had come in, but to her surprise, a pair of soft white linen trousers and a white linen top had been laid out for her, along with a white lace bra and matching underwear.

It looked positively bridal, which was ridiculous, because he wasn't even pretending that they were to be married.

No, he was aiming to parade her before the world as his mistress. And she knew what he really thought of that. What that meant to him. It was exactly what he saw her mother as. And she did understand. They had both been traumatized by aspects of their lives, and she knew that.

It was just that… It was just that she despised how small this made her feel. It wasn't even her fear of the press. She had no remaining fear of them in truth. They'd already skinned her alive when she'd been a younger, more tender person.

It was how much it reminded her of being that needy, lonely girl, who wanted so badly to be whatever he might have wanted her to be. To be whatever her mother might've wanted her to be. She had become who Eloise wanted to be, and she was happy with that. Except…

Well, she had shut down the part of herself that wanted to be seen as attractive by men. The way that her mother was, the way that her mother had always been in those relationships concerned her. And what had happened with Vincenzo had worried her even more. Had convinced her that she could not be trusted to enter into that sort of relationship. And this only confirmed it, really. Because she was back to being insecure, back to feeling uncomfortable, back to being all of the things that she had tried to let go of. She was thinking about her body through the lens of other people, and she had determined to stop that.

Are you thinking about it in terms of other people, or him?

No. He had been... Complimentary.

The memory made her face warm.

There was a stern knock at the door, and she went to open it. And there he was, resplendent in a fresh dark suit, his black hair pushed off his forehead, his expression enigmatic.

He was far too much, this man. Perhaps he always had been. At any rate, he was far too much for her.

"We will begin our descent soon," he said. "Come and sit."

Her stomach tightened up, butterflies swirling around. Arista.

She had lived in America until she was six, until her mother had met King Giovanni Moretti at a party where she had been with another man, and he had been with his wife. Up until then, Eloise had enjoyed a fairly comfortable life with a nanny who had cared a great deal for her.

She had not seen her mother often, but when she had it had been nice enough.

Then the King had brought them to Arista to live. And everything had changed. She had been turned into a secret. Isolated. Kept separate from the rest of the world. From friends. From everything.

Her palms felt sweaty. She had never thought that she would return to Arista. Being confident and healthy and happy was easy in Virginia. It was easy in the new life she had carved out for herself, which consisted of quiet evenings at home, gardening and monthly meetings with her flower arranging club. She had made for herself a quiet life with people who didn't know who she was. With people who didn't know who her mother was. With people who didn't have any idea what she had been like when she was younger. Where she had been headed.

But now she was going back to the scene

of all she had been created to be, to her mother's barbs and his father's cold indifference.

Two yawning, empty corridors that recognized her loneliness and amplified it. Created an echo in her chest that expanded throughout her entire body.

She hated it. And she hated the idea of it even more.

But what if he's right? What if this is your chance at redemption? Revenge.

"You do not look well," Vincenzo commented as she sat down on the leather sofa.

"I am not," she said, shaking off her uncomfortable thoughts. "I don't enjoy the prospect of going back to Arista."

"You said you'd had therapy."

"I did. And it has all served me well far away from my mother and the site of all my trauma."

"Trauma?"

He asked the question with a faint hint of mocking to his tone, but she was past caring what he thought about anything. It didn't matter.

"Yes, I found life at the palace quite traumatic. Did you not?"

"I do not think in terms of my own

trauma," he said, lifting his glass of whiskey to his lips.

"Can you say that you were happy there? Because it seems that you were away more than you were ever there. Unusual for the heir to the throne, don't you agree?"

"I will never take the throne. And I will never have an heir. It dies with me. It will be turned over to the people."

"Your father will be devastated by that."

His grin took on a wicked curve. "I hope so."

"Revenge," she said. "You did mention that."

"Do you not take any joy in this?"

She frowned, looking down at her hands. "I don't know. If I'm being honest with you, I don't know. I came with you, so maybe I… Maybe a part of me wants to hurt both of them. Maybe. I would hope not. I would hope that…"

"You would hope that you were somehow more enlightened than me while offering to come back as my friend and help me in my endeavors?"

"Yes," she said. "I'm sorry if you don't understand that. I'm not sure that I understand much of anything in regard to my own feelings right now."

"Something I never suffer from. But then, I believe that is because I am honest. I am honest about what I want. I am honest about who I am."

"And you don't believe that I am?"

He stared at her for a long moment. "You are many things, *cara*. I do not believe that honest is one of them. But you are beautiful. And you will make an excellent weapon to be wielded against my father, and that is all I require of you."

With those words settled like a brand in her breast, the plane touched down.

They were ushered into a car, and they began to drive on the narrow, cobbled roads that felt like a distant dream to her now.

A part of a person that she no longer acknowledged.

Eloise St. George.

Who wanted to be beautiful, like her mother. Who wanted to be special. Who just wanted, and felt so hungry for whatever might make her feel whole. Feel real.

The approval of her mother.

The attention of Prince Vincenzo.

That poor girl. She did not know what love was.

And you do now?

She knew what it was not. She would accept that as progress.

"I never spent much time in the city," she said, looking out the window as they moved away from the small brick buildings into modern skyscrapers. The business district in Arista was as bright and modern as any other major city. It was only around the edges that the ancient charm of the place was still preserved.

"Of course, you wouldn't have."

"We would travel with your father's staff. We spent most of our time in Paris. I haven't been back to Paris since I was fifteen."

"Why not?"

"I told you. I have been living and working in Virginia. Do you think that I have the funds to be a jet-setter? I took the check you gave me and I made something from it. But it was hardly enough to make me independently wealthy for life. I am on a budget."

"And your many benefactors since have not flown you off to Europe?"

"My many benefactors? Do you mean my employers? Because no."

"No, I mean your *lovers*."

"What makes you assume I have lovers paying for my life?"

He stared at her for a long moment. "Are you telling me that you don't?"

The way he looked at her made her stomach feel tight.

"I'm not telling you anything," she said. "I am asking you a question. What about anything that I am, or any of my life you have seen, suggests to you that I have an endless array of sugar daddies trotting me about the globe?"

"It is only that your mother…"

"Yes. My mother. We are not the same. We don't look the same. We don't act the same. My mother has spent the last twenty years with your father. Living a strange half-life. They cheat on each other, of course. My mother takes other lovers. But still, she is a creature of the night, wandering around European cities after dark because she can never be connected to him. Because she cannot have the notoriety she would prefer. Because she must trade that in for money. The most glittering, celebrated, reviled socialite America had to offer way back at the turn of the millennium, and now she is obscure.

That's who you think I am? An undercover piece on the side? Managing to stay out of the tabloids because I have taken up with someone so lofty that I am a secret? Or perhaps you imagine I am more of a common tart, and none of the men that I associate with need to be quite so careful of the press?"

It wasn't the first time people had assumed things about her because of her mother. There was no excuse for it, ever. She hated it. It made her feel small and grim and sad.

"You forget," he said, his tone dark. "You forget what we all know to be true."

"You think I'm a whore. Go ahead and say it."

It wouldn't be the first time one of the Moretti men had accused her of such.

"I assumed you had continued on in the lifestyle you'd begun at the palace."

"Because you think you know the truth? Because of something your mother told you? As if she had any reason to…as if she would have ever wanted you to like me, Vincenzo."

"Be careful what you accuse my mother of," he said, his teeth gritted.

"Why? She was not careful of what she accused me of. And even if it were true? Are you better than me?"

"Eloise..."

"No. Admit it. You are just like your father. Just like all those sorts of men. You think you can judge a woman by the way she dresses, and you think that you know her moral character based on the amount of men you think she might've slept with. That doesn't teach you anything about a woman. How many women have you slept with? And were they wealthy? You have paraded all around the globe with great glittering creatures on your arm. What am I to learn about your morals from that?"

He laughed. Bitter and hard-edged. "You mistake me. I never said that I was better. I never said that I was better than my father. Or than you. I am simply different. I hardly lead a life worth canonizing. Nor do I pretend to. I am steeped in all manner of immorality, and I have never acted differently. And that is the only real difference between myself and my father. That and the fact that my liaisons affect only me. And I will not seek to flex my power over my people. That, perhaps, is my only real redeeming feature. I am not power hungry. I have power. I find that with it, I am able to ignore any appetite for more. I have money. I am not afraid of losing my status. I know who I am. My father is small. He fears being deposed. He fears being unmasked. He fears that in the end all that he is, all that he cares for and all that he pretends to be will be unveiled. Will be destroyed. I will see that it is. As for me? There are no surprises. There is nothing to destroy. I have been working to restore Arista to its former glory behind the scenes for many years. I will give all that must be given to the country and its people. And yes, I will continue on as a whoremonger. But I will not enforce morality that I do not myself believe in upon my people. I will not put on a mask. You mistake me. I do not care what you do. I do not care who you have slept with. And I do not care who is bankrolling your life. Only that I do not wish to be lied to."

"You have not earned the right to my honesty," she said, her chest feeling tight. "I don't like to give people access to my secrets."

"And why is that?"

"Other than the fact the press already tried to make me a public commodity? Somewhere in the middle of your secrets, all your insecurities are buried. And what do people love more than anything else? To use those against you. I will not expose myself to such a thing. I will not make myself an easy target. I refuse. So I will not prostrate myself for the enjoyment of any man. Least of all you."

"So long as you're a good actress, I suppose in the end it doesn't matter."

He shifted, and she smelled the spicy scent of him. Her entire being fluttered.

The real concern was that she would not have to pretend at all to act as if she was attracted to him. The real concern was that she wore it with obvious ease.

The real concern was that anyone might know.

But most especially, him.

The car pulled up to the front of a grand building made entirely of glass and steel. The windows reflected the mountains in the distance, and the intensity and magnitude of it sucked the breath straight from her lungs. This was his palace. A palace so unlike the traditional palace where they would go later tonight. The deliberate flex of his distinct power was obvious here. He was younger. A man who had earned his money, not a man who had taken it out of the pockets of the citizens of Arista. They got out of the car, and the doors to the building opened automatically. The lobby was stunning. All

modern architecture that gleamed with gold
rather than the expected chrome. It was not
ornate or tacky, rather there was something
like fire about it that made the entire place
burn hotter.

The doors to the elevator had that same
gold, brushed bright. He put his fingerprint
on a panel, and the doors opened.

"This is my private elevator. It is the only
way to get to my suite of rooms."

"And so you have made yourself the King
of Arista after all."

The back wall to the elevator faced the
city, and as they rose high above the buildings, looking out over the expansive view,
she could see what she said being proven.
He had no rejoinder, because there was nothing to be said.

"All of our things will be sent soon. You
may have a rest."

"I should like some food."

"We are having dinner at the palace."

"Yes. But by then I will have a stomach
full of anxiety, and I would like something
to eat."

He gestured across the barren, modern
space. The floors were black, the counter

cement. But yet again the details in gold. "Be my guest."

She walked into the kitchen area and opened the refrigerator. She noted that the handles were also gold.

Inside were fruit platters. Meat and cheese trays. It was as if appetizers for an upcoming party had been prepared. And she took them all out, happily examining them.

"These will do nicely."

She put them on the countertop and uncovered them, scrounging until she found a plate and filling it with a generous portion from each tray. Then she hunted around until she found sparkling water and poured herself a glass.

And all the while he watched her, leaning back against the island, his palms pressed down into the surface, his forearms flexed.

"I have staff for that," he said.

"Well, I was able to dish myself an entire plate without you summoning anyone, so I think it all worked out in the end."

She looked around and saw that there was no dining table in the space. So she took it all to the low, leather couch that faced floor-to-ceiling windows that overlooked the city.

She sat down and popped a grape into her mouth. "This is quite nice."

"Thank you," he said, dryly.

"I always try to be polite."

"What game are you playing?"

"I'm not playing a game. I feel that you are a game player, and therefore cannot figure out what I'm doing. And what confuses you most is that I'm not doing anything. I'm not. I am not doing anything, and I do not wish to be doing anything, and I am no threat to you at all. I am simply me. I have changed. I was only ever the Eloise that you knew because of my mother. And I have worked very hard to become the Eloise that I am. Stop looking for the snake in the grass. It isn't me."

"How do I…"

"You came to me, Vincenzo. If you had not, I would never have come back here."

"You acquiesced easily."

"Yes. Because I meant what I said. If you need help, I wish to help you. You are trying to rescue your country, at least, as far as I can tell, reading between the lines of your grim threats. I respect that. Your father has done a terrible job with this country, and it sounds to me as if you are the only person willing to do something to save it. And the fact that you are willing to turn the power over to the people… For all your bluster I do believe that you are well-meaning. I do believe that you want to do the right thing by your country. The palace staff were always kind to me. Regardless of the drama happening between your parents and my mother. They were always so very kind. I feel… Even though it was isolated, Arista has been my home for as long as anywhere else. It matters to me what you're doing. So I'll help. But I don't want to enrich myself or anything like that." She ate a piece of cheese. "Though, I'm not averse to enjoying some nice food."

And for his part, he was actually stunned into silence, which was really quite something.

But it wasn't long after that her clothing arrived. And she was whisked off to change yet again. Wrapped in that brilliant green gown that was now custom fitted to her curves.

And when they exited the hotel, the press was there. Flashbulbs went off, the melee surrounding them intense.

"Is that Eloise St. George? Your father's mistress? Where has she been hiding?" The press volleyed questions, a pounding insistent drum, and it took her back.

All the way to when she'd been eighteen and heartbroken, tender in her feelings for Vincenzo still and somehow being cast as a whore in a play with his father on the world stage.

Her heart was pounding so hard she thought she might vomit.

"Yes, it is Eloise St. George," he answered. "And you know the old stories about her. But you do not know the truth of how she came to be at the palace. Her mother has lived as my father's mistress since Eloise was six. Eloise and I have known each other since childhood. I, like many of you, blamed her for my father's behavior at the time. She was eighteen. My father was a king. I am not blameless, but the press hounded her, treated her as the villain in the piece. We are here to unmask the real villain."

"Your father's mistress?" one of the men asked. "It was reported that the indiscretion with Eloise St George was the only…"

"You will find that my father is economical with the truth as it suits. That the King has not held himself to the same standards that he holds his people. You may be quite shocked to learn just how deeply my father has let down Arista."

"Do you have proof?" another reporter asked.

"I have lots of proof," he said. "I will happily give it to you. But now I must take Eloise to dine at the palace. It has been a long time coming for her. I am here to tell my father that he is ruined."

He grinned then, the smile of a predator that made her shiver down to her bones. "And believe me when I tell you, you will have all the information you need to ensure the ruination is complete."

CHAPTER FIVE

HE ALMOST FELT sorry for Eloise. Almost. She was pale and drawn and quiet as the limousine inched ever closer to the palace.

She had been nearly silent ever since the reporters had ambushed them outside his penthouse. And it had only become more pronounced with each passing moment since. He could feel her dread, feel it radiating off her.

"You are nervous?" he asked.

For the first time he felt... He had miscalculated. She was hurt by all of this. More distressed than he'd assumed. He had thought her hard. He had made assumptions about who and what she was based on his belief in her guilt when it came to her relationship with his father.

And he'd let that form his image of her all

these years. Anything to replace the one he'd had back when they'd been young.

They arrived at the palace, and he felt his own stomach tense. He felt her entire body go rigid.

He had not been back here since his mother had died. And it had been her death a year ago that had triggered this plan.

He'd come only to say goodbye to her, and he could still remember the stale feeling in the room. All the bitterness from so many years steeped in it.

It lingered. In the air. In him.

They got out of the car at the front entrance, the grand double doors opening slowly. The palace was a gleaming white, a testament to the unending purity of its ruler. The spires were gold. It was not an accident that in his own building he employed the use of concrete and gold. An echo of what his father was, and the lack of pretense with which Vincenzo presented himself.

Symbolism that no one would ever appreciate except for him, he had a feeling. And yet, appreciate it he did.

He took her arm, and the two of them stood at the threshold to the palace, and suddenly she began to… Laugh.

"What?"

"Oh, I just… This would've been my dream. When I was sixteen years old. Arriving at the palace with you. I would've felt… I would have felt like the luckiest girl in the world."

"Well, you are quite undermining my presence, at the moment. As it is intended to be a bit more ominous. Giggling is hardly the tone we want to set."

"What you're sharing with the world is ominous enough. We have to belabor it by acting like a funeral procession?"

"Did you want it to be a family reunion?"

"Hardly." She made a strange, strangled sound. "We are practically stepsiblings."

He nearly recoiled. "We are nothing of the kind. Our parents are not married."

They stopped and looked at each other for a beat. And he felt a burn start in his blood. But it wasn't just that. It was an unexpected solidarity.

He had thought to force her here, but she had offered to come.

As a friend.

Even after everything, she had offered that.

They were announced and led through the grand corridors of the palace, on through to the great dining hall, where his father was seated at the head of the table and there, at his right-hand side was Eloise's mother.

She looked up, her eyes like glittering bright jewels. Her fingernails were long, red claws.

She had not been permitted to sit in that position when his mother had still been living. And he could see that she took a great joy in flaunting this change in his face.

"How wonderful that you could join us this evening," she said, acting the part of hostess.

It made his stomach curdle.

"Of course."

"The other guests will arrive shortly," his father said.

And it took a moment. Just a moment. For Eloise's mother to recognize her. And a moment longer for his father to do the same.

"What is this?" his father asked.

"Oh," he said. "Eloise is here. As my mistress. I find that I have taken a great liking to her of late."

Her mother looked at her daughter with a dismissive sneer.

"That is impossible," she said. "She has gained at least two stone since she was here last. I should think that a man of your pedigree would have better taste."

What surprised him, as much as the moment of camaraderie he'd felt with her outside, was the rage he felt toward her mother just then. Had he not himself been hard on her when he'd first encountered her again? He knew he had been. But it was not this.

The way she looked at Eloise...

She hated her, he realized. Because she was young and beautiful, whatever the woman said. Her own daughter outshone her and she couldn't stand it.

"Oh, my taste is impeccable," he said. "And I find each and every curve of her body to my liking. More than that, I have decided to go public with it. And with our relationship."

"All the guests here tonight are well aware of the nature of my relationship with Cressida St. George. It is my inner circle."

"I'm sure, Father," he said. "But your cronies are one thing—the public is quite another. I have already spoken with the press. Of course, they all remember the one sin you were ever caught in. But you made sure to assassinate her character. To make it seem as if you were only a victim. But I have evidence to the contrary, and I will make sure the world knows. Not only of your sexual indiscretion but of all you have stolen from Arista. You have defrauded this land, and its people, and I intend to see your wrongs exposed, and made right."

His father began to turn a particular shade of purple, but it was then that the other dignitaries and diplomats began to line the table.

Eloise, for her part, looked subdued. Then as he made conversation with the men around him, making provocative statements about the economy of Arista, he felt her shrinking beside him.

And again the urge to protect her was strong. He could not explain it; he was here on a mission that concerned his country, his revenge. And yet he felt consumed by her. And that had not been part of the plan.

Tonight, he decided he would say no more to his father. Tonight, he made it his mission to speak only to the other men present. And he also left the table at the precise moment all of the other guests did. His father tried to catch him.

"Eloise and I are returning to my flat," he said. "I rather would like an early night with her. Surely that's something you can understand."

"You were raised with her," he said.

"And you took advantage of her," Vincenzo said. "Which I will not do. But you did that often, didn't you?"

"You will not make these things public," his father said.

"I already have."

But then his father reached out and grabbed Eloise by the arm. "If you wish to play the whore…"

"I never did," she said. "And you know it. But you let the story go out as it did because you thought it such a great distraction to the reality of what you were doing. I understand that now. That my image, my body, was something you could trade on. A way to try and play the victim. Someone got too close to the truth, but they were just wrong enough that being handed me as a scandal kept them from my mother."

Vincenzo only stood, frozen. There were few times in his life when he had felt that he might be outside his understanding. Once had been when Eloise had kissed him, and he'd sent her away in spite of a roaring need to drive himself inside her.

And now.

He'd had no idea. He never had.

"I didn't know why I came back," she said, her voice sounding strangely detached now. "But I realize now. It was to have a front seat at your deposition. You destroyed me for all the world to see, but I refused to let that be the last word. It will be mine. The last word will be mine. You could not force me to be your mistress, you could not shame me into vanishing and you will not cow me into silence. You are a twisted, perverse old man, and you may have made my mother your puppet, but you never succeeded in making me anything. Neither did you, Mother," she said, looking her mother in the eye. "All that I am, I am because of myself."

She turned then, walking out of the ballroom. He stood for a moment and realized that his place was with her for now. For had he not brought her here? Was her distress, her pain not his fault?

He had believed a lie for years. He had been his father's pawn much the same as anyone else, and it galled as much as the guilt that now assaulted him.

"Eloise," he said, following her. "Tell me."

"Now you want to know? You should have

always known, Vincenzo. You of all people should have always known."

"How?" he asked, and yet he felt his failure like a howling beast inside his lungs.

"You knew me."

"I thought I did. But then you kissed me."

"And that made me a whore?"

"No," he said. "You said you loved me. I thought anyone who loved me… I could not believe it. I could much more easily believe you were using me all along."

In those words was a sadness he never wanted to examine.

"I was never using you," she said, unshed tears in her eyes.

"Eloise…"

"After all of that I just wanted to start over. I never wanted to be here again. I never wanted any of this. I thought… I thought I could just put it behind me."

"But you came with me. When I asked. You came with me."

Her eyes glittered. "Yes. I did. I thought I was fine. I thought therapy fixed all of this but… I'm angry. I am angry. My mother made me hate my body—your father made me afraid of it."

And for the first time, true sympathy

curled inside him. Not just the first time he had ever felt sympathy for her. Possibly the first time he had ever felt sympathy for anyone.

And he felt a black sort of blinding rage at his father that was different than the rage he had carried around inside him all this time. It was different.

They went back to the penthouse, and when they walked inside, he looked at her silhouette against the city lights below.

"Are you all right to continue?"

"I knew the history between myself and your father. Even if you did not."

"He did not ever…"

"No. But I fear that he would have."

"You're very brave, Eloise," he said, the compliment foreign on his lips.

She turned and looked over her shoulder, smiling. Her blond hair cascaded down her back in golden waves, and he had the urge to touch it, but also… In the wake of what she had told him, he felt he ought not to.

"Thank you," she said. "I do not feel brave sometimes. Rather I have chosen to hide myself away, and there are times when I question that. But I am happy. I am content. Is there more to life than that?"

"I am not happy or content," he said. "So I suppose we can debate whether or not there is more than that."

"Indeed." She looked at him for a long moment. "I wanted you," she said. "Please know that. It was not simply manipulation or loneliness. I know that I was too young. But what I felt for you was genuine. That means something to me."

Then she turned and walked into her bedroom, leaving him standing there feeling speechless. And there was nothing half so remarkable as that.

CHAPTER SIX

WELL, SHE HAD done it. She had confronted
the King. She had spoken the truth.

She knew the King's behavior wasn't her
fault. She knew that it was the kind of man
the King was. It had nothing to do with the
kind of woman she was. Nothing to do with
anything she put off, nothing to do with the
shape of her body. There was nothing wrong
with her.

But she still felt shame, especially when
the King had looked at her last night, and
she hated that.

What a strange thing to be back. To be
confronted with all these things that she had
been convinced she had dealt with on some
level. She supposed that she had. She wasn't
reduced to a crying mess or anything like
that. It was just that she felt… It was just that
she felt. And tonight they were to return to

the palace for a ball celebrating the five hundredth year of the Moretti Rule.

It was tonight, she knew, that Vincenzo would ensure it all burned.

She knew that because it would be poetic to him. Of that she was certain. This claim that he was going to disrupt the line, he would do it on the anniversary of his family's rule, because he liked the symmetry of it. Because he would like the poetic bent to the justice.

She wasn't sure justice sounded anything like poetry to her.

But it appeased some dark piece of her heart she'd thought long dealt with.

Who didn't want to stand before their abusers and tell them what they thought?

When the news had broken of her supposed relationship with the King she'd been devastated. And she'd lost the one ally she'd thought she had.

Vincenzo.

She had to wonder if, in the end, it was Vincenzo who had hurt her worst of all.

Because she'd never believed in her mother, or his father for that matter.

But she'd believed in him.

She shook off those thoughts and decided

on a walk. She went down through the marketplace, away from the center of the city, and found a farmers market. She bought flowers. So many flowers. Enough that her arms were completely full by the time she left. Then she went up to the penthouse—her thumbprint granting her access for the time she was staying there—and began to place flowers in vases on every available surface.

When Vincenzo appeared, he was shirtless. There was sweat rolling down his chest, and his cheekbones were highlighted by slashes of red. "What the hell is this?"

"Oh," she said. "I thought you were… In bed."

"I've been out for a run," he said. "What is this?"

"I thought that some flowers would brighten the place. I love flowers."

He blinked. "I have never had flowers in here."

"You also don't really have any color. This is much nicer, don't you think?"

He shook his head. "I do not think."

"Do not be a beast, Vincenzo," she said, continuing to arrange the flowers.

He took a deep breath and crossed his

arms. "I've been thinking about my father," Vincenzo said.

"Yes?"

"He is a bastard."

"No argument from me."

"If you do not wish to participate in this…"

Her fingers stilled, her eyes lifting to his. "Are you asking what I want?"

His expression was grim. "Yes."

Her heart felt tender. She could leave. She could go right now. Forget this was happening in Arista. He could complete his vengeance without her.

"Vincenzo, do you believe me now?"

"Yes," he said, his voice tight. "I am… sorry."

"Have you ever told anyone you're sorry before?"

He looked away. "I have never been sorry before. I am now."

She thought her chest might crack. "I accept your apology."

"Would you like to leave?"

"No," she said. "I might be having difficulty sorting through my feelings on the matter. And I am not entirely certain that I'm… Happy. Or enjoying this, but I do think it needs to be done. And in some ways I think it is good that I'm bearing witness to it. But in the meantime, I would like to collect flowers, and do things to make myself feel more comfortable."

"Of course."

"There is the matter of the gold dress…"

It was so revealing. And she had felt sick over that when he had first put her in it. For a variety of reasons. But now…

She did not want to act out of a sense of fear. Or a sense of shame. She wanted to be… Well, if he thought she was beautiful, then she wanted to be that kind of beautiful. For her. For him.

Maybe she shouldn't want to be beautiful for him. But she did.

Because it was a tender bloom in the center of her, of a girlish fantasy that had been as breathless as it was innocent. Something that she had lost later.

Something that had been tainted thereafter."You are worried about it?"

She was, but she…decided to let it go. "Really, the thing that I'm most worried about is having to dance."

"We do have to dance," he said.

"I figured as much. But we are making a statement, are we not?" She imitated his tone and arched a brow in what she hoped was a decent impression of his arrogant expressions. "We must make a show."

"Are you mocking me?"

"If you have to ask, I'm not doing a very good job."

"No one dares to mock me."

"I dare. And quite handily too. I am sorry if it disagrees with your royal constitution."

"I'm glad to see you are not quite so timid as you were last night."

"I was not timid in the end."

"No," he said, smiling. "You were not."

It was his smile that undid her.

"Shall we practice dancing?"

"No," he said.

"Please?"

"You wish to practice now?"

He gestured to his bare chest, and she could not help but take a visual tour of his body. Glistening and tan, with just the right amount of dark hair sprinkled over his muscles. His pectorals, his abs. She wanted to touch him. And the inclination she felt toward him was quite a bit different than the one she had felt when she was eighteen. For she had imagined gauzy things. Sweet kisses and touches, and him laying her down on the soft mattress. Here she could easily imagine his hot skin. Sweat slicked. She knew his mouth would be firm, and that his whiskers would scratch her face. She could picture him putting his hand between her legs and...

She bit her lip.

Her fantasies had certainly progressed, even if her experience had not.

But she could imagine—vividly—what she wanted from him. She wanted to inhale all that testosterone. She could remember vaguely being concerned about his chest hair back when she had been eighteen. In fact, she had been afraid that she would not like to touch it, which was a problem, as she did want him, she had told herself.

Now she wished to run her hands over his body, chest hair and all. She wanted to lick him. Even sweaty. Maybe most especially sweaty.

The desire was deep, and it was visceral. And she was not ashamed. She wasn't ashamed.

She was a woman. And he was a man. An attractive man, and she wanted him.

Her body was her own. But he could borrow it. And he could use it. She would greatly enjoy that.

"If you wish," she said.

And he took two steps toward her, his dark eyes blazing, and she realized then that he was certain he was calling her bluff. Instead, she took a step toward him and held out her hand. "Let us dance."

He pulled her up against him, and she could feel that his chest was damp through the fabric of her top. He was hard. And just as hot as she had imagined. She put her hand on his bare shoulder, could feel the play of his muscles beneath her fingertips. And he grasped her hand in his. "I have made it no secret that I think you're beautiful."

"It is only our connection that prevents you from finding me… How did you put it? Beddable?"

She was being more bold, more forward than she had ever intended to be.

And she felt… Giddy with it. Not ashamed. Not worried.

"Yes. I believe I did."

A great many words bottled up in her throat. He thought her a victim now, or something close to it. Did that mean he no longer found her beddable? Or did it mean he found her more so because he found her innocent in that way?

She didn't know. And she supposed the only way to find out would be to make an actual move on him. But she stopped herself just short of that.

And instead, tried to focus on what it felt like to be held in his arms. To follow the steady rhythm of the dance. Even though there was no music.

And the absurdity of it all would've made her laugh if she could breathe. But she couldn't.

"You're a very good dancer," she said, her eyes focused on his chest. The golden skin there. The muscle definition. The hair…

"Hazard of my upbringing."

"I didn't learn to dance."

"You seem perfectly competent at it."

"Oh, I am. I used to watch. I used to watch from upstairs. When your family would have balls."

"Your mother went."

"Yes," she said. "But there was… My mother enjoyed the attention. The drama. In a way that I never could. Anyway, it was thought that I would draw attention. The kind they didn't want. The kind they didn't like."

"I've never been able to figure out exactly what manner of sadist my father is. The way that he hurt my mother. And the way that he... The way that he treated yours."

"I think you'll find my mother quite likes being involved in the pain, whether she's dishing it out or taking it."

"That may be. But there is an element to it that I... I can't absolve him of. Not anymore. After knowing what he did to you."

"My mother knew. She is still with him. Do not absolve her simply because you are refocusing your anger. No, your father isn't a good man. There is no disputing that, but my mother is not a victim."

"Perhaps it is possible to be both. The predator and the prey."

She frowned. She wanted only to focus on him. On his body, on his beauty. She wanted to focus on the warmth of his body, the strength of his hold. The fantasy inherent in this moment, and not the reality of their lives. Never that.

One thing was certain—they had both suffered for the games their parents played. Whoever's door had most of the blame heaped at it.

"It will be fascinating," she said. "To be down in the ballroom tonight."

"Yes. No longer the secret."

Recognition bloomed in her chest. "I think I must want that."

"What?"

"I am marveling at my own motives," she said. "I cannot say that I have figured them out entirely. I have lived a quiet life these last few years, and I said that I would never return here. That I would never... That I would never see you again. And that I was happy for it."

"I see."

"Yet here I am. Dancing with you. Here I am, leaping headfirst into this retribution."

"Perhaps you are just as filled with hate as I am."

She smiled up at him, but she felt the expression falter as her eyes collided with his. "But that can't be. Because I have worked very hard and I..."

"All that therapy," he said. "You think you should be more enlightened than I am?"

"I know I should be," she said.

"Reality is often a difficult thing. What we might like is not always what is. Aren't our entire lives a testament to that? Isn't all that we've been through a testament to that?"

"Maybe that's why I prefer the fantasy. Of gardens and a quiet life. A little stone house."

"I can see how it might appeal," he said.

She looked up at him again, and she felt something electric when their eyes clashed.

"You can?"

"For a moment. Like smelling the scent of roses on the breeze. And it catches you, for a breath. And then it's gone and you're left to wonder if it was there at all. I can sense it that way. I can feel it that way. The impression of a life lived quietly. Of a life lived only for yourself."

"I hadn't thought of it that way." But he was not wrong. She had removed every responsibility she might feel toward another person. Every hint of caring about outside expectations. She had sunk deeply into her own reality. Only her. Only her flowers. Only the things that made her happy and none of the things that didn't. And so she had been unprepared. Her emotions still in that same deep freeze when he had come to see her. She had been unprepared for what it would do to her. Unprepared for what being back in Arista would mean. Or maybe *unprepared* was the wrong word. Blissfully, intentionally disconnected from it.

But now she was here. And she felt anger.

For the girl she had been. And a heady rush of need for the man that he was.

He felt like the reward she had been hoping for all this time. The reward that she deserved after living a life so disconnected. After being denied so many things when she was a girl.

And without thought, she moved her hand from his shoulder and slid it down the front of his chest. Pressed over where his heartbeat was, and she felt it raging. She looked up at him, her heart pounding an intense tattoo in time.

"Vincenzo..."

"That is enough," he said, moving away from her. "Tonight is the night that I tell my father no matter what. No matter how he tries to clean up after this, it is no use. I am his heir, and I refuse to carry the line forward. And he will have to face that."

"I admire your rage," she said.

"Why is that?"

She felt separation between them like she had been stabbed. "Because it's clean. And bright. Because it is...real. It is that which I admire most. The honesty in it."

"You seem quite honest, Eloise."

"I try to be. But then I wonder. If I have

been the least bit honest with myself. I didn't think I was angry anymore. I thought I'd put it all away. What does it mean that I haven't?"

He stopped, his hand lifting, hovering over her cheek, as if he wished to touch her. To maybe offer comfort?

"You are human," he said, lowering his hand.

She ignored her disappointment. "Is that what you are? Human?"

"I cannot afford to be human. I must be the cleanup crew. I must fix all that he has broken. And I cannot allow myself to be distracted."

He strode from the room, leaving her standing there. Her hand burned where she had touched him, and her heart… Her heart burned too. Her heart burned with an intensity that she could not identify.

She felt like she was on the edges of her own life. The pull to Virginia was strong, but she wasn't there. She was here. And she felt like… Something was going to break.

She was afraid that it was going to be her.

And it shamed him, tenfold.

Because even if she had slept with him, that would have been true.

He had somehow realized she was young and a victim of circumstance when she had kissed him. When she had come to his room.

And he had forgotten it all when he'd been hurt by her. Had recast her as the villain the moment he'd found it convenient.

It shamed him.

But now Eloise was standing before him wearing that revealing gold dress and looking like a goddess reborn. Like she had just emerged from fire, a glorious avenging sexuality that he wanted to hold against his body. She was glorious. When he could think of nothing more poetic than his father having to witness her being part of his downfall. She was a fresh-faced glory, her cheeks pink and tinged with something gold like the dress, her lips a glossy rose with an underlying flame.

And he could not help himself. He wanted her.

But it was not Eloise who was unworthy.

It was him.

One thing was for sure, she might've had therapy. She might arrive in a place that she

CHAPTER SEVEN

WHEN ELOISE EMERGED, ready for the ball, his gut tightened with the need that defied everything else. He'd had to walk away from her earlier. The touch of her delicate fingertips against his skin almost more than he could bear. He did not wish to be so attracted to her.

What he'd said to her when she was eighteen was just as true now. She was bound to him in ways she had not chosen. They were bound to one another in this sadistic farce.

He was a man who owned his appetites. But he was also a man who protected those weaker than himself. A man who did not believe in using his power against others. Eloise had chosen to be here, but he had to wonder how much of the past's sins had dictated that.

His father had hurt her unforgivably—he could see that now.

considered healthy, but healthy was the furthest thing from his mind. Because his life was not divorced of responsibility. Because he could not go off and live that quiet life that called to him like a rose petal on the wind. He could not. Because he had to save Arista. Because he had to make sure his father's legacy wasn't immortalized in glowing terms and song, but that he was remembered as he'd truly been.

He must.

And so if all the things inside him remained twisted, it was because they were twisted around these inevitabilities.

He could not be another man, and he would not seek to try. He would not turn away from all that he must do.

But he did not wish to turn away from the beauty that was before him either.

Whatever he might deserve.

He held his hand out, and she took it. A tentative light in her eyes.

And he wanted to banish that tentativeness. He wanted to tell her definitively that he would defend her. That he would slay every dragon.

Because he was piecing together these things, these events that had occurred. From the first time he had seen her when she was six years old to that time she had gone to his room and confessed her love to him in what he thought to be a brazen sort of manipulation. But if he saw it differently. If he looked at her differently, if he banished that cynicism that was so forceful inside of him...

Maybe she had loved him.

Maybe when she'd come to his room, when she'd kissed him, it had been with more sincerity and heart than he'd ever had inside his body.

A gift he had not known how to receive.

It made his chest feel like fire.

She had gone away and hidden, protected herself in the wake of his betrayal, because he could see that clearly now.

He had been the one who had wronged her.

Enormously.

He was not a man who understood love, but loyalty at least, he had made it a point to know. Honor. He had not acted with honor. She had been his friend, all because she had reached out to him. All because of her spirit, which was lovelier than his would ever be.

He had accused her of whoring herself out. He had paid her to leave.

She had gone away and made a quiet life

for herself. And she was correct. He was
the one who had sought her out. So if he
removed all of his presuppositions and the
deep, entrenched and unfair thoughts that
he had been directing at her for all these
years… He was left with the woman standing before him. Strong when those around
her who should've protected her had not
been. Filled with honor and integrity. With
strength. A girl who had thrived in spite of
the lack of care.

A wildflower left to grow on her own
in the garden, who had fought her way
through,without being consumed by weeds.

She was that wild garden at the house in
Virginia that he had thought was unkempt.
It was not.

For it tended itself, and it thrived in
the wild.

Just as Eloise did.

They should all be so lucky as to have that
kind of strength inside of them.

He himself? He was oriented to vengeance. But she had seen to her healing.

There was a power in her choice that
he had never known before. That he had
never seen.

They got in the limousine and were silent

on the drive to the palace this time. His own thoughts were turning. He was ready for this. More than ready.

But he had not anticipated that so much of his thought would be with her. How could he have? For his entire opinion on her had changed in just a couple of days.

The palace was open, brightly lit and glittering. Lights were strong over the courtyards, with guests spilling outside.

One of his father's perfectly immaculate glittering affairs.

These were not the sorts of debauched parties he had in secret. No. These were demonstrations of wealth and goodness, and only if you knew, only if you really knew, could you sense that hint of disreputability beneath it all.

But it was there.

And he knew it well.

The truth of the fact was that his father was often sleeping with his friends' wives. That there were no fences built by marriage vows, none that could not be handily crushed by the cavalier nature of the way all of these people treated relationships. But that was only what you would see if you wished to dig beneath the surface.

And none of the casual guests would. They would all simply enjoy the opulence around them and not dig at all into the glittering, terrible underbelly.

But, as he and Eloise walked into the ballroom, a hush came over the room, and he knew that his statements from yesterday had done their job. They had been in the media. And everyone here had heard the rumors, and here he was, and here she was. A bright beacon of truth. Substantiating those claims.

Here they were together. A reckoning.

"They know," he said. "And tonight, they have all turned up to see what will happen."

"It is amazing your father hasn't disbarred you from the event," she said.

"He won't. He won't because he knows that doing so will only create more rumor. And at this point, the scandal is already out of his control. He will not wish to be pressed."

"And you will press him," she said.

"Without hesitation," he responded. "But first, a dance."

He led her out to the middle of the dance floor and pressed her luscious body against his. For a moment, he forgot where they were. For a moment, he forgot why they were here.

Every eye in the room was on them. Every eye filled with curiosity, but he did not care. For what he wanted, what he really wanted was to have Eloise in his arms. Her soft skin beneath his hands.

She had become a symbol of his retribution. She had become a symbol of all of this. While she most of all was suddenly what he now wanted to avenge. More even than his mother.

As he looked at her angelic face, he could not explain why it had become suddenly the driving force, the driving need.

But it had.

She was the most important thing. She was everything.

Eloise.

The desire for her was like a fire in his blood, and for a moment, that thought gave him pause. Because he wondered if this heat in his blood was anything like his father's.

Vincenzo had never wanted a woman. Not a specific woman.

He desired women. He liked them in all their shapes and forms. But… He had never been sick with his desire for a specific one.

And here he was.

He wanted her above all else. He wanted

her more than revenge. He wanted her more than his next breath.

He traced his finger along the line of her jaw, and he felt her shiver beneath his touch.

He lowered his head, a breath away. "You are beautiful," he said.

"I feel beautiful."

Not foolish. For she had said so many times that she feared feeling foolish. But she did not feel as if her body was the sort that would create the reaction that he anticipated, but he could not see what she saw. He could only see desirability. He could only see beauty. But he could also see that it mattered what she thought of her own self. What she thought of her body. And he cared about that.

Another foreign feeling. Caring about another person in this way.

He had cared only about justice for a very long time.

Now he found he cared about her feelings.

And that was a novelty.

But he could not call it anything half so light as a novelty, not with any honesty. It was a pain that started at the center of his chest and burned outward like a wildfire. He looked over her shoulder and saw his father. Watching.

Even the King was watching.

Good.

He hoped that he was anticipating what came next.

The gaze of his father made him refocus. On his revenge. And that was when he decided to lean in and taste her lips. He felt her breath draw in just as his mouth touched hers. And he tasted that sweetness.

That rose petal on the wind. That glorious hint that filled his lungs if only for a moment before vanishing. Like a bright white moment of clarity. Of possibility. And suddenly, with that soft mouth beneath his own, everything seemed possible. They seemed possible.

And when they parted, it was gone. A hint of a memory that might've been a dream, because all that remained was Vincenzo. And all that he had yet to do.

"It is time," he said.

He moved away from her and made his way over to his father. "Congratulations," he said. "On the long-standing lineage of the Moretti family. Is that not why we are all here to celebrate?"

"It is why I could not bar you from the festivities. Yes."

"A tragedy for you," he said, feeling his mouth curve into a cruel smile even as he spoke. "But I think what I have to say about the Moretti family is something that all the guests in attendance may wish to hear."

He turned and, with an effortless ease, projected his voice over the din of the crowd. And he did not sound like an unhinged voice in the street, rather he spoke with the confidence and authority that flowed through his veins. "The Moretti family bloodline is filled with poison," he said. "There is no one who knows this better than Eloise St. George and myself. We have joined together, united as one in this common belief. The Moretti line must end. And it must be exposed for what it is. You, who have sat here in riches while your people starved. Who have rained the judgment down upon them while you engaged in every kind of debauchery. While you kept a mistress for more than twenty years in the same home as your wife, flaunting her as an assistant, using state funds to support the lifestyle. And then attempting to manipulate her daughter into an affair with you, and allowing the media to crucify her when she refused you. Using your power and position and lording it over the

women around you. You are a man with no
honor. You are a man with no dignity. You
are no kind of man. And I will take over the
throne, and when I do I will begin to dismantle the line. Your precious bloodline. As
destroyed as your reputation will be, once
the truth I have about you is disseminated
in the media."

"Whatever it is you're doing," his father
said. "It will not work. The country needs
me. The country needs the monarchy."

"The country needs nothing of the kind. I
have been building the infrastructure right
beneath your nose. Establishing the scaffold-
ing required for everything to go on when
you are no longer at the helm." His blood
burned with anger, but this was different.
This was a righteous, unending anger that
flowed through him. And it did not feel toxic
or calcified.

It was alive and so was he.

"Oh, yes. I have been pouring money
into this nation for years. Under the guise
of being an anonymous benefactor, foreign
aid. Foreign aid you should be ashamed to
accept given the amount of money that flows
through your coffers. But you are not. Because you are greedy. Because you are cor-

rupt. And when I ascend the throne, it will be to dismantle everything that you have built. The machine that you have created. And having me killed will solve nothing. Nothing at all. For even then you will lose your bloodline. I am not your ally, old man. And I have never been. And the line will die with me. For I will never have an heir. And the government will be turned over to the people. The Moretti line will not prevail for another five hundred years. It will not even prevail past the end of my life. I will deny you that. You will not live to see it, but you will live knowing it. You will watch the foundation of all that you are crumble. The rewriting of what will be in the history books after you are gone."

The room around them might have been a hundred yards in the distance, for in this moment, there was only him. Only his father.

"No one cares about a few women," his father sneered.

"Perhaps. Many do not. A small sin in this world. But it is not your only sin. And the rest? Do you think it was only my mother's life that spared you my wrath? I cared about her, but if I'd had all the evidence I needed to make sure your reign ended, unequivocally, when I revealed you, I would have done so on any given Tuesday. I don't require theatrics."

His father looked truly afraid now, and Vincenzo relished it. "I don't mind them, though." He grinned, and he knew it was filled with all the hatred that insulated his heart. "I have everything now. It is all in order. I was finally able to pay off one of your most trusted accountants to get me absolute proof of how you siphon money away from the people, and there may be those who will turn a blind eye to your sexual exploits, but what you have done to Arista? The name of Moretti will cease to exist. And what was it all for?"

He took a step closer to his father, and he felt as if someone had grabbed hold of his heart and taken it in their hand. Was holding it in place. Keeping it from beating. For he saw... Not the raging monster of his mind. But a man coming to the end of his years.

A man who was only a man.

"You are nothing but an old man who has left a legacy of pain. That is what you will leave in this world. It will be fixed when you are gone, and no one will think of you. You will die, and that will be the end of you."

"You would not dare. You would not dare do this. It does not benefit you."

"I don't care about power," Vincenzo said. "It is of no consequence to me."

"You… You think you're better than me. And here you are parading in with the same sort of whore that I have favored these many years. She would've warmed my bed if she had stayed longer. They all do in the end."

"That's a lie," Eloise said, her voice cutting over the sound of the gasps in the room. "I would never have warmed your bed. I denied you. When you came for me when I was only eighteen years old. I denied you."

His father's face contorted then, into an ugly, hateful sneer, and Vincenzo felt as if they were all watching him unmask himself. "You can say whatever you like, but the newspapers already spoke their piece. And people will always wonder."

"But I won't," she said. "And I am not hungry for a certain kind of reputation. I am only hungry for freedom. And I can have that. I will have it. You are nothing but a bitter, sad old man. Twisted. If you did not have power and money, no woman would touch you. And that is the difference between you and Vincenzo."

Vincenzo felt as if he'd been shot. Her defense of him, after all he had done.

"He does not crave it because he does not need it," she continued, all her righteous fire spilling from her, filling the room. "You do. You need to have power over the people that you manipulate into your sphere. Over the women that you manipulate into your bed. They must be afraid of you. You would've forced me, and we both know it. Even though the rumors leaked to the press were wrong, they were what rescued me. Because it was the rumors that made Vincenzo give me the money to leave. And I am grateful for that every day. Had I not been rescued by default of being sent away, I know that you would've forced me into your bed. You would've made me into another of your secrets. And I know what it's like to live my life as a secret. But I will not. Not anymore. Hiding was easier, because it allowed me to make my life mine. But I will not be cowed. Not for any reason. Not for anything. I am not afraid of you. I am not a powerless girl. And no one should be afraid of you. Everyone should know what you are, openly. So that no one is keeping your secrets, and no one is trying to pretend."

"You bitch of a girl," he said.

"That is enough," Vincenzo said, stepping forward. "Eloise is a woman. Filled with bravery and integrity, and she makes the world better for being in it. Something you will never ever understand. You are nothing but a coward. Your entire kingdom is built upon perfidy. It is built upon lies. And tonight it is finished. In the future it will be finished for good."

"You are dead to me," his father said.

Vincenzo turned. "I would love to say that you were dead to me. But you are not. You are very much alive. And until you are dead, you will not be able to be dead to me. Because I must fight against you. You have made it so. I refuse to allow you to exist as you do. To be as you are. What I want you to know is that you are a fool. Believing that I was simply distant. Believing that I was not secretly acting against you all this time. You are a man of great manipulation. But it did not occur to you that your own son might have secrets of his own. Did not occur to you that your own son might be hiding the truth of the matter from you. And of course it never occurred to you that you might miss something."

"You cannot do this."

"I have. The ball is in motion. All the information that I've compiled about you is being sent out to various news sources automatically tonight. And I daresay there will be a reckoning about what took place in this very ballroom. I cannot imagine that all your guests will remain tight-lipped. Many of them will be rushing to speak against you. To make it clear that they do not wish to associate with you in any way. They will all flee from you like rats from a sinking ship. Even your mistress would be wise to do the same."

"You cannot…"

"I have done my part," Vincenzo said. "The rest will unfold on its own. It is over now. You do not deserve silence. And no one here deserves protection. I would remember that when you all go out into the world. You must choose a side. I would advise you choose the side that stands against him."

He looked over at Eloise, who was burning bright, her breath coming in harsh, sharp bursts. Eloise. She would not be broken by this. Because she was not the fragile wisp of a creature he had deemed her when she'd come to his bed and kissed him. She was not the great manipulator he had allowed himself to believe she was thereafter.

She was strong. And she was brilliant.

And he was trying to think now of all that he could give her.

Make her your mistress.

No. It was impossible. That was the only thing that burned now. She could not be his mistress, because he would not dishonor her in that way. And he would not take a wife.

But she could be his. For the night.

He would give her everything they could have had then.

Because now triumph burned in his veins, and need burned in his gut, and he needed her. He needed her more than he needed to breathe.

He needed her more than he needed anything.

Like atonement.

Like redemption.

He took her hand and escorted her from the room.

When they were outside the palace, Eloise did something entirely unexpected. She threw her arms around his neck, and kissed him.

CHAPTER EIGHT

ELOISE COULD NOT explain what was happening to her. She couldn't explain the feeling that was fizzing through her veins.

But she felt like she was ready to crawl out of her own skin. She felt like she was ready for something. For something big. For something changing. Altering.

She needed him. As she had felt when she was eighteen, but this time that burned brighter and hotter.

This time she burned brighter and hotter. Incandescent.

Rage.

She was so angry. For the shame the King had made her feel all these years. For the way she had been written about. She had tried to push all that aside, to reconcile it. But it was wrong, and it had hurt. She had been called a whore countless times, wrapped in the language of smug men wielding pens and trying to sell clicks.

And she had never let herself be angry. She had tried to move on. She had tried to let it go, but here she was, back in the thick of everything, and she could not let it go. She did not feel placid and healed and normal. She did not feel like a lazy day gardening. She felt like a thwarted warrior who needed only a sword so that she could take it out and cut off the head of her accuser.

She was furious. And right then she did want revenge. Right now she wanted satisfaction for all the things that she had been through. For the life spent ignored, for the girl that she had been walking these palace halls, for the young woman she had become who had fallen in love with Vincenzo only to be cruelly rejected. Who had been paid off by the one person she'd cared about, and he hadn't believed in her any more than anyone else. Who'd had to forge a life by herself. Who had only ever been able to find contentment by herself, and never with another person. And certainly never in the arms of another person.

It was hell.

And she felt like she was burning.

She had tried. She had tried so hard to be… Above it. But right now she was in it. And she was being roasted in these flames, and she wanted to burn more. Burn brighter. Burn until it was not only anger. Burn until she was not just a victim. She wanted to burn it all away. All of it. And so, without thinking, she kissed him. And it was everything she had ever imagined. More than that kiss out on the dance floor, which had sparked something in her. More than touching his chest during their dance lesson this morning—had it really been this morning? She could hardly believe it. More than anything. Ever.

It was all him. It always had been. And maybe tonight was about reclaiming something. Reclaiming something for her own. Reclaiming a piece of her that had never experienced satisfaction.

Maybe that's what it was.

And so she kissed him. He put his hand on the back of her head and held her close. Angled his head so that he could take the kiss deeper. And when his tongue touched hers, it was gasoline to the lit match that was Eloise.

They were standing there in front of the palace, and it might as well be a burning building behind them. Ready to explode with the powder keg they had set off there. And still they were kissing. Absurdly, and perhaps appropriately.

"Let's go," he growled against her mouth.

He growled.

He did want her.

And everything else could wait. All of the complicated feelings she had about tonight, all of her concerns for the future. All of it could wait until tonight was over. Because tonight she felt beautiful, and it didn't feel like it had teeth. Didn't feel like the cost of her beauty was her dignity or her agency. Didn't feel like her beauty could only exist if it took the shape her mother tried to force her into.

She felt both in and out of control in the most glorious, delicious way. And she wanted to claim it. As she staked a claim on herself and on him. He had been a wound. An old wound that had lived deep inside her, not because she didn't understand that their age difference at the time had made it perfectly reasonable that he had rejected her. It was that she had felt like she had revealed a part of herself, for the first time, to another person, and she had been rejected. She had felt

fragile all these years. And now she felt…
Reborn. Like she was reclaiming something
that had been twisted and perverted, taken
from her.

Tonight she felt giddy with her excitement over him. With the hope of what it
might mean.

No, not a future together. He had made
it abundantly clear that was never going to
happen for him. And as for her…

She could not tie herself to this family. To
this place. This was the end of it. Her eyes
filled with tears, because she did not want
to think of that. So she leaned in and kissed
him again, and she pushed all thoughts of
the future away.

They got into the limo, and he pulled her
onto his lap. She put her thighs on either side
of his and kissed him, uncertain where her
confidence came from. Where her reckless
abandon had come from.

She rocked her hips against the hard ridge
of his arousal and she ignited.

She was slick and hot and ready for him,
and a childhood crush had not prepared her
for the desire she would feel as a woman.

No. It had not. "We still have to get into

my penthouse," he growled. "Or I would strip you naked now."

The dark promise sent a thrill through her entire body. She would not be opposed to that. Not really. They could have the driver go around the block and he could take her here, right in the back of the car. They wouldn't have to pause to think; they wouldn't have to pause for breath. They wouldn't have to pause for anything, and that was what she wanted. Because thought felt like the enemy right now. She didn't want thoughts. She wanted feelings. Nothing more than the deep, intense feelings that existed between them. The unending desire that he had built inside her. It felt magical. And few things in her life ever felt magical.

She nearly laughed.

Because she could remember when she had been a girl, and she had thought that moving to the palace meant she was a princess.

There was nothing half so terrible as a nightmare adjacent to a fantasy. She knew, because she had lived it. She had never been a princess. She had been a ghost.

A ghost in her own life. A ghost in the life of those around her, and she would not do it. Not now. Not anymore.

And so she rolled her hips forward and reached between them, undoing the button on his pants and undoing the zipper as well, reaching her hand inside and gripping the hot, hard evidence of his desire for her.

His breath hissed through his teeth, and she marveled her own boldness.

But she was not a girl. She might not have practical experience of men and sex, but she knew all about it. She had read plenty of books that described the act in glorious metaphor and had seen quite a few TV series that had presented it in less than metaphorical visuals.

She knew that it was all right for a woman to be bold. In fact, it was appreciated.

And she knew what to do to follow her own desire. That felt somehow miraculously like a gift. Like an inbuilt sort of magic she hadn't known was there.

His head fell back onto the seat, his breath hissing through his lips. And she pushed herself off his lap, down onto the floor of the limo. She looked up at him, at the strong, hard column of his arousal.

She leaned in, flicking her tongue over the head of him. And he reached back, grabbing her hair and guiding her movements as she took him deep between her lips, sliding her tongue over his hardened length.

She was lost in it. In the glory. In her power.

For here she was on her knees with the most vulnerable part of him in her mouth. And he was at her mercy.

It didn't matter that she was less experienced. It didn't matter that she was younger. Here, they were equals. Here, on her knees before the Prince, perhaps she was even the one in charge of things.

It was a heady discovery. A deep, intense experience that she hadn't known she had wanted. But hadn't she spent all of her life feeling helpless? Surrounded by people with more money, more power and more powers of manipulation than she would ever have.

She was in charge now. She was.

He growled, bucking his hips upward, the hard length of him touching the back of her throat, and she steeled herself against that surge of power. And found that she loved it. Because it spoke of his lack of control. Because it spoke of his need for her.

She continued to pleasure him like that, until the limo pulled up to the front of the building. He looked down at her, his black eyes glittering.

"Maybe you should tell him to go around the block," she said, sliding her tongue from his base to his tip.

The tension in his neck was evident, the tendons there standing out, the tension in his jaw live with electricity.

"No," he said.

He righted his trousers, putting himself away and pulling her back up to the seat.

"We will finish this properly."

And she hated the underlying truth in those words, because what he was not saying was that they would finish it in a bed because tonight would be the only night they ever had.

Because this was their only moment.

It made her feel a sense of profound grief, and she couldn't understand it.

She didn't want to understand it.

He got out of the car, then reached in, taking her hand and drawing her out onto the street as though she had not just been tasting him intimately. They looked for all the world like a proper couple who had not been engaged in sex acts in the back of a car.

It gave her a secret, giddy thrill.

It made her feel like she never had before.

Because she had given herself that quiet life, had disappeared into her garden and her flowers.

Those flowers that were simply beautiful as they grew and didn't have to strive for it. Those flowers that were not victimized for their beauty.

She had done it because it was healing, but her version of healing had had a cost. It was far too quiet. At the end of all things, it felt too sedate.

At the end of everything, what she had done was sand all the hard edges off her life, but with that she had taken the excitement. The thrill.

In truth, she had never really had a thrill. In truth, all of her life had been decided by others. There had been pain, there had been grief and sadness and neglect. There had been danger.

But no one had ever thrown her a birthday party. She had been surrounded by evidence that the capacity for lavish celebrations existed, but none had ever been wasted on her.

Not a kind word had ever been thrown her way.

Living amongst all that wealth… And no

one had ever distributed even the smallest bit to her. She was fed, and she was clothed.

But she did not have beautiful Christmas trees and Christmas presents.

Because she was not a princess. And she never had been.

And so for this night, to seize the thrill of it all… It seemed worth it. But she mourned already that it could not go on.

At least she had a quiet life to return to. A safe life.

At least she had that.

The elevator ride was a study in torture, and they stood with just a scant amount of space between their bodies. And she did her best to breathe. To breathe in and out and to stop her thoughts. Her body was rioting with desire. She could still taste him on her tongue, and she was slick between her thighs with the anticipation of what was to come.

The elevator doors opened, and he walked out ahead of her and extended his hand, as he had done out on the street, but this time they were not going out into public. This time he was beckoning her into his lair.

This time he was inviting her to a private night of sin, and she was going to accept. She reached out, and her fingertips brushed his.

A shudder went down her spine. The desire that was growing inside her was almost pain.

He drew her out, his dark eyes never leaving hers. Her mouth went dry.

No, it wasn't almost pain. Now it was pain. A deep, aching emptiness, and the desire to be filled by him.

She wanted him. She might be a virgin, but she knew full well what was going to happen here, and that she would receive it with great relish. She wasn't concerned about the pain.

Pain was familiar to her. And pain passed. That was one thing she had learned. You could live through unimaginable emotional pain. Betrayal, fear. You just had to find a way to get through the moment. A bit of physical pain didn't concern her at all.

It was amazing, really. That she had no nerves. That she didn't feel a sense of worry over what she did not know. Because she was with Vincenzo. And everything would be fine. That knowledge echoed deep within her soul, and she could not have explained it to anyone, let alone herself.

But it was Vincenzo.

The man she had fallen in love with when

she was a teenager. The man she had never forgotten.

The man she had always wanted. This... This was inevitable in a way that she could never explain.

It felt right.

Sad in a way, but in a way that she was determined not to think about. Because this was their night.

The culmination of all that she had felt for him from the time she was a girl.

Vincenzo.

And then he swept her into his arms, and he kissed her, with a deep, unyielding need that stoked a fire down in her belly and made her feel like she was the flame itself.

She stood back away from him; she needed to do this. She reached around behind herself and grabbed the zipper tab on the revealing dress that she had worn all evening and un-zipped it. Let it fall down to her waist, let it reveal her bare breasts. She needed to do this. To choose to reveal her body to him.

To stand proud in it.

Because it was the evidence of the shape that her life had taken. Of the things that she loved. Of the fact that she enjoyed baking bread and eating it too. That she liked cakes,

and always had. That she also worked outside in the sun, and had freckles on her arms
and shoulders from being out in it. That her
nails were short because you could not garden with long fingernails, at least not nicely
and easily.

This was the Eloise that she had chosen to
be. And now she was choosing to give herself to him.

She pushed the dress down over her hips,
leaving herself standing there in only her
glorious, gold shoes and a pair of gold panties. She knew, because she had looked at herself in the mirror, that they made a slight dent
in her hips, and she had known a moment of
insecurity about that. Because it revealed her
body was not perfectly taut or toned.

But then she looked at his face and saw
the hunger there. She did not feel regretful
about anything. About herself.

She took a step toward him, and she saw
a muscle in his jaw jump.

"You are beautiful," he rasped, the words
scraping over his throat.

Her cheeks heated.

"I'm glad you think so."

"I would never say that your body is made
for sex. Not when it clearly accomplishes so

many other wonderful things. But I do believe that sex...with me...may be one of its highest purposes."

She should not appreciate that. But she did.

She stopped, and she put her hand on his chest. "Only if you concede that your body was definitely made for sex. And most especially with me." His lips curved into a smile, and it made her stomach dip. Because how often did this man smile? So rarely. If ever.

She began to undo the buttons on his shirt, slowly, and there was an increased thrill to seeing his chest when she was the one uncovering it. It had been glorious when he had come in shirtless, and she had danced with him only this morning, but this...

This was unmistakably sexual. An unmistakable expression of their need for one another. She moved her hands over the hard planes of his chest, his stomach, then slid them back up to his shoulders, pushing his shirt and jacket down onto the floor.

He was glorious. Just standing there in a low-slung pair of black pants, all his hard-cut muscles on display.

He was physical perfection. In the classic sense. A man who seemed carved from rock rather than flesh, and yet he was hot to the touch, and she could not deny that he was every inch a man. He made her mouth water.

And she had thought that she wanted to lick him. So now she would.

She leaned in, kissing his chest, then pressing the flat of her tongue there, drawing it over his nipple and up his neck, before biting the edge of his jaw.

And he moved, grabbing hold of her, taking her wrists and pinning them behind her back, down at the base of her spine.

"Little minx."

"Maybe."

She didn't feel like herself. Or rather, she did. She felt like herself unfettered, even as he held her there captive.

She had wondered what it might be like to live in a moment where she didn't carry pain or baggage from the past. Where she didn't carry inhibition, and she seemed to be living in that fantasy.

For everything just felt right. Everything felt free. And so did she.

He kissed her, holding her captive as he did so. And then he lifted her up off the ground and carried her back to his bedroom.

He deposited her at the center of the bed and reached out, hooking his finger through the waistband of her panties and dragging them down her legs. Then he took hold of her ankles, undid the delicate buckles on her shoes, one by one, slid them off and discarded them on the floor.

"Sit back against the pillows," he commanded. "And spread your legs."

For a moment, she knew embarrassment, because it was a frank command. And she did not know that she could withstand it.

"Spread them," he repeated, and so she found herself obeying, sliding back and leaning against the pillows on the headboard, parting her thighs, even though she felt as if there was a magnet between them trying to get her to put them back shut. To conceal herself.

It was one thing to stand before him bare, and imagine herself a classical painting, but quite another to do something so openly sexual.

This was not the kind of thing you could walk into a museum and see.

This was something else altogether.

But she did it. And when she saw the effect that it had on him, when she could see the outline of his arousal through the fabric of his pants, her embarrassment faded away.

And she found herself unconsciously moving her hand toward the heart of herself, drawing her finger slowly through her own slick folds.

"Dammit, Eloise," he ground out. "This is not going to last as long as I wanted it to."

"But we have all night," she said, her breath coming in short bursts as her arousal began to reach a fever pitch.

The need for him combined with the teasing touch of her own fingers.

And the view of his desire for her.

"Yes," he agreed.

He kicked his shoes and socks off, and then moved his hands to his belt buckle, undoing it slowly before pushing his pants down his lean hips and revealing his flesh to her.

She arched her hips up off the bed, beseeching.

Because she was so hungry for him.

His lips curved slightly.

He wrapped his masculine hand around his own desire, squeezing himself, and then he made his way to the bed, still holding his arousal in hand. He slid his hand around the back of her head and forced her head upward, kissing her. Then he moved between her thighs and replaced the touch of her hand with the head of him. He slid it back and forth through her slick folds, and she shuddered, that hollow sensation there growing more pronounced. Growing wider.

"Please," she whispered.

"Not yet," he growled. He moved down her body, kissing her breasts, sucking one nipple into his mouth before turning his attention to the other one. Then he kissed his way down her stomach, until his face was scant inches from the most intimate part of her, his hands on her hips. Then he started to lick her. He was not delicate in the strokes he made against her body. He was decisive. Firm. The flat of his tongue moving over the most sensitized part of her. And then he moved his lips to that centralized bundle of nerves and sucked it in deep.

She screamed. Her climax broke over her in a wave, pounding against her, never-ending.

And when he came back to her, kissed her, let her taste her own desire, there was no fear in her.

Only need.

The need for him that she'd had for so many years.

This man who had felt like the other half of her soul at one time.

Leaving him had felt like losing herself.

But he was here now.

And he was there, between her thighs again, the blunt head of him now probing the entrance to her body. And she could feel herself stretching, could feel a slight bit of pain.

Then he growled and thrust into her in one smooth stroke, pain and pleasure bursting behind her eyes, for this was what she had wanted. More than anything. This was the answer to the need in her, and while there was pain there, it was offset by the deep sense of satisfaction that she felt. And she understood it. She understood why women did this even though it hurt.

Because it hurt not to. Because it was the only way to find true satisfaction.

Because there was no other answer.

He looked at her, his expression strange, but it faded. And then he began to move. Building the desire in her stroke by glorious stroke.

Impossibly, she felt need begin to build inside of her again. And when it broke over her, he went right along with her, growling out his pleasure as he found his own release. As he spilled himself inside of her.

And when it was over, he lay beside her, stroking her face.

"You should've told me," he said.

"I should've told you what?"

"You either have not been with a man for a very long time, or you have never been with a man at all."

She closed her eyes. She could lie. She could lie to protect herself. But why? This was tonight.

And they got to have tonight. And why should there be any lies between them?

"I have not been with a man," she said. "Not with anyone."

"No, Eloise," he said. "I was appalling to you."

"Yes," she said. "You were. But I'm used to that."

"I hate that even more. That it did not affect you because I'm just one of the many people who have treated you cruelly."

"The world is cruel, Vincenzo. And we either hide from it as I have done, or we learn to become cruel in it, as you have done. At least you fight for the right things. You try. You have honor."

And she realized as she said the words, just how true they were. That this was why it could only be one night. For Vincenzo had chosen his path, and she had chosen hers. And tonight they were able to meet in this bright place of glory. Tonight, they were able to meet at this place of pleasure. Where neither the world nor either of them needed to be cruel.

But she would have to go back. Because she had chosen her way, and he had chosen his.

And she had to admit to herself that his way… It was hard and sharp. Like living in a battlefield, but it at least helped people. What did her method do? It did nothing. It did not protect anyone else.

It made her feel ashamed.

But they had tonight. And she would not let anything else matter.

"Why have you not been with another man?"

"You know why not," she said. "You know why."

"My father."

"It's part of it. But I never felt like my body was right. And I never felt like it was mine. And I was afraid… I was afraid of becoming my mother. She has made terrible choices in the pursuit of men. In the pursuit of her desire for them. Or for what they can give her, and I never wanted that. You must understand, what happened between the two of us made me question myself in a very deep way. And I did not wish to question that. I did not wish to find myself lacking in that way."

"The very fact that you have a concern about that proves that you are not your mother."

"Perhaps."

"It doesn't matter. Tonight you are mine."

She smiled. "Yes. Tonight I'm yours.

They made love all night and slept in between. At one point he got up and made them a platter of fruit, cheese and honey. All the things that he already knew that she loved, and it made her ache. Because this could not last. Because she could not stay with him. With her Vincenzo. She had to get away from here. She had to go back to the safe space that she had created for herself. But they had tonight. And it had been glorious. That would be enough.

It would have to be.

When the sun rose up over the mountains, she dressed in the clothing that was hers and sneaked out of the penthouse. It did not take long for her to find a flight that would take her back to Virginia by way of England.

She turned her phone off so that when Vincenzo discovered that she was gone he would not be able to contact her. Because if he did… She would not be able to be strong.

CHAPTER NINE

WHEN HE HAD awakened to find that Eloise was gone, it had come as a shock to him. A shock that had faded with the passage of these many months, especially as the media storm that he had brought down upon his father, and on Arista, had had some unexpected results.

His father had abdicated. And fled before legal proceedings could be taken up against him. Whether or not he had taken Cressida St George along with him was a mystery, but she had vanished as well.

Leaving Vincenzo on the cusp of being crowned King. His coronation would coincide with the new year. Though it was merely a formality, as he was even now acting the part of ruler.

It gave him little time to ponder Eloise. But he did. In those quiet moments when there was nothing but the breeze and he thought of roses.

It was an impossibility, anyway. The two of them. An impossibility that they should ever have anything more than that single night.

It was perfect, poetic in many ways. As if they had somehow consummated the vengeance itself.

And yet he dreamed of her.

And he wanted no other woman. Though he told himself there was no time for women anyway.

He was rearranging a country.

He was not going to plunge them straight into democracy, but rather he was establishing oversight. Parliament. He would not abolish the monarchy overnight, for there was no practicality there.

The people were used to being ruled with an iron fist, and when it came to restrictions, Vincenzo was opening the floodgates.

There were many older citizens, however, who wondered at the security if they did not have a king.

And Vincenzo was happy to see that everything ran the way that he thought it should, and that everyone felt secure.

He was thankful, also, for his friends from Oxford, who had been his lifeline through all of this.

Rafael, bastard though he was, in every sense of the word, had been the acting Regent of his nation for years, waiting for his younger brother, the true heir, to come into majority.

Jag was well established in his own country, and Zeus was god of all he surveyed. Though he was not the ruler of his country as yet, he certainly behaved as though he ran the world.

It was not unusual for them to clear their schedules and fly to the nearest major city to meet up for a drink or two. Even less unusual for them to make video calls to one another. He felt privileged to be surrounded by them as advisors. Though he often thought it funny, given the hell they had raised in their youths. Age, he thought, came for everyone.

So it was not entirely unexpected when his computer chimed, and he answered, that the first face that popped up was Rafael. Followed by Zeus and then Jag.

"It's late here," Jag said.

"Apologies," Rafael said, but he did not sound at all sorry.

He could see that Rafael was in his study, a fire roaring behind him. It was cold in his mountainous country near Spain, as it was in Arista.

"You've never been apologetic a day in your life," Zeus said. "It's one of the things I like about you."

Rafael waved a hand, dismissing them. Then his black eyes met Vincenzo's through the screen. "You have not seen," he said.

"Seen what?"

"I knew it. For if you had seen it, you would've phoned us. Or, at least would've looked like thunder when you answered."

"I always look like thunder. The cost of figuring out how to repair a country so badly managed."

"No," Rafael said. "This is worse than the state of your country."

"What?"

Rafael picked up a newspaper and held it up. It took a moment for it to come into focus on the screen, but when it did…

"What is the meaning of this?"

"Why, it looks as though your lover is round with child," Zeus said, looking darkly amused. "So much for all of your proclamations regarding the ending of your line. It seems that your seed is prodigious."

"I will thank you to not speak of my seed," Vincenzo said, continuing to stare at the image before him.

For it was indeed Eloise. At a grocery store, with a very clear and obvious baby bump beneath her sweater.

"Why is this..."

But the headline made it all clear. The former lover of King Vincenzo, who had disappeared seven months prior without a word after dropping bombshells regarding the previous King of Arista, was now looking about as pregnant as one might be had they conceived during that time. So of course the speculation was that she carried the heir to the throne of Arista.

She carried the heir to the throne of Arista.

The truth of it hit him hard.

He had failed.

He had made one vow. He had said that he would not carry on his father's line, and that bastard yet lived, and he was likely bringing a child into the world. It filled him with rage.

"No," he said. "This must be... It must be doctored."

"You did not sleep with the delectable

woman that you brought to help destroy your father?" Jag asked.

"That is beside the matter. I have slept with many women, and none of them have ended up carrying my child."

"Yes, but did you use a condom?" Rafael asked.

"Excuse me?"

"A condom," Zeus said. "They've been around for quite some time. Known by many names. French letters. Surely even in your little backward country you are familiar with the concept of keeping it under wraps."

"I…"

He had not used a condom. And he was only just realizing this. He had been… It had been an intense night. Filled with the revelations of the day and the rather unpleasant business of the ball. And he had been swept away. Just as she had been. But she was a virgin. He should've…

"Yeah," Zeus said. "No condom. Excellent."

"You must marry her," Rafael said.

"I'm sorry, am I taking orders from you now?"

"No," Rafael said. "But as the bastard in this group of legitimized men, I feel I must speak to my own experience. The Crown was denied to me. Because my father would not marry my mother. And here I am, doing all the work, planning my brother's wedding, in fact, so that he might take the throne. Managing all the things that come with it, as if I am a glorified nanny, all for want of legal documentation between my parents. I could've been king. Instead of a nanny."

"It is my will that none should be king," Vincenzo said.

"So abolish the monarchy. Carry on as you intended," Jag said. "There is no reason for you to change your plans. But Rafael is right. A real man does not impregnate a woman and allow her to go unwed."

"We do not all live in the Dark Ages," Zeus said. "I don't know. You could set her up in a very nice home. Adjacent to yours, if you ever plan on visiting the child. Though, children are quite boring."

"Thank you," Vincenzo said. "For your concerns regarding the entertainment factor of the child that I may have created. However, whether or not I find it amusing to become a father is irrelevant. If I am to become one… Then I will do as I must."

"You will marry her," Rafael said.

"Not because you told me to," Vincenzo said.

"Petulant," Zeus said.

"Hardly. As if you would obey the dictates of that asshole."

"Absolutely not," Zeus said. "I cannot be tamed. By anyone. But, I use condoms. So."

"God help you when you meet a vixen who matches the appeal of Eloise St. George."

It was foolish to even attempt to defend himself, and yet he did.

"I have met any number of vixens," Zeus said. "Minxes, scarlet women and temptresses. And still. No bastards."

"Marry her quickly," Rafael said. "We will all be at your wedding."

"We'd better be *in* the wedding," Zeus said.

"I should think so," Jag said. "It is the only wedding we are likely to take part in."

And all Vincenzo could think was that he would be incredibly, darkly amused if any one of them ended up in the position where they were forced to marry. "Just don't make it around the new year," Rafael said. "It is my brother's wedding."

"Yes," Zeus said. "He is marrying that fresh-faced little princess from Santa Castelia. She is quite delectable."

Rafael's face turned to stone. "She is barely twenty-two years of age. I would prefer you keep your opinions on my future sister-in-law and her beauty to yourself."

There was a thread of steel in his voice that was always present, but it was much more intense than usual.

He had not given full credit to the rather unfair nature of the situation Rafael found himself in. Because of course, he was a placeholder. For his younger brother, who he must herd through life as if he was his son.

All after their father gave no thought at all to Rafael himself.

But Rafael's problems were of no real concern to him right now. The biggest issue was the fact that he was going to be a father.

He was going to be a father.

He had never wanted this. He had sworn that he would not...

He was here in Arista, on the cusp of keeping his promise to his father. Working to dismantle everything.

But Eloise was carrying his baby. And that changed everything. Eloise, who he had not been able to stop thinking of since their time together. Eloise.

"I must charter a private jet to Virginia."

"When?" Zeus asked.

"Tonight."

Eloise was sitting at the kitchen table, solemnly looking around at all her decorations. She had imagined that when she was an adult she might have a different sort of holiday season. That she would decorate festively and cheerfully and capture the magic of Christmas that she had always missed as a girl.

She had always done her house up beautifully, and yet it still never felt... Magic. But even now, nursing a broken heart, she felt a tingling of magic. Because by next Christmas she would have a child to share the holiday with.

The thought made her heart nearly overflow.

She had been terrified, ever since she had taken that pregnancy test and it had come back positive. But she had known... She had known that she wanted the child. She had also known with perfect clarity that Vincenzo did not. He had vowed never to have an heir. It meant something to him. That promise.

Vincenzo was on a path. And nothing would change his mind about that path. Nothing. She didn't want their child to be a source of contention. She had returned to her quiet life, and that was a gift. She had her cottage; it was paid for. And she wanted the baby. She wanted to be a mother. And she had not fully realized what that would mean until this moment. Sitting there in her house surrounded by the Christmas decorations that had never really created the feeling in her that she wanted to have.

Holidays in the palace had been—as had everything—for the enjoyment of the adults. There had been parties she was not allowed to attend and gifts that had not been for her.

She had never had anyone to share it with.

She had never had family to sit by the Christmas tree with. And now she would. And her child... She would throw them birthday parties and Christmas celebrations. She would delight in their achievements and comfort them when they failed. She would do for her child what no one had ever done for her.

And there was something hopeful in that. In knowing that she could change something about the world. And knowing that she could take a little piece of the hurt inside of herself and transform it into something different. Into something new.

No, she could never have the relationship with her mother that she might have wished for as a child, but she could be the kind of mother that she had wished for. She would have another person in her life that she could love and...

Well, very much of her had wished that she could love Vincenzo but... This was better. It was.

She would raise the child far away from Arista. Far away from the palace, and all that pain. It would be better. She would be better.

No. She couldn't have Vincenzo.

But that was all right.

She had accepted that. Before she had gotten into his bed. She wished, just slightly, that she might have thought a little more clearly about the consequences of their joining. But...

Now? Now she felt happy. Even now, sitting there by herself with the snow falling outside the window...

There was a knock at the door. Skerret leaped onto the table and knocked her ball of yarn off onto the floor.

"Skerret," she scolded.

The cat jumped down, startling again when there was another knock on the door.

She got up, and she walked over to the door, looking out the side window. Her heart fell down to her feet.

Because standing there on the doorstep, snowflakes collecting on the shoulder of his dark wool coat, was Vincenzo.

Oh, she didn't know what to do. She hadn't wanted him to know about this... She glanced down at her rounded stomach. But she couldn't avoid him. He was here.

It didn't matter. She would simply face it. It was her decision after all. She was pregnant, and she wanted the baby.

She took a deep breath and opened the door. But what she was about to say died on her lips. Because she had forgotten how beautiful he was. Or maybe it was simply that a mere memory could not hold within it the intensity and brilliance that was Vincenzo Moretti.

"Hi," she said.

Well, that was just perfect. That was not at all what she had meant to say.

He looked down at her stomach, then back up at her. "It is true," he said.

"What's true?"

From the interior pocket of his jacket he

took a folded-up newspaper and held it out toward her.

And then she recognized herself. Standing in front of a rack of candy bars, with her baby bump clear and visible. And the headline read: King's Lover Pregnant with Heir?

"Oh, no," she said. "I don't… Vincenzo, I don't know how they got this…"

"Do not tell me the baby is not mine, *cara mia*. For we both know that it is. You were a virgin when you came to my bed, and I hardly think that you leaped straight from my bed into a different one."

"How do you know?" She scowled, indignant at his assumption. "For all you know, I decided sex is actually quite fun and I should like to have more of it. Maybe I went straight from your bed to someone else's. I did leave very quickly." She was practically breathing fire. He'd thought all of this about her easily before, why not now?

Standing there in a rage as if she'd betrayed him, when she knew damned well, as did he, that he'd emphatically stated he did not want a child. As if she'd taken something from him when he had said from the beginning he wanted nothing to do with it.

"Do not play games, Eloise," he said. "I'm not amenable to them."

"Well, what you are or aren't amenable to is my highest concern, Vincenzo."

"Come with me."

She should have known that if he found out he would be inflexible, obnoxious and demanding. On account of the fact he was inflexible, obnoxious and demanding.

"I cannot come with you," she said. "I have a Christmas tree. And a cat."

"Is the cat not outdoors?"

"No. When it began to snow I brought Skerret in."

His lips flattened into a stark line. "That is a ridiculous name for a cat."

"Well, it just kind of… It fits her. Because she gets scared very easily. And also she is sort of slinky like a ferret. And so she's a Skerret."

"It is still ridiculous."

She was pregnant, he had come to take her away and they were debating the merits of her cat's name. "I can't go with you," she said forcefully.

"You can't or you won't?"

"It amounts to the same thing. And anyway, you said you didn't want a child. You in fact vowed never to have one."

"I did. But you are having one. So… It does not matter what I said."

"Yes, it does," she said. "Vincenzo, you can pretend it doesn't matter but it does. Look, you don't have to do anything with this child. I am prepared to care for him or her myself."

"You don't know what you're having?"

"No. I declined to find out. I wanted to be surprised. I know it sounds strange, but I'm very happy. The idea of being a mother… I didn't know that I wanted it. I had told myself that I would be better off living a quiet life by myself. But now… I quite like the idea of sharing it with someone. It pleases me. I'm very… I'm very content with the way things are turning out. You have to trust me. I… I'm not unhappy."

"You mistake me," he said, stepping into the cottage and filling the space. She had forgotten, too, how commanding his presence was. "I did not come here to see to your well-being, Eloise. I came here to claim my child. This is not a welfare check. This is a proposal. Or kidnap, if need be."

"A *proposal*?"

"You will marry me."

"That is a demand, not a proposal. And I will not," she said.

"You will," he said. "I am about to be King, and we must marry before my coronation or the child will be a bastard. Do you understand the implications of that?"

"I… I guess I don't. I… This isn't the Dark Ages. Surely that doesn't mean a thing."

"It does. It means he or she will not be able to inherit the throne."

"You did not want the throne to carry on," she said.

"I don't know what I want now," he said, shaking his head. "There was a way of things. That I had planned, and none of this fits into it. None of this is what I wanted. None of it is right. And yet it is what is. So I must adjust my plans accordingly, must I not?"

"I'm set to have Christmas here."

"It does not matter. You will come with me."

"Don't you want to know why I left?"

He looked as if she had slapped him.

"Why you left?"

"Yes. The morning after we… After we

were together. Don't you want to know why I left?"

"Why then? As you are surely intent on telling me."

"I left because I could not stand the idea of…being in Arista any longer. I do not want to be in the palace. All of it, the royal protocol, the location, the walls themselves are nothing more than a terrible memory for me. And it is not something that I can…fathom living with for the rest of my life. Vincenzo, this is my home. And in it I made a place for myself, and I do not wish to go back to being that sad girl lost in a royal life that she was never meant to live."

"I am not my father," he whispered.

"I didn't say that you were. But that does not change the fact that I do not feel at home there. Nor do I want to."

She had just been sitting there, feeling excited about her future. About what she might have with her child. She had been imagining the simple, quiet life where they did not have to consider anyone. Where they did not have to conform, or hide in the shadows.

The very idea of returning and marrying Vincenzo… And he was to be King! It was everything she didn't want. It was so many connections, so much responsibility. It was a nightmare.

"No. I cannot."

"Come back with me," he said.

"No, Vincenzo."

"You must come back with me," he said. "Or I will have no choice but to take the child."

"You wouldn't." She searched his face, tried to put aside her own fear, her own anger and see what on earth he was thinking. Feeling. He'd said he didn't want this, and yet here he was. One thing she knew was Vincenzo was a man driven by his own code of honor, consumed by it, and it didn't matter if she could make sense of it or not. When he decided something, it was the way of things. "You don't want the child," she reminded him. "You said as much yourself."

"I said I didn't want a child. Now there will be one. And that is simply the way of it. I am not turning away from my responsibility. I will not do it. I am a man who knows what is right. And I will do it. I will do my duty. In this as in all things." His voice sounded shattered, and it was the only thing on earth keeping her from lashing out at him entirely.

The only thing that was pressing her to go with him.

"So you really will blackmail me, then?"

"If I have to. I was always willing to, Eloise. That must've been clear."

"I'm bringing my cat," she said.

He looked down at the small creature, the disdain he felt for the little scrappy tabby apparent. "It shall not be loose on the plane."

"Of course not," she said. "What a silly suggestion. She cannot be loose on the plane. It would terrify her. She will be in a crate."

"And what else?"

"What do you care what else I want? It does not matter to you."

"It may shock you, Eloise, but your misery is not actually my goal. What I want is my child."

"Why?"

"Is it not the most natural thing in the world to want your child?"

She stared at him. "You and I both know that it is not. You cannot simply expect that someone will. Did my mother really want me?"

"Eloise…"

She shook her head. "You might be able to take the baby from me, but you cannot force me to marry you. And then the child will not be legitimate."

"Eloise…"

"No. I know that I don't have a lot of power here, but I have had so little choice in my life, Vincenzo. Surely you must want to do better for me than my own mother did. Surely you must want more than to hide me away in this place. Surely I deserve more than that."

"What is it you want?" he said.

It came to her in a moment, because the truth was, it would be… A wonderful thing for her child to know its father.

It was only her fears of that palace, of that life, that truly held her back.

"Make me a beautiful Christmas there at the palace. Show me that there's something there other than what I remember. Other than that dreadful…awful empty feeling that I always get in the palace. You show me. Show me that there is something else. Show me that there can be more. That there can be happiness."

"As you wish," he said. But he looked angry. And he did not look happy at all.

"Gather your cat," he said.

"And my Christmas tree," she said. Because on this she would not budge. And maybe she was just throwing out a ridiculous thing she did not think that Vincenzo could or would accomplish. But if she was going to subject herself to being married to him, if she was going to go back there, she needed him to try. But as she packed her things to go, her heart nearly cracked with an unimaginable grief at the thought of leaving this place.

This safety.

And then Vincenzo went into her living room, picked the tree up and put it over his shoulder. Three ornaments dropped on the floor. "Be careful with that," she said.

"You told me you wanted to bring your tree. I cannot guarantee the manner in which it will arrive."

"I don't…"

"The plane is waiting. I will drive us there. And I will strap your tree to the roof."

"You really will?"

"Yes. Make your commands of me, and I will show you that I am equal to whatever task you assign. You asked me once if I wanted a quiet life. The truth of the matter is, I do not get to choose that. Because of my birth. Because of who my father is.

"The same is true for our child. And I do not want to limit their choices. And you…"

She nodded slowly. Because she knew. She knew she had a responsibility to her child. To their child. To doing what was best for them. No matter what. It was the one thing that his father and her mother had not been able to do. They had not been able to think of anyone else. They had thought only of themselves. And she could cling to her quiet life, her desire to stay away from Arista, but if she denied her child that which they were due by rights, if she denied her child the chance to know their father, when Vincenzo clearly wanted them? Then she would not be any better than her own mother. She simply could not do it. "Let's go."

And she knew she had no choice, not because he would pick her up like the tree and carry her out if she refused, but because there simply wasn't another choice. There simply wasn't.

CHAPTER TEN

"YOU'VE DONE WHAT?"

"I brought her back to the palace," he growled at his computer screen, and more specifically at Rafael.

"Did you kidnap her?" Zeus asked.

He shrugged. "Borderline."

"No one likes an indecisive kidnapping, Vincenzo," Zeus said.

"It was decisive enough. She is here, is she not?"

"Is she *marrying* you?" Rafael asked.

"Most likely."

"Most likely," Jag said. "That is…"

"Weak," Zeus said.

"Mmm," Rafael agreed.

"I cannot force her to marry me."

"Untrue," Jag said. "You can absolutely force her to marry you."

"Perhaps I do not *wish* to force her to marry me," he said.

"And why not?" Rafael said.

In truth, Vincenzo did quite want to force her to marry him. When he had opened the door and seen her standing there, round and pregnant with his child he had... Well, he had picked up her Christmas tree, tossed it over his shoulder and brought it back with them to Arista! That was how strange and primal the response had been to seeing her like that. All he had known was that he would do anything to have her.

And yes, he actually would force her to marry him. If he had to.

"I am hoping to make her think it was her idea," he said.

"Oh," Zeus said. "That is smart."

"All she has asked is that I give her a Merry Christmas. She said if I can make her forget how difficult life was here at the palace when she was a child then she might be more... Amenable to staying with me."

"Buy her a pony, then," Zeus said.

"She did not ask for a pony."

Zeus looked at him as if he were insane. "All women want a pony."

"Then I will buy one. I will fill a stable with them for her. I will do it now."

"No one likes a reluctant gift giver," Zeus said.

"I do not care about any of this. Not ponies or Christmas."

His words landed in this group of men, for none of them had ever experienced the kind of happiness many associated with the holidays. They had never spoken of it, he simply knew.

Because they had never spoken of it.

That silence spoke volumes, like many other silences they had shared over the years.

"Let us send gifts," Rafael said. "To welcome her. Your new Queen."

He narrowed his gaze. "You don't need to do that."

"Yes, we do," Jag said. "I will have…" He snapped his fingers. "Yes. I have an idea. All will be sent tomorrow."

"I…"

"It is settled," Rafael said.

"Settled," Jag confirmed.

And then they vanished from the screen, and Vincenzo had a feeling he would not enjoy what came next.

He pushed the button on his desk and summoned the house manager. Who came quickly. "I wish to decorate the palace for

Christmas. Every single room. From floor to ceiling. No expenses to be spared. The money is to be taken from my personal account. None of the money shall come from Arista."

"Your Majesty…"

"It is for Eloise. We must make this place beautiful for her. For she is to be my Queen," he said.

The manager looked delighted at that. "Your mother would be very pleased," the woman said.

"Perhaps," he said. "Perhaps not." He could not imagine his mother being happy with him taking Eloise as his bride. Considering the history of it all.

"Well I am pleased," the house manager said. "She was always a nice girl. Very quiet. She never got the childhood she deserved."

A strange pang of regret echoed in Vincenzo's chest. "No," he said. "She didn't."

One thing he was utterly determined in— he had been given a challenge to woo his princess in a specific way, and he would do it. He might not understand finer feelings. Might not be a man who knew much about emotion. But he had a capable staff more than able to ensure that any decorating needs might be met.

And when it came to him personally... Well. He knew about seduction. And that, he was confident, would do the real work.

One thing he was certain of. Eloise would not be able to resist him.

Let his friends send gifts. He would take a different approach.

Eloise didn't emerge from her room until late. She was jet-lagged and had a terrible time sleeping the previous night. She felt out of sorts and unhappy to be back at the palace. Except... It was not that simple. It was not so simple as unhappy. Because in spite of herself that was something that she wanted—to be close to Vincenzo.

And she couldn't even be angry about the fact that he wanted their child.

No. What frightened her was the warmth that filled her at the thought. What frightened her was how much she wanted him to want their child.

When she emerged, she was met with a sight she had not expected.

It was magic. There were twinkling icicles hanging from the ceiling. Glittering rich green and red garlands swirled around every column, every balustrade. Every bannister. Wreaths were hung on every wall. There were gold candelabras with lit white taper candles casting a glow over the room.

The white palace was bedazzled. And trees. There were trees in every room. When she went into the dining room, there were four trees. One that stretched all the way to the ceiling, impossibly tall, two beside it a bit shorter. And in the center, her humble little tree that had come all the way from Virginia. She could not believe it. She simply couldn't believe it.

"I..."

"Good morning."

Elizabeth, the housekeeper, came into the room. She had always liked Elizabeth. There was a distance between them that had been ordered by the King, but she had never felt any chill coming from the other woman. And now, with the King gone, there was no reservation at all.

"Breakfast is set to be brought out upon your arrival. If you are ready?"

"Oh," she said. "Yes, I am."

"Coffee?"

"Herbal tea. Thank you." She had been

quite happy that coffee didn't sound appealing, since strictly speaking you needed to limit it with pregnancy. She had thought it sounded unimaginable, but then she had attempted to drink the permitted one cup, and her stomach had turned.

All for the best.

"Right away."

She was only left alone for a moment when the double doors swung open, and one of the other members of staff, Pietro, came in and bowed with a flourish. "Ms. Eloise," he said. "Some gifts have been sent for you."

"Gifts?"

But she did not have to wait to see what that meant. For in through the doors came a veritable procession of staff. The first wave of them carrying bowls made of precious metals. Inside of them was dried fruit that sparkled like jewels. There were flowers, crystal bottles of perfume and woven rugs.

"From Sheikh Jahangir Hassan Umar Al Hayat," one of the men said, placing all of the bounty on the table in front of her. She sat down, overwhelmed. "Sent upon a hand-carved troika, for the lady to keep as her own."

"I… That's incredible."

"There is more."

Following that came another wave of staff, carrying baskets filled with olives, platters of cured meat, fruits and nuts.

"From Regent Rafael Navarro. The finest goods from his country." He handed her a stack of papers. "Also stocks," he said, "in the Regent's personal company. Should you need to make a bid for your freedom."

Eloise blinked. "Oh, well, that is very nice of him."

And then, at the very end, came a young woman, with a very small horse on a lead.

A horse.

"This is from Prince Zeus. With the message that, if at all possible. women should be given the world. But failing that, they ought to have a pony."

And she couldn't help it. It was ridiculous. She laughed. "How wonderful."

She looked up then and saw Vincenzo standing in the doorway looking like a thunderstorm.

"That bastard did not send a horse into my palace."

"Who?"

"Zeus," he said curling his lip. "I should've known he would do it."

"Who are these men who sent these gifts?"

"They are my…" He looked like the word he was about to say was causing him pain. "My friends."

Her eyes widened. "You have *friends*, Vincenzo?"

He arched a dark brow. "Endeavor to not sound so surprised about it, Eloise."

"Well, I am."

"They did not decorate the palace," he said. "I did. Well, I had it done."

"It's glorious," she beamed.

Her breakfast came out, which took the form of baskets full of pastries, butter, jam. It was all a bit much.

"I don't think I will be able to eat all of this," she said, considering the fruit baskets as well.

"I will help."

He sat down next to her. Next to her. This man who was King. It was such a small gesture, and yet it felt…

Don't go romanticizing things like this.

He wanted something from her, and he was willing to do anything to get it.

Yes. And she had wanted him to. So was it so bad that he was acting consistently in that manner? She swallowed. This was all she had wanted. All those years ago.

Well, she had wanted to kiss him. But there was something to this simple connection, here in the palace that… It felt intimate in a way. It felt right.

And no, it wasn't simple. It was complicated. All of this was complicated. There was a horse in the dining room for crying out loud.

"The horse should probably be taken outside," she said.

He nodded. "Have the pony taken to the stables," he ordered.

"I will go see her," she said. "After I'm finished."

"I do not think you have hurt the pony's feelings."

"I shouldn't like to hurt the pony's feelings."

"And how is… Skerret finding his new residence?"

"I believe he quite likes the back right side of my bed. Beneath it. He has not come out. But he has eaten. And has used his box."

"Good to know," he said.

"It will take some time to adjust. The palace is very large."

She didn't just mean the cat.

She stared at him, and she knew that he didn't really care how her cat was finding the adjustment. He was trying. She just wished she could understand more deeply why. Because he had said so firmly that he didn't want a child. And she could understand him making gestures toward it now out of a sense of duty, but the degree to which he seemed to be taking up the cause was… That was what she could not understand.

"Why do you want this child?"

"Because it is the right thing to do."

"Is it only important to do the right thing? In this way?"

"My father never did. Not on behalf of anyone but himself. All I know is, in this life, I will make the decision to do what I know to be right. Whether I understand it, whether I want to… It is the path I have chosen."

"Right. That path of revenge."

"I removed my father from the throne, essentially. And now here I am, striving to set the nation on a better path, but grappling with the reality that the people are not completely happy with the idea of losing the monarchy. Even though they had no real love for my father. They like a symbol. And I am trying to affect change…"

"But it isn't as easy as coming in and ordering things to be done your way?"

"Do not sound so pleased about that, Eloise."

"I'm not. Actually… Vincenzo, you must know one wonderful thing about going off and having my simple life is that I have not been responsible for anyone else. Skerret. She is the only thing I've been responsible for all this time, other than my own happiness. And that is very easy. It is very easy. What you must do… It isn't. You are beholden to an entire nation, and I do not envy you that position. I never have. I was so happy to leave Arista. So happy to escape all of this. But you are right. There are other things to consider. I cannot face the idea of our child growing up in this palace as it was for us."

"It will not be."

"Down to ponies in the dining room. Apparently."

"That was not me," he said. "Let me make that very clear."

"Not wanting to take credit for your

friend's idea?" A smile tugged at her lips, in spite of everything.

"Not wanting to take blame."

"She's very charming. And perhaps our… Perhaps our child will enjoy riding." Her eyes stung. "We get this chance. Not just to do this because it's right. But to give our child what we did not have."

"And that is?"

"Love."

"What is love to you?"

It was not a question she had expected him to ask. "You know," she said. "Love."

"I confess that I do not. I was never exposed to love as a child. Nor have I been exposed to it as an adult. At least, not in any way that I recognize." There was a cool detachment to his voice that was somehow more painful than a wrenching sob, and Eloise could only stare, stunned at the pain his admission created in her. Stunned at this easy admission of his own deficits. And even more, that he did not seem hurt by it. Only accepting. "On top of that, we have very different ideas of what love is presented throughout time in history. There is, of course, the modern concept of loving yourself before all others. There is romantic love. The love of a friend. There is the classic biblical interpretation. Love is patient. Love is kind. It speaks more of a concept than anything specific. So what is it you mean when you say *love*?"

She was taken aback by that absolutely, because she found she did not have an answer. Because it was only a feeling, and he wanted to know what it looked like practically.

"I…"

"You say that you want our child to have love, because as a society we're encouraged to talk about love as though it is free and easy. As though every parent loves their child, and every child their parent in return, but we know that is not the case, do we not?"

"Yes."

"And then there is romantic love. Look at my parents' marriage. Is that love, do you think?"

"I do not think your father or my mother have ever truly loved anyone."

"And yet, I imagine they would say they do. Maybe they didn't think that they do. Because we are conditioned to believe these feelings simply are. That they are easy. That they are created inside of us perhaps the same time as our physical hearts. But what is love in a meaningful sense? In a way that you can touch, and a way that you can taste and feel. What is it? Because if it is not an action, then it does not matter, does it? So when you speak of loving our child, if you mean I will care for them, if you mean I will offer support. Yes, I will. All of those things. Everything we did not get from our parents. In the same manner that I'm delivering your Christmas."

"But to you that isn't love?"

"I think perhaps love is a mass societal hallucination," he said, his voice grim. "If less people professed it as easily as they sneezed, then perhaps it might return to some original weight. Perhaps there would be something to understand. But I find myself cynical about the concept."

"Your mother loved you, surely."

He lifted a shoulder, and his gaze grew distant. "If she did, she never said. But my mother was the most stable influence in my life, that is certain. She saw to her duties, she inquired about my well-being. She was a good queen, and for all that my father offered her no recognition. Nothing but scorn."

She could hardly breathe after that scathing takedown of the entire institution of an emotion that she had believed to be the greatest thing in the entire world. Except... He had made it feel cracked. Crumbling. Was love and care the same thing? Duty and responsibility? Because when she thought of what she had been denied by her parents, those were the things that she would list. And yet it felt like there was more. Something self-sacrificial. Something self-sacrificial by choice.

"Would you have rather your mother said it?"

"Maybe at one time. But in the end of all things, it doesn't matter."

"You have a very grim view of the world."

"Is it? I don't think so. I think what is grim is how cheap words have become. We say them, we ask for them, we do not think about what they might mean. What they should mean. Perhaps if we did, people like our parents could not exist in such denial about their own behavior."

"Do you think they are in denial?"

"I hope so," he said. "Because if either of them has any real idea of the depth of their own depravity, if they realize how morally bankrupt they truly are and choose to walk that path anyway, I find that infinitely more upsetting."

"I suppose," she said. She felt chilled, all the way down to her soul.

She looked at him. And she felt like she understood something deeper about him than she had before.

She had wondered why. Why he wanted this child when he had been so dead set against the idea of children at all. Why he had come to get her. Why he wanted to marry her.

But she could see that he was actually a man of great depth and feeling, though ironically, after his previous statement about the awareness a person had of themselves, she knew that he did not see himself that way.

But he was a man who wished to intensely understand love before he ever professed it. And she realized, that was the cost of him.

She had escaped to that simple life, and nothing would ever be simple with Vincenzo. She let that sink in deep. Down through her skin, down into her blood. Her bones. Yes. Being with him would be a choice. A choice that would take her far away from where she had been before. From what she had known.

But perhaps she was ready now. Strong

enough now. Perhaps she could be with him. She leaned in, across the small space of the dining table, and she pressed a kiss to his mouth.

He went still. And so did she. And it was like fire in her blood. Fire that joined in with that deep acceptance of the fact that there was no simplicity with a man like him.

And there never would be.

"I wish to go for a ride in the troika," she said.

"The pony cannot pull the troika," he said.

"Perhaps not. But we are in a winter wonderland. And you have promised me Christmas."

"I did. But I must call my friends first and tell them what manner of monster they have created."

"And what manner of monster is that?" she asked.

"Well, a kind very similar to them, I suppose."

"Tell me about your friends," she said.

"There isn't much to tell," he said, straightening. "We met at Oxford."

"I find that very interesting."

"What exactly?"

"Well, that you have friends. I wasn't trying to be mean when I said something about that. I don't really have friends. I have made casual acquaintances in the world of horticulture. Don't laugh. But I have never really known how to…" What she was about to say was dishonest in some ways. "I have struggled in my life to know how to connect to another person. Weirdly, my upbringing isn't very relatable."

It was one reason, she supposed, that it had been him from very early on.

"We are connected very much by similar pain," he said. "Each of them has their own… Difficulties. We are wealthy, powerful men, by any standards. And that made others in our sphere either seek to use us—which is foolish, because none of us would allow it—or it made them hate us. We found each other, and over the course of years confessed the great bleeding wounds our parents had left in us. You can have the entire world at your feet and still be missing a great many things."

She knew that to be true.

"If you want your troika ride, I suggest you get ready. I will have the staff prepare the horses in the stable. And I will have an outfit appropriate for the weather sent to you."

198 CROWNED FOR HIS CHRISTMAS BABY

"Oh…"

"I think the word you're looking for is *thank you.*"

"Yes," she said. "Thank you." And she suddenly felt foolish that she had kissed him. Because he had kissed her back, but it had been solicitous, not filled with heat.

But then, perhaps he was not attracted to her when she was like this. She was incredibly round. She could not blame him. She was surprised, honestly, that she was attracted to him still. She would've thought that her present condition excluded her from such feelings. How interesting that it did not. For she felt as if she would happily strip off all her clothes and climb into his lap, baby bump notwithstanding.

"I will meet you in an hour."

"All right."

CHAPTER ELEVEN

IN THE END, Vincenzo decided to prepare the horses himself and did the rigorous task of getting them in the bridles on the troika. He would be sending Jag a picture of his middle finger later.

But it was a lovely sleigh, with intricate hand carvings on it and he knew that the gold leaf paint contained real gold, because Jag would never settle for anything less.

When Eloise appeared, it was like the sun coming out from behind the clouds. She was wearing a furry white hat, and a long white coat with fur around the edges. It went all the way down to the ground, sloping gently over her bump. There was a border of blue thread that ran from the collar all the way down to the floor.

She looked like a snow queen. Standing out there in the cold, her cheeks red, wisps of blond hair escaping the hat. When she had kissed him earlier, it had taken all of his strength not to clear the table and ravish her upon it. But he knew that he could not. He was trying to convince her to marry him, and ravishing her in her present state was not going to help with that. He had to show her that they had something that went beyond attraction. Attraction they knew they had. That was not up for debate. Attraction was what had gotten them into this situation in the first place. But she was asking for something else from him, and he was determined to give it. Determined to secure her acceptance of marriage.

His staff had packed a grand lunch in the sleigh, and they had placed thermoses of hot chocolate in the front. He wished that he'd asked them to add liquor to his own, but he had thought that it might be distasteful, considering Eloise's condition.

Still, he regretted it now.

"Oh," she said. "It's beautiful."

One of the horses shook their head, tossing their caramel-colored mane. And the harness jingled. There were, of course, bells upon the red leather straps.

"This is a Christmas fantasy," she said, her eyes jewel bright.

He had noticed that when they had flown on the private plane, she did not seem inured to excess. She had been raised in the palace, and yet, she did not seem to take luxury for granted. But perhaps that was because she had been kept adjacent to it, rather like an urchin with her nose pressed against the glass. For she might as well have been, as the use of it was denied to her.

It made him want to give her everything. Everything she had been denied.

"Leave it to Jag to go over-the-top."

"It's wonderful. I do rather wish Zeus's pony could lead the team."

"He will have to be content with being a stand-in in a live-action manger scene. That is perhaps more to his scale."

"Poor little thing. I'm afraid to ask why the pony. It seems as if it's some sort of inside joke."

"Zeus is under the impression that all women want a pony."

She laughed, the sound crystal like the snow all around them. "You know, I don't think he's wrong."

"He would tell you that he never is."

"And what do you think?"

"I think he is only wrong when he disagrees with me."

"I see."

Then they got into the troika, and there was a soft blanket inside, mottled gray and thick and plush. He draped it over her lap. And when she looked at him, her cheeks were crimson.

"Yes?"

"Nothing. No one has ever taken care of me before."

"Did you not ask for care? Is that not what a request for Christmas is?"

"I like it. But it occurs to me I have never really taken care of anyone either. And I suppose I will be. Soon." She looked down at her stomach and placed her hand on the rounded bump there."

"I have never cared for anyone either."

"I don't think that's true," she said. "You have your friends. And it sounds to me like you've been there for each other when you've needed one another. I think that is quite commendable."

"I will accept any and all commendations as they come," he said.

"Naturally," she said.

He took his seat in the driver's spot and picked up the reins.

"It did not even occur to me to ask you if you knew how to drive it. Why would you know how to drive a Russian sleigh?"

"It is easy," he said, slapping the reins gently and urging the team forward.

These horses were soft mouthed and easily steered, the best. And the sleigh moved smoothly through the snow. They went away from the grounds of the palace, toward snow-dusted pines, going along the path that went through a thick canopy of trees.

She looked around, an expression of wonder on her face. "I half expect to see a lamppost."

He chuckled. "How about if I offered you some Turkish delight in exchange for betraying your entire family."

"You have essentially done that. But my family was easy to betray." She sighed. "Turkish delight really isn't good enough to justify that sort of betrayal. Not if your family is good."

"Is that your firm stance?"

"Yes. I would need chocolate cake."

He chuckled. "Good to know."

"I am happy," she said quietly. "That your

father has lost the throne. I am happy that my mother has lost her position here at the palace finally. I am… I am glad they were exposed. And I have to wonder what all that therapy was for if I can still take such pleasure in their downfall."

"I believe that is just called being human."

"It is an inconvenient thing. To be human. I think I tried really hard not to be."

"What do you mean?"

"Moving away the way that I did. Going off on my own, ensconcing myself in gardening and all of that. It was my very best attempt at not being vulnerable."

"You can hardly be blamed for wanting to avoid vulnerability."

"Maybe. But I wonder about all I have missed. And how… Well, how deeply in denial I am about my own human nature. I do not think I am half so benevolent as I let myself believe. When you and I met in the garden all those months ago, I told myself that I was going with you as a friend. But by the time I left your bed that morning, I knew. I knew that I was glorying in their destruction. And I was so judgmental of you. I felt above you. I felt better than you, but it was not fair."

"Do not be concerned about that. I feel better than most people."

She laughed. She couldn't help herself. She utterly howled. "I imagine you do." They lapsed into silence again, as the troika went deeper into the trees, the bells jingling.

"We shall take the baby out like this," she said, "for Christmas."

"Shall we?" he asked, his chest getting tight.

"Don't you think we ought to make some Christmas traditions?"

This was the first time she had really talked like she would stay.

"I don't know. Do you think they are important?"

"I do," she said.

"And how will we know?" he asked. "How will we know what matters?"

"Well," she said slowly. "I would think, we should try and remember everything that it felt like we were missing back when we were children. And make sure our child does not miss that?"

"A long list," he said.

And he suddenly wondered if he had never wanted a child because he wanted to end his line, or if he had known that…

That it would be difficult for a man who had never experienced having a real father.

A father who cared.

He wanted to be the right kind of father.

And he had no real idea what that meant.

Right then, he made a decision to show her something he had never shown another person. As the road forked, he went to the left, and it narrowed and went windy, and the ground became thicker with snow as they exited the trees.

"Where are we going?"

"You'll see."

They rounded a curve, and the mountains in front of them disappeared. And about twenty feet ahead, so did the snow.

"Vincenzo," she said, putting her hand on his thigh.

"No worries."

He stopped the team of horses, just at the edge of a ravine that overlooked a crystal lake, frozen over with ice, the sun sparkling over the surface.

"Vincenzo…"

"It's beautiful," he said. "Is it not?"

"Yes. What is this place?"

"I used to come here as a boy. It is part of the unspoiled wilderness in Arista. As far as

I know, there is no path to get down to the lake, though I thought as a boy of many different methods to try and get there. I wanted to be part of the wilderness. Most of all, I wanted to escape the oppression of the palace. And so I used to come here. And I used to sit. And I used to think of escape. But there was no way to escape. Not from where I was. It was then that I had to accept that… in the end of all things, I had to turn back and confront the evil in my world. I could not simply run away into the wilderness. There was no path."

"That must've been terrifying to realize as a child."

"Did I ever tell you when I realized that my father was bad?"

"No," she said.

He had never told anyone this story. Not even Rafael, Jag and Zeus.

"When the antiliquor laws in Arista went into effect, I remember seeing my father drink a glass of wine with dinner every night. And when I tried to question him about it, he said that some men made the rules, and others had to live by them. And I knew it was wrong. Down in my soul, I knew it was wrong. That one life should be lived here in the palace, while another would be lived among the people. I knew that his control was simply for the sake of control, and not out of conviction. And at first, like I said, I wanted to run. But I realized someone had to fix it. Someone had to. And the longer things went on, I only saw more contradictions between the rules my father made in the edicts he issued and the way that he lived. And no one did anything to stop him. No one spoke against him. I realized that person would have to be me."

She nodded slowly. "What a terrible realization."

"It was a powerful realization, and I am glad for it. You cannot wait for others to do the right thing. It is up to us. Each of us. We cannot claim something is not our problem. If it exists in the world, it is a problem for all of us."

"You are a very good man. You cover it quite skillfully with hardness. But you are a warrior."

He did not know what to say to that, so he simply looked out at the view. He felt like a warrior at times. But rather than wearing armor, his whole body was covered over in a protective layer. Calcified. He looked at her, and he felt drawn to her. Pulled toward her like there was a magnet between them. Something he could not deny.

But she had wanted a nice outing; she did not ask to be ravished. Again, he would have to practice self-control. Damned inconvenient when he wanted to do anything but. "We should go back."

"We haven't even had a hot chocolate."

"I do not wish you to catch too much of a cold."

"I'm fine. I'm pregnant. I'm not broken."

Pregnant. With his child. They really were standing on the brink of everything changing.

But it was not that escape he dreamed of as a boy. And it wasn't that simple life she had talked about either. It was something else. Something he couldn't say that he understood.

"The doctor said you were healthy?"

She nodded. "Yes. I had my standard checkups and…"

"Are you due another one?"

"Soon. But I'm not concerned."

"Good to hear."

"Women have been doing this for a very long time."

"Yes," he said. "But it is not always safe."

"But there's no reason to believe that mine will not be."

Suddenly, his chest went tight, clutched with something unfamiliar. He could not figure out what it was. He had never experienced anything like it before in his life. He had the sudden urge to grab her and gather her up close to his chest. And all around him the world seemed precarious. The trees laden with snow that might tip from the weight of it. The precipice in front of them, and the lake down below. All of these sights that he had wanted to show her suddenly seemed like they might rebel against them both. He was aware of how fragile she looked. In all that white.

He had been prepared to seduce her, to entice her into his plan of vengeance. He had made love to her that night months ago with both of them burning white-hot from battle, the thrill of victory.

And now it was his own need. A great, ravenous beast that burned in him like a monster he feared could consume them both.

But she was pregnant with his child. He could not touch her like this.

"Let's go," he said.

The farther away they got from the precipice, the more the feeling faded. But he only wished that he could understand what had started it in the first place.

Or perhaps, he did not.

CHAPTER TWELVE

ELOISE COULDN'T UNDERSTAND. Vincenzo had been so sweet to her today. And it was weird. Because he was many things, but he was hardly sweet, and he was being solicitous in a way that… It seemed odd. She had kissed him this morning, and he had not done anything to follow up on it.

She paced back and forth in her room, wearing a soft, gauzy white nightgown that made her feel elegant, or rather like a cloud. A round, fluffy cloud. Perhaps she simply didn't appeal to him. He had been sweet to her on the trip in the troika. And he had shown her the view of the water and she felt… In many ways she felt closer to him than she ever had. But she missed the heat. She missed the fire. And she hoped that this was not the compromise that had to occur. That in order for them to have conversations.

In order for them to connect, in order for them not to be bogged down in misunderstandings and recriminations, they had to be... Friends.

Not that there was anything bad about being friends. But she wanted the fire. He had always felt like more to her than that. A connection that had come from nowhere. A connection that had taken root deep inside of her chest. He had never been anything quite so bland as a friend, and she did not wish him to be now.

She remembered the wildness between them, that moment when they had been rejoicing in their accomplishments. In taking down his father.

She was remorseful about that emotion, but there was something about the dark edge of that experience that had affected her. That had made her feel... Wild.

Did she have to be glorying in something so dark in order to experience that kind of explosion of passion? In order to create it in someone else?

Without thinking, she exited the bedroom. She began to walk down the hallway, her throat dry. Her heart was thundering in her chest.

She already knew what she was doing without it even forming in her mind as a coherent thought. She wanted him. And she wanted to be brave.

She was trying to find a way to join up these pieces of herself. This girl who loved planting, who wanted a Christmas and who wanted birthday parties. Who wanted these soft, simple things. And who felt the dark turn to light when her enemies were slain, and who wanted to tear Vincenzo's clothes off and wanted him to do the same to her.

Who had gloried in the animalistic need between them, and who had sat in the troika watching the falling snow all around them. Who had enjoyed the silence and that lake view.

Because it was all inside of her. All the same, but right now it felt distinct. Separate. She had been certain that he had chosen a path and she had chosen another and those paths could not meet.

But they could. They did. She had the feeling they met at that cliff side. Tranquil beauty and a sense of danger.

But she could not quite figure out how to make sense of it. That's what she was searching for now.

She had the sense that he would not be in his room. She knew where his study was in the palace. Where his father's had been before him. It was funny to wander around the palace now, this place that had always been filled with dark foreboding, but now was covered in icicles and lights. All for her. And he didn't understand it, but he had done it anyway, and surely there must be something of emotion in that.

Or he's just trying to manipulate you.

What was manipulation? And what was caring?

Did either of them even know the difference?

Her heart was pounding in her head now. Making it difficult to breathe. She pushed open the door to his study and found him there, sitting at the desk. There was a fire in the grand fireplace, and she could see snow falling outside the window in the darkness.

"What are you doing here?" he asked.

"I came looking for you." She walked toward him.

"Is everything all right?"

"Everything is fine. It's just… It's just that… Am I repulsive to you now?"

"What?"

"Me. In this…" She swished her nightgown around. "In this shape. Do you not want me?"

He stared at her from the desk, the firelight illuminating the hollows of his face. His eyes looked black. Like coal.

"Is that what you think?"

"Yes. I kissed you."

"You did. And asked me to take you on a sleigh ride."

"And you did not try to kiss me."

"No. But you did not ask me to. You asked me for a ride in the troika."

"And you gave it to me. And I appreciate it. But I did expect you to try and…"

"I thought that you wanted me to give you Christmas."

"I want both. I want Christmas, and I want you to look at me as if you want to devour me. I want conversation, but I also want you to kiss me."

"A kiss… Eloise, I could not stop at just a kiss."

"You couldn't?"

He stood and rounded the desk slowly, his mannerisms that of a prowling cat. "Eloise," he said, his voice frayed. "It is a torture to be so near you and not touch you. To see your body so luscious and round with the evidence that you carry my child, and to keep my hands off you. I have wanted nothing more than to grab hold of you and crush you to my body from the moment I first saw you standing in your house. But I have been restrained, because I did not want to put you under undue stress. And I have commanded that you marry me. And I am... I am at your mercy," he said, the words splintering like thin ice. "I would not wish to do something to distress you, for fear that you would refuse me."

"You're afraid that I will refuse you?"

"Of course I am. You have not agreed to be my wife. You have not agreed to be mine, and it all hangs by a thread. This balance is... It is precarious." He dropped to his knees before her, and she startled. Then his thumb was at her ankle, massaging her there. And he continued up, sweeping the nightgown up her thighs, past her hips, and pulling it over her head, leaving her completely nude in the firelight. And she felt... She felt beautiful. The way he looked at her, the way the fire glowed across her curves. He made her feel like a goddess.

"*Diana*," he said.

And it made her feel warm all over, because she knew that he was thinking the same that she had been. A goddess.

"Goddess of the hunt. But it is I who would have been in pursuit of you."

"I'm the one that came to your study," she said, her breath a whisper.

"Perhaps... Perhaps we hunt for each other."

"Perhaps," she said, the words coming out soft as a feather.

He stood away from her, unbuttoned his shirt slowly, his body bathed in an orange glow. The dips and hollows of his body highlighted by the harsh flame. He removed all his clothes, and he looked like a god himself. Or perhaps simply... A predator. Like he had said. Perhaps they both hunted one another. Then he moved to her and kissed her. But this was not tentative. Not the polite kiss between two people seated at the dining table, where others could walk in at any moment. It was deep and hard, carnal. It held in it the promise of everything he had just said. It made his words into truth, as he devoured her mouth, licking deep and stealing her breath away. He kissed her neck and then moved down to her breasts. He cupped her, squeezing them, drawing his thumbs over her nipples. "Beautiful," he rasped. "I love your curves. You were concerned, about your roundness, even before you carried the baby. I find you lush. Feminine. Exquisite. And this new shape... It is unbearable. I cannot breathe for how exquisite you are."

She moaned as he lowered his head, drawing one tightened bud between his lips and sucking hard. She was so sensitive there now, she felt it all echo between her legs. Felt her desire for him erupt like sparks. She was very nearly there, just from the attention to her breast. He sank lower, trailing a line of kisses over her rounded bump. And she felt the baby shift inside her. He stopped and looked up at her, his expression fierce. "Was that?"

"Yes," she said, softly. "The baby moves."

He got to his feet and pressed his palm against her stomach. "It moves?"

"Yes," she said.

He caught her gaze and held it there for a long moment. And something swelled inside her chest, and she was sure looking into his eyes the same thing was in him. And she wanted to tell him. Wanted to say it.

Because this was love. It was pure, and it was real. And it was more than a responsibility. It was more than an attachment. It was a miracle. A miracle that defied explanation. "It is incredible," he said.

"I know," she said.

He kissed her hungrily then, breaking the softness of the moment, driving her back and then guiding her gently down into a chair. Then he knelt down before her and spread her legs, lifting her thighs up over his shoulder and tasting her as he had done the first time they were together. She gasped, arching into him, enjoying his loss of control. But it was the combination of this moment and the moment just prior that sent her over the edge. That fierceness in his face. The realization that this was real. Everything.

She sobbed out her pleasure, and he rose up from the floor, picking her up off the chair and wrapping her thighs around his body, before seating them both again. Then he thrust up inside her, and she let her head fall back. He gripped her hips, driving up into her, his eyes wild. And she lost herself.

Because here it was. The sweetness combined with the passion. Need combined with want too.

The simplicity of creation, of life and the dark broken pieces of their desire for one another. It filled her. Consumed her. Changed her. This man, who was the father of her child, her future husband, her lover.

He was everything, just as she was.

He was a warrior, a protector. He could touch her gently and with passion.

And when her desire broke over her, it burst behind her eyelids with every color under the sun, bright and brilliant, sweet and pastel, dark and rich, and for the first time she understood what it was to be Eloise. Not Eloise ignored. Not Eloise hidden. But Eloise, fully in charge of herself. In command of her desires. Then he cried out his own release, and their eyes met. And right then, she felt whole.

He rested his head against her neck and whispered, "I smell roses."

She didn't know what it meant. But it felt like a declaration. "Vincenzo," she whispered. "I'll marry you."

He looked up at her, the intensity in his gaze burning hotter than the fire. "You'll marry me?"

"Yes."

"We will marry on Christmas Eve."

"Yes."

He gripped her chin, holding it tight. "Say it again."

"Yes," she said again.

CHAPTER THIRTEEN

"WE ARE GETTING married on Christmas Eve," he said, speaking to his friends through the computer screen.

"What a shock—Vincenzo Moretti's had his way," Jag said.

"It was the stock options," Rafael said.

"I think we all know it was the pony."

"It was the troika," Vincenzo said.

"Is that what the kids are calling it these days?" Zeus quipped.

"I expect you all to be there."

"Absolutely. I would not stay away from court if you were being sentenced to life in prison," Jag said. "I will certainly not miss your marriage."

"Nice," Zeus said.

"You're doing the right thing," Rafael said. "It is right that you marry the mother of your child."

"Do you always do what is right, Rafael?" Zeus asked, his tone dry.

"Yes. Do you not?"

"I think you know I avoid it at all costs whenever possible."

"Not me. Honor is everything. It is all a man has," Rafael responded.

"Well," Zeus said. "We all have thrones. You do not. At least not permanently."

"It may shock you to learn I don't care," Rafael returned.

"Enough of this," Vincenzo said. "You must all come, and you must all be kind to her."

"Of course we'll be kind to her," Jag said.

"*You* are another matter," Zeus finished.

"Friendship is overrated," Vincenzo said. But he did not think that was true. Friendship had been the only good thing in his life. The friendship with these men. But then there was Eloise. The memory of last night made him burn. Eloise was perfect. Brilliant. She had been exquisite in the firelight. All glowing curves and pleasure.

"We will see you Christmas Eve," Zeus said.

"See you Christmas Eve." He rang off the

call and paced the length of the room. There were only three days until the wedding. And he intended it to be a massive celebration. He would make a wedding so bright and brilliant that Eloise would be radiant with it. And he found that drove him most of all. Something had changed inside him that night all those months ago. He had begun to want things, not for himself, not for the greater good, but for her. When he was in her arms, what seemed faint became all the more clear. As if the intangible suddenly made sense in a way it never had before.

It was a feeling that rested somewhere next to the fear he had felt when he was out in the troika with her. But it was something different. Something more. And when he had put his hand on her stomach and felt the baby moving...

It had made everything all the more real. That was certain.

He left his study and went down to the dining room, where she was already sitting, chatting with the housekeeper. The smile on her face made him stop where he stood. She was radiant. But there was something more. There was something to the light in her expression. Something bright in her eyes. And he could not fully fathom what it was. Only that it immobilized him. Utterly. Completely. He didn't think he had ever seen anyone look quite so happy in this palace.

Perhaps it would be all right.

"All plans are going forward for the wedding," he said, moving deeper into the room.

"Oh, good," she said. "A Christmas Eve wedding really is so exciting."

She beamed. The smile quite unlike anything he had ever seen before. She was beautiful.

One of his staff came in then, holding an envelope. "A message for you," he said, addressing Eloise.

"Oh," she said. "Thank you."

She took the envelope from his hand and opened it. As she began to read, her expression fell. It was like a light had been extinguished, and it made his chest seize up.

"What is it?"

"It's nothing," she said, holding the letter close to her chest.

"It is something," he said. He held his hand out, the demand obvious. She gave in, placing the paper in his palm.

He looked down at the letter. And his blood turned to ice.

Congratulations on whoring yourself out to royalty. Do you honestly think you're any different from me? You're smart, though. You're carrying the heir. But all your principles, and his, look foolish. You are no different. Just remember that.

It was from her mother.

"That snake," he said.

"She's not wrong. Except... She's all wrong." She looked up at him, but her expression was sad now, and he hated her mother for that.

"Explain."

"It's not the same between us as it was between her and my father. And I am not carrying this child to get your money. You know that."

He did. Because she had been happy to hide the baby away from him. He did not suspect Eloise of being at all like her mother. But still it was a terrible thing, to watch that haunted look in her eyes. Because no matter what she said, she felt the pain from this letter very deeply. It didn't matter that she shouldn't. It didn't matter that she knew she wasn't her mother. She felt it.

And he felt a burden of responsibility for causing this pain.

"Is it bad?" he asked. "Being here?"

"I'm not going to pretend it's my favorite."

"Of course not," he said.

"But… Where else would I be?"

He gritted his teeth together. "Yes. Where else…"

But in his mind's eye, he saw her back in her garden. Surrounded by her flowers.

That was where she would be.

If not for him. If not for this.

She had been brave, a warrior in all of this, but she had not chosen this path in the beginning. He had. Or rather he had been put on it in a way that felt fated. Unavoidable.

But she wanted love.

And he did not know what it was.

The evils of the past would always be there. This letter proved it.

He had dragged her back into hell along with him, and he did not know what to make of that revelation.

"I am taking dinner in my study tonight. I hope you enjoy your meal."

Then he turned and left her there, feeling like a coward. Feeling ineffective. Feeling like...

He felt like an ass. And he was.

But there was nothing to be done about it.

CHAPTER FOURTEEN

HE HAD BEEN distant for two days. And now it was the eve of their wedding, and she didn't understand. She didn't understand why this man, who had taken her out and showed her his favorite view, something he had never shown anyone before, was suddenly like a stone again.

Because she and Vincenzo had nearly become friends, and then after the way they had made love by the fire, it had all become more. And she just couldn't credit what had happened because of this distance between them. It was disturbing and upsetting. And she wished… She wished that she knew exactly how to reach him.

What is love?

She had been thinking so much about that statement. And she knew the answer, but she didn't know how to tell him. That was the problem. Because she knew that she loved him. And she knew that she loved their child. And that he did too. She had seen it in his eyes when he had felt that miracle. But how...

You have to tell him.

But it scared her. The idea of telling him. Because she had tried... It reminded her of being eighteen. Of trying to forge that connection between them that he had not felt at the time. It reminded her of that humiliation. Of that sadness. And she didn't want to experience it again.

But what other choice was there?

She had had a moment of wholeness. Of being Eloise as she was intended to be. Rather than Eloise, fragmented by the life she had been given. But she would live her entire life in fragments, only experiencing that blinding, wonderful feeling of being complete when he was inside her. When she had a feeling that she might be able to experience it all the time. Yes. She might.

And wasn't that worth it? Wasn't that worth the risk?

It was only her feelings, after all. And whatever happened with those, she could survive them. It was only feelings.

She had a doctor's appointment today, and he was going to accompany her. She had been wanting to leave the gender of the child a surprise, but having a scan done this late in the game might reveal everything.

But it would be okay if he… She wondered if he would connect even more, having seen the child. Knowing if it was a son or a daughter.

Those thoughts were all swirling around in her head when the doctor arrived at her bedroom.

How different it was to be treated when one was going to be a queen. The doctor was followed closely by Vincenzo, who appeared in a cloud of ferocity and intensity. As he was wont to do.

But this seemed even more pronounced than usual.

"Good afternoon," the doctor said. "It is an honor to treat you today."

"Oh," she said, feeling her cheeks heat. "Thank you."

"Let us get this started," Vincenzo said.

She readied herself, lay on the bed and waited.

The doctor shifted her nightgown, pushing it up over her bump. Then put a warmed gel on her skin, gliding the Doppler over the top of it.

And then the sound of the baby's heartbeat filled the screen, and she saw the silhouette of their head. An arm pressed right up by their face.

"Vincenzo," she whispered.

She hadn't seen the baby in a few months, and it was incredible how much more like a baby it looked.

"Oh, Vincenzo."

She heard Vincenzo draw close to the bed, and then felt him as he dropped to his knees beside it. She looked at him, at the way his dark eyes were rapt on the screen. The doctor was moving over various parts now, the baby's belly, legs, feet. Then back up to the head, where they could see the profile.

Vincenzo said nothing. His face was simply set in stone, caught somewhere between terror and awe. She understood. She felt that way too. "This is it," she whispered. "Vincenzo. This is it."

And she knew that he understood what she meant. This was love. It was as certain as she could ever be that he would understand. Because she could see it. She could see it in his eyes. And she felt it reflected inside her. This terrifying, momentous, wondrous thing.

"And do you want to know the gender?" The doctor asked.

"No," Vincenzo said. "No."

But there was something strange in his voice that she could not quite understand.

The doctor finished the exam, and then Vincenzo turned to leave at the same time as the doctor. "Stay with me," she said.

He stopped.

Skerret chose that moment to come out from under the bed and jump up onto the mattress. Investigating the extra person in the room, not brave enough exactly to take on two. The little gray creature was no less mangy now in looks than she had been when Eloise had first adopted her. She would always look like a ditch cat. There was no getting around it.

"I think Skerret is requesting your affection," she said, feeling mildly amused when she jumped down from the bed and wove between Vincenzo's legs.

"Skerret will have to be disappointed on that score."

"She's not afraid of disappointment. In

fact, I think she's quite inured to it. She'll wear you down eventually."

She felt for a moment like she was actually talking about herself.

"And how have you been? Since your mother's letter?"

She frowned. "Oh. It's not unexpected. She's spiteful. It has nothing to do with us. Nothing to do with where we are going."

"I do not think we should get married."

"What?" she asked, feeling as if she'd been struck, the pain of those words a physical blow.

"I do not think we should get married. I think you should go back to Virginia." His words were hard, and so was his face.

She felt as if the bottom had dropped out of the world.

"Are you… Angry at me?" It was all she could think. That she had done something wrong. Again. He had sent her away once before with offers of money because he believed the worst of her. Had something happened again?

"Vincenzo," she said, a pleading note in her voice. "What is it? You know I am… You know I care for you…"

"It is not you," he said. "But this place…

There is poison in these walls. And no amount of Christmas lights is ever going to make it different. You deserve better than this. Our child deserves better than this."

"Better than being the heir to a throne? Better than this country?" Tears filled her eyes. "Better than having his father?"

"I will still be his father. But if we do not marry, then he is not the heir. If we do not marry, then... All will go according to plan on my end, and you will not have to spend your life trapped here."

"Did I say that I was trapped?"

"No. You didn't. But I see it. I see it even if you do not."

"You... You utter bastard. I did not ask you for this." Anger boiled over inside her. He was talking about walls, but the only wall here was him. He was so hard. And he would not tell her the truth. He was shut down and merciless in his coldness, and what was she supposed to do with that? "How... How can you do this? After you've just seen our child?"

"This why I have to do this. It is why I have to."

"I love you," she said. "I love you, Vincenzo, and I didn't tell you this before because you want to know things about this feeling that I don't think I can answer. Because it is something in my blood. Something that feels as much a part of me as anything else that I am. And I cannot come up with a way to explain. I cannot think of how I might define it. I know that you want that. But I can only tell you what I feel. In my heart. And it is love for you. A love that has been there for... Well more than ten years. I love you. The more that I get to know you, the more that I feel it. And it is more than simply wanting to take care of you. Wanting to protect you. Wanting to sleep with you. I am carrying a piece of you inside of me. This evidence of the passion between us..."

"Yes," he said, "and I am the result of my mother and father's union. But there was no love between them. What of your father? You've never even met him. That is not evidence of love, Eloise. It is simply an aftereffect of sex."

"But the child..."

"I don't feel it," he said. "I don't feel it. You said this was it. And if I cannot... I refuse to have our child grow up as we did. I refuse it."

He didn't feel it. He didn't feel it even for their child.

"Maybe it is because I never saw it," he said. "Never heard it."

"Neither did I. But I still know enough to understand it when I am fortunate enough to have it. Why can't you?"

"Perhaps I'm just broken, more so than you."

"Your friends," she said. "Do you not love them?"

"It's different."

"It's not. It all comes from here." She pressed her hand to his chest. "It all comes from here. From who you are. And I cannot… How can you think that there isn't love there?"

"I will send you back to Virginia."

"No," she said.

"I am sending you back."

"You can't."

"Then you will live here as you did as a child. Ignored. Unwanted. Is that what you would like?"

She drew back, feeling as if he had struck her. He might as well have.

"Vincenzo…"

"I will ready the plane immediately."

"Vincenzo!" She screamed his name, because he would not yell. She unleashed her fury because he had closed everything inside of him.

And he stood there, his breath coming hard, his chest heaving with it. "It is not this place that is poison, Eloise. It is me. It is my blood. And I will not poison us all."

And that was how she found herself bundled onto a private plane, numb. Crying. She had no recollection of the flight. None at all. She was just suddenly standing in front of her door in Virginia with the snow falling softly behind her, and her cat carrier in hand.

She walked inside and looked into the corner where her Christmas tree had been. She realized it was still at the palace. And for some reason it was that, that stupid thing, that made her burst into tears. That made it all feel like too much. For some reason, it was the tree that pushed it beyond the pale. She began to weep. Like her heart was broken. Because it was. Because she no longer had Vincenzo, and nothing would ever be right again.

You have your child.

Yes, she did. And her simple life. Except Eloise was not simple. Not anymore, and perhaps she never had been. Eloise had learned to want it all.

And taking half felt unacceptable.

* * *

He did not expect his friends to show up early. But they did.

And he was drunk.

"What the hell is this?" Zeus asked.

"Nothing," he said, straightening at his desk, feeling worse for wear.

"Liar," Rafael said. "You look like hell. And you smell worse."

"I find you offensive in every way," Jag said. "Where is your woman?"

"She is not my woman," he said.

"Then something's changed," Rafael said.

"Nothing has changed. I simply realized that I was allowing her to live through what we had already endured as children. It was not right. I sent her home."

"You did what?" Jag asked. "You sent your pregnant fiancée home the day before your wedding?"

"It had to be done."

"Did it?" he asked. "I do not believe you."

"I didn't ask for your belief, friend. I, in fact asked for nothing. Least of all for the three of you to be standing in my study."

"Too bad for you," Zeus said. "This is what friends are for. Get yourself together."

"I'm together. I am doing the right thing."

"You're not doing the right thing. You're doing the easy thing," Rafael said. "You saw her struggling, and rather than doing something to fix it, you sent her where you didn't have to look at it. Rather than doing the work to figure out exactly how you needed to change this place so that it was not the same place that you grew up in, you removed her. And you're going to what? Sink away in your misery?"

"How dare any of you lecture me on feelings."

"You do not have any, you are a coward. Not a King."

"And you are in my palace."

"How quickly he has come to view it as his palace," Jag said. "For all his talk of not even wanting the throne."

"What would you have me do? You'd have me keep a woman with me who professes to love me when I cannot offer her the same in return?"

Zeus lifted a brow. "I am hardly one to advocate for the institution of marriage, or love. But I can hardly see why you're standing there acting as if the woman carrying your child being in love with you is some conundrum you cannot get past."

"Because of her happiness. It is for her."

"Or is it for your own protection?"

Vincenzo didn't want to speak to them anymore. Instead, he strode out of the study and down the stairs, and before he knew what he was doing, he was walking. In the snow. Walking until he reached that spot on the hill that overlooked the lake. The wind whipped up furiously around him, his coat blowing around his knees. He stared into the snowflakes, which burned holes through his skin with the freezing cold.

But he didn't care. "Eloise," he said.

This is it.

He could not understand what she meant. He couldn't.

Because all he felt was pain. The same pain that had been in his chest from the time he was a boy. When he looked at his mother and saw her sad. When he looked at his father and found him lacking. When he felt lonely. When he had been isolated as a boy. This feeling was…

He thought of his mother again, and a great pain burst in his chest.

This is it.

He recognized this feeling as grief. Not as love. And then he saw his mother's face.

I love you.

The words exited his mouth before he could even think them through.

He looked at his mother, and that was what he thought.

But it was painful. It was not a glory.

No one has ever said it to me.

No one except for Eloise.

And then, even in the midst of the snow, it was like he could smell roses.

And he knew.

It wasn't the simple life that called to him. And it wasn't a rose petal on the wind.

It was Eloise. And loving her.

Love had been grief for all his life because there had been no one there to return it. And when he had looked upon his own child, he had felt that same pain because he felt ill-equipped to deal with it.

But Eloise was right. It was love. And it was something more than he had ever imagined it could be. Because pain was part of it. And perhaps this was why people did not love in this way. Unless they couldn't help it.

Unless they had to.

He loved her.

He loved her. He loved their baby.

He had loved all along. He had loved his

mother, who had never said it to him as she wallowed in her own grief. He had loved his father, even while knowing the man was flawed.

Love had always been inside him.

And now, it finally had a chance to take a shape other than this pain.

If only Eloise did not hate him.

He hoped that she didn't. To have come this far, only to lose love again would be unbearable.

He walked back to the palace, completely unaware of the cold now. "We must go," he said to his friends. "To Virginia."

"Really?" Zeus asked. "That's so surprising. You had a change of heart after your isolated self-flagellation walk."

"Shut your mouth for once and gather up as many Christmas decorations as you can. And we must make sure to get her wedding dress."

CHAPTER FIFTEEN

SHE HAD NOT put up a new Christmas tree, and she was slightly regretful. There was no reason to compound her misery, after all. And yet part of her wished to. Wished to wallow in it. In the pain of not having him with her.

Vincenzo.

She loved him. The fact that he had done this to her didn't change that.

It was Christmas Eve, and she was miserable.

Skerret was sitting by the fire in the sweater that she had knitted for her, looking as fine as a ditch cat could.

"At least one of us is content."

The cat said nothing. She only stared back with contemptuous yellow eyes.

Then suddenly there was a knock on the door, and she had a terrible flash of the two other times this had occurred. But twice was perhaps possible, three times, after he had so soundly rejected her, was not. But who else would be at the door on Christmas Eve?

She scrambled out of her chair and waddled to the door.

And when she opened it, it was not just Vincenzo standing there, wearing a dark suit, but three other men, just as tall and imposing, and all so handsome it was stunning.

These men had to be his friends. They had all gone to school together. How had the women on campus gotten anything done?

"Oh," she said.

"She's beautiful," one of the men said.

"Luminous," another said, walking in past her.

"A goddess," said the third. And then suddenly all but Vincenzo were in her house.

"Agreed," Vincenzo said. "I have brought your wedding dress. Because I would still very much like to marry you."

She blinked, then took a step out of the house, closing the front door behind her and isolating them. "What?"

"I realized something. I realized that I love you. Because I found an answer to my question. I was wrong. Love is something born into all of us. What I think we learn is how to suppress it in favor of selfishness. What I think we learn is to ignore it when it hurts too much. And so, for me, all love was pain. When I looked at our baby, all I saw was grief, and when you told me you loved me, all I felt was loneliness. Because that is all I have ever known when it comes to love."

"Oh, Vincenzo."

"You do not need to pity me. For I was a fool. And I hurt you. I regret that. Bitterly."

"But…"

"But I'm here. I'm here because I love you. I'm here because I want you. I've never said those words to anyone. I have never realized that feeling before now. And I hope that is enough. I hope that it is clear that what I say is true."

"Even if I didn't believe you, I wouldn't be strong enough to tell you no." She flung her arms around his neck and kissed him. "Because I love you. I was willing to love you through you figuring out what love was. I didn't need to hear it back right away."

"I know," he said. "But I was just so… I cannot explain." He shook his head. "Except that I was terrified. And I hated admitting that. More than anything."

"I'm sure."

"Zeus is ordained. And he is ready to perform the wedding now. I'm ready to marry you now."

She blinked back tears. "That's good. Because I'm ready too."

From behind the garment bag he pulled a bouquet of roses and extended it to her. "When you told me about your simple life, I could feel the longing for it in a fleeting way. The scent of roses on the wind. But I realized today it was deeper than that. It was my longing for you. Not simplicity. But simply to be where you are. And I got these roses because, for me, it is that intangible thing made real."

She put on her dress, floaty and ethereal, skimming over her bump, and clutched her roses to her chest, looking at herself in the mirror and feeling... Whole.

They were all out in the garden. In the snow. And as she and Vincenzo exchanged vows, just them and Vincenzo's closest friends, she felt she understood love in the truest, most complete way possible.

"I now pronounce you husband and wife. King and Queen."

"You cannot pronounce me King," Vincenzo said. "There is to be a coronation."

"I can pronounce you whatever I like," Zeus said. "I'm officiating."

And with that, they kissed. And it didn't matter what they were called. It didn't matter if the monarchy was abolished or not. It didn't matter if they lived in this cottage in Virginia, or in the palace. They were each other's home. And that was all that mattered.

The coronation was met with great enthusiasm by the people of Arista. Jag and Zeus were in attendance, but not Rafael, who had the wedding of his brother to see to. And it was shocking when they heard the news later. That the wedding had not in fact gone on as intended. But the bride had been taken—by Rafael himself!

"Now that was unexpected," Zeus said.

"Entirely," Jag said. "He never breaks the rules. Or does anything half so interesting as kidnapping women."

"There is a story there," Zeus said. "And I am going to get it."

Eloise thought that she had been filled up with love, more than she could ever hold inside of herself, with her husband, his friends, the people of Arista. But when their son, Mauro Moretti was born, they knew different. Both of them. And they found that the miraculous thing about love was the way that it expanded. To fit everything. The way that it colored every breath, the way that it informed absolutely everything.

After much restructuring, and a vote, it was decided that Arista would retain the monarchy, at least as stabilizing figureheads. And the people were happy to welcome Vincenzo as their King, and Mauro as the next. Especially with more freedom to choose the laws of the land and the knowledge that their leader was just. And that his son would be raised in the same way.

That summer, they went back to Virginia. And spent time in the garden where Vincenzo had first found her.

She had planted roses. Everywhere. For they would always be that concrete symbol of their love. And much to her surprise, with the baby strapped to his chest, Vincenzo rolled up his sleeves and knelt in the dirt beside her, digging a hole with his hands for the new rosebush she had bought.

"I never thought I would see King Vincenzo Moretti on his knees in the dirt, much less beside me."

"And I never thought I would be loved. Yet now I find myself overfilled with it. And I've never been so happy."

"Neither have I, Vincenzo. Neither have I."

There were no sad places left in the world for them. No dark, deep hollows of loneliness. For their love filled them up.

Eloise had wanted a simple life. And in some way she supposed she had one.

Simply perfect.

She started humming.

* * * * *

Blown away by
Crowned for His Christmas Baby?
*Look out for the next instalments in
the Pregnant Princesses quartet,
coming soon from Jackie Ashenden,
Caitlin Crews and Marcella Bell!*

*In the meantime, why not get lost in these
other Maisey Yates stories?*

His Forbidden Pregnant Princess
The Queen's Baby Scandal
Crowning His Convenient Princess
Crowned for My Royal Baby
A Bride for the Lost King

Available now!

"Hi," Susannah said.

The girl pointed to the cast that protruded from the left sleeve of Susannah's sweater. "Did you hurt your arm?"

"I broke my wrist."

"Does it hurt?" the child asked.

"Not so much now, but it did in the beginning. The doctor put this on to make it better." The girl kept staring at it, seemingly fascinated. "Would you like to see?"

She nodded, and Susannah pushed up her sweater. The cast covered her hand, except for her fingers and thumb, and went up to just below her elbow.

"How come you don't got any of your friends' names on it?"

"Well, that's a very good question. Do you think you could do it for me?"

Her eyes lit up. "Uh-huh. I even got a marker." Hastily she took off her backpack and rummaged around until she came up with two. She slowly and carefully wrote the name Nia in black. Instead of dotting the *i* she drew a red heart.

"How beautiful," Sussannah said. "Thank you."

Nia looked quickly over her shoulder, as if realizing she'd strayed too far from the person who'd brought her. "I got to go."

"Are you here with your mother?"

"My daddy. My mama's dead."

Dear Reader,

I wish you and your family a wonderful holiday. I'm so pleased this month to bring you my first Christmas book. I had great fun researching, particularly the customs and history of the Cherokee in western North Carolina. The mountains are spectacular, the people warm and generous.

My story is about Ryan Whitepath, a Cherokee and talented artist…and Susannah Pelton, a woman who has lost everyone she loves. I hope you'll enjoy the Cherokee legends in this book, the language and the love story. I think Ryan's "Nana" will tickle you, and his little daughter, Nia, will steal your heart.

Happy reading—and Merry Christmas!

Fay Robinson

P.S. Write me at fayrobinson@mindspring.com. To learn more about the research behind this book, please visit my Web site at www.fayrobinson.com. Or come chat with me at www.eHarlequin.com.

Books by Fay Robinson

HARLEQUIN SUPERROMANCE

911—A MAN LIKE MAC
961—COMING HOME TO YOU
1012—MR. AND MRS. WRONG
1068—THE NOTORIOUS MRS. WRIGHT

Christmas on Snowbird Mountain
Fay Robinson

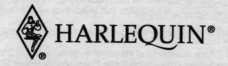

HARLEQUIN®

TORONTO • NEW YORK • LONDON
AMSTERDAM • PARIS • SYDNEY • HAMBURG
STOCKHOLM • ATHENS • TOKYO • MILAN • MADRID
PRAGUE • WARSAW • BUDAPEST • AUCKLAND

ISBN 0-373-71094-1

CHRISTMAS ON SNOWBIRD MOUNTAIN

For my mother…who was fearless.

And for Sherry, Brenda, Jackie and all the other
good sons and daughters taking care of elderly parents.

ACKNOWLEDGMENTS

I'd like to send my appreciation to the people of
Graham County, North Carolina, the city of Robbinsville
and the community of Snowbird for their hospitality and
willingness to answer my questions. I also found the
following works valuable in my research: *Snowbird Cherokees:
People of Persistence* by Sharlotte Neely, The University of
Georgia Press; *Meditations with the Cherokee: Prayers, Songs, and
Stories of Healing and Harmony* by J. T. Garrett of the Eastern
Band of the Cherokee, Bear and Company; *Medicine of the
Cherokee: The Way of Right Relationship* by J. T. Garrett and
Michael Tlanusta Garrett of the Eastern Band of the
Cherokee, Bear and Company; *Another Country: Journeying
Toward the Cherokee Mountains* by Christopher Camuto, The
University of Georgia Press; *Aunt Mary Told Me a Story:
A Collection of Cherokee Legends and Tales* as told by
Mary Ulmer Chiltoskey, edited and compiled by
Mary Regina Ulmer Galloway, North Carolina Publications;
Cherokee Plants: Their Uses—A 400 Year History
by Paul B. Hamel and Mary U. Chiltoskey, Cherokee
Publications; *Cherokee Cooklore* by Mary and
Goingback Chiltoskey, Cherokee Publications;
Walk in My Soul by Lucia St. Clair Robson, Ballantine Books;
Beginning Cherokee by Ruth Bradley Holmes and
Betty Sharp Smith, University of Oklahoma Press;
*Celebrate the Solstice: Honoring the Earth's Seasonal Rhythms
Through Festival and Ceremony* by Richard Heinberg,
Quest Books; *The Winter Solstice: The Sacred Traditions of
Christmas* by John Matthews, Quest Books; *The Encyclopedia of
Mosaic Techniques* by Emma Biggs, Running Press; *Mosaics*
by Kaffe Fassett and Candace Bahouth, The Taunton Press;
Working with Tile by Jim Barrett, Creative Homeowner;
Decorating with Tile by Margaret Sabo Wills,
Creative Homeowner and *Setting Tile* by Michael Byrne,
The Taunton Press.

CHAPTER ONE

Fayetteville, West Virginia
Late October

SUSANNAH LOOKED DOWN into New River Gorge at the rapids nearly nine hundred feet below. Understanding why Native Americans had once called this the River of Death was easy. Even if you miraculously survived a fall here, you'd die on the boulders that dotted the banks, or face the possibility of being swept away in the cold, rushing water.

In the past twenty-three years, two men had drowned after jumps from the steel-spanned bridge where Susannah stood waiting to leap. A third had died when his pilot chute failed to open properly.

"Are you scared?" the older woman in front of her asked. Kay was her name. They'd met at last night's party and agreed to give each other moral support. Like Susannah, Kay was a first-timer.

"I'm a little uneasy," Susannah admitted, "but excited, too."

As far as jumps went, this wasn't one of the

worst. Another plus was that it was legal—at least
for the next six hours during the annual Bridge Day
event. Many other BASE jumps from natural and
man-made structures had been outlawed in the U.S.
The acronym stood for Building, Antenna, Span and
Earth. Bridges and cliffs were two of the most popular places for take-offs.

But Susannah accepted the fact that, sanctioned
by the National Park Service or not, flinging her
body off a fixed object and plummeting toward the
earth at more than forty miles an hour was dangerous, much more so than skydiving, another sport
she'd taken up in the past year. The low altitude left
little room for the deployment of a reserve chute if
her main one failed. Her canopy or lines could also
become tangled in the structure.

Even now rescue workers, or "trolls" as they'd
been nicknamed, were below on the bridge supports,
dangling like spiders from rappelling ropes.

Susannah wasn't worried so much about hitting a
beam as she was overcoming the hazards of the
landing. The designated area on the right shore was
only a few meters wide, wooded and strewn with
rocks.

She'd trained to land safely in wet places and water, her maneuvering skills were good and boats
were positioned below to help if needed, but she
remained a weak swimmer despite classes. A boat

wasn't much help if you couldn't keep your head above water long enough for it to get to you.

The river was freezing and swollen from a week of hard rains, and setting down in it today was Susannah's option of last resort.

But she had to go through with this regardless of the danger, or rather *because* of the danger. During the nine years she'd taken care of her sick mother, she'd forgotten what it meant to feel carefree or excited. She certainly hadn't done anything adventurous.

"A good daughter." That was what the nurses had called her. Reliable. Sensible. Responsible. She was all those things and proud of it.

Alzheimer's, though, destroyed not only the patients but the people who loved them. That was what it had done to Susannah, devastated her emotionally. And now that her mother was gone, she felt a longing to be less reliable, less sensible and responsible. To be less *everything,* or at least different from the dull, unimaginative person she'd grown into.

She had the opportunity to live a different life and take chances—like with this jump—and she intended to do it.

If she chickened out, she might as well go back to the bleak existence she'd had until eighteen months ago, when her mother had died.

The new-and-improved Susannah wouldn't lose

her nerve. This person took risks. This person no longer had to worry about being suffocated by responsibility. Her new approach to life was simple: see everything, experience everything and never forget that each day might be her last.

She'd sold the house and quit her job as an office manager for a law firm in Waycross, Georgia. Anything that wouldn't fit under the camper shell of her new pickup truck she'd given away or taken to the Salvation Army.

In no particular order, she'd committed her desires to paper. Her *Life List,* as she called it, was a blueprint for happiness and fulfillment.

While the items changed and the list continued to grow, so far she'd gone for a dip with dolphins, run a marathon, raised money to protect the endangered black rhino, belly danced, helped Habitat For Humanity build a house for a low-income family and visited the capitals of thirteen states. Thirty-seven more to go.

She'd confronted her fear of heights by taking skydiving lessons, and said goodbye to a lifetime of claustrophobia by going on a three-day caving trip with a group of experienced spelunkers.

Growing her short auburn hair to her waist would take more time; so far, it had only reached her chin. And some of the things she dreamed of accomplishing—like performing in a ballet and being the star of a movie—were perhaps a bit too ambitious, but she wasn't discounting any possibility.

If she didn't at least try, she'd certainly never eat real French onion soup in Paris or dance the tango in Brazil. She'd never have wild, uninhibited sex with a handsome stranger.

The line moved forward more quickly than Susannah expected, bringing her focus back to *this* item on her list. She was among three hundred people awarded slots to jump today. The weather was fair and no one had experienced any problems yet. Soon it would be Susannah's turn.

Kay mumbled over her shoulder, "I don't think I can do this."

"If you don't, you'll lose your entry fee and the couple hundred more you spent on the adaptive rigging."

"Money I can replace," Kay told her. "My life I can't."

"Very true, and I don't want to push you into doing this if you're afraid, but you told me last night that you've been planning this for months and asked me to give you a nudge if you backed out. Didn't you say you begged your family to let you come?"

"Yes."

"If you don't follow through, how would you face them?"

"I'd face them just fine. My husband would be

relieved. He said I was crazy when I took up sky-diving last year, but when I told him I wanted to try this—'' she snorted ''—he said I'd gone completely nuts. I'm beginning to believe he's right.'' Nervousness had her chewing her fingernails. ''What insanity made you sign up?''

''I watched a TV program one night where BASE jumping was featured. The idea of it terrified me, so I knew I had to do it—you know, to prove I could.''

''You *are* insane.''

''Probably so, since I'm afraid of heights and I can't swim.''

''But you skydive. How can you do that if you're afraid of heights?''

''I don't know. I just force myself. I figure going ahead while being scared is better than hiding from the fear.''

Kay looked over the side and grimaced. ''*Hiding* is starting to sound pretty good to me right now. This seems a whole lot scarier than skydiving.''

''But that's the whole point, to do something a little off-the-wall, even if it's scary. If you weren't here, what else would you be doing?''

''I'd probably be raking leaves or cleaning house.''

''I bet this'll be more fun.''

''Yeah, you're right.'' Kay nodded, seemingly reassured, but when it came time for her to jump, she balked. "I can't," she said, scrambling down off the exit platform.

Some of the hundred thousand spectators around them began to boo.

"Come on," Susannah urged. "You said you wanted to add adventure to your dull life. Here's your chance."

"I know, but I was wrong. The truth is, I love my life. I have a great husband and two kids who need me and think I'm perfect. So what if I'm nearly forty, overweight and the most exciting thing I do all week is laundry? I can live with that." She squeezed Susannah's arm. "I'm sorry."

"It's okay. I understand." And she truly did. Kay had her family to think about. Susannah no longer had family, or anyone who mattered. She especially didn't have anyone who thought her perfect.

She'd been the only child of elderly parents, now both dead along with both sets of her grandparents. Her friends had all drifted away when her mother's Alzheimer's worsened and her behavior had become more bizarre.

Even Andrew, the man she'd planned to spend the rest of her life with, had abandoned her when she needed him most. He'd been unable to cope with having his needs placed behind those of a sick person.

At twenty-eight, Susannah was alone in the world.

If she died today, not a soul would care except this woman from Arkansas whose last name she didn't even know.

The crowd started to chant, urging Susannah into action. "Jump...jump...jump."

The official controlling the line gave her a hard look. "Are you going or not?"

"Yes, I'm going."

She climbed the platform straddling the bridge rails and visualized what she had to do once she took off. By arching her body and pointing her hips at the horizon, she could stay upright until the wind turned her naturally into a face-to-earth position. Two seconds into the freefall, she'd reach to the small of her back and grab her pilot chute, tossing it toward the sky.

If everything went right, the chute would unfurl and she'd feel the reassuring tug upward, when the canopy fills. And if it didn't, she'd be seven seconds away from death.

"Hey," she called out to Kay. "What's your last name?"

"Murphy. Yours?"

"Pelton."

"I enjoyed meeting you, Kay Murphy."

"Same here, Susannah Pelton. Have a great life."

"I plan to."

Susannah took a deep breath to shore up her resolve, and with three running steps, launched herself into the air.

Sitting Dog, North Carolina
One week later

THE ONLY SOUNDS in the forest were the faint chattering of the birds as they foraged for seeds and the crunch of Ryan Whitepath's boots in the snow.

He could have driven the four miles to the school bus stop to get Nia, but he preferred the half-mile shortcut down the mountain, where he could free his mind from the projects he had to finish this week.

Work was going well. Professionally and financially he was successful. He had more commissions than he could handle and three upcoming gallery shows featuring his handcrafted tiles and display mosaics. But the obligations of his career were keeping him inside too much lately, and his personal life had gone to hell.

Disconnected was a good description of how he felt. His once-strong connection with the earth, which had always brought him peace and was the very foundation of his art, had experienced a short circuit over the past year. He needed to restore it before his creativity suffered.

He missed the feel of the wind on his face and the way it carried the faint smell of wood smoke on a brisk day. He missed witnessing the change of seasons up close, the brilliance of fall fading to the gray of winter, then the revival of color in the spring and summer.

All this land, as far as he could see across the Snowbird and Unicoi ranges, had once been the home of the *Ani Yunwiya,* the Principal People, but the nine hundred acres his family owned now had come to them only fifty years ago.

His father had taught him about the mountains as a boy, the places where the deer wallow and the wild boar root, where caves exist that can hide a man forever and wild berries grow in such abundance that you never have to worry about hunger.

Such secrets, gifts from parent to child for countless generations, were bonds to Elohi, Mother Earth, the Center. Ryan had neglected his obligation to pass along what he had learned to his daughter. Perhaps she felt disconnected, as well, and that was part of her problem.

She wouldn't like that he hadn't brought the truck, but maybe on the walk home they'd see wild turkeys or the pair of comical mink that had taken up residence near the stream, and it would make her smile. So little did these days.

The death of her mother from pancreatic cancer last March had been hard on the six-year-old, even though Nia had never lived with Carla nor visited her in London more than a handful of times.

Nia was experiencing what the therapist called Separation Anxiety Disorder. She'd lost one parent. Now she was afraid of losing the other.

Ryan had tried explaining about the eternity of the soul, that it's alive before it goes into the body and remains alive after it leaves, but she was too young to fully understand. So he'd sent her to psychologists to help her deal with the grief. After three months of meetings with one and then four months with a second, he couldn't see much progress. Nia remained confused and unhappy.

His vibrant, outgoing daughter was gone. In her place was a quiet child who cried for no reason and didn't want to be alone, sleep or even go to school.

The doctor had suggested trying drug therapy after Christmas to control the anxiety attacks that had begun in the last month, but the thought frightened him. Nia was only a baby. Medications carried risks, especially in someone so young.

He didn't know what to do. His grandmother counseled patience. She believed something besides Carla's death was bothering Nia.

Nana Sipsey had taken of the sacred tobacco one night and had a vision: a redbird with a broken wing would heal his child's heart and, in so doing, heal itself.

Ryan hadn't voiced his skepticism, but it existed. His grandmother came from a long line of healers of the *Ani Wodi,* the Red Paint Clan. He trusted her knowledge of medicines for simple cures of headaches, colds and such.

Accepting prophecy was difficult for him, though, especially when something as important as the emotional stability of his daughter was at stake.

Ahead, John Taylor's Trading Post came into view. The school bus pulled up outside just as Ryan left the woods.

This short stretch of road was the heart of Sitting Dog. A gas station-grocery store, an activities center and a volunteer fire station were the only buildings, but the eighty-four residents could find just about anything they needed, from tools to eggs, without driving the twenty miles to Robbinsville.

Their small community didn't have a McDonald's or a Blockbuster, but the store had videos for rent and its lunch counter served food that appealed to both Indians and whites.

A bank would be nice, but people who worked over on the reservation, Qualla Boundary, fifty miles to the northeast, took care of check cashing and deposits before driving home.

"Sa Sa," he called out, and Nia turned. She'd gotten off the bus with two friends who lived nearby, Iva Williams and Mary Throwing Stick.

"Hi, girls," he said as he walked up. "How was school?"

Mary answered for them. "Buddy Henderson brought his tonsils in a jar and made Iva sick. It was so gross."

"I didn't puke, though," Iva said proudly.

Ryan tried not to laugh, but it was impossible. "I'm glad to hear it." He pulled Mary's braid. "You didn't puke on anybody, did you, Pretty Miss Mary?"

She giggled and wrinkled her nose. "Uh-uh."

"Nia, how was your day?"

Nia shrugged and didn't say anything. Ryan didn't press. Simply getting her to *go* to school this morning had been a triumph. He was thankful she'd made it through the day without coming down with one of her stomachaches or headaches.

"How's your dog?" Ryan asked Mary. "Did she have her puppies yet?"

"Six of them. All black. Can Nia come by for a minute and see them?"

"Maybe another day." Darkness would fall soon and he still needed to recheck a couple of measurements at the activities center before the trek home. Workers were building an addition to use as a child care center and small library. Ryan had promised to complete a wall mosaic in time for the reopening, during the Christian holiday next month, and he was sorely behind. "I'll bring Nia to visit this weekend, Mary. We have chores to do right now."

"Can she come to my slumber party on Saturday? Iva's coming. And Tracie. And Kimberly. And…" She rattled off the names of ten or more little girls in their class. They were going to make banana splits and play games, she added with excitement.

Nia didn't jump in and beg to go, so Ryan hedged. "We'll see. Her grandmother might have other plans for her. She can let you know tomorrow."

The girls' mothers arrived to drive them home, and Nia finally spoke, telling her friends goodbye.

Once they were alone, Ryan tried to talk to her about her reluctance to attend the sleep-over party. "Sounds like a lot of fun, doesn't it?"

"I guess so."

"You like Mary. And all your friends will be there. Don't you want to go?"

"I want to stay home with you."

Ryan didn't push it. When she didn't want to do something, no amount of cajoling would work. She was like her mother in that respect. In the few months he'd dated Carla, he'd learned two things: to let her have her way and to leave her alone when she curled up inside herself.

"I need to go into the center for a few minutes," he told Nia. "Do you want to come with me or wait in John Taylor's where it's warmer? You can buy some paper to practice your writing."

The buildings were adjacent. She'd be safe in the trading post among his neighbors. And it would be good for her to go in by herself.

"Can I go with you?" she asked.

"The heat's turned down, since there aren't any activities today. You'd be cold."

She looked around. "Can't I stay in the truck?"

"I came down the trail today."

"We got to walk in the snow?"

"Walking is good for you, and the snow's not deep. Besides, I told your grandmother and Nana Sipsey I'd see if I could find some possum wood grapes for a pie. You can help me pick them."

"But...the dark might get us. Or we could get lost."

"We'll be home by nightfall." His answer didn't seem to reassure her. He knelt down. "Hey, I'd never let anything hurt you. I know every inch of these woods."

"What if we meet a bear?"

"Mr. Bear is probably sleeping right now. He's snoring in his cave."

"But he could hear us and wake up."

"I'll wrestle him if he does."

"He might bite you."

"I'll bite him back."

She smiled a tiny bit. "Oh, Daddy."

"Will you go into the store? Show Daddy what a big girl you are and buy the paper yourself."

"I'm scared to."

"Remember what Dr. Thompson said. When something scares you, ask yourself why. What do you think's in there that can hurt you?"

"I don't know," she said with a shrug.

"You've known John Taylor and his wife since you were a little baby, and you've been in the store hundreds of times. Nothing in there will hurt you."

"You come, too."

"You can do it by yourself."

Her frightened little face almost made him cave in.

"Will you try, sweetheart?"

She nodded.

He walked her to the front door and gave her money, enough to buy some gum and a pad of paper.

"Stay inside. Don't leave the building for any reason. I'll come for you in a few minutes. I promise everything will be okay."

He said a silent prayer as she let go of his hand and went into the store alone.

CHAPTER TWO

SUSANNAH PARKED the truck at the pumps, filled the tank and checked the tires. This area here was beautiful, like a Christmas card scene. Snow frosted the branches of the trees and a blue mist veiled the mountains in the distance, making them seem painted.

Despite the beauty, driving the winding roads in icy conditions had made her tense. She was tired and hungry and her thermos was empty. A cup of hot coffee and a sandwich would be heaven. She also needed to get directions to see how far she was from Sitting Dog and the studio of the artist she wanted to talk to. She hoped he gave lessons. If he'd work with her, she might be able to mark another item off her list.

First, though, she had to find a place to stay for the night. When possible, and to save money, she stopped at RV parks and slept on the truck seat or used her sleeping bag in the back, under the camper. Tonight would be too cold for that. She'd have to squeeze money out of her tight budget for a motel room.

Well, at least she'd be able to take a hot shower. That alone was worth the extra expense.

Sleeping in a real bed and being able to go online to update her Web site were other pluses of a night indoors. Her travel diary, or "Web log" as the people on the Internet preferred to call it, was getting more than a hundred thousand hits a month from visitors signing on to read about her adventures.

Cranking the truck, she pulled away from the pumps so others could use them. She found a parking space in front of the store.

The warmth of the store was welcome. The building, much larger than it looked from outside, had three parts. The entry room held groceries, clothing and household items. At the back were two doorways. Through one was a self-service laundry. The other appeared to be a small restaurant.

Four old men sat near a gas heater playing a game with rectangular blocks. Cherokee, she guessed they were. Full-blooded or close to it.

She'd seen photographs of Native Americans, but had met very few in person. She hadn't imagined them to be so beautiful or their faces to hold so much expression.

Her fingers itched to get her art pad out of the truck and sketch them, but as a stranger in this isolated place she was already the center of attention. Everyone had turned to look at her as she walked in. They continued to stare as she picked up toothpaste and deodorant and walked to the cash register.

"Hello," she said brightly to the men. She gave them her warmest smile.

A man in a brown shirt threw up his hand in response and smiled back. "Welcome."

"Thank you." After paying for the gas and toiletries, she went to the rest room to freshen up and wandered over to the restaurant to have a look at what they offered. She took a seat at the counter, where one large woman seemed to be both taking orders and fixing meals. Bitsy, as one of the other patrons called her, had to weigh three hundred pounds.

"What would you like?" she asked.

"I'd love a cup of coffee. And do you have soup or sandwiches?"

"Both. I have ham, turkey, barbecued pork or venison sandwiches. Pumpkin soup, walnut, tomato or chicken noodle, all homemade. If you want a hot dinner, your choices are vegetables, hamburger steak or chicken gizzards." She handed her a small chalkboard that listed the vegetables; many were traditional and some—like ramps—Susannah had never heard of.

She wavered between being adventurous and satisfying her hunger.

"I'd like to try something exotic, but I'm also starving and don't want to order and then not like what you bring. Any suggestions for something unique, but that I'll probably enjoy?"

"What are you leaning toward?"

"Well, definitely not the gizzards, but the venison sounds intriguing. And the pumpkin soup. And the walnut soup. But, then again, ham I know I like. Maybe I should play it safe."

"I can make you a half ham, half deer meat sandwich and put the two kinds of soup in small cups instead of bowls so you can have a taste of both for the same price. And I make a nice bean bread that goes well with soup."

"Oh, sounds perfect."

"It'll be right up."

"Can you also tell me how far it is to Sitting Dog?"

"You're here."

"But where's the *town?*"

"You're smack-dab in the middle of it. If you want a town, then Robbinsville, fifteen or twenty miles to the northeast, is the place to head. They've got, oh, maybe seven hundred folks."

"That doesn't sound like much of a town."

"Sugar, you're in Graham County. We've got

plenty of mountains, creeks and trees, but we're way short on people. Only about eight thousand of us are crazy enough to live here.''

''In the whole county?''

''Yep. The land's mostly government-owned national forest. We're the only county in North Carolina that doesn't even have a four-lane road.''

''I passed through some of the forest land. I went nearly fifty miles without seeing another car.''

''Which way did you come in?''

''From Tellico Plains, Tennessee, over the Cherohala Skyway.''

''Lord, girl! You took a chance in this weather. That's a desolate trip this time of the year, and this early snow must've made the going even tougher. Some of those curves never get enough sun to melt the ice.''

''The scenery was worth it. I've never seen anything more beautiful in my life.''

''It *is* pretty.''

''Is there a motel close by?''

''No, sorry. We don't get many tourists this late in the year. In warm weather we attract nature lovers who hike the back country, but they mostly camp out.''

''I imagine with this fresh snowfall everyone's farther upstate at the ski resorts.''

''Probably. We don't normally get our first snowfall for a couple more weeks, so I'm sure the skiers have headed up to Maggie Valley. But they're missing a treat. These mountains are the place to be in winter, especially during the holidays.'' She refilled the coffee of a man two seats down. ''You only passing through?'' she asked Susannah.

''I'm not sure yet. Do you have a bed-and-breakfast? Even a boardinghouse would do.''

''A couple B-and-Bs. And there's a lodge, but they're probably closed for the season and won't open up again until late March or mid-April. When you've finished eating, you can borrow my phone book and call around. Maybe someone around here is open.''

''Thanks. I appreciate that.''

Several people sat down to order and the woman got busy filling orders. The venison she brought Susannah a few minutes later was delicious, the pumpkin and walnut soups interesting. The best part was the bread—simply out of this world. Susannah was glad she'd taken a chance on something different.

She was finishing her coffee when she felt a presence. She glanced to her side and found a young girl with huge brown eyes staring up at her.

''Hi,'' Susannah said.

''*Si yo,*'' the girl answered. Her front teeth on the top and bottom were missing, making her whistle slightly when she talked.

"I'm sorry. I don't speak your language."

"I said hello."

"Oh, well, then *si yo* to you, too."

The girl pointed to the cast that protruded from the left sleeve of Susannah's sweater. "Did you hurt your arm?"

"I broke my wrist."

"How?"

"Mm, I guess you could say I tried to fly and found out I wasn't any good at it."

Actually, the flying part had gone well. She'd jumped from the bridge, her chute had opened perfectly and she'd drifted down toward the landing area without problems. At the last second the wind had shifted. In an attempt to stay out of the water, Susannah had overcompensated and hit the rocks.

"Does it hurt?" the child asked.

"Not so much now, but it did in the beginning. The doctor put this on to make it better." The girl kept staring at it, seemingly fascinated. "Would you like to see?"

She nodded.

Susannah turned on the stool and pushed up her sweater. The cast covered her hand, except for her fingers and thumb, and went up to below her elbow.

"It's white. My friend Iva broke her arm last year and her thing was purple."

"That's because this one's made out of plaster.

Your friend Iva's was probably made out of fiber-glass and those come in purple and other colors.''

"How come you didn't get a pretty one?" She reached out and lightly rubbed her fingers over it.

"Because the pretty ones cost a lot more money and I was being frugal."

"Fruit girl?"

"Frugal," Susannah repeated with a smile. "That means I was trying not to spend too much money."

"How come you don't got any of your friends' names on it?"

"Well, that's a very good question." And one Susannah didn't know how to answer for a child. How did you explain to someone her age that you didn't have any friends? Fortunately she didn't have to.

"We printed our names on Iva's," the girl said, forging ahead. "I put mine right there." She placed her index finger in the middle of Susannah's forearm.

"That sounds pretty."

"I could only print then, but I can write my name in cursive now." She looked up with expectation, her sweet face showing exactly what she longed to do. "I can write it real good."

"You can already write in cursive? Goodness. How old are you?"

"*Sudali.*" She held up six fingers.

"Well, this must be my lucky day because I've been looking all over for a six-year-old to write her name on my cast and couldn't find one. Do you think you could do it for me?"

Her eyes lit up. "Uh-huh. I even got a marker." Hastily she took off her school backpack and rummaged around until she came out with two. Susannah held her arm steady in her lap while the girl slowly and carefully wrote the name *Nia* in black. Instead of dotting the *I* she drew a red heart.

"How beautiful. Thank you."

"You won't wash it off?"

"No."

"Promise?"

"I promise." The cast would be removed and thrown away in four to six weeks, but the child probably hadn't thought about that.

Nia looked quickly over her shoulder, as if realizing she'd strayed too far from the person who'd brought her. "I got to go." She returned her things to her pack.

"Are you here with your mother?"

"My daddy. My mama's dead. She got the cancer in her stomach."

"I'm sorry."

"You got a mama?"

"No, not anymore."

"Did she get the cancer?"

"Something like that."

"Do you miss her?"

"Very much."

"You got a daddy?"

"No, I'm afraid not."

"Who tucks you in at night?"

"I…" The question sent a sharp pain through Susannah's heart. "I tuck myself in."

"My daddy tucks me in. I got a Gran and a Nana Sipsey to help."

"Then I'd say you're a very lucky little girl to have so many people who love you."

The child said goodbye and left. Susannah ordered another cup of coffee. "Anything else?" the waitress asked when she'd finished.

"No, thanks. Everything was delicious."

"Glad you enjoyed it. Want that phone book now?"

"Yes, please." Susannah paid for her meal, then Bitsy helped her look up numbers for places where she might stay the night. She wrote them down.

While she had the book, she flipped over to the *W* section and skimmed the listings.

"Do you know Ryan Whitepath, the artist? This lists only a post office address and I'd like to drop by and speak to him."

"Sure. Everybody knows the Whitepaths.

They've lived here all their lives. That was Ryan's little girl you were talking to.''

''You're kidding!''

''He usually picks her up out front when she gets off the school bus. Hurry and you might catch him.''

Susannah raced through the store and outside. She scanned the parking lot for Nia, but didn't see her anywhere. Damn! So close to Whitepath and she'd missed him.

The one item on her Life List that had caused her the most concern was ''Create something beautiful and lasting.'' For months she'd pondered what that should be and the training she needed to accomplish it. A painting maybe? An exquisite photograph? A sculpture? None of those things seemed exactly right, but she couldn't explain why. She wanted the whatever she made to be admired long after she died, but it also had to ''speak'' to her heart, to be part of her somehow.

While waiting in the emergency room in Fayetteville to have her wrist set, she'd wandered off in search of a rest room and wound up in the lobby for the recently completed heart center. The floor had been the most stunning mosaic she'd ever seen, hundreds of thousands of tiny pieces of tile expertly placed so that they gave the illusion of walking on a leafy forest floor in autumn. Looking at it had literally taken her breath away.

A pamphlet about the heart center credited the work to Cherokee artist Ryan Whitepath of Sitting Dog, North Carolina.

A mosaic. Perfect! They were beautiful and durable. She'd found out on the Internet that one dating back thirty-five hundred years had recently been uncovered by archaeologists and was still intact.

She believed she had the talent to learn the craft. She'd started college as an art major, planning to be a portrait painter. Her mother's illness had killed that dream the following year, but in the last few months she'd taken up drawing again.

She possessed a sense of color and understood perspective. And it wasn't as if she wanted to be an expert, only make a little piece of something Ryan Whitepath could insert in a larger work. *If* she could talk him into giving her lessons and letting her help in his studio.

That request, she felt, was best made in person rather than by telephone. So she'd rearranged her schedule and backtracked into North Carolina.

The timing was perfect. She planned to be in New York City to watch the ball drop in Times Square on New Year's Eve. That gave her eight weeks before she had to move on.

She reentered the store and went back to the lunch counter. "I wasn't quick enough. Can you tell me how to get to Mr. Whitepath's studio or home?"

"Be glad to." The waitress picked up a napkin and started drawing a map. "I hope you have four-wheel drive."

RYAN ENJOYED the walk back, but Nia struggled to keep up. He put her on his shoulders and carried her.

"Am I heavy, Daddy?" she asked in *Tsalagi*.

"Yes, you're heavy. And you squirm like a trout. I can hardly hold on to you."

She wriggled her behind, teasing him. "There was a lady with pretty hair in the store. She tried to fly and fell down and hurt herself."

"She tried to fly in the store?"

"No, Daddy, not in the *store*." She giggled, a welcome sound.

"Was she an eagle?"

"Uh-uh."

"A big owl?"

"No."

"A moth?"

"No!"

"Maybe she was a goose like you, Sa Sa."

"No, silly. She was a *lady*."

They came to the possum wood trees, persimmons some people called them. He set Nia on the ground and took a sack from his jacket pocket to hold their bounty. Deer and raccoons considered the tart fruit a treat, and the many tracks in the snow told him the animals had already found the ripe ones that had fallen.

"Help me dig down and get some good ones for a pie. The cold will have turned them sweet."

They gathered enough for several pies, along with a few large pinecones Nia wanted to use for a Thanksgiving project at school. Few Indian families celebrated the holiday, but Nia, like all children in this area, went to the county school where such things were usual.

He and Nia thanked the earth for the possum wood berries and pinecones and then started back up the trail.

"We made it before the dark got us, Daddy," Nia said as the house came into view.

"And I didn't have to wrestle a single bear."

Ryan didn't stop at his place. A few years ago he'd converted the old equipment barn from his father's defunct furniture-making business into a modern workshop with two kilns in the back and living quarters in the loft for him and Nia, but Nia most often ate in the house and sometimes slept there. Ryan did, too, unless he worked late, which was happening more often than he liked.

A vehicle he didn't recognize was parked in the yard. "We have company."

"Is it Uncle Joe?"

"No, not unless he's bought a new truck." That wasn't likely. His youngest brother didn't have money for luxuries. Joseph was a carpenter and furniture maker and worked hard, but employment opportunities were limited in the sparsely populated county. Most of the land was virgin forest. Only six percent was appropriate for cultivation. Except for one factory, they had no industry.

Just inside the door, he helped Nia take off her boots and coat. He followed her through the house to the kitchen.

A pretty young woman with red hair sat at the table with his mother and grandmother drinking tea. "You're here!" Nia exclaimed. To his amazement, she rushed over and climbed into the stranger's lap.

"Hi, sweetheart." The woman playfully tugged on one of Nia's long braids.

"Look, Daddy! I wrote my name on her arm."

Nia badgered the woman into pushing up the sleeve of her sweater to reveal a cast with her signature.

Ryan couldn't have been more stunned. The fiery hair. The broken "wing."

His grandmother nodded to him with a satisfied smile. "Rejoice," she said in their native tongue. "The redbird has come."

CHAPTER THREE

RYAN WHITEPATH hadn't moved or said a word since he arrived. He stood in the doorway holding a sack and stared at Susannah as if she had a second head. She stared back. Not that it was a hardship. On the contrary, she was having a difficult time dragging her eyes away.

The man was extraordinary looking, with black hair falling in shiny soft waves past his shoulders, and rugged, almost harsh, features. If not for the flannel shirt and jeans, he could've stepped out of a nineteenth-century painting by Frederic Remington, or been the model for Maynard Dixon's warrior in *The Medicine Robe*.

"The woman wishes to speak to you about your art, Ryan," his mother said. Mrs. Whitepath had offered Susannah a sweet, herbal tea and kept her entertained while they waited for her son and granddaughter to come home.

The older woman—eighty, at least, and no bigger than a twig—was the other woman's widowed mother-in-law, Sipsey Whitepath, the "Nana Sipsey'' Nia had mentioned. She spoke Cherokee and broken English, which meant she was sometimes hard to understand. She also acted as if Susannah had been expected, and that made her a bit uncomfortable.

"Hi," Susannah said to the man. "I was at the store earlier and met Nia, but I didn't realize she was your daughter."

"Who did you say you are?"

"I'm sorry. I should've introduced myself. My name is Susannah Pelton."

He put his sack down on the table. Instead of sitting, he chose to lean with his back against the counter and his arms crossed over an impressive set of chest muscles.

"And you're from where?" he asked.

"Originally Waycross, Georgia, but the last year or so not from anywhere in particular. I've been traveling the country." She took the hospital pamphlet out of her purse and passed it to his mother who, in turn, handed it to him. "I saw the floor you did for the hospital in Fayetteville, West Virginia, and thought it was exquisite. I was wondering if you'd consider giving me lessons in designing and creating mosaics. I have a couple of months of free time and I'm eager to learn."

"You drove three-hundred miles to ask me that?"

"And to see more of your work, of course, if it wouldn't be an imposition."

"I'm sorry, Miss Pelton. If you'd called I could have saved you the trouble of a trip. I don't give lessons."

"Not ever?"

"Occasionally in the summer months I take on an intern from one of the universities, but right now I have too much to do and too little time to do it in. I can't possibly work with anyone who has no prior experience."

"I'll gladly pay you." She'd already calculated what she could afford, not much, but this was so important she was prepared to dip into her emergency fund.

"Money's not the issue," Whitepath said. "I can't give you lessons. I'm overwhelmed with contracts and it's going to take every free minute I have to fulfill them. In fact, I should be working right now."

"I see." Susannah's hope dimmed. "Won't you make an exception this one time? I've taken art classes and I have a sketchbook in my truck with examples of my work."

"I'm sorry. Like I said, I'm too busy to train anyone. It would only put me further behind."

"I believe I could be a help to you rather than a hindrance."

"With a broken arm?"

"The break isn't severe."

"How did you do it?"

Nia piped up, "She tried to fly, Daddy. I told you."

"*Did* you try to fly?" he asked.

"I jumped off a bridge using a parachute," Susannah explained. "It feels a bit like flying. My landing was off, though, and I hit some rocks."

He grunted and she could hear censure in it. He thought her a fool for doing something so ridiculous.

"I'm sorry you came this far for nothing, but I can't help you." He pushed away from the counter. Apparently he'd decided his discussion with Susannah was over. "Nia, do you have homework?"

"I got to read aloud. And I got to look up ten words in my dictionary."

"Let's do it before it's too late. Go wash your hands so you won't get the book dirty."

"Can I read to the pretty lady?" She cocked her head and exchanged smiles with Susannah. Again, Whitepath's gaze seemed puzzled, as if Susannah had said or done something peculiar.

"We'll see. Go wash your hands, goosey. Be a good girl. Find a book you'd like to try."

His expression softened when he spoke to his child, making him look different. Susannah wouldn't say *handsome* because it didn't fit. *Less severe* was more accurate.

Nia scooted off Susannah's lap. When she'd left the room, the older woman mumbled a few words in Cherokee. That prompted a quick response from Whitepath. Judging by his scowl, his grandmother had clearly said something he didn't want to hear.

"Ryan, don't be rude," his mother admonished. She turned to Susannah. "Forgive my son. He forgets not all people speak *Tsalagi*."

"Sorry, Miss Pelton. I didn't mean to exclude you."

"Call me Susannah, please."

"Susannah."

She'd never liked her name, but it sounded... appealing coming from his lips. Pleasurable, like the brush of silk against her skin.

"Don't apologize," she told him. "I love listening to your language being spoken. I wish I'd bought some books so I could learn a few basic phrases. *Tsalagi*." Susannah pronounced it slowly. "I assume that means Cherokee?"

"Yes, the word refers to our language and is one of only a few common to Cherokee here and out west."

"I don't understand. You speak a different language from other Cherokees?"

"A different *dialect*."

His mother jumped in and explained. "The Eastern Band is a separate entity from the Cherokee Nation in Oklahoma. Most Cherokee here in North Carolina and surrounding states speak *Atali* and those in Oklahoma *Kituhwa.* We in Sitting Dog, however, have a mixed dialect that's not really used on the nearby reservation. I'm afraid a book of phrases would do you little good. You must hear the language spoken, the subtleties of it, to truly understand the meaning of the words."

"Why is there a difference in dialects if the reservation is so close?"

"We've been isolated from each other until recent years because of the mountains. Traditions and lifestyles have evolved differently, as well. Like Qualla Boundary, we have a few mixed-race families because we've lived among our white neighbors for many years, but most of our residents are full-blooded. English is our *second* language rather than our first. We speak mostly *Kituhwa,* as our ancestors did centuries ago. The dialect is similar to that once spoken by the Cherokee who were relocated to Oklahoma, but with colloquial differences. We borrow from both the Eastern and Western dialects."

"Well, it's lovely. Very musical."

"Yes, a good description. That's why we so often express ourselves through song."

"Is Nia fluent in *Tsalagi* and English?"

"She speaks both and is learning to read and write both. She's been brought up to learn and respect the language and customs of both races. Her mother was white."

Susannah had thought so. The child's skin was light, not dark like her father's. Her hair was a warm brown rather than black. She could pass for white or Native American.

"Nia mentioned that her mother had passed away. I'm very sorry."

Whitepath made a strangled sound. He straightened, taking several steps toward her. "She told you that?"

"She said her mother died of cancer."

He and his mother stared at her strangely again. His grandmother only nodded, as if she wasn't surprised.

"I'm sorry," Susannah said. "Was talking to her about it a mistake? If I did something wrong, I apologize."

"No, no," Mrs. Whitepath said. "You did nothing wrong. We're only amazed that Nia confided in anyone. She's rarely so open with strangers, and she never speaks about her mother. She seems to have taken a great liking to you, though. That's what Ryan and his grandmother were discussing."

"I see," Susannah said, but she suspected there was more to it than that. There was some kind of conflict between the man and the old woman. Sipsey Whitepath seemed pleased, but Ryan looked downright unhappy.

AT HIS MOTHER'S insistence and to Susannah's delight, Ryan Whitepath agreed to take her on a quick tour of his studio.

"I'll help Nia with her words while you're gone," his mother told him, ushering them out the front door with their coats.

They stood on the steps to appreciate the beauty of the landscape. The old house and its outbuildings sat about halfway up a mountain in a small clearing bordered by hardwoods and evergreens. A panorama of hills and valleys stretched out before them. Dusk had arrived, turning the trees to dark figures and streaking the sky with multiple shades of orange and pink. The scene was breathtaking.

"My God," Susannah said with a long sigh. "Everything seems too beautiful to be real."

"The sunrises are just as spectacular. And when a storm rolls through…it's like nothing else you can imagine."

"Have you always lived here, Mr. Whitepath? In these mountains, I mean."

"Call me Ryan. And yes, I've lived in the mountains and, for the most part, in this house all my life, except for the years I was away at school. I was born in one of the back rooms. So were my father, uncle, two younger brothers and my sister. My grandmother delivered all of us.''

''Do your siblings live in Sitting Dog?''

''Joseph does. Charlie's in Winston-Salem and Anita's a sophomore at the University of North Carolina at Asheville.''

''Is that where you went to school, UNC?''

''I did my undergraduate studies there in painting, but I was lucky enough to get a couple of corporate grants that allowed me to do graduate work in Ravenna, Italy, at The School of Mosaic Restoration.''

''I'm impressed.''

''For my family it was a very big deal, since I was the first Whitepath to ever go to college—actually, the first to even graduate from high school.''

''Really? But your mother seems so well educated.''

''Because she works hard to improve herself. She's become an expert on the history of our people. She's also one of the founders of a national project to make sure every child has the opportunity to learn his or her native language.''

''That's ambitious.''

''But important. Fewer than 150 native languages in the U.S. have survived out of several thousand, and we've already lost a major dialect of Cherokee called *Elati.* She's determined not to let that happen again.''

''I admire her for preserving your heritage.''

''I do, too. Because of her, I know who my ancestors are. That's important to me, to my understanding of who I am.''

''What about your father? Is he Cherokee?''

''Yes. His great-great-great-grandparents hid out in these mountains and eluded the soldiers who came in 1838 to relocate them. Their son was born later that year. They named him *Numma hi tsune ga,* Whitepath, after a chief of the same name from North Georgia who was a half-blood brother to Sequoyah. Chief Whitepath tried to warn against the government's treachery. But he wasn't successful at rousing the tribal elders to take a stand and was among those rounded up and marched west. Old and sick, he was one of the four thousand who died.''

''The Trail of Tears. I remember reading about it in my American History classes.''

''My family carries Chief Whitepath's name in remembrance of what he tried to do. We adopted it around 1900 as a surname.''

''Does it mean anything?''

''To an Indian, everything has a meaning. The *white path* is the path of happiness in the Green Corn Dance ceremony our ancestors practiced. For a Cherokee of the old time to say he was *white* meant he was taking the path of happiness, of peace."

"So where does *Ryan* come from? That's obviously not Cherokee."

"Ryan MacDougal was a childhood friend of my mother's who died in a fall. She named me for him. These mountains are full of families with Scottish and Irish heritage. You'll notice the cross-influences in the languages. Our legends are similar, too. Ever heard of the Little People from Irish folktales?"

"Of course. They're leprechauns. When I was little, I believed they lived in our den."

"The Cherokee also know of the Little People, the good and bad spirits who inhabit the forest. The Little People are said to take things or move them. Sometimes they'll leave you a gift, and you're expected to reciprocate. My father used to swear they were constantly moving his tools."

"What does your father do?"

"He used to run a shop here on the property with my grandfather and uncle. They made furniture. For the past fifteen years, he's lived in a little town called Lineville and worked for a trucking company. He and my mother are divorced."

"Sorry," she said with a grimace. "I assumed your dad was at work. Am I being too nosy? I find your family fascinating."

"No, no problem. The breakup was economic

more than anything. The business wasn't profitable anymore, so after Granddaddy died, my dad wanted to move to the city. My mother didn't. At first he was pretty good about coming home on weekends and holidays, and they tried to keep the marriage going. But over time the visits got more infrequent and then stopped. I haven't seen him in three or four years.''

"That has to be tough.''

"Everyone took it hard when he moved out, especially my brother Joe who was only seven and particularly close to him.''

"How old were you?''

"Fifteen. I'm the oldest.''

"So that made you the man of the house?''

He shrugged as if it were no big deal, but Susannah didn't believe that. Fifteen—thrust into adulthood... The situation must've been difficult for him.

He walked down the steps and motioned for her to follow.

"Get your sketchbook and I'll look at it,'' he said, striding over to her truck.

"You mean you might reconsider teaching me?''

"No, but if you want my opinion on your work, I'll give it.''

WITH HER SKETCHBOOK under her arm, Susannah fell in next to him, trying to keep up with his long strides as they made their way down the driveway. She thought he'd head to a cabin on the right, but instead he turned left toward a long barn.

"My studio's over there," he said.

The air was crisp and smelled of sawdust, and in the fading light she could see piles of the stuff rotting behind the building. Snow had begun to fall again.

"This used to be my dad's workshop," Ryan explained. The long structure had double barn doors in the middle and a regular door to the left, with an opening below for a pet to go in and out. He opened the smaller door and they went inside. "I needed a large space nearby so I closed in the sides, added plumbing and a floor and made a workshop and apartment."

Susannah had expected something rustic and dark, considering the exterior, but when he flipped on the lights, she couldn't hold back her surprise. The interior was spacious and airy, as modern as any dwelling in a big city.

"Wow! This is wonderful."

"It works well for the business and for me personally. I'm close enough to take care of my mother and grandmother and for them to help me with Nia, but I have my own space and privacy. At least, I feel the illusion of privacy."

The main floor was his workshop. Long plywood

tables made an L along one side and across the back, holding projects in various states of completion. Sketches and vibrant paintings covered the walls. The stairs on the left led to a loft where he lived.

He showed her around the main floor. Shelves under the tables held glass jars filled with tiny tiles of every conceivable color and hue. Larger tiles were stacked in bins along the right wall.

"Do you use commercial tiles or make your own?" she asked, as they walked through the kiln room.

"Both. It depends on the project and · what I'm trying to accomplish. If I can't get the color, texture or durability I'm looking for, I'll make my own. A good part of my business is restoration, which involves hand-making or painting tiles to match older or antique ones. I often have to experiment with pigments, glazes, bisques and firing techniques."

"You do all the work here?"

"Mostly. I create manageable sections of tile by attaching it to a special backing I designed myself. When the whole piece is done, I ship, reconstruct and install. I prefer to work from scratch on-site, but that's not practical because of the time and expense involved."

They came back to the main room and he showed her his office, in the corner area by the stairs. Papers were strewn haphazardly on his desk, as well as the light table. Everywhere, actually. The whole office needed a good tidying.

A white Persian cat lay stretched out on top of a tall bookcase, and it watched Susannah with eyes like gold jewels, expression haughty.

"Hello," Susannah called up. "What's your name?"

"That's Abigail," Ryan supplied. "I thought it would be good for Nia to learn responsibility for taking care of a living thing, but I have a suspicion Abigail owns us and we're *her* pets rather than the other way around."

"Cats can be a bit independent. She's so beautiful."

"She knows it, too."

He took Susannah's jacket and flung it over a chair, then shed his own. Grabbing a rubber band out of his desk drawer, he drew his dark hair off his face, into a ponytail.

"Do you wear your hair long because you're Native American?" Susannah asked.

"I prefer *Indian*."

"Sorry."

"That's okay. I'm not offended by *Native American*. The term is just a little too politically correct for me. Others like it, and that's fine. And to answer your question, no, I don't wear my hair long to appear more Indian. It's vanity. With short hair I look about twelve.''

She smiled at his honesty.

"I thought maybe you were trying to look authentic.''

"To do that, I'd have to cut it to stand up in a ridge along the back of my head down to my neck, and then shave the rest.''

She wrinkled her nose but didn't say anything.

"That was the style for Cherokee men before about 1800, except for the Long Hair or Twister Clan.''

"I don't think you'd look too good bald.''

"Neither do I.''

"I'm envious of how long and glossy your hair is. And the color's gorgeous.''

"I was just thinking the same thing about yours.''

He reached out and picked up a strand, gently rubbing it between his fingertips. She hardly breathed.

"To tsu hwa," he said softly.

"What?''

"Redbird.'' He must have realized he was still touching her, because he suddenly let the hair drop, thrusting both hands in the pockets of his jeans.

"Your grandmother called me that earlier.''

"Consider it an honor. The cardinal, or redbird, plays an important role in our legends.''

"How so?"

"It's revered by my people. There's a story behind how the bird got its color."

She waited, but he didn't go on. "Well, don't keep me in suspense."

"I can't tell the story like my grandmother can."

"Your grandmother's not here. Come on, don't leave me hanging."

Finally he acquiesced.

"Years ago the redbird wasn't red. He was plain and brown. One day, while gathering food for his family, he came upon a hurt wolf lying on a riverbank. The wolf had chased a raccoon up a tree and the raccoon had sneaked up on him while he was exhausted and plastered his eyes shut with mud. Thankful for the bird's compassion in helping him remove the mud, the wolf broke open a paint rock, a geode left from a volcanic eruption, and used it to give the bird a bright red coat. When the redbird flew home, his mate was so excited by his new color, she wanted some for herself. But she was afraid to leave their babies too long so she went and got only a little bit of the paint for herself. She was a good mother and hurried back to the nest. Today redbirds are symbols of beauty, kindness, compassion and dedication to family."

Susannah was thrilled to be compared to the little

bird. She'd always hated her hair color, but he'd made her see it in a whole new way.

"That was so lovely. How do you say 'redbird' again? *To-tso…*"

"*To tsu hwa.*"

"*To tsu hwa,*" she repeated several times until she'd memorized it. "Thank you for the story. I feel like…like I've been given a gift."

"You're welcome." He stared at her a moment longer than was healthy for her heart, then looked away. "I need to check my messages and return my calls. Do you mind?"

"No, go ahead. I'll wander about, if that's okay."

"Sure. On that table is a mosaic I'm repairing for a 1930s era pool, and over there's a ceiling I'm designing in conjunction with another company in California. The rest are…I don't know…different jobs and separate pieces for a museum show. Look all you want."

FIFTEEN MINUTES LATER, after reviewing his work and overhearing his telephone conversations, Susannah had decided that Ryan Whitepath was the most gifted person she'd ever met, but also the most disorganized.

She supposed his problem was a right brain, left brain thing, or that his overabundance of creativity had been offset by his lack of order.

His mosaics were brilliant, the colors earthy and the designs so stunning that Susannah felt spiritually changed just looking at them. But from a business standpoint, the man was hopeless.

He had no system for organizing his quotes and keeping up with correspondence, and apparently hadn't sent out invoices for work he'd completed weeks ago. The clutter on his desk made her cringe.

He tried to pull up a letter he'd typed on his computer to discuss with someone on the phone, but he couldn't find it. After several failed attempts, a lot of grumbling under his breath and the accidental deletion of a file, Susannah walked toward him.

"Here," she said, leaning over his shoulder. "Let me help before you do something you can't repair. What's the customer's name?"

"Health Systems of North Carolina." He spoke into the phone receiver. "Hold on a minute longer, Mr. Baker. We've almost got it."

She couldn't find a folder that resembled the name so she did a search and came up with one document called healthnc.doc.

"That's it," he said. He read off the figures to his customer and promised him an invoice within the week. When he'd ended the call, he asked Susannah how to print it, since he couldn't remember the procedure.

"You can go into your File menu and down to

Print, hit Control-P on your keyboard, or click on this icon on the toolbar. See how it looks like a little printer?''

He tried to print, but got an error message. ''What the—? I did what you said.''

She reached over and pushed a switch. ''It helps if you turn on the printer.''

''Oh, yeah. That makes sense.''

She printed two copies. He seemed surprised when they actually came out into the tray. After, she used a utility program to retrieve the file he'd deleted and restore it to its original folder.

''Thanks for the help. I bought the computer expecting it to save me time. But I forget from one day to the next how to use it. Pretty stupid, huh?''

''Success takes practice.''

''Nia's better at it than I am. It's downright embarrassing to have to ask a six-year-old for help when I do something wrong.''

She cleared off a spot on the corner of his desk so she could sit.

''May I make a suggestion? You'd be able to find things more easily if you kept your quotes, correspondence and billing linked in this one program. It would also reduce your aggravation, especially at tax time.''

''I don't know how to do all that. Typing a letter takes me two hours as it is, and then I can never find where I saved them—if I remember to save them.''

"I could set up a billing system and teach you how to use it and your computer in exchange for a few mosaic lessons. Until I quit my job to travel, I ran an office for twenty-three attorneys. I'm proficient in all the software programs you have here, and I'm available for the next eight weeks. I could really have you rolling on this thing by Christmas. And I *know* that being more organized would save you a lot of time.''

"Thanks for the offer, Susannah, but like I said earlier, I'm overwhelmed with contracts and I don't have time to train anyone. Or to learn anything new myself. On three separate occasions I've tried hiring office staff, but nobody worked out. Having someone nearby asking questions all the time proved to be too distracting. I couldn't concentrate.''

Dispirited, she nonetheless couldn't blame him. "I understand.''

"But let's take a look at your work. Maybe I can recommend someone else who can give you lessons.''

He reached for the sketchbook she'd left propped against the chair holding her jacket, but she jumped up and grabbed it first. She clutched it to her chest. "I've changed my mind.''

"Why?''

"Because I'm embarrassed. Your work is so incredible and mine, I realize now, is amateurish."

"With your enthusiasm, I doubt that. Where did you study?"

"I didn't, not really. I had a year of basic drawing classes at Auburn University and grand dreams of being a portrait artist, but then...well, something happened in my personal life that forced me to return home. I ended up getting a two-year business degree at a community college."

"How many years ago were those drawing classes?"

"Nine, unfortunately."

"That's a lot of time. Have you been drawing or painting since then?"

"Only sporadically. Recently I've started back in earnest, though."

"Let me see." He held out his hand. "I won't sugarcoat my opinion, but I'm rarely brutal."

With nervousness, Susannah gave up her art pad. He sat down in the office chair again while she reclaimed her former position on the edge of the desk.

He took his time examining each drawing, without making a comment about any of them. He'd flip a page, study for a minute or so, and then flip again.

Most of the drawings were of people she'd met in the past few months. Some were of her mother as she'd been before her illness, when she still remembered how to laugh and her eyes weren't clouded by confusion.

A piece of loose yellow paper fluttered from the pad to the floor when he turned a page, and Susannah realized with horror that it was her Life List.

Ryan picked it up, gave it a cursory look and stuck it in the back of the pad. He went on to the next drawing.

Thank you, God. She'd never intended anyone to ever see her desires so blatantly scribbled.

He closed the sketchbook and handed it to her. "Your drawings aren't bad. I wouldn't call them good, but considering that you haven't had a chance to develop your skills, you've done okay."

"So do I have any talent?"

"I see evidence of it. You probably won't ever be a professional artist, but with some practice you could develop into a gifted amateur."

"I'd be happy with that," she told him, pleased. "I'm really only drawing for myself. I don't expect to make a living at it."

"Then keep doing it. Draw what you like and do it often. You'll see a big improvement fairly soon."

"And what about mosaics and tile-making? Do you think I could learn the techniques?"

"I think so, although I warn you that crafting people in tile is extremely hard and that's the subject you seem to like drawing the most."

"Oh, I don't care what kind of design I do. A leaf or a cloud would satisfy me as long as whatever I make will be around for a long time."

He pulled out an address book, jotted down the names of teachers in the southeast and included phone numbers.

"Try some of these people." He passed her the list. "Tell them I recommended you."

"I will. Thanks for your help. And your honest opinion. It means a lot to me."

They put on their jackets. Outside, the temperature had dropped dramatically with the coming of the dark, but yard lights guided their way. The snow was now ice in the low spots of the gravel driveway. Walking was difficult; twice she slipped and nearly fell. Only Ryan's quick action saved her.

"You need real boots," he said, supporting her under her good arm. "Those designer things are worthless up here."

"I have sturdy boots in the truck, but I didn't expect to be hiking through a blizzard when I got dressed this morning."

"If you think this is a blizzard, you've never been in one."

When, for the third time, she nearly went down on her backside, Ryan cursed. He picked her up and kept walking as though she didn't weigh anything.

"What are you *doing?*"

"Keeping you from breaking another bone."

Susannah should have protested, but he was warm, his arms were strong and, oh boy, he smelled good. The scent was masculine, woodsy.

"Do you usually carry your guests?"

"Only the klutzy ones," he answered playfully. He smiled, and the transformation truly shocked her.

She'd been wrong before. The man was handsome as hell.

CHAPTER FOUR

"'...AND...mouse...and...' What's this word?" Nia asked.

"Cricket," the woman told her.

"'Cricket...carr-ie-d...'"

"Carried."

"'Carried...the pea...to...get...her. To-get... Together'!"

"Very good. You're an excellent reader."

Ryan watched the exchange from the other side of the kitchen table. After he and Susannah had returned to the house, he'd been put to work peeling potatoes for supper, penance ordered by his grandmother for sassing her earlier.

Nana Sipsey had threatened to take a hickory switch to his backside if he didn't watch his tongue. She'd do it, too, no matter that he was a grown man and outweighed her by seventy pounds.

He hadn't meant to be disrespectful, but he didn't share his grandmother's quick acceptance of this woman. *Susannah.* The name fit her. He'd never seen skin so creamy. Her eyes were as blue as a robin's egg.

She seemed nice, friendly. He'd enjoyed talking to her at his workshop. Still, she was a stranger, a drifter who had no more regard for her own safety than to throw herself off a bridge.

Going by the quick look he'd gotten at that list of hers, she had a skewed perspective on what was important in life, too. And Nia didn't need to get attached to someone who would inevitably leave.

Regardless of his grandmother's insistence that Susannah had been sent to heal his daughter, he was *not* allowing her to stay. She could be bad for Nia, and a distraction for him, as well.

They were alone in the kitchen except for Nia. His mother and grandmother had suspiciously disappeared to the second floor. Susannah looked up and her smile turned his insides liquid.

Pretty. Too pretty. He'd never get any work done if she was around.

"You've done a great job teaching Nia to read," she said. "You should be proud."

"The praise belongs to her. She learns quickly."

Nia touched Susannah's necklace. "Why is your ring here?"

"Because I outgrew it. My mother gave it to me when I was a little girl about your age. When it wouldn't fit anymore I put it on this chain so I could still wear it.''

"The blue rock is pretty.''

"That's a sapphire, my birthstone. I used to believe the ring was magic and would give me courage.''

Nia wanted to slip it on, but Ryan told her she couldn't. He was afraid she'd break the slender chain.

"Can we read another book?'' she asked Susannah.

"I'm sorry, sweetheart, but I need to be going. I enjoyed having you read this one to me, though. I don't think I've ever met a little girl who reads as well as you do.''

"When will you be back?''

"Well...'' She appealed to Ryan for help explaining.

"Susannah has to go home, Nia,'' he told his daughter. "She won't be back because she doesn't live around here.''

Nia wrinkled up her face, confused. "Where do you live?''

"I used to have a house in a state called Georgia, right below this one, but I don't anymore. I sold it because I wanted to sleep in different places, to travel and see new things.''

"Sleep here.''

"No, I can't do that."

"Daddy can tuck you in. You *said* you don't got nobody to tuck you in."

His gaze met Susannah's and her pale complexion flushed slightly.

"I can't stay, Nia."

"He gets the covers just right and everything. Please, please?"

"Nia," Ryan warned. "Don't pester Susannah. She's already told you she has to go."

"But I don't want her to." She slammed the book on the table, crossed her arms in defiance and stuck out her bottom lip. Her eyes narrowed.

"Nia," Ryan warned in a low voice.

Instead of apologizing, she knocked the book to the floor.

He ordered her to go to her room until she could behave better. She climbed off Susannah's lap and stomped down the hall in her socks, smacking her fist loudly against the wall because she couldn't make any noise with her feet. He made her come back and return the book to the table.

"Don't leave that room until I tell you to, young lady."

"You don't love me," she spat.

He knew she didn't believe it, but the words still broke his heart.

"I love you more than anything in this world, but

I don't like being around you when you act like this. Tell Susannah goodbye and that you're sorry for being so naughty.''

He wasn't sure she'd do it, but she finally whispered it through her tears. She ran off to her bedroom.

"Sorry about that," he said. "She's had a rough time lately. Normally she's a great kid."

"Did your wife die recently?"

"Carla wasn't my wife, only Nia's mother," he felt compelled to explain for some reason. "She died in March, not long after being diagnosed."

"Stomach cancer? I believe that's what Nia said."

"Actually it was her pancreas, but Nia calls it stomach. She's had trouble dealing with her mother's death, although Carla lived abroad and never had custody of her."

"I lost my mother last year, so I know some of what she's feeling. Healing takes time." Her expression turned sad. "I don't think it's possible for a child, regardless of age, to ever completely get over losing a parent."

"Was your mother's death from illness or accident?"

"Complications from Alzheimer's."

"I've heard that's really hard on a family. Emotionally. Financially. Physically."

"*Hard* doesn't even begin to describe it. Luckily my dad had done well in the plumbing business, and he and my mom invested wisely. Money wasn't a problem until the last couple of years of her life. The physical part, though, was very difficult."

"And the emotional part?"

"Devastating."

"How long was she ill?"

"Nine years."

"Damn! How did you deal with it?"

"Not easily, and probably not with much grace, but when you're in that kind of situation you do what you have to and hope it's enough. By the end of her life, my mother no longer knew who I was and had become abusive. That was really hard. She'd been a gentle, lovely person before, and the disease changed her."

"Is that the personal problem you mentioned, the one that caused you to leave school?"

"Yes. She needed me at home. I was all she had."

"Where was your dad?"

"Dad died of a heart attack when I was four. All I remember about him was that he had a loud laugh and kept butterscotch candies in his pockets for me. Growing up, it was just me and Mom."

"No brothers or sisters?"

She shook her head. "My parents didn't think

they could have children. They'd tried for nearly twenty years without success and were resigned to being childless, and then, surprise! When my mom was forty-two and my dad forty-eight, she suddenly found herself pregnant.''

''Were you and your mom close?''

''Very close.'' Her voice trembled. ''She was my best friend. Watching her slowly die was the hardest thing I've ever had to do.''

He'd judged her too quickly. He'd assumed her to be flighty and irresponsible, but that didn't mesh with the portrait now forming—a daughter who had loved her mother and been willing to give up her dreams to take care of her.

She was on the verge of crying, and he felt guilty that his question had upset her. She recovered by glancing at her watch.

''Gosh, look at the time.'' She stood abruptly. ''I need to go. I still have to find a place to stay.''

''You don't have one?''

''No, but the lady at the store gave me numbers for a couple of places. Do you mind if I use your phone to see if any of them has a room?''

''Go ahead.''

She discovered that all the guest houses in the area were closed for the season. Ryan told her the owners of one were good friends of his. He called and asked them to take in Susannah for tonight.

"You can follow me over," Ryan said. "Bascombe and Helen Miller's place is only a few minutes from here."

"I think I've already taken up enough of your time. I can find my way if you'll give me directions."

"I can't send you out in the dark alone. The roads are dangerous, particularly for someone who's unfamiliar with them and driving at night. You'd end up in a ditch, or worse."

"Then I'll accept the offer. Thanks."

RYAN TOLD HIS MOTHER and grandmother of his plans, and then went out and started both his and Susannah's trucks to warm them. He checked on Nia while Susannah said her goodbyes to the women.

Nia was still sulking, lying on her bed with tears on her sweet face and one arm around her favorite toy, a bear his mother had made from an old brown blanket.

Hell, he felt like a failure. All he wanted in life was to make this child happy, and he seemed incapable of it.

"I have to go out for a few minutes," he told her, sitting down. He stroked her hair. "Gran and Nana Sipsey will be here. Gran is making you something to eat, and then she's going to help you take a bath."

She didn't respond.

"I guess you're still mad at me, huh?"

She nodded.

"Too bad. I was hoping for a kiss. I haven't had one since this morning, and you know I can't go very long without some of that good Nia sugar."

She shook her head.

"No deal, huh? Okay, then." He started to rise, but she sat up, threw her arms around his neck and began to bawl.

"I'm sorry, Daddy. I didn't mean to be bad."

"I know you didn't, baby."

"Please don't give me away."

"Give you away? Sa Sa…" He untangled her arms, sat her in his lap and made her look at him. "Where did you get a crazy idea like that? I would *never* give you away."

"You'll love me for ever and ever?"

"Of course I will. Why would you think I'd give you away?"

"Because."

"Because why?"

"Just because."

He tried to coax her into talking, but she didn't seem to understand why she felt the way she did. Neither did he. He'd never given her any reason to believe she wasn't wanted. She was his life, his most important reason for existing.

"Baby, there's no need to worry. Daddy wouldn't do that. Not ever. No matter what."

"Promise?"

"I promise."

"If I was *really* bad?"

"Not even then. Listen to me, Nia. Nothing you could do would ever make me give you away or leave you. I love you too much. Do you understand?"

She said she did, and wiped her tears with the back of her hand.

"Good girl. Now stop crying. Everything's okay." Ryan took his handkerchief out of his pocket. "Let's blow that nose before it runs away." He held the cloth and she blew hard, making the honking sound that had led to her nickname. "That's my little goose."

"Cooper's nose is running, too."

"Uh-oh. We can't have that." He picked up the bear from the floor where he'd fallen and pretended to let him blow his nose. "Any other critters that need attention? No? Then, can I have a kiss?"

She gave him a big sloppy one.

"Where's Susannah?" she asked.

Oh, hell.

"She's downstairs saying goodbye to Gran and Nana Sipsey. She's about to leave."

"I want to."

"Want to what? Say goodbye?"

"Uh-huh."

"Do you promise to do it right this time and not make a fuss?"

"Uh-huh."

"Okay, then. Come on."

SUSANNAH TOOK the sack Ryan's mother handed her. "Thank you. I can't wait to taste it. I didn't know you could make jelly out of kudzu."

"We use only the blossoms, not the vine," Mrs. Whitepath told her. "Be sure and have Helen open a jar for your breakfast in the morning."

"I will."

Nana Sipsey also had a gift for her. She pressed a small cloth pouch into her hand.

"Med-cine," she said.

"Oh, thank you, but I already have medicine for my arm." The doctor had prescribed painkillers. She hadn't used them, though, the bottle was still full and tucked away in her makeup bag.

"No, no," the old woman said. She rattled off several words in Cherokee that Susannah didn't understand.

"Pardon?"

Mrs. Whitepath interpreted. "She says the medicine isn't for your arm, it's for your headache. Feverfew. It can taste bitter taken alone, so mix a few of the leaves in with your dinner tonight.''

"How did—?"

Ryan and Nia came into the kitchen then and Susannah never got the chance to ask how the old woman had known she had a headache. The pounding at her temples had started only a few minutes ago.

Nia ran over and immediately wanted Susannah to push up the sleeve of her sweater again. "Is my name still there?"

"Right here." Susannah put down the jelly and showed the child. "Having your name on my arm will be almost like having *you* with me wherever I go. We'll be together."

Nia thought about that, and shook her head. "Uh-uh, because I don't got your name anywhere."

Bright kid.

"My goodness, you're absolutely right. How silly of me. Would you like me to write my name on something of yours?"

Her eyes lit up. "Uh-huh." She turned to Ryan. "Can she, Daddy?"

"Does she have an old T-shirt I could sign?" Susannah asked Ryan.

"I think we can find something."

"Cooper!" Nia said, and ran off to get what Ryan explained was a stuffed toy.

When she returned, Susannah knelt and used a craft marker Mrs. Whitepath gave her to write her name on the shirt worn by Nia's teddy bear.

"There you go."

"Tell Susannah thank you," Ryan said.

"Thank you."

"You're welcome, Nia."

"Do you got to go away?"

"Yes, sweetheart, I do. I'm sorry."

"Can I kiss you goodbye?"

The request took Susannah off guard, but also touched her heart.

"Oh, I'd like that very much."

Nia clung to her after the kiss, and Ryan had to gently coax his daughter to let go. "Remember your promise, Sa Sa."

Once out the door, Ryan walked Susannah to the driver's door of her truck and helped her get in with her jelly.

"I appreciate your being so nice to Nia," he said.

"Being nice to her is easy. She's adorable. So sweet and loving."

"I know. Sometimes I can't believe how lucky I am to have her."

Susannah wanted to ask why he'd gotten custody instead of her mother, but she let the question slide. The subject was too personal. She didn't need to know, anyway. After tonight, she'd never see Ryan Whitepath or his family again.

The thought saddened her. She liked these people. For a few hours, she'd felt connected again, a part of something.

But maybe it was best that Ryan hadn't been able to take her on as a student. Caring about this family would be too easy, and she didn't ever want to care about anyone again. Love inevitably brought pain.

Some doors, she knew from experience, should be left closed and locked, especially those that led to the heart.

TEN MINUTES LATER, Ryan pulled his truck into the yard of Helen and Bascombe Miller. Susannah parked beside him.

Ryan had grown up with Bass and was as close to him as he was to his own brothers. Ryan also had high regard for Helen, who was eight months pregnant with their first child.

The couple was mixed race—he was Indian and she was white—and that had created a rift between Helen and her rich, upper-class parents.

He couldn't understand their reaction, but he was familiar with it. He'd been a victim of the same kind of prejudice when he'd left the mountain to go to school. Some people hadn't been able to see past his skin color.

"Thanks for doing this, Bass," Ryan told his friend while Helen helped Susannah settle in her room. "I didn't feel right letting her fend for herself."

"No problem."

Ryan followed him into the kitchen and poured himself a glass of tea from the pitcher in the fridge.

"Wait," Bass whispered. "I've got something to show you in the basement. My new toy."

In the dimly lit room below, Bass removed a long, thin case from behind a workbench cabinet and opened it. Inside was a new fishing rod. Bascombe loved fishing almost as much as he loved being a sheriff's deputy. He had more gadgets, rods, reels and tackle than anyone Ryan knew.

"Pure graphite with a custom-made Tennessee foregrip," Bass told him. He stroked the rod the way he would a favorite dog. "See the thread wraps on the guides? Tight. That's quality."

Ryan had to admit the workmanship was good. "How much?"

"Three twenty."

"Yow!"

"Yeah, expensive, but it's made to fit my hand."

"Let me know when you plan to tell Helen so I can go out of town that day."

"I thought I'd wait to mention it until after the baby comes and she doesn't feel so miserable."

"Smart move."

Bass put the fishing rod back in its hiding place. "So what's Susannah's story? How'd you meet her?"

"She's traveling around the country, and showed up at the house this afternoon wanting art lessons, but I'm busy right now with a couple of major contracts. I told her I couldn't do it."

"Too bad. She's a looker, or didn't you notice?"

"I noticed."

"Couldn't you find time?"

"Probably, but Nana's got this crazy idea that Susannah's been sent to help Nia, and the last thing I want to do is encourage that kind of thinking."

"I don't know, man. Your grandmother sensed before Helen did that she was pregnant."

"Yeah, but you were trying to have a baby. She made a lucky guess."

"What about old man Litton and the vision she had of him surrounded by flames? A month later his place was gone."

"He smoked like a chimney, Bass. I'm surprised he didn't burn the house down a long time ago."

"I'm just saying your grandmother's been right before and maybe you should put more stock in what she's telling you. Take a chance for once. Loosen up a little and stop thinking you have to be in control of everything."

"I can't afford to do anything that might hurt Nia. She's already formed an attachment to Susannah."

"I don't see what it would hurt for Nia to spend some time with her. Or you either, for that matter."

"It's a moot point. I've made my decision."

Helen yelled down the stairs, "What mischief is going on down there? I don't trust you two alone."

"Nothing's going on," Bass called out, and muttered to Ryan, "I'm still in the doghouse over that boat you talked me into bringing home."

"*I* talked you into? Hey, friend, spending eight thousand dollars on a used fishing boat without consulting your wife was *your* idea."

"I got a great deal! It was seventeen thousand new."

"Didn't I tell you she'd pitch a fit? You don't go out and buy a boat when your wife's getting ready to have a baby."

"She nearly didn't let me in the house. Hell, I still haven't made it back into the bed, not that there's much activity going on there right now, but it's the principle of the thing. A man should be king of his castle, you know?"

Ryan guffawed at that statement. "How would I know? I live with three females. Four if you count the cat. I'm the peon of my castle, not the king."

"She says we can't go off together again. You corrupt me."

His friend smiled broadly. *Bass* was the corrupter, and had been since they were both boys. Ryan had gotten in more trouble as a kid from following Bascombe than he cared to recall.

"I guess you told her it was my fault," Ryan said.

"Of course I did."

"Then I'm glad she's making you sleep alone."

Going back upstairs, they found the women putting plates on the table. Helen looked like she was about to whelp a whole litter rather than one baby and Ryan told her so. In the past week it seemed as if she'd gained twenty pounds.

"What a terrible thing to say to a woman three weeks from her due date." She pinched him playfully on the arm. "But I'll forgive you. Will you stay and eat supper with us?"

"I'd love to, but I need to get back and spend some time with Nia before she goes to bed."

"How's she doing?"

"About the same."

"I'm sorry. Why don't you come back when she's asleep and visit for a while? We haven't seen you in weeks."

"Can't. Got to work."

"That's all you do these days, Ryan."

"I know, but it's a busy time for me. Thanks for the invitation, but I'll do it some other night." He kissed her on the cheek. "See ya, Bass."

Susannah walked him to his truck. He got in and rolled down the window.

"It's been nice meeting you, Ryan."

"Same here. If I wasn't so bogged down—"

She waved away his apology over not being available to teach her. "Don't worry about it."

"Good luck with your list."

"My...?" She cringed with embarrassment. "I was hoping you hadn't read that stupid thing."

"Sorry. I saw part of it when I picked up the paper."

"You probably think it's silly."

"No, I don't."

"I wrote it because I don't want to look back on my life with regret. Now that I'm free of the responsibility of taking care of my mother, I want to try new things and go places I've never been before."

"I can understand that. Sometimes I wish I could start the truck, take off and drive wherever the road takes me."

"Exactly. I don't want to be tied down. I never again want to have to worry about anyone but myself."

"So your top item's what brought you here—your desire to create something that'll outlast you?"

"Yes."

"Sorry things didn't work out. I mean that, Susannah."

"I know."

He remembered some of the more personal items she'd included on her list and chuckled.

"What?" she asked.

"I was just thinking that having a shot at helping you out with number nine might've been a lot more interesting than number one."

"Number nine? What was that one?"

"I think," he said with a grin, "maybe I'd better let you look it up after I'm gone."

SUSANNAH RACED upstairs to her room when Ryan pulled out of the drive and went straight for her sketchbook.

She pulled out her Life List. Number nine read, "Wild uninhibited sex with a stranger."

"Oh, no!"

Dismay turned to amusement. She giggled and fell on the bed, laughing loudly.

Well, he was right. Working on number nine with the attractive Ryan Whitepath would have been very interesting indeed.

CHAPTER FIVE

NIA HAD ONE of her stomachaches, so Ryan put her to bed in her room at the barn, where he could work and still be close. According to the doctor, her pains were physical manifestations of the emotional pain she couldn't verbally express, but Ryan never discounted them. To Nia they felt real.

He read her an extra story and then another, staying until she felt better and went to sleep. The cat lay curled in her favorite spot at the foot of the bed. Ryan stroked Nia's dark head and kissed her, then scratched Abigail under the chin. He made sure the night-light was on, and he left the door open so he could hear if Nia stirred.

At two o'clock in the morning, a scream pierced the air. He was already up the stairs and at Nia's bedroom door when he heard the crash and the sound of breaking glass from inside. Abigail raced out as if being chased by hounds.

He flipped on the light. He found his daughter thrashing about, fighting some unknown demon in her sleep. She'd knocked over the lamp and the base lay in shards on the rug.

"Daddyyy!"

He scooped her up and held her against his chest. "I'm here, baby. Daddy's here."

Sobs racked her slender body. Her arms continued to flail.

"Wake up, Nia. You're having a bad dream."

"Daddy, help me!"

"Nia, wake up."

After a moment she pulled back and blinked at him with unfocused eyes. "Daddy?" Her voice remained pitiful, but at least she was starting to come around. She began to sob.

"I'm here, sweetheart. You're safe. It was only a bad dream."

"I'm scared."

"Of what?"

She said she didn't know. She couldn't remember what had frightened her in the dream.

He sat on the side of the bed and rocked her, but his efforts to calm her fears didn't seem to be doing any good. Her breathing was too heavy. She continued to cry and gasp for air until she hyperventilated, making the situation worse.

When her hands and feet started to go numb from too much oxygen, she thought she was dying and that scared her even more. Ryan took her to the bathroom, set her on the vanity and washed her face.

"You need to settle down, sweetheart. Stop crying and don't breathe so fast."

"I ca-n't," she said with a hitch in her voice.

"Yes, you can. Look at Daddy. Watch how I'm breathing." He took a couple of slow, shallow breaths. "See?"

"I ca-n't do it."

Without warning she vomited her dinner down the front of her pajamas. He helped her to the toilet, where she threw up a second time.

He washed her face again.

"That it?" he asked.

She nodded.

Ryan felt her brow and cheeks. She didn't seem feverish. She'd made herself sick from anxiety before, but never this bad.

He considered calling the rescue squad, or running her down to the emergency room in Andrews, but either one would take too long. She needed to calm herself and she needed to do it now. He did, too. His heart beat so hard he feared it might jump out of his chest.

He wasn't sure what to do.

"Baby, lie down on the floor. That's good." He wet the washcloth again, wrung it out and placed it on her forehead. "Close your eyes and try to think of something nice while Daddy calls Dr. Thompson."

"Don't le-ave me."

"I'm only going to get the phone. I'll be right back."

He raced downstairs and grabbed the portable from his workbench. He dialed the doctor's emergency number on his way back to Nia. The doctor returned the call within a couple of minutes. Ryan explained the problem.

"Put Nia on the phone," she said.

Dr. Thompson was able to do what Ryan couldn't. Thankfully, Nia's breathing eased as they talked. She stopped crying and began to respond to the doctor's questions.

Ryan waited until he was satisfied she was all right. Then, while Nia was still speaking to the doctor, he slipped out to clean up the glass in her bedroom. He was trembling so badly he had to sit for a moment. He put his face in his hands and willed himself not to break down.

He didn't know how much more of this he could take. The worry, the frustration of not being able to help his child... His nerves were shot.

Nights were hell. He never slept well anymore, but drifted in and out, his ears trained to listen for any sound from her bedroom.

Days when he was able to coax her into going to

school, he worried about her being so far away. And the tension didn't leave during the days she was home. *Those* times he worried about her not being in school and falling behind in her class work. She was already in danger of having to repeat first grade.

He'd done everything he knew to do, but Nia wasn't getting better. If there was an answer to this problem, he had no idea where to find it.

Several minutes passed before he'd composed himself. He vacuumed the carpet, got a clean pajama top out of the drawer for Nia and returned to the bathroom, where she sat cross-legged on the floor mat. She actually tried to smile when he came in.

"She wants to talk to you, Daddy."

Ryan took the phone and put it in the crook of his neck so he could talk and remove Nia's soiled top at the same time.

"I think she'll be okay now," the doctor told him.

"I'm sorry I had to wake you. I didn't know what else to do."

"That's perfectly all right, Mr. Whitepath. That's why I'm here. Please call me back first thing in the morning so we can talk further. I'd like to know more about Nia's new friend."

"New friend?"

"Susannah."

RYAN HAD mixed feelings about his next conversation with Dr. Thompson. As arranged, they talked a second time at 6:00 a.m. Ryan explained the events of the day before, how Nia had come to know Susannah and how she'd responded to her.

"Interesting," the doctor said. "You might want to reconsider your decision not to give this woman lessons. For some reason, your daughter feels a connection to her, and that could be utilized. In the months I've been counseling Nia, this is the first time I've heard her animated about anything. She has a spark when she mentions Susannah."

"Which doesn't make sense to me. They were only together for a couple of hours. Nia's spent much more time with my sister, yet she hardly ever asks about Anita since she went back to school."

"Perhaps she identifies with Susannah because the woman also recently lost her mother. Her presence is comforting because here, finally, is someone who can understand how Nia feels. Or so Nia believes…"

Okay, Ryan conceded, but he relayed his concern about his daughter becoming too attached. "Couldn't she be hurt even more by Susannah leaving a second time?"

"That's certainly a risk, and I won't tell you she wouldn't be upset, but this could be a way to reinforce an important lesson. People Nia cares about are inevitably going to go out of her life. You have an elderly grandmother, for example, who in all like-lihood will die before Nia reaches adulthood. If she can learn to appreciate the time she has with people rather than focusing on their departure, her life will be much more fulfilling.''

"I've tried to explain that already. And it's not like she hasn't lost people. She's had friends move away. And my brother and his wife moved out of town last year. That didn't seem to upset her."

"I know, but her sole experience with *traumatic* separation has been her mother's death, and that was so sudden she never had time to prepare for the loss."

True. Carla had died within twenty-four hours of his and Nia's arrival at her home in London. Her quick passing had been a shock even to him.

"If Nia understands from the outset that Susan-nah's stay is temporary," the doctor continued, "she has time to understand and accept it. It would also do her good to see someone else dealing with death and doing it appropriately. Do you believe this woman is stable?''

"I think so.''

"I hear reservation in your voice.''

He told her about Susannah selling her house, quitting her job and flitting around the country. "That's not something I'd do, but after learning she nursed her mother all those years, I can see where she'd want to cut her ties to the past and have a little adventure. What's your opinion?''

''I haven't met her, so it's difficult for me to render one, but her reaction is common. One of the steps of the grieving process is to suppress grief, to detach and distance ourselves from the trauma. You've seen that same behavior in Nia when she put away her mother's photograph and the dolls she gave her.''

''At least Susannah will talk about her mother. I try to get Nia to talk and she acts like Carla never existed.''

''Yet you say Nia had no problem speaking of her mother to Susannah.''

''No, apparently not.''

''Then having her spend a few weeks with Nia is an idea worth considering—if she's agreeable, of course, and if it wouldn't interfere with your work.''

''I'll give it some thought.''

And he did. He argued with himself until daylight, first about whether he should ask Susannah to stick around. He would, he decided. And second, about how much he should tell her. That decision was harder.

She'd made it clear she didn't want any entanglements. What was it she'd said? *I never again want to have to worry about anyone but myself.*

She might not stay if she understood the depth of

Nia's illness—or that *she* was the magic pill prescribed as part of the cure.

"So don't tell her," he mumbled to himself as he turned on the shower and prepared to make himself look more presentable. He'd dust off what little charm he had and offer her a deal she couldn't refuse.

He didn't like subterfuge. He'd been taught to be honest in his dealings with people and to respect them as he did his blood brothers and sisters. But after Nia's frightening episode last night, he was willing to try anything. Even lie to Susannah about the real reason he'd changed his mind about the job.

SUSANNAH WOKE early enough the next morning to watch the first rays of sunlight spread across the snow-covered trees. Standing in a robe on the private balcony outside her second-floor room, she breathed in the fresh air and experienced a rare moment of happiness.

If it was true that some places on earth were sacred, then these mountains were surely among them. She'd slept soundly for the first time in months. No nightmares. No waking up thinking she was back home and that her mother had cried out in the darkness.

Her good night's sleep might have been because of her exhaustion or the comfort of the wonderfully soft sheets and down pillows Helen had on the bed. The room was homey and comfortable and the quiet enveloped her like loving arms.

The "medicine" Ryan's grandmother had given her also played a part in her restful sleep. Assured by Bascombe that the leaves were harmless and would help her headache, Susannah had crumbled them in her dinner salad last night. Within ten minutes her pain had disappeared.

The crunch of footsteps below made her look down. Bass, dressed in his deputy's uniform and carrying a thermos, was walking his way to his truck.

"Morning," she called out.

He turned and looked up. "Morning. You're up early."

"Hard to sleep with views like this."

"That's what all our guests say. Helen's in the kitchen and I've already made coffee. Go get yourself a cup."

"Thanks, I will. And thanks for letting me stay last night, Bass. You have a lovely place."

"Anytime, Susannah. I hope you'll come back and see us again." He raised his hand in parting.

Susannah took a quick shower and laid out jeans and a long-sleeved red shirt.

Helen knocked gently. "Susannah?"

"I'm up." She slipped her robe back on and opened the door.

"Oh, good. I thought I heard the water running. Ryan's here. He wants to talk to you."

"Is something wrong? What did he say?"

"Only that he wanted to catch you before you left."

"Okay. Tell him I'll be right down."

She dressed quickly, ran a brush through her hair, and jogged downstairs to the kitchen, where Helen was cutting dough into biscuits on the counter. Ryan sat at the table with his hands around a steaming cup of coffee. He stood as she entered. He had a haggard look and dark circles under his eyes.

"Is your family okay?" she asked.

"Can we talk a minute?"

"Nia?"

"She's fine. My mother's getting her ready for school."

"You don't look well, Ryan. Are you okay?"

He ran a hand through his loose hair. "I haven't been to bed yet. I worked all night."

"That can't be good for you."

"Actually that's why I'm here." He glanced at Helen. "Do you mind if Susannah and I talk in the den?"

"Of course not. I'll make you both some breakfast."

"Thanks, Helen," he said, "but none for me."

Susannah poured herself a cup of coffee and they

walked to the den with its rustic beams and rough wood walls. The house was more like a lodge—four bedrooms and a private bath for each on the second floor, plus several large rooms downstairs for eating and entertaining. Helen and Bass had their own bedroom, bath and small sitting room off the kitchen.

A fire burned in the massive stone fireplace. Susannah took a seat on the leather couch in front of it. Ryan preferred a chair.

"What's up?" she asked.

"I've been giving a lot of thought to what you said yesterday about how learning the computer would save me time. I want to take you up on your offer to help. In exchange, I'll give you the mosaic lessons you want, let you work with me on a project or two and also pay you a salary. You can live in the cabin across from the workshop while you're here. My interns have found it comfortable."

Susannah didn't know how to respond.

"Interested?" he asked.

"Why the sudden turnabout?"

"Like you said, I need to get better organized. I've been thinking about trying again to hire someone to handle bills and deal with customer calls. You're a nice person and apparently competent. I doubt you'll drive me crazy like the last woman. It's a plus that you also have artistic talent. And that my family likes you."

"I like them, too."

"So you'll do it?"

"You understand I could only stay here for about eight weeks. Until Christmas, or a few days before it. I want to be in New York for New Year's Eve."

"That's fine."

"Does your family observe Christmas? It didn't occur to me until this moment that you might not."

"We do, but more traditionally than most people. Our celebration also involves the Winter Solstice, which falls on December 22. We decorate, burn a Yule log, light fires and say prayers to bring back the sun. Our gifts are made by hand rather than purchased."

"That sounds lovely. I wouldn't be an intrusion to your holiday plans if I stay?"

"No, not at all."

"I wish I had more time to offer you, but I don't."

"A few weeks will be enough. You can get me started on the computer and help clean up the files. Maybe we could spend a couple of hours every morning. After that, I'll teach you about mosaics as we tackle some projects. You can help me with a mural I'm doing for the community center here and knock number one off your list."

"You'd trust me with that?"

"You can follow instructions and a pattern, can't you?"

"Yes."

"Then I trust you. How's five hundred dollars a week sound?"

"Too generous for what you're expecting. You wouldn't have to pay me. I'm thrilled to simply be able to work with you."

"No, I insist. You'll be putting in a lot of hours and you deserve a salary."

"But you'd already be giving me lessons *and* a place to live. That's enough."

"If I hired you or anyone else with your experience as my permanent office manager, I'd have to shell out a lot more than that."

"True."

"Then it's settled."

"Not quite. One more thing." She was embarrassed to bring this up, but felt she needed to clear the air. "So there won't be any misunderstandings between us…I'm really not looking for a relationship, even a temporary one." Heat crept up her neck. "Just because I put something on my list doesn't mean I'm actively seeking to do it right now. Do you get my meaning?"

He smiled, amused. "You mean we can't do number nine? Well, hell."

"Don't tease me, Ryan. I'm mortified enough as it is."

"I can't help it. Your face is redder than your shirt."

"I just don't want you to think... Not that you aren't attractive, because you are, but..." She rolled her eyes. Oh, good Lord! Had she really said that out loud? "You know what I mean. This has to be a business arrangement."

"Don't worry, Susannah," he told her with a chuckle. "I'm only offering a job."

"Sorry. I had to make sure."

"You have to negotiate separately for sex."

She tried not to blush any more than she already had, but didn't succeed. "You really enjoy making me squirm, don't you?"

"Yeah."

"Can we please just get back to business?"

"All right," he said, nodding, but he didn't stop smiling. "Let's settle this. If you accept my offer I only have one condition. You have to stay the whole two months. Until December twenty-third, let's say. You can't up and leave if you get bored and decide there's someplace else you'd rather be."

"I wouldn't do that. I'd honor my commitment."

"I'd want your word. I can't rearrange my work schedule only to have you run out on me."

"That's reasonable."

"Then let's give it a go."

She still had some reservations. His change of heart seemed a bit odd, given how adamant he'd been last night. But she'd be getting to train with someone whose work she admired *and* getting money for it, which she could use.

"Sounds great," she told him. "When do we start?"

AFTER HE RETURNED home and had taken Nia to the bus, Ryan's next stop should have been bed, but he had one more thing he needed to do before getting some sleep.

He parked at the barn and walked to the house. Thankfully, he could see Nana Sipsey in her workroom checking her dried herbs, so he didn't have to face her again right now. He couldn't stand another one of her gleeful, I-told-you-so looks.

"Etsi?" he called out. He found his mother folding clothes in the laundry off the kitchen. He said he was headed up the mountain for a little while.

"Halayv dvhilutsi?" she asked. *When will you return?*

"In a couple of hours."

She nodded, but didn't say anything more, and Ryan sighed. He couldn't understand why she was upset with him.

"I thought you'd be as happy as Nana that I asked

Susannah to stay. You're the one who believes in Nana's prophesy mumbo jumbo, not me."

"I *am* happy. I like Susannah very much. But your dishonesty disturbs me. She's a nice woman and you should have told her the truth."

"She never would've agreed to stay if I had."

"You have no faith in people, son. And for someone who embraces his heritage as strongly as you do, you turn a blind eye to our teachings rather a lot—whenever it suits you, in fact."

"Meaning?"

"We are all part of something larger than ourselves. These connections—one thing to another, one person to another, spirit world to physical world—support us. Alone, the flower couldn't reproduce so *Elohi* has made the bee to carry the pollen from plant to plant. The tree drops its branches and the bird uses the twigs to build its nest. Surprising, isn't it, how when something is needed, it's given?"

"What does this have to do with Susannah?"

"You've been sent a gift, perhaps the very thing you need for Nia, and yet you don't accept it as offered. You still try to manipulate and control it."

"Because I have a responsibility to my daughter and her welfare."

"Yes, but sometimes you forget you are not alone in your responsibility—and not only to your child."

"You're not making sense."

"When your father left, you stepped in and helped take care of all of us, even though you were only a boy. You've continued to do that, sending Charlie and Anita to school, helping Joseph start his carpentry business, providing for me and your grandmother. We all appreciate what you've done. But I worry about the heavy burden you carry, even more so since Nia was born."

"I don't mind that, and you know it. I've got the money."

"It's not the financial burden, but the emotional one you must share, along with yourself."

"Myself? Huh?"

She pinched his ear, as she used to do when he was little and being thick-headed. "You've grown into a fine man, but you still have much to learn."

THE CAVE where his ancestors had hidden from the soldiers back in the 1830s was a forty-five minute hike through difficult terrain, but Ryan could follow the trail in the dark if he had to.

Branches, small rocks and boards hid the secret entrance and prevented bears and other creatures from using it. Years ago he'd covered a hole in the rocks above with heavy wire mesh. The grate kept out bats, but still allowed the rising smoke from campfires within the cave to disperse.

You could smell a fire if you were close enough, but the smoke mingled with the blue haze this far up and wasn't detectable by sight.

His ancestors had been blessed with good fortune. The cave, the abundance of natural resources and the inaccessibility from the outside world, had allowed *Numma hi tsune ga* and his parents to avoid capture until the government granted amnesty to them and the others who'd held out against relocation.

Ryan moved aside the obstruction and crawled in. Three feet beyond the opening, the tunnel opened out and became a room, the larger of two. He stood and brushed the dirt and snow from his clothes. Using the flashlight he'd brought, he found his supplies and the oil lantern and matches he kept among them.

As a boy he'd camped out here hundreds of times, even staying overnight, and strangely he'd never been affected by the isolation or the sounds of the creatures who moved about in the night.

This place gave him peace. He came here when he sought answers or his problems seemed unbearable.

He struck a match and the lantern came to life, illuminating his favorite part of the cave—the walls—decorated by the former inhabitants with crude pictures of animals and their own handprints.

His grandfather, upon purchasing the land, had

added his handprint and identified it with his Indian name. Ryan's father's was to the right of it, painted when he was still a young boy.

At nine, Ryan had placed his own hand against the wall and written his name, *Siquuitsets,* possum, underneath.

His siblings, as was now tradition, had added theirs when they'd been old enough to understand the significance of it.

He removed his jacket and shirt. He drew a large circle in the dirt and in the center of it built a fire to say prayers to The Great One and to the seven sacred directions, using sycamore wood for east, beech for south, oak for west, birch for north, pine for center, locust for above and hickory for below.

His grandmother had taught him how to find and grind the red paint. Putting some in a wooden bowl, he mixed it with water from the trickling drops of melted snow that had collected in a rock depression. He smeared lines down his face and across his naked chest. He lit the fire and stood before it.

"To the Fire Spirit in the East,

"To the Earth Spirit in the South,

"To the Water Spirit in the West,

"To the Wind Sprit in the North,

"To Elohi, Mother Earth,

"To Galunlati, the Above World,

"To Adanvdo, the Center that connects all things,

"To Ogedoda, The Great One and creator,

"I give thanks for your wisdom and your patience.

"I humbly ask forgiveness for any hurt I've caused any living thing.

"I honor those who came before me, those who are with me and those who will come after me.

"Hear me, Ogedoda. I seek your healing power for my daughter. Guide me in my decisions so that she may grow up strong in body and mind. Show me the path to knowledge and understanding.

"May the smoke carry my prayers to you."

He watched as it curled upward, went through the hole and journeyed toward the sky.

"And so it is good."

CHAPTER SIX

THE CABIN WAS ONE rectangular room with a tiny adjoining bathroom, but Susannah liked the old iron bed. The other furniture was either handmade or high-quality reproductions.

A covered porch ran the length of the building. The back door stood directly opposite the front and a colorful floor runner stretched between them. That divided the space into halves.

A couple of chairs and a table big enough for eating or working on her computer occupied the kitchen. A door on that side led to the bathroom.

On the left was a stone fireplace, the double bed, a couch with cushions covered in a striped Indian print, a small trunk that served as a coffee table and a waist-high bookcase holding several local guide-books and assorted paperbacks. The last resident had obviously been a hiker and mystery-novel reader.

Large picture windows set in both the front and back walls made her feel as if she were outside. She could look out the rear window or door and see the mountain with the house nestled at one edge of the clearing.

Ryan's place sat about a hundred yards away to the right, on the other side of the driveway leading to the house.

From the front window she had the same awe-inspiring view she'd admired last evening from Mrs. Whitepath's steps.

She puzzled over the position of the claw-footed tub in the kitchen until Ryan's mother showed up and explained.

"My husband built us this place thirty-one years ago when we got married so we could be away from his parents. He called it our honeymoon cabin. I loved it except for one thing. Ned only installed a shower, which wouldn't do. I like my baths."

"Same here."

"I cajoled, whined and begged for a bathtub until he finally gave in, but the bathroom didn't have space, even for a small one. Hence, it wound up out here. The pleasure you'll get from using it, though, is worth its unusual location."

"I'll bet it is." The thing was huge. Susannah couldn't wait to fill it up and soak. "Who made the furniture?"

"Ned and his father. They built the cabinets, too. I've had the couch reupholstered a few times since then, but the rest is original."

"Everything's lovely."

"Unfortunately, I didn't get to enjoy it very long. When I got pregnant with Ryan, moving to the house with Nana Sipsey and Papa George seemed the practical thing to do since they had plenty of room, but I came to miss this little place." She looked about wistfully. "Ned and I had some good times here."

"Are you sure you don't mind me using it? I could make other arrangements."

"No, I'm happy to have you." She handed Susannah towels and clean linens for the bed, then drew her finger across the table. "The furniture could use a bit of dusting, I'm afraid. I haven't cleaned in here in a while."

"That's okay. I'll take care of it."

"Ryan called Joe, my youngest boy, to come over and turn the water back on—he's handy with things like that. He also checked the chimney and water heater to make sure everything's working as it should."

"I appreciate that."

"Joe said he'd bring you some more wood when he got a chance, although there seems to be enough in the woodpile for a week or so. You have electric heat, too." She motioned to a wall heater that was blasting hot air. "You might prefer to use that all the time and forget about struggling with the fireplace. I always found it inconvenient. Light it or not—that's up to you. If you do use it, just be careful about going off and leaving the fire unattended.''

''Okay.''

''There's no phone, but you're welcome to use mine whenever you need.''

''Ryan's already offered me his.''

''Would you like me to bring down a small television? There's one in Anita's room you could have.''

''Don't bother. I have a CD player I like listening to. Even when I have a TV in the room, I rarely turn it on.''

She helped Susannah make the bed, then got blankets out of a built-in storage cabinet. On the table she placed a bouquet of dried flowers in a vase, a present from Ryan's grandmother.

''I'll leave you alone now so you can settle in. Ryan's trying to catch a couple of hours' sleep, but I'm sure he'll be over shortly. Let me know if you need anything else.''

''You've been wonderful, Mrs. Whitepath. Your whole family has.''

''I'd be delighted if you'd call me Annie. And Ryan's grandmother is Nana Sipsey—Nana to everyone.''

''Thank you, Annie. And please thank Nana Sipsey for the flowers.''

After Annie left, Susannah set about moving in. She had few possessions, but that was fine because there wasn't much space, anyway.

The small closet had a hanging rod and a couple of shelves and was adequate for what she owned— a jacket, one summer and one winter dress with matching shoes and a few casual outfits. For ease, she'd kept her wardrobe to a minimum.

The only personal articles she'd held on to were the family photo albums and her mother's jewelry.

She dusted the furniture and put her albums on the trunk. Her chores finished, she stepped back and looked around.

For the first time, she felt a longing for the things she'd given up when she sold the house, even those she'd never imagined she'd miss—like the grand- father clock that sat in the hallway for more than twenty-five years and annoyingly chimed on the quarter hour.

That sound, she realized now, had provided com- fort to her when she was growing up. She missed it.

She missed the ugly lamps, too, the ones with peonies on them that her mother had found for a dollar a piece at a yard sale years ago and insisted on putting in the living room. She missed that awful dressing table with its frilly skirt trimmed in white eyelet. And the tea pitcher that, despite its hairline crack, had never leaked a drop and sat on the table at nearly every meal.

The cabin was charming, but it belonged to someone else and was decorated with someone else's things.

Be content with that, Susannah.

She had to remind herself that her life was different now. The people she'd loved were lost to her by one means or another. And no place would ever feel like home again.

"SHE'S REALLY, really gonna live with us?" Nia asked Ryan, her face showing her excitement.

He'd driven into Robbinsville and picked her up from school instead of letting her ride the bus. He figured he needed the quiet time alone with her to explain the situation, why Susannah was suddenly around again.

"Not *live* with us. For a few weeks, Susannah will be staying in the cabin and helping me with my work. Do you remember Brian with the long beard who stayed there two summers ago? He used to tease and tell you his name was Booger."

"Uh-uh." She shook her head.

"I guess you were too little. How about when Uncle Charlie and Aunt Barbara moved to the city and they stayed in the cabin for a couple of weeks until their new place was ready?"

"Aunt Barbara let me put pictures on the 'frigerator."

"That's right. She did. This'll be sort of the same. Susannah will stay in the cabin but only for a little while. Then she'll be going away."

"Where?"

"To New York."

"Where's that?"

"We'll get out the atlas tonight and I'll show you."

He parked the truck at the barn and told Nia to go in and hang up her backpack. "We'll say hello to Susannah before we look up your word definitions."

"Are we staying here tonight, Daddy, or with Gran and Nana?"

Shuttling back and forth between their place and his mother's and having two bedrooms got to be confusing for her at times.

"We're *home* tonight."

Nia hung her backpack and jacket in the kitchen, while Ryan went through the mail and put away the groceries he'd bought in town. He took a minute to slip a couple of steaks into marinade and pat out a hamburger to cook for Nia.

She insisted on taking time to draw a picture for Susannah with her crayons. Afterward, the two of them walked over to the cabin. Nia kept running ahead and Ryan had to keep ordering her to slow down. That part of the drive still had a few icy spots.

They found Susannah sitting on the porch, enjoying the day's pleasant weather. Their arrival frightened the snowbirds pecking for seeds beneath the melting snow. The creatures scattered with a flurry of wings.

Nia threw herself excitedly into Susannah's arms.

"Hey, be careful," Ryan warned her. "Remember her wrist."

"Sorry."

"That's okay," Susannah told her. "You didn't hurt me."

"I made you a present."

"You did?" She beamed a smile. "Let me see." Nia showed her the drawing with its crude house and stick people, and from Susannah's reaction, you would've thought his daughter was Picasso. "You made this? I can't believe how talented you are. Why, you draw as well as your daddy."

She winked at Ryan over the top of Nia's head and he felt a tightening where he shouldn't.

Too pretty, all right. Too nice. Too damn sexy. He was going to have a hell of a time behaving himself.

"The picture's for your 'frigerator," Nia told her.

"Let's go put it up."

Nia went ahead, with Susannah a few steps behind. Ryan followed them in.

"Do you have everything you need?" he asked Susannah, looking around.

"Yes, thanks. Your mother helped me."

"Did she warn you not to put any garbage outside?"

"No, she didn't mention that."

"Separate the recyclables, if you don't mind—glass, paper, aluminum—and put any vegetable-based waste in a bucket to throw in Nana's compost bin. And when you have a bagful of garbage, let me know and I'll take care of it. I don't want you scared by some four-footed visitor scrounging for meat scraps in the middle of the night."

"Uh, neither do I."

"I'll bring you some containers."

She told him again how much she appreciated his letting her use the cabin and said she was ready to start her job.

"Tomorrow's soon enough," he told her. "Or we can wait until Monday, since tomorrow's Friday."

"I'd rather get started immediately."

"Okay. That's fine."

"What time?"

"I take Nia to the bus stop every morning, but I'm back by eight. Walk over anytime after that."

"What's your schedule?"

"I work whenever I can get a minute, but you should plan on helping weekdays from around eight to three with a break for lunch. I leave again at three-thirty to pick up Nia and we're home by four except on Tuesdays, when she has ballet down at the community center. She's in bed and usually asleep by eight on school nights. I go back to the studio after that."

Every second Monday he also took her to her therapist after school, but her next appointment wasn't for a week. This information was best left unsaid, for the moment anyway.

"Do you work weekends?"

"Saturdays."

"And how often do you try to kill yourself working all night?" Susannah asked.

"Not often. Last night was an exception." Sleep had eluded him after Nia's episode. He'd simply put the time to good use.

"Don't hesitate to let me know how I can help, Ryan. I can run errands and get supplies. I could even take Nia to catch the bus and pick her up, if it'll save you time."

He almost confessed his deceit then. Obviously she liked Nia and didn't mind being with her. Maybe she wouldn't care that he'd hired her only to befriend his daughter.

"Thanks," he told her instead. With Nia there,

now wasn't the time to be making such revelations. "I'm sure we'll find plenty for you to do."

She got some tape so Nia could attach her drawing and commented on what a lovely present it was.

"I can make you more," Nia told her. "I draw flowers real pretty, don't I, Daddy?"

"She's an A-Number-One flower artist," Ryan agreed.

"Then flowers it is," Susannah told her. "I could use some pictures in here."

"Do you got crayons?"

"Mm, afraid not. Maybe you can draw it for me at your house and bring it over the next time you come. Would that be okay?"

Nia agreed it would.

"Well, we'd better go," Ryan told her.

"You just got here."

"I know, but Nia has homework, and I like to get that out of the way. We also need to spend a few minutes with Mom and Nana." He hesitated, hoping he wasn't about to make a fool of himself. "How about joining Nia and me for supper? I picked up steaks to grill."

"You don't eat at your mother's?"

"Some nights, but not tonight. I already told her not to expect us and that I was going to ask you over."

"Oh? Well, then I'd love to come. I haven't had

a chance to buy any supplies yet. All I have is a pack of peanut-butter crackers. Steak sounds much better. But are you sure? I wouldn't want to intrude on your time with Nia.''

''You won't. We'd enjoy the company. Wouldn't we, Sa Sa?''

Nia jumped up and down and begged her to say yes. ''I can show you Dora, Boo and Jessie.''

''Are those kittens?''

Nia giggled. ''No, they're my babies.''

Ryan explained that they were dolls associated with her favorite TV shows and movies.

''Ah…babies. I see. Okay, but I don't change diapers, young lady, especially stinky ones.''

Nia fell into a new fit of giggles.

Ryan couldn't help chuckling himself. A weight seemed to lift from his shoulders. He'd done the right thing in asking Susannah to stay. She was going to be good for Nia.

''We won't ask you to do any diaper-changing,'' he told her, ''but we might put you to work making a salad.''

''Vegetables I can handle. No problem.''

''Then we'll expect you about six. I'll leave the door unlocked.''

SHE NEEDED new clothes. Her ''best'' jeans had somehow acquired a hole in the knee. The back pocket was coming off the only other clean pair she had.

Sighing, Susannah decided the second pair, although more faded, would have to do. With a sweater, maybe the rip wouldn't be noticeable.

After a long bath, she covered the freckles on her nose as well as she could with makeup, and applied a hint of mascara and lipstick. A quick brush through her hair to give it shine and she was ready to go.

Once at the barn, she let herself in the door. The kitchen and den of Ryan's living area were at the rear of the loft. Glass walls made those rooms visible from below. The drapes were drawn back and she could see Ryan puttering around in the kitchen; Nia sat at the counter watching him.

Abigail approached her on the stairs, wearing a dress and an old-fashioned granny cap tied under her neck. Unhappy about it, she swished her tail.

"Oh, dear, what happened to you?"

The cat mewed pitifully in response.

Susannah entered the door to the den and called out a greeting. Ryan waved her in. "Perfect timing," he announced.

Nia met her with a hug and the present of another drawing. Susannah took off her jacket, tossing it over a chair.

"Does your cat have a date? She looks pretty snazzy."

"What?" Ryan asked.

"The cat has a dress and hat on."

"Nia," Ryan said, giving her a stern look, "what did I tell you about putting your doll clothes on Abigail?"

"I forgot."

"No, you didn't forget. You just ignored what I said."

"But, Daddy, we were having a tea party and you can't go to a tea party without clothes on."

"What did I say about dressing the cat?"

"That she could get tangled up and hurt."

"That's right. And you wouldn't want to do anything to hurt her, would you?"

"Uh-uh. I love Abigail."

"Then go take them off. And if you *forget* again, no watching Powerpuff Girls for a week."

She looked like she was going to sulk for being scolded. Not wanting a repeat of last night's temper tantrum, Susannah jumped in. "Come on, I'll help you and then you can show me your room. I'm anxious to meet your babies." To Ryan she said, "Can you do without me for a few minutes?"

"Go ahead. I'm not ready to put the steaks on yet."

They freed poor Abigail from her outfit. Still

miffed, she streaked away and disappeared out the pet door.

Once in Nia's room, Susannah sat on the bed with Nia next to her and was introduced to each doll and stuffed animal. The child had dozens of toys.

"But Cooper's my favorite," she said, hugging the bear. "He's not a real bear. He only looks like one."

"Is that so? I'm glad to know that."

"Real bears are scary. They eat people. We have bears out there in the woods so you better be careful."

"Oh, I will. Thanks for warning me."

"Daddy says you're going to New Ork. He showed me on the map. He says I've been there before but I don't remember."

"It's called New *York*. They have interesting things I've always wanted to see."

"We have int'resting things. Last summer Daddy and Uncle Bass took me out in a boat and I had to be real quiet. Uncle Bass said 'damn' when the fish ate the food. That's a bad word."

"Oops, it sure is."

"I'm not supposed to say that, but it's okay 'cause I'm only telling you what Uncle Bass said."

"I think this one time it's all right."

"Uncle Bass isn't my real uncle, but Daddy says

to call him that 'cause he's like a real uncle. Him and Aunt Helen.''

"I met them. They're very nice.''

"I liked riding in a boat, but it don't got a place for little girls to tee tee.''

Susannah's lips twitched. She tried not to laugh. "I can see that would be a problem.''

"If you don't go away, maybe Daddy and Uncle Bass will give us a ride.''

"That sounds like fun, but I can't stay. I'm only going to be here a few weeks.''

"When are you going away?''

"Around Christmas.''

"Do you got to?'' Her face was so solemn, Susannah felt bad for making her unhappy.

"I'm afraid I do.'' Her instincts warned her to be careful. She could easily break this child's heart— or her own—if she foolishly allowed herself to get too close. "Friends sometimes have to go away, Nia. But we can have a good time while I'm here. We can draw and play with your dolls.''

"Can we bake brownies?''

"I guess we could. I'll ask about that.''

"I like the gooey ones with nuts.''

"Yum, me too.'' She patted her leg. "No need to be sad. We'll have lots of fun. Now, come on. Your daddy's going to wonder what happened to us.''

THE STEAKS were delicious. After dinner they played two quick games of Chinese checkers with

Nia. Susannah loaded the dishwasher while Ryan supervised Nia's bath and put her to bed.

Susannah said a quick good-night to the child. She left father and daughter picking out a story to read.

Ryan returned to the kitchen ten minutes later. "I told you I'd clean up."

"I didn't mind. Nia asleep?"

"Yeah, she dropped off by the time I got to the third page."

"Poor kid. She could hardly keep her eyes open during the game. She fought and fought to stay awake."

"She didn't sleep well last night. Nightmares."

"Does that happen often?"

"Occasionally."

"I guess that's one thing that never changes. I used to dream about road machinery chasing me when I was little. Cranes. Big dump trucks. That sort of thing. What about you? What did you find scary?"

"The usual stuff. Monsters. Falling. Going to school without my clothes on."

"I've dreamed about the last one," she said, smiling. "What about forgetting the combination to your locker?"

"Oh, yeah. And not knowing you were having a test until you got to class."

"Funny how universal nightmares are."

"I didn't really have that much of a problem with them. Charlie did, though. He had a thing about chickens."

"Chickens?" She wiped her hands on the dish-towel and hung it on the rack. "What's scary about chickens?"

"My great-uncle, Nana's brother, had a henhouse. To keep me from stealing the eggs, he said the hens would peck me to death if I got near them. At first, I didn't believe it. I was ten and thought I was pretty hot stuff. But I wasn't taking any chances. I paid Charlie to go in to see if they'd attack him. He was five and you could get him to do anything if you gave him a penny."

"You used your little brother as bait?"

"In those days, I thought that's all they were good for. But the plan backfired. One of the hens flew near his face and scared him. He fell down and started screaming bloody murder and sent all the birds into a panic. When Nana Sipsey found out what I'd done, she took a switch to my backside and blistered it good. And she blistered Charlie's be-cause he was gullible enough to listen to me."

"You're too funny."

"He still hasn't forgiven me. He had bad dreams for years about killer chickens."

"I don't blame him."

He got a bag of coffee out of the refrigerator and started to measure some into the drip machine on the counter.

"Can I interest you in a cup?" he asked.

"No, none for me. I should be going anyway and let you get back to work."

"Don't rush off. Talk to me while this brews."

"Okay, for a few minutes."

She took a stool at the island separating the kitchen from the den. When Ryan remained standing on the other side, she said a silent prayer of thanks. Her body was doing crazy things tonight, reacting to his smell, his voice. The farther away he stayed, the better.

The dark-green shirt seemed tailor-made to fit his broad shoulders. The tan corduroys showed off his flat stomach and narrow hips.

Had he dressed up for her? The thought made her a bit breathless.

"What will we work on tomorrow?" she asked, trying to keep her mind—and gaze—directed toward something safer than Ryan Whitepath's splendid body. "What mosaics are priority?"

"The tile repairs for a mosque ceiling in California. Very detailed. Very old. The new pieces have to be aged to match perfectly or they'll stand out.''

"Sounds interesting. And what's the community center project you said I could help you with?"

"We'll run over there sometime tomorrow and you can see where it's going. I've completed the majority of the panels, but there's still a couple more, plus grouting. If Helen doesn't screw me up with her delivery, we should have that finished in time for the Christmas opening.''

"What's Helen got to do with it?"

"The mural has caricatures of the people of Sitting Dog. I want to include the baby in a pink or blue blanket, but Helen doesn't want to know the sex until it's born.''

"Neither would I.''

"Bass is also reluctant to put up an image representative of the baby before its birth. He's afraid we'd be asking for trouble.''

"That's a bit odd, isn't it?"

"What can I say?" Ryan grinned. "He's superstitious.''

"Are you the same way?"

"Yeah, I guess I am to some extent. I've been brought up to believe in good spirits and bad ones and not to tempt the bad ones.''

"Angels and demons?"

"You could call them that. My mother is Christian but my grandmother, although she goes to church with us, holds fast to the old ways of our tribe. They brought me up to be open to the beliefs of each and my faith is an amalgamation of what they've both taught me. I believe in what some call God, but I know Him by another name. My understanding of creation, temptation, the flood, paradise…probably isn't very different from yours, only it has a *Tsalagi* twist to it."

"I suppose my faith is all that kept me going during my mother's illness, but I have to admit it also wavered at times. I found it difficult to understand why *her.* I guess everyone who's ever had a relative die feels like that. Life isn't fair. Death has no rules."

"Some things are beyond our ability to comprehend. Carla was only twenty-nine when she died and she'd been a fanatic about taking care of herself. Exercised every day. Ate right. Her job was stressful, I guess, but in a good way. She loved it. She was the last person I'd ever have imagined would die from disease."

"What kind of work did she do?"

"She was in acquisitions and appraisals for Christie's London auction house. Her specialty was Art Deco jewelry."

"What a great job. She must've been very smart."

"She was. And a nice person. We just weren't right for each other."

"I know how that is. I've had experience with it myself. How did you meet her?"

"On the way home after finishing my graduate work, I stopped in London to catch an auction of Impressionist paintings, not that I could afford any of them, but some hadn't been available for public viewing in decades. Carla offered to show me around the city and I ended up extending my stay by two weeks. I'd been home a month when she called and said she was pregnant."

The coffee stopped dripping. He poured himself a cup. "I guess you've been wondering why Nia lives with me."

"Well…yes, but it's not that unusual these days for a father to raise a child."

"Carla didn't want children. She'd worked hard to establish herself in a tough field. Luckily for me, she was willing to sign over full custody."

"Did Nia visit?"

"Once a year. They weren't close, though. Carla really never had time for her and Nia sensed it, but she still feels a loss now that her mother's gone."

"Nia must take after her mother in appearance."

"Yeah, Carla wasn't what you'd call beautiful, but she was an attractive woman and Nia resembles her. I see it more and more every day. She inherited her mother's light skin and brown eyes.''

He looked toward the doorway and cocked his head, listening.

She turned around and looked, too, but didn't see anything. "Something wrong?" she asked.

"I thought I heard Nia." They were both quiet for a moment. "Probably my imagination but let me go check on her. Be right back."

He returned a minute later, saying she was still asleep.

Susannah glanced at her watch. Eight-thirty. "I should go. If you don't get back to work, you'll be up too late, and I don't want a crabby boss tomorrow."

"Me, crabby?" he teased. "Never." He put down his cup. "I'll walk you to the door."

They reached it, and she felt awkward saying good-night. Her attraction to him had caught her by surprise.

"Thanks for dinner. I enjoyed it."

"Me, too, Susannah. Thanks for coming."

He helped her put on her jacket. The collar got turned under and he straightened it, his fingers lingering a bit longer than necessary. His touch, even through the heavy fabric, had the same effect as if he'd caressed her bare skin. She had to force herself to be still and not jump away.

"See you in the morning," she said.

"Lock your doors. And remember what I said about the trash."

"I will."

He watched until she went inside the back door of the cabin. She waved, indicating she was safe, and then did what he'd said and bolted everything up tight.

As she crawled into bed later, she admitted that he was right. Danger existed for her here—but not from nocturnal animals. Ryan Whitepath was interesting and sexy. His daughter took first prize as the most adorable kid on the planet.

"Damn," she said out loud with a groan. What the hell had she gotten herself into?

CHAPTER SEVEN

SUSANNAH ARRIVED for work the next morning shortly after Ryan got back from putting Nia on the bus. He figured she must've been watching for him out her window.

"Hey," she said, yawning.

"Hey, sleepyhead. I picked up biscuits if you're hungry. There's also coffee."

"Coffee would be great." She opened the lid on one of the foam cups and took a sip. "Mmm, that's good."

Her hair was still a bit tousled and she hadn't tried to hide the splattering of freckles across the bridge of her nose as she'd done last night. Some women, like Carla, improved with makeup. This one had an appealing earthiness, a natural beauty that didn't need it.

"How'd you sleep?" he asked.

"Like a log. I zonked out immediately. I had a terrible time waking up."

"The mountain air will do that to you."

"I guess that was it."

"Hopefully it wasn't the after-dinner conversation."

"Don't be silly. I had a great time."

"I was afraid I bored you talking about Carla."

"No, I'm glad you told me. Knowing helps me understand Nia better. I wouldn't want to do or say anything out of ignorance that might make her grief worse."

"I appreciate that, Susannah. She could use a friend right now."

"How *was* she this morning?"

"Good."

"Any bad dreams?"

"No, she slept okay."

She'd wet her bed, something she hadn't done in a while, but Ryan wasn't too concerned about it.

He emptied cream and two sugars into his coffee and stirred it. "Last night you said you understood about people not being compatible. You looked sad. Were you speaking from experience?"

"That's a big question to ask me so early in the morning."

"Hey, I told you my story. It's only fair you tell me yours."

"There's not much to tell. I was engaged. He dumped me."

"Who was he?"

"An attorney."

"One of your bosses?"

"Heavens, I wasn't that crazy." She yawned again. "He worked for another firm."

"What happened? Why did the relationship go sour?"

"He couldn't cope with my family responsibilities. Mother was in the late stages of her disease at the time. He broke it off and asked me to give back his ring."

"Jerk."

"I'd argue, but you're right. I'm at least thankful he realized he didn't want to marry me *before* we walked down the aisle."

"Is he one of the reasons you decided to hit the road?"

"I guess he was part of it. I needed a change in my life. Everything around me was a reminder of the sickness and heartache the past several years had brought me. I also regretted that I'd never done anything important or exciting."

"But you can't ramble forever."

"True. When the money runs out, I'll have to find a place to settle and start fresh. But I can hold out a year longer, even two if I'm careful. And maybe by then I'll have done enough of the things on my list that I won't feel like I've wasted my life."

"The infamous list," he said with a chuckle.

"It's not *that* infamous," she said, chuckling too.

"Most of my goals are pretty tame. You just happened to see one of the, uh, racier items."

"One? You mean there's something that beats *sex with a stranger?*"

"Of course. Number 14. Or Number 27. Ooh, Number 33 is really hot."

"Okay, okay, I deserved that for teasing you the other day."

"Yes, you did."

"Seriously, Susannah, I can understand your desire to change your life, but did you have to completely give up the old one?"

"There wasn't really anything left to give up."

"What about the friends you left behind?"

"Friends? What friends? By the end of my mother's illness everyone had stopped coming by. They didn't want to sit down in the same room with a woman who poured vinegar on her cornflakes and had a reputation for walking around in nothing but her birthday suit."

"You're serious?"

"Those were good days. She could get away from me and out of the house before I knew what had happened. At night she'd wander off in her nightgown. And she grew increasingly paranoid—she believed I was hurting her or stealing from her. Once I thought she was asleep but she'd somehow managed to crawl out the window. The police found her miles away. When they brought her home she told them I'd tried to kill her.''

"Her own daughter?"

"She didn't know what she was saying or who I was most of the time. Sometimes she'd recognize me. The next hour she'd think I was her nurse. For a while she believed I was her mother." His expression made her shake her head. "Don't feel sorry for me, Ryan. I had a lot of good years with her before she got sick."

"I'm thankful Nana Sipsey hasn't had those problems. She complains of arthritis in one hip and her hands, but her mind is good. She's still full of spit and fire."

"Maybe she'll stay that way."

"Maybe. With luck." He finished off his biscuit and dusted the crumbs from his shirt. "You ready to get to work?"

"Sure. Tell me where you want me to start."

"Look over what I have on the computer and in the files and begin setting up a workable system for record keeping. Remember, I'm a dummy."

"I'll make it simple, dummy."

He playfully tweaked her nose.

"We'll drive down to the center later, and I'll show you where the mural's going. After lunch I'll give you your first lesson."

"Okay."

They worked separately for a few hours, he on the design for the mosque, Susannah on the computer. Every now and then she asked a question about a file, but for the most part she left him alone, which he appreciated.

Not that he wasn't aware of her. A man would have to be dead not to be affected by the sexual heat the woman generated.

He knew each time she shifted in her chair or chewed on the end of her pen. The soft sigh she let out when she encountered some crazy thing he'd done raced down his body and settled in his groin.

Other than that, he couldn't complain, at least not about her work. Only once did he have to stop and talk to a customer directly. All the other calls she handled, either taking messages or finding out what the person needed. They had a productive morning.

Close to eleven, Joe ambled in and blew that all to hell. Ryan had asked him to make more shipping crates, and his brother had promised to stop by and get measurements.

Joe grinned widely when he got a good look at Susannah. He ignored Ryan and went straight for her.

"You must be Susannah. I'm Joe."

"Oh, hi!"

"I'm the *handsome* brother."

Susannah giggled and Ryan shook his head. Ten seconds and the kid had charmed her. Amazing.

Had Ryan been so cocky at Joe's age? He didn't think so. Then again, he didn't have Joe's looks or his easygoing way with people.

"Thanks so much for what you did at the cabin yesterday," Susannah told him.

"Glad to help. I've got some firewood for you on the truck. I'll drop it off on my way out. Let me know when you need more."

"Aren't you sweet."

Ryan snorted. Sweet. That was a new one.

"Morning, big brother," Joe called over his shoulder without turning.

"Morning, little brother."

"You didn't tell me Susannah was such a beauty."

"Because I didn't want you over here all the time bothering her."

"Ignore him," Joe said. "Pretend like he's not even here." He took Susannah's hand. "Have dinner with me tonight and we'll go out dancing after."

"And just how old are you?" she asked.

"Twenty-seven."

"Twenty-two," Ryan corrected.

Joe turned and looked at him. "Do you mind? I'm trying to have a conversation with the lady."

"Court on your own time and in your own age

bracket, squirt. I need you to look at those pieces and I don't have all day.''

Joe sighed. "Duty calls. Don't you go away, sweet thing. I'll be right back.''

RYAN'S BROTHER was funny. The two of them together were a riot. Their good-natured bantering as they discussed crates and wrote down measurements amused Susannah. They obviously had a close relationship.

Physically, Joe was a younger, more perfect version of Ryan, at least in the face. He was softer-looking, his features less chiseled. But she couldn't agree he was handsomer. Ryan's maturity added a quality Joe didn't have.

He was shorter and thinner than Ryan, not as well built. He also didn't have his older brother's beautiful hands.

When the two of them were finished, Ryan went back to his worktable, but Joe sat down on the corner of her desk and continued to flirt outrageously.

"Is it true what they say about redheads?" he asked.

"I don't know. What do they say?"

"That you're all fire and heat.''

Ryan made a noise deep in his throat.

"Did you say something?" Susannah asked.

"No.''

"So what about dinner?" Joe pressed again.

"Sorry. You're a smidgen too young for me."

"Aw." He clasped his chest with both hands. "Don't reject me."

"I suspect you won't be sitting at home tonight crying."

"Well, probably not," he admitted, grinning. That smile had probably thrown many a female heart into palpitations.

"I'm sure there's some sweet young thing out there who'd love to have you call her up. More than one."

"That's a fact, but I'd rather be with you. I can think of a lot of ways we could entertain each other."

"I'll just bet you can."

Ryan mumbled a remark she couldn't decipher, put down his straight-edge ruler and walked over. "Okay, Romeo, time for you to go." He grabbed him by the collar and lifted him easily to his feet. "Say goodbye."

"Bye, Susannah."

"Bye, Joe."

SUSANNAH LIKED her work, and the day seemed to race by. Around one they picked up sandwiches at Taylor's, the country store. Ryan had a key to the community center, but they didn't need it. A group of women were inside weaving baskets.

Ryan explained they were part of an arts cooperative whose members made native crafts to take to the reservation and sell to tourists during the summer months.

The money raised bought more supplies and helped fund community projects like the ballet class Nia attended, equipment for the volunteer fire station and expansion of the center.

He introduced her, but they didn't linger. He wanted to get back and work a while longer before he had to pick up Nia.

They entered a larger room under construction to the rear. Ryan had brought sketches to show her. She'd already seen three of the five panels back at the workshop, but as he explained where each would go and held up the drawings, she began to understand his vision more clearly.

The mountains were the background and were being done in broken tile of irregular shapes and sizes. Similar tonal values gave them depth and perspective.

A horizontal band about twenty-four inches in height ran midway through each panel. These sections would feature a series of vignettes. Because the subjects included faces and figures, he was putting this part together in what he called *micromosaic* tile. Some of the pieces were smaller than the head of a pin and had to be laid with tweezers.

"Do you see?" he asked. "The people are the heart of the community and will be the heart of the mural. Each person will be represented in a way that others are accustomed to seeing them. Here's the store with Bitsy at the counter and her husband running the cash register. Here are the old men who play dominoes there every afternoon."

As he went through the sketches, he told stories about some of the people. Mrs. McCaffrey, who'd taught school for thirty-five years, would be holding schoolbooks and an apple in the mural. "Doc" Summerfield, a bird watcher, would be shown with his binoculars.

"Ryan, it's wonderful! Do you really know all these people personally?"

"Every one of them."

"How are you handling deaths?"

"All the people living here as of last January when we drew up the construction plans are included, even if they've since died. We've only lost two in that time. We haven't had a birth yet—Helen will be the first this year. Her baby will be our eighty-fifth resident."

"These insets have to be time-consuming to make with pieces of tiles that tiny."

"I've been working on them for ten months in

my spare time. Here's the palette of colors I'm using and this—'' he unfolded a watercolor rendering ''—is basically what it'll look like when it's finished, with a few adjustments. The first panel goes over there and then they progress down that wall, around the corner and across the back.''

The watercolor itself was so beautiful it could have been framed and hanging in a gallery, but the finished mosaic would be stunning.

''I'm overwhelmed,'' she told him. ''This will be incredible.''

''I hope so. One thing I ask. You can't tell anybody what it looks like. A committee approved the general design, but no one will actually see the finished panels until I unveil them at the dedication.''

''I won't give the secret away.''

''When I begin installing, I'll have to keep this inner door locked, but I'm not at that stage yet. The construction crew still has a few things left to finish.''

''What part will I be able to tile?''

''Some of these background areas. They have random pieces you can nip with hand cutters and not have to use the wet saw. I'll show you what I mean when it's time. You need to practice first.''

''I'm excited. I've never been part of anything so beautiful.''

"Hold on to that enthusiasm. You're going to need it over the next few weeks working with me."

THAT AFTERNOON she got her first lesson in grouting, great fun, but harder than she'd imagined. The movement didn't hurt her broken wrist, although she had to hold the little scraper thing just right to get enough of the thick mixture of cement and fine sand to press down between the tiles. She found it easier to push into place with her hands.

Ryan had put together a practice piece so she wouldn't mess anything up.

"Where the hell are your rubber gloves?" he barked, making her jump. He'd been in the back room for the past hour setting up to test-fire some tiles over the weekend and she hadn't heard him approach.

"I can't work with them on. They're too big. The fingers are three inches longer than mine."

"Then you should've said something. You don't want direct contact with grout or any of the adhesives. They all have chemicals in them and they'll eat up your skin."

"Did you explain that?"

"I didn't think I had to. Giving you the gloves and telling you to put them on should've been enough."

"You're right. I'm sorry."

He wiped her fingers with a clean rag until he'd gotten rid of all the excess. Pulling her off her stool to the sink, he doused her hands liberally with vinegar and made her scrub them.

"Being so fair, I'll bet you have sensitive skin, too," he grumbled, handing her a towel. "Some people even have allergic reactions."

She didn't say anything. What *could* she say? She'd done something stupid, and on her very first day of work, too.

The excitement she'd felt only hours earlier dwindled.

Her changed mood must have shown in her face because Ryan's tone softened. He told her not to worry; he'd get her gloves that fit. He had cream that would help if her skin broke out.

"No Powerpuff Girls for you for a week," he teased, smiling tentatively.

Susannah smiled back. "Sorry I screwed up."

"You didn't know any better. Let's clean up and call it a day. I have to go get Nia and you've probably had enough of my foul temper, anyway. Sorry I barked. I'm bad about that."

"That's okay."

"I'm used to working alone. When other people are around, I forget they don't know the fundamentals."

"Or are too stupid to follow directions…"

"Don't sell yourself short. You've been a big help today."

His praise made her feel better.

She cleaned her tools and put the grout in a plastic holding bucket under Ryan's watchful eye. Periodically, he said, once the cement settled to the bottom, he poured away the water and bagged up the residue for disposal. He did the same with the resin-based grouts and adhesives so as not to mess up the plumbing.

She tidied the workbench.

"I meant to ask if I could take some photographs while we're working. I've been documenting my travels and posting photos on my Web site. I'd love to include shots of you, along with some of the finished pieces."

"I don't know about me, but I have no problem with your shooting the mosaics. Are you any good? I wouldn't mind having copies."

"Very good. Actually it's the camera that's good, a very high resolution five megapixel that gives quality comparable to a 35 mm SLR."

"I have no idea what you just said."

"Any dummy can take a clear, brilliant photo with it."

"Now you're speaking my language."

"The images are digital, meaning we can plug the camera into your computer or mine and import them for dropping into Web pages, brochures to send out, business cards. Everything's instantaneous. No film to develop.''

''I know nothing about this stuff.''

''The technology today is amazing. Have you considered setting up a Web site to advertise?''

''Joe's tried to get me to do it. He has one for the furniture he makes. But I already have too many contracts and my business is nearly all word of mouth, anyway. I'm not sure a Web site would help me much.''

''You may be right. To hire someone to set up and maintain it can get expensive. But you wouldn't need anything complicated—only simple informational pages to highlight your work and let potential customers know how to contact you. Those aren't difficult to design yourself if you have the right program. It's all wizzie wig.''

''Remember who you're talking to.''

''W-Y-S-I-W-Y-G. What You See Is What You Get. The program has a graphical interface. You design the page the way you want it to look, and the program automatically generates the HTML code, or language, needed to display it to visitors.''

''If you say so.''

''You're technologically challenged now, but by the time I get through with you, you're going to be a different man.''

"Don't count on it. I can't even figure out how to set the answering machine to catch my calls."

"I know, but I fixed that already. I recorded a message and set it to pick up after six rings."

"Are you always so efficient?"

"Yes, or so I'm told. I have one of those structured minds that thrives on order. Being able to file and categorize today—I've been in heaven."

"I'm the opposite. Anything orderly frightens me."

"We should make a good team, then. You create the chaos and I'll have fun cleaning it up."

They both laughed.

He followed her out and locked the door.

"Friday is usually pizza night for me and Nia," he said. "Come with us."

"I'd like to, but I need to buy groceries and wash clothes. I thought I'd go to town now before it gets dark."

"We can stop and pick up your groceries while we're out. And you can use the washer and dryer upstairs any time. No use paying a laundry. Throw them in when we get back."

"Okay, but only if you promise to let me buy the pizza, since you cooked last night."

"I'll flip you for it at the restaurant."

"If you win, you shouldn't have to pay," Susannah argued, picking up the bill from the table.

"*Because* I won, I get the right to choose." Ryan reached across and snatched the slip of paper from her hand. "I choose to pay."

"I've never played the game like that."

"Then you haven't been doing it right."

Next to Susannah in the booth, Nia giggled.

"What's so funny?" Susannah asked. She tickled the child's side. "You sure do have a bad case of the sillies tonight."

"You and Daddy are funny. You fuss all the time."

"He's the funny one. Look how his head is all lopsided. And his nose sticks out so far we might have to put a flag on the end so cars won't run into it."

Nia giggled again. "Nah-ah. My daddy is beautiful."

"Beautiful? You think so?"

"Uh-huh."

"Well, let's see." She studied Ryan's face. His eyebrows lifted in question, waiting for her response. "You know, I think you're right. He *is* beautiful in a weird, lopsided, long-nosed kind of way."

"Thanks a lot," he said.

Nia yanked on her sleeve.

"I know a secret about Daddy's quarter."

"What kind of secret?"

Nia looked at him. He shook his head.

"I can't tell."

"Oh, I get it. He tricked me somehow, didn't he?"

"Uh-huh, it's got a man on both—" Nia slapped her hands over her mouth, realizing she'd almost given away what she knew.

Susannah pretended to be mad at him. She held out her palm. "Okay, buster, show me the quarter."

"Not on your life."

"You don't play fair."

"As fair as you."

"You flipped the coin *and* you called first."

"So?"

"So that's not how you do it."

"Next time we'll use *your* quarter and *I'll* call first."

"Okay," she said, then realized he'd tricked her again and sputtered, "Wait a minute, that's not right."

"You already agreed. Too late."

They argued again at the grocery store when Ryan tried to pay for a pair of rubber gloves she bought for work. The man had a streak of hardheadedness in him. This time, he gave in because she threatened to slug him.

Her hands were a little dry and itchy from the

exposure to the grout. She didn't tell Ryan, only added a bottle of moisturizing cream to her basket.

They checked out, and he loaded her groceries into the truck's back seat with Nia. "Do you need anything else while we're in town?" he asked, getting in.

"I got everything."

"Anyplace you want to stop?"

"Can't think of one."

Robbinsville was a sweet place, nestled in a valley among the mountains, but Susannah couldn't see much to do after dark. During the quick tour Ryan gave her, she admired the courthouse made of native stone. Ryan showed her the sheriff's office where Bass worked.

The surrounding "downtown" of a handful of streets was quaint and had some interesting antique and period clothing shops, but all were closed now. Tomorrow she'd drive back and have a better look around in daylight, maybe see if she could find another pair of jeans.

The only road with any traffic was a one-street "bypass" with a few fast-food restaurants, a couple of motels and a convenience store. Ryan stopped at the store and pulled up to the pumps to get gas.

While he was inside paying, Nia took off her seat belt and leaned over to talk to Susannah.

"When are we going to make the brownies?" she

asked. Susannah had bought a boxed mix at the store.

"Maybe this weekend, but first we have to see if your grandmother will let us borrow a pan. Your daddy isn't sure he has one that'll work."

"My friend Mary is making banana splits at her sleep-over party tomorrow."

"Then we should wait to make brownies another time. Eating brownies and banana splits on the same day wouldn't be good."

"Daddy says I don't have to go to the party if I don't want to."

"But you want to go, don't you?" Nia didn't seem too sure. "You're not too young to start spending the night away from home. And sleep-overs are great fun. I went to a lot of them when I was a little girl."

"But what happens if you miss your daddy?"

"You'll be playing so many games and laughing so much, you won't have time to miss him. But if you *were* to miss him, you could always call."

"I could come home?"

"If you really, really felt you had to, I guess he could drive over and get you, but I don't think you'd want to leave."

"What if I got sick?"

"Of course you could come home if you got sick,

but you're feeling okay now, aren't you?'' She said she was. ''Then I wouldn't worry.''

''Susannah?'' Nia's demeanor turned more serious. She obviously had something else to ask, but seemed reluctant to continue.

''What is it, sweetheart?''

''If Daddy doesn't want me anymore and gives me away, can I come live with you?''

''Doesn't want…?'' The question stunned her. If ever a child was doted on and loved, it was this one. Her father adored her. That was obvious to anyone who saw them together.

''Nia, that's not something you ever have to worry about. Your daddy loves you very much. He'd never give you away.''

''But if he did, would you let me be your little girl?''

Susannah had no idea how to answer.

SHE DEBATED whether she should tell Ryan about her conversation with his daughter. Nia had seemed genuinely worried about her father giving her away. Yet all young children had fears about being unwanted, didn't they?

She could remember feeling that way herself a few times as a child. Once she'd gotten in trouble for coloring on the wall of the freshly painted living room. Convinced her mother wouldn't want her anymore, she'd run away—as far as the neighbor's back porch.

The child had no reason to worry. Ryan loved her. Still…something didn't seem quite right in the Whitepath household.

Nia didn't go to her party Saturday night and she also backed out of baking brownies. She didn't feel good, she said, but her complaints were vague. First it was her head, then her stomach, then both her head and her stomach.

Ryan said not to be concerned. She did this sometimes.

"I think she was afraid she'd get homesick at the sleep-over and embarrass herself in front of her friends," he said.

Susannah decided that was reasonable, but it didn't explain why Nia didn't want to be around *her*.

She felt she'd handled her answer to the child's question poorly. As much as she'd love Nia to be her little girl, she'd told the child, she wasn't planning on ever being a mommy.

Nia was herself again on Sunday morning when Susannah joined the family for church. Later, during dinner at Ryan's mother's house, Joe and Nia told jokes to each other and laughed throughout the meal, making Nana Sipsey threaten to take a switch to both of them. Nia seemed completely recovered.

"Annie, this roast is delicious," Susannah told her.

Everyone echoed the sentiment.

"Thank you. How did you enjoy the service? Was it very different from what you're used to?"

"A little different, but interesting." A few of the hymns were the same, sung in Cherokee or English. The program had provided a translation of the Cherokee prayers.

The best part, though, was seeing Ryan dressed in a suit.

"Daddy has Susannah's underpants in his pocket," Nia suddenly announced.

Ryan nearly choked on his food.

Every person at the table stopped eating and stared at him.

"Do tell," Joe said with a grin.

"Uh, I found them in the dryer," Ryan explained when he'd stopped coughing. His face had turned crimson. Susannah imagined her face was the same lovely shade. "She washed her clothes over at our place the other night."

"That's a good one, brother," Joe told him.

"Joseph!" His mother warned him to behave.

Susannah was mortified, especially when Ryan later took the silky scrap of red fabric from the pocket of his jacket and handed it to her.

"Nice color," was all he said.

CHAPTER EIGHT

SUSANNAH FELL into a routine at work and the first month passed swiftly. Before she knew it, her time in Sitting Dog was already half gone.

Thanksgiving came. The Whitepaths didn't observe the holiday, but Ryan's brother Charlie, his wife and their two boys drove over from Winston-Salem to visit for the day. His sister came home from college for the weekend.

Ryan's mother invited the man she'd been dating, Bob Humphreys, over for everyone to meet.

Susannah tried to keep to her cabin and not intrude on the family's time together, but they insisted on including her.

As it turned out, there *was* cause for celebration. Helen Miller went into labor and gave birth to a healthy little girl.

Margaret Ann Miller, weighing eight pounds and one ounce, burst into the world Saturday afternoon. That night, Ryan and Susannah drove to the hospital in Andrews to see mother and baby.

Susannah couldn't say she was close to Helen.

Twice she'd brought her meals at Annie's request. Three or four times, when Ryan had driven over to talk to Bass or check on Helen while Bass was at work, Susannah had ridden along with him.

Once, she'd picked up Nia from the bus stop and the two of them had dropped by with a basket for Helen. It was hand-woven by Nana and contained two loaves of banana-nut bread.

She liked the woman. With more time to develop a friendship, she sensed the two of them might become close.

When she and Ryan arrived, Helen was sitting up in the bed holding baby Maggie in her arms.

"She's the spitting image of her daddy," Bass crowed proudly over his newborn daughter.

"She's too pretty to look like you," Ryan told him. He kissed Helen on the forehead. "I'm proud of you. How are you feeling? Okay?"

"A little sore, but much better than this morning. Any woman who says childbirth is a good kind of pain is a liar."

Susannah laid presents on the bed. "This is from Annie and Nana Sipsey. I think you'll love what they did. They've been working on something for the baby. The rectangular package is from Ryan."

"And Susannah," he added quickly. "She helped me pick it out."

"Nia made you a card," Susannah said. "And

Anita told me to tell you she'd come by tomorrow before she heads back to school. She also has a little something for you.''

"That's so nice. Open the gifts for me, would you, please?"

Ryan's mother and Nana had crocheted a darling white outfit and matching blanket. Susannah had suggested Ryan get something for Helen rather than the baby, since giving birth could be tiring and emotional. They'd shopped on the way over and found an exquisite bed-jacket in a colorful Asian print.

"How gorgeous! Ryan, you doll! And thank you, Susannah, for helping him choose this. I love it!"

"You're welcome."

"Ryan, please thank your mother and grandmother for me. And tell Nia her card was exactly what I needed."

"I will."

Helen wanted to try nursing the baby again, so Ryan and Bass went outside, where Bass planned to smoke one of the pink-wrapped cigars he'd been handing out. Susannah stayed with Helen.

"Neither one of us has gotten the hang of this yet," Helen explained. "The nurses said not to worry, though." After several attempts, the baby finally latched on and began to suckle. Helen brushed her hand softly, lovingly across the tiny dark head. "That's my good girl."

"She really is beautiful," Susannah said. "She has your features, I think, but her skin is the same lovely brown as Bass's."

"Some people wouldn't call it lovely."

"Your parents?"

"Susannah, they haven't even bothered to find out if Maggie and I are okay. Can you believe that? What kind of people could ignore their own grandchild?"

"Maybe they're on the way down from Pennsylvania."

"I wish that was true, but it's not. Even though he didn't want to, I forced Bass to call them when we got to the hospital. They said they didn't care to know about the *half-breed* child and hung up on him."

"Oh, Helen, I'm so sorry."

"If it was only me I wouldn't care." Her eyes filled with tears. "But I don't want my daughter to grow up thinking there's something wrong with her because of her Native American blood. And I hate that they've treated Bass so horribly. They've hardly been civil to him in the five years we've been married. I've kept in touch. I prayed that one day... But when I told them I was pregnant, they even stopped talking to me on the phone."

She broke down and cried. Susannah sat next to

her on the bed, put an arm around her shoulders and tried to comfort her.

"I can't begin to understand why they feel the way they do, but Helen, you have to accept that it's *their* problem. You have a great husband who's crazy about you and a beautiful new baby. If your mom and dad don't want to know them, I'm not sure what you can do to change that. Feel sorry for them. Keep hoping they'll change. But don't let them ruin your happiness."

"You're absolutely right." She wiped her eyes. "I shouldn't let it get to me. I'm probably feeling a bit of postpartum depression. Hold the baby for me a minute, will you? I need to wash my face before Bass comes back. I don't want him to know I've been crying."

Susannah looked at the tiny bundle with horror. "Don't you want to put her in the bassinet?"

"Are you afraid of her?"

"Honestly? Yes. I'm terrified. I've never held a baby before."

"Never?"

"I was an only child. I never even did any baby-sitting. I know zero about kids."

"But you're so wonderful with Nia. That day the two of you dropped by, she was as lively and happy as I've seen her in ages."

"Nia's an exception. I feel comfortable around

her because…I don't know. I was going to say because she's old enough to reason with, but that's not always the case.''

''Maybe you're comfortable because you've grown to care about her?''

''I suppose that's true. She can be moody and she gets her feelings hurt easily, but most of the time she's great fun to be around. I enjoy her. Babies—now that's a new experience for me.''

''For me, too, but Bass and I plan on having a houseful. And we're also going to adopt. We're waiting for a child right now.''

''Are you? That's wonderful!''

''So many children out there need homes.''

Helen tried to hand the baby to her again.

Susannah shook her head. ''Helen, I'm not sure about this. I might drop her.''

''You won't. Besides, you *have* to take her. I'm too sore to get out of this bed and hold her at the same time.''

Helen passed over the warm bundle and Susannah accepted her with trepidation.

''See, it's not so scary,'' Helen said. She struggled to sit and swing her legs over the side of the bed. She eased to a standing position and put on her robe and slippers.

''Do you need help? I can buzz for the nurse.''

''No, I can do it. The doctor said I should get up

and begin taking short walks. This will do me good.''

Susannah sat in the chair and cradled Maggie to her chest while Helen took short, shuffling steps to the bathroom. Having the small body in her arms felt good, felt right somehow. Susannah had to admit the sensation wasn't at all unpleasant.

''You're an angel,'' she told her. The baby's face was red and wrinkly and she had scratches on her cheeks where her fingernails had raked them, but she was adorable. She had a full head of dark hair, which Susannah found amazing.

''How is everything with Ryan?'' Helen called out. ''Are you enjoying working with him?''

''Very much. He's a great teacher. I only wish I had a tenth of his talent.''

Helen came back a few minutes later with her hair combed and her face washed. She'd taken the time to put on a little lipstick.

''Ryan's a good person,'' she said, sitting slowly down on the bed. ''Not too many single men would've taken on the responsibility of raising a child. And he's doing a wonderful job with Nia.''

Susannah agreed. ''He's a good father.''

''I remember the first time I met him. Bass and I weren't married yet, but we'd gotten serious. I already had a pretty good idea I wanted to marry him. I was living out of town and I came down for the weekend to suffer through the big introduction to his parents and friends. Boy, was I nervous. But Ryan was wonderful. He treated me like he'd known me all his life.''

''He has a way of doing that.''

''Nia was about two months old then, I guess. Here was this big muscular guy with this tiny baby strapped to his chest. They were so cute.''

''I'd love to have seen that.''

''I have pictures at the house. Remind me next time you're over and I'll show them to you.''

''Oh, I'm glad you said that. I nearly forgot. I brought my camera.''

She handed Maggie back to Helen.

''Do you mind getting a few of Bass and the baby before you leave?'' Helen asked after Susannah had taken multiple shots. ''He recorded the birth with the video camera, but I'd love some stills.''

''Of course not. And we can do a family photo with the three of you, if you want.''

''I'd love a family photo! I could put copies in my birth announcements. Let me know how much I owe you for the prints.''

''Don't worry about it. Once you get home and settled, I'll bring over my computer and we'll look at all the shots. You can decide which ones you like. The prints will be my gift.''

"You're incredibly nice. I understand why Ryan's so crazy about you."

Her comment piqued Susannah's interest. "What makes you think that?"

"The way he looks at you. The expression on his face when he talks about you."

"When has he talked about me?"

"One night when he dropped over to the house. He said you're a hard worker."

Susannah sighed inwardly. How disappointing. Not the most flattering of remarks.

"He also said he likes having you around. You make him laugh."

Ugh! That was little improvement over *hard worker.*

"He makes me laugh, too," Susannah told her.

"I sense he's conflicted about his feelings. You won't be here that much longer, and that's a problem. But if you gave him the slightest indication you were interested in him, he'd probably overlook his worries and make a move."

"You're mistaken, Helen. Ryan and I are only friends. He's never even hinted that he's attracted to me."

"Hasn't he?"

"A couple of times I thought... No, I'm sure it was only my imagination."

"Maybe I'm asking the wrong question here. Are *you* attracted to *him?*"

Susannah opened her mouth to deny it, but she couldn't. With each passing day she'd grown to respect Ryan more and more, not only for his talent, but for the honorable way in which he conducted his business and for the loving way he treated his family.

From a physical standpoint, she found it hard to look at him without imagining a few naughty things she'd like to do.

He had this old pair of overalls he wore when he was firing tiles. She'd never thought of overalls as sexy until she'd seen them on Ryan Whitepath, both clasps undone so the bib hung down. With his shirt off, skin glistening with sweat, chest and arm muscles bulging, she found it hard to watch him and breathe at the same time.

Her silence made Helen chuckle.

"I thought so. You *are* attracted to him. Now, my next question is, what do you plan to do about it?"

"CUTE BABY, isn't she?" Ryan said when the silence in the truck became too much. Susannah had hardly spoken a word since they left the hospital.

"Very cute."

"Anything wrong? You're pretty quiet tonight."

"Nothing's wrong."

"Tired?"

"Not particularly."

There was obviously something on her mind, but he let it drop. He took her to the door of the cabin and said good-night, then hurried to the house to collect Nia.

His grandmother was reading a magazine while watching TV. At eighty-two she could still follow both the article and the show.

"Elisi." He leaned down and kissed her.

She patted his arm. *"Gvgeyu."* I love you.

His sister, she said, had gone out to see friends.

Ryan found his mother in the kitchen, trying to deal with leftover food. Nia had already been put to bed. She urged him not to disturb her.

"Let her sleep. If you wake her now, you might have trouble getting her back down."

"I'll sleep here, then. If she has a nightmare..."

"When was her last one?"

"A couple of weeks ago."

"She's better. You said the doctor told you as much."

"Dr. Thompson said she *seemed* better. Nia was more talkative the last visit. And she didn't cry like she normally does."

"Ogedoda has heard your prayers. Your daughter is healing."

"I want to believe that, but I'm afraid to get my hopes up."

"Have hope, but remember that difficult problems take time to correct themselves. Be patient."

"I'll try."

"It's early. Go out and have fun for a change. Sleep at your own house so you can rest. Let me watch my granddaughter."

"I shouldn't." He rubbed the back of his neck, feeling the tension there.

"You've been working too hard. A young man needs the company of other young people. For once, follow Joseph's example."

"I don't believe you're telling me to act like *Joe.*"

"Your brother is young and often foolish, but at least *he* knows how to relax. Isn't there a young woman who would enjoy your company for the night?"

"Etsi!"

She chuckled at his shocked face. "You think I'm so old I don't understand the comfort of lying in someone's arms?"

"Yes! I mean, no!"

Hell! Did she have to go and put an image of *that* in his head? Every time he looked at Bob Humphreys from now on, he'd think of his mother having sex with the guy.

"I get your point without the illustrations," he told her.

He felt guilty about leaving. He worried that Nia might wake up and need him. But he could use a break. And it was still early, not yet nine o'clock.

"Okay, I'll go out for a little while, but I'll keep my cell phone on. Call if anything happens."

"I will. Now, off with you. And if I should wake up early in the morning and see your truck parked down at the cabin, I will pretend not to notice."

Ryan swore under his breath. The sly old bird. She'd set him up.

HE HEADED DOWN the drive, telling himself he wouldn't give in to his desires and go to Susannah's. He'd see if Bass had gotten home yet. They'd shoot pool and smoke a few cigars.

Not until he'd parked at the cabin did he admit to himself that this was his intended destination all along. So many nights he'd wanted to come here, but he'd stopped himself.

He didn't get out immediately. After he turned off the engine, he sat there for several minutes. In a month, she'd be gone. He had no business being here, starting something that had no future.

He got out and walked up to the porch.

No damn business at all.

He lifted his hand to knock, but before he could, the door swung open.

"I wondered if you were going to stay out there all night," she said.

"I was…thinking."

"About whether or not you should come in?"

He nodded slowly. "I'm not sure being alone with you like this is a good idea."

"Yet here you are."

"Yeah, here I am."

She stepped aside and he entered. Somehow she'd made the cabin seem like her own. Little touches of her were everywhere—oranges and apples in a bowl on the table, a branch of evergreen draped across the mantel.

She'd created cardboard frames to display photographs she'd taken of the family and hung a patchwork quilt on the wall.

The couch and table had been pushed back, and she'd placed a small rug he didn't recognize in front of the hearth.

"I was about to try starting a fire," she said.

"Let me do it."

He brought in logs. In the wood box he scavenged until he found a thin piece of lighter, a resin-filled shard of pine he used to ignite the kindling. Within a few minutes, he had a blaze going.

Taking her lead, he sat down on the rug, his arm propped across his knee.

"Are you in a no-furniture mode?" he asked.

"I like it better on the floor. That's why I scooted the couch back from the fireplace." She smiled. "Sometimes I get silly and pretend it's 1850. I light the oil lamp and read a book by its light. I imagine there's no electricity or computers or microwaves."

"Strange behavior for a techno-geek like you."

"I suppose it is, but since I've been here, I've come to appreciate a simpler way of life."

"Tomorrow I'll help you toss out your computer."

"I don't think I'm ready for *that* drastic a step."

"I'd say it's a good thing you didn't really live here in the 1850s. You would never have survived it."

"Oh, I don't know. Raising my own food, cooking over an open fire... Sounds like fun, don't you think?"

"What about giving birth without a doctor in case you had problems? Having to climb the mountain on foot to visit a neighbor? Or kill a deer and skin it so your kids won't starve?"

"Uh, okay. Not so much fun. But I still admire the relationship people used to have with the environment. They depended on it for their survival. Folks today don't appreciate the natural world as much. I'm ashamed to admit I was one of them until I came to visit this mountain."

"When I was younger, my grandfather used to take me into the backcountry and tell me stories about the First People and how, through the grace of *Elohi,* the mother spirit of the earth, they lived in peace with her. Everything they needed was provided—food, skins, medicines. In return, the people protected her, honored her."

"That's the way it should be."

"I've watched my grandmother in her garden, gathering her leaves and roots, and each time she takes something from the earth she thanks it. Each spring she makes me plant trees and scatter seeds in the nearby woods to make up for what *Elohi* gives our family."

"We should all live like your grandmother. She's a very intuitive woman."

"Yes, she is."

"She spooked me a bit when I first got here, the way she seemed to know how people were feeling without being told. I figured out it's because she's such a good listener. And she notices things that others don't."

"Listen or your tongue will make you deaf. It's an old Cherokee saying."

"I like that."

"Nana's ancestors were all Medicine Elders of

the *Ani Wodi* clan, as is she. She was raised to understand natural, physical and spiritual healing."

"I love sitting at the kitchen table with her while we're preparing supper and talking."

"She likes that, too. She's told me so."

"And her stories are wonderful. I don't understand half the words, but somehow I know what she's trying to tell me. The other day she was talking about turtles."

"Ah, how turtle got the lines on his shell."

"That's it. Another day, it was why the possum's tail is bare."

"And why he plays dead?"

"Yes. I'll miss my visits with Nana when I leave. I'll miss her."

"Is she the only one you'll miss?"

She looked away. "You know she isn't. I've grown to care about all of you."

He traced the line of her jaw with his index finger, turning her head to make her look at him again. "Any of us more than others?"

"Yes."

He slipped his hand behind her head and pulled her forward for a gentle kiss. Sweet. He knew it would be. The second time he pressed harder, demanded more, and like the flower that opens wider with the warmth of sun, so did her lips. She welcomed him inside.

Desire raced through him. She was forbidden, dangerous, and every cell in his brain warned him he should back away. But he couldn't force himself. He wanted her. Almost from that first day, when he'd watched as she read with his daughter, he'd ached to feel her body against his.

Four long weeks he'd endured the torture of hearing her laugh, witnessing the way her face lit up when she was having fun or learning something new.

He'd come to care about her a little more with each passing day, but aside from that, he'd come to *enjoy* her. She was funny. She amused him. He looked forward to getting up each morning because he knew he'd be with Susannah.

"Mmm," she murmured as the kiss ended. She opened her eyes and smiled softly. "That was as nice as I imagined it would be."

"Have you been thinking about my kissing you?"

"At least a hundred times a day."

"You should've said something. I might have done it sooner."

"No, you wouldn't have. You're as afraid of me as I am of you. Maybe even more so. You have Nia's feelings to worry about. I only have my own."

"Starting a relationship with no future is pretty crazy."

"I agree."

"I don't want to hurt you. I don't want to *get* hurt."

"I feel the same way," she told him. "But if we both understand it isn't permanent, how can anyone get hurt?"

He gazed into her eyes and saw a reflection of his own heart. This woman was his life mate. He knew it suddenly with a clarity that astounded him.

"What's wrong?" she asked. "You have the strangest look on your face."

"Nothing." He shook his head.

If this was meant to be, then he had to trust that somehow it would work out. And he couldn't be with her without honesty.

"Susannah?"

"Yes, Ryan?"

"I have things to tell you and you're probably not going to like hearing them. But if we're going to have any kind of relationship, I don't want any lies or secrets between us."

"That sounds ominous. What is it?"

"Since Nia's mother died, she hasn't been herself. She worries when she's separated from me. Emotionally she's...ill. When I sometimes disappear on Monday afternoons, I take her to a doctor for treatment of depression and anxiety. In addition to the nightmares, she has panic attacks. Bad ones."

"I had no idea her problems were so serious."

"Yeah, well, I've hidden it from you as much as I could. I'm not proud to tell anyone I've failed my daughter."

"You have no reason to be ashamed. It isn't your fault."

"I feel like it is. I should be able to make her feel better, to prove to her that everything's going to be all right."

"Ryan, that's not always the way it works. Illnesses like Nia's are caused by chemical imbalances in the brain, and they can be brought on by a trauma. I struggled with depression and anxiety myself when my mother died. I felt terrible guilt for being glad that I no longer had to take care of her. For weeks I could barely leave the house."

"How did you get past it?"

"With medication and therapy. Is Nia taking anything?"

"Not at the moment. We're holding out until after the first of the year to see if her condition improves. The doctor said a lot of the adult drugs haven't been tested for pediatric use, or have bad side effects."

"What about a support group? She might benefit from interacting with other children who've also lost parents."

"We tried that with a group in Charlottesville. Nia didn't want to go. Forcing her only made the panic attacks worse."

"Poor little thing."

"There's more. And it has to do with you. Will you promise to keep an open mind and not get mad? You seemed my best hope."

"Your best...?" She stopped suddenly. "Oh, wait. You expected *me* to help her?"

"She responds to you. She likes you."

"And I like her. But Ryan, I'm not a therapist! I'm not trained to handle the problems of a sick child. And I told you when you hired me that I'd be leaving soon."

Obviously agitated, she jumped up. Ryan also got to his feet.

"I didn't—don't—expect you to handle her problems. Dr. Thompson thought it would be good for her just to be around someone who's dealing with the same kind of loss."

"Oh, great. You talked to Nia's doctor about me?"

"Nia did—she mentioned her new friend. But yes, the doctor and I have had a few conversations in which you were the subject. She felt you'd be a positive influence on Nia. And you have been."

"This is why you so abruptly changed your mind and decided to hire me, isn't it? You and the good doctor had a little chat and decided to conspire against me."

"Dr. Thompson assumes I discussed this with

you, so I'm the one at fault, not her. I'm sorry for not leveling with you. I wanted to, but I was afraid if I did you'd leave.''

''I would have. I can't believe you've done this. It's not fair, Ryan.''

''Come on, Susannah. Have I asked you to do anything special for Nia in the past few weeks? You've picked her up at the bus stop, but other than that, have I asked you to do anything you normally wouldn't?''

''No, not really.''

''You're a good person with a good heart. You've played with her, read her stories and been her friend because you *wanted* to, not because I asked you to.''

''All right, I admit that's true, but you shouldn't have schemed against me. I don't like being used.''

''I'm sorry. You deserve better. And once you came to work, I realized how much I needed you, too. What can I do to make this up to you?''

''I'll have to think about it.''

''Do you want me to leave?''

''Maybe.'' Her expression softened. ''No,'' she said, shaking her head.

He let out his breath. ''So am I forgiven?''

''I don't know yet. Ask me again in a little while.''

CHAPTER NINE

THEY TALKED for a long time. Susannah found it hard to stay angry with Ryan when she knew he was only trying to help his daughter.

He told her frightening stories, about Nia's panic attacks and about the dreams that terrified her but that she could never remember.

"Never?"

"No, she wakes up screaming for me. I don't know if she's being chased or hurt in those dreams. And she's gotten it into her head that I might abandon her, which sends her into a panic when I'm out of her sight for more than a few hours. Keeping her in school has been hell, although she's been better about that since you got here. She's been better about a lot of things...."

"She asked me once if she could be my little girl if you gave her away."

"When was this?"

"Soon after I came here. That first time we went grocery shopping. You were paying for your gas. She leaned over the seat and dropped that bombshell on me. I was concerned about it, but then shrugged it off as normal childhood anxiety. Now I realize I should have told you. I'm sorry.''

"It doesn't matter. I already know she's frightened. The question is *why?* The doctor says it was triggered by Carla's death.''

"I wish I knew what to do.''

"Being able to talk to you has helped a lot. I try not to tell Mom and Nana too much. They worry.''

"You can talk to me anytime.''

He threaded his fingers through hers. "That jerk you were engaged to...what was his name?''

"Andrew.''

"Andrew was a fool to give you up.''

He kissed her and warmth eased into every part of her body. As insane as it was, she wound her arms around his neck and drew him closer.

"It feels like maybe you've forgiven me,'' he said against her lips.

"You think so?''

He urged her down to the floor.

"If you don't want me to make love to you, tell me to go home now.''

She gave him his answer by undoing his buttons, then sliding her hands across his naked chest.

"Last chance. If you don't want me to make love to you…"

She smiled and began removing his pants.

RYAN TREMBLED with the touch of her fingers on his zipper. He tried his best to be patient, but he'd never wanted a woman more than this one and she was undressing him so damn slow.

"Here, let me help you," he offered, quickly discarding his boots, socks and jeans.

"A bit anxious, aren't we?" she teased. "Can *I* do the rest?"

"Go ahead."

She slowly lowered his briefs. As he kissed her, he helped her undo the buttons on her shirt and shed her jeans. She dragged her nails lightly along his ribs, across his stomach and down his thighs, skimming his growing erection with each pass, but not lingering on it. He decided she was intentionally trying to drive him crazy—and succeeding.

Her panties were hot pink and matched her bra. She lay on her side facing him, the firelight making her pale skin seem translucent.

"I like your freckles," he said. "Are they everywhere?"

"I don't know. I've never really thought about it."

"I'll look and see."

He removed the rest of her clothes. She giggled as he rolled her onto her stomach and conducted a thorough inspection of every inch of her back and legs.

"Well?" she asked. "What's the verdict?"

"Yep, they're all over everything on this side. They even make pictures. You have a flower right down here." He kissed the small of her back. "And right here—" he touched his lips to the back of one of her knees "—you have a cloud."

"That feels so good. Where else?"

He pretended to find bears and trees and dogs. He kissed every one.

She turned over, and her eyes had become heavy-lidded with desire. "And what about this side? Any interesting pictures on it?"

"A thousand."

"Will you kiss them, too?"

"Gladly."

"I know there are a couple right here," she said, touching her breasts. He kissed both rosy tips. "And here," she said, indicating the insides of her thighs. Her back arched from the floor when he kissed her there. "Oh, Ryan! I'd forgotten how wonderful it feels to make love."

"How long has it been for you?"

"Two years."

It had been about that long for him, too. Since Nia came to live with him, he hadn't dated much or given sex priority. He enjoyed it, and sometimes physically his body needed it, but in the seven-year stretch between Carla and Susannah, he hadn't felt attracted to anyone, and sex had been more of a chore than a pleasure.

He wasn't going to last long this first time and neither was she, so they brought each other quickly to climax. With that out of the way, they were free to take their time, to enjoy the slow road back to arousal.

At least, he *thought* the journey was going to be slow. He was wrong. When she gave him a massage, he tried to give her one, but she squirmed under his palms and decided she'd had enough foreplay.

"Make love to me," she said, guiding him.

"Yes, ma'am. Whatever you want."

The floor wasn't the most comfortable place to do this, but after a couple of minutes he no longer cared. Susannah delighted him by being a very vocal lover. She wasn't shy about asking for what she wanted or letting him know she was enjoying herself. Pretty soon he was spiraling out of control, no longer able to hold back.

But he didn't need to. She came with him. Her climax exploded within seconds of his. The pleasure was so pure and so intense, he was afraid it had stopped his heart.

"Mmm, that was incredible," she said. "I wouldn't mind doing that a hundred more times tonight."

Ryan groaned. "Give me a few minutes to rest and then I'll see what I can do."

SUSANNAH TRIED to move but Ryan had his leg partly over hers. He'd pinned her to the mattress. Thank God they'd moved to the bed the second time they'd made love. That hard floor had nearly broken her bones.

He mumbled in his sleep and grasped her left breast. In the pale light from the dying fire, his brown hand looked strange against her white flesh.

He was all hard sculptured muscle, a living work of art, and she'd never seen anything more beautiful in her life.

His body fascinated her, from the long hair that draped her like a tent when he made love, to his cute bony toes.

He was perfectly made and flawless, except for one scar. Stitches, he'd told her. He'd fallen from a tree and cut open his right knee when he was seven.

With Andrew, sex had been enjoyable, but it had always included questions afterward: "Was that good? Did you come?"

Sometimes she'd wanted to scream at him, "Stop with the quiz! This isn't school!"

Ryan didn't have to ask. He'd known by her cry that she'd enjoyed every spiraling wave of ecstasy.

He stirred, opened his eyes and saw she was awake. "Sorry, I must've dozed off. What time is it?"

"Midnight."

"I should go home."

"Probably." She stroked his shoulder. "I don't want your mother knowing what we've been doing for the last two hours."

He chuckled and rolled onto his back.

"What's so funny?"

"I doubt she'd be surprised."

"That may be true, but we shouldn't change how we act in front of your family, and our working relationship needs to stay professional."

"Can I carry your panties around in my pocket while I work?"

"No!"

"Dadgum. That's the only reason I slept with you. I was hoping you'd give me a pair."

She sat up so she could talk to him. "You're such a comedian. I don't know how I stand you."

"You stood me just fine a while ago—twice."

"I was only humoring you. I don't really find you all that attractive."

"Oh, is that right?" He pulled her down on top of him. "So how come you begged me to make love to you?"

"*Begged* you? You're having a hallucination, mister."

"Oh, Ryan, touch me there," he said in a high feminine voice, imitating exactly how she'd sounded during lovemaking. "That feels so good. And you're so huge."

She laughed so hard she had to put her head down on his chest. "You added the 'huge.' I didn't say that."

"Okay, I embellished a bit."

The body part under discussion was currently rigid against her leg and demanding attention. One slight movement, and she'd be in trouble.

As much as she wanted to make love to him again, they had a major problem. They'd used both of the small packets in his wallet.

"Uh, before you get too worked up, remember we have no more condoms."

"Ah, hell."

"Sorry, but I don't have any. And I don't think we should take the risk of not using one. This is a safe time for me, but accidents can happen."

"Yeah, I was conceived in this bed."

"Oh, boy, I forgot about that. Then we'd better not tempt the spirits."

"You're right."

She expected him to get up. Instead, he rolled and took her with him, reversing their positions. Now she was on the bottom.

He sought out the soft red curls between her legs

and stroked beneath them with his fingers. Slick with her own moisture and on fire, she feared she might spontaneously combust, but he wouldn't let her come. Again and again, he'd let her get close, but not go over the edge.

"Are you trying to kill me?" she croaked out.

"Yes."

The next time, he waited until she was a breath away and replaced his fingers with his mouth. Tremors shook her whole body. Even after she climaxed, he continued to make love to her with his lips and tongue.

A second and a third wave of incredible pleasure washed along her nerve endings.

"Oh!"

She really *had* died.

And gone to heaven.

When she could speak and move again, she told him she'd do the same for him, but he said no.

"That was a gift. Gifts should always be given because you want to, not because you expect the other person to reciprocate."

"I feel a bit stingy getting and not giving."

"Nothing says sex has to be equal."

She nodded. "I'll give you a gift another time."

"I'll tell you what you *can* do for me. Get that crazy list. I want to see it and mark off Number 9."

She made a quick run to the bathroom. When she

came back she turned on the lamp, found the list and got a pen. He propped a pillow behind his head. She crawled in next to him and pulled the covers over them both.

He chuckled and snorted a few times as he read.

"Cruise the Amazon River? When do you think you'll ever have a chance to do that?"

"I don't know. Stranger things have happened. Remember this is a list of things for my whole life. Twenty or thirty years from now, who's to say what I might be doing?"

"Star in a movie," he read. "Like that's going to happen."

"You're missing the point."

"Visit Paris in April. That one's probably doable, but *Dance in a ballet?* Are you even a dancer?"

She snatched the list from his hand. "If you're going to make fun of me, you can leave." She tried to get up, but he grabbed her and made her sit down again. He wrapped his arms around her from behind and held her tight against his chest.

"I'm sorry. I didn't mean to hurt your feelings."

"Well, you did."

He kissed her neck, nipped at her ear. "I like the one about growing your pretty hair to your waist, *To tsu hwa.*"

"Call me that again."

"To tsu hwa."

"Talk to me in your language."

The words he spoke were melodious, like a beautiful song.

"What did you say?"

"I said...your smile is brighter than a thousand suns and the blue of your eyes makes the sky weep."

"That's lovely. Did you read it somewhere?"

"No, my heart wrote it."

She sighed and nestled in the curve of his shoulder. "Tell your heart to say some more."

RYAN SHIFTED on the church pew and wished the preacher wasn't so long-winded this morning. The sermon was about sin. Each time he mentioned the word *sinners,* Susannah poked him in the ribs with her elbow. Trying to keep a straight face was becoming impossible.

Covertly, she took something out of her purse, made sure no one was watching and stuffed it in the pocket of his suit pants.

He waited fifteen second, then stuck his hand in and felt. His fingers identified silken panties. He smiled.

"A gift," she whispered. "No need to reciprocate."

AFTER LUNCH, since it was a lovely day, he asked her if she'd like to ride up the Skyway with him and

Nia and look at the mountains. They'd had a light snowfall early that morning, but the sun had since been trying to come out.

Anita had left to go back to school and his mother had other plans. She wanted to take some soup to a sick neighbor. Nana said she was "done going" for the day and preferred to stay home.

"The mountains will be beautiful with the rays hitting the snow and ice," Ryan told Susannah. "How about it?"

"I'd love to go. I can get some photos."

Nia wasn't happy with the decision. She wanted to drive into town and see the Christmas lights that had been turned on the day before.

"We'll do both," he said.

When they'd changed out of their good clothes, Susannah met them at the front door of the barn. Her attitude toward Nia didn't seem any different than the day before and he was glad of that. In minutes Susannah had her giggling as usual.

"We'll head up into the mountains first and then swing through town on the way back," he said. "After that, we'll go see Helen for a minute. That okay with everyone?"

They agreed.

Over the next half hour, they climbed steadily upward along the curving road. Ryan pulled off into one of the scenic overlooks.

"Are all these mountains the Snowbirds?" Susannah asked as they got out of the truck. They walked toward the edge.

"No, but each is part of the Appalachians. The Nantahala Mountains come in from the east and the Unicoi from the west. To the north are the Great Smokies."

"And most of this land is national forest?"

"That's right. The Skyway goes through both the Nantahala and Cherokee National Forests, but we have other forests and wilderness areas, as well. We drove through a different part of the Nantahala when we went down to see Helen last night in Andrews. Remember the steep gorges? You were scared we'd go off the road."

"That was a terrible drive. Worried me to death."

Nia asked, "Were you scared, Susannah?"

"For a minute, but your daddy reminded me that he was familiar with the road and knew what he was doing. So I wasn't scared after that."

"We'll come back through before dark this time. I promise."

Ryan sat on the stone wall while Susannah walked around and took her photos. He warned Nia not to go near the edge, but kept an eye on her. She seemed content to play nearby.

Susannah came back, cheeks rosy and puffing from the high altitude. "I can tell we're high up."

"About 5,300 feet."

"I need to get in better shape. Whew!" She bent over, put her hands on her knees and took a few deep breaths.

He glanced at Nia. She wasn't paying them any attention and was out of earshot. "There's nothing wrong with your shape," he said in a low voice. "And I should know. I've touched every inch of it."

"I have a fondness for your shape, too."

"Enough that you might consider staying around past Christmas?"

She straightened. "Ryan, we talked about this last night. We agreed we'd enjoy what time we have together but not make any promises."

"I'm not asking for a commitment and I'm not prepared to give one, but I *would* like time to build on what we've started. Maybe we'd be good together and maybe we wouldn't, but how are we going to know if you run off?"

"And if I stayed? What then? How would I support myself?"

"Doing what you're doing now, working for me. You like the job, don't you?"

"Yes."

"And you're great at it. In the past month you've already brought me three new clients and convinced that gallery in Atlanta to sell my museum-quality pieces. I should make you my agent. But if you'd rather not work with me, then do whatever you enjoy. You're a great natural photographer. Maybe you could take some classes and learn to do that professionally. Or teach computing. Do bookkeeping. Design and build Web sites. Hell, you have a number of talents you could use to make a living."

"I have other concerns." She nodded toward Nia. "The longer I stay, the harder it'll be on her—and me—if our...relationship doesn't work out."

"Sometimes life is a risk. You know that."

"My body I'm prepared to risk. But my heart...I couldn't go through another break-up. I laugh and call Andrew a jerk, but he *hurt* me."

"I wouldn't hurt you."

"You can't be sure of that. You have the capacity for hurting me even more deeply than he did."

"And why is that?"

"Because my heart's already tender. And because...in the short time we've known each other, I've come to care for you so much it frightens me. I don't *want* to feel this way."

"Susannah..." He stood and drew her closer. "Don't dismiss what you feel. Give us a chance."

"I'm afraid to, Ryan, and not only because of what happened with Andrew. Those years I spent caring for my mother were like being in prison—

worse than prison, because I lived every day with the knowledge that my escape would only come with the death of the person I loved. The guilt and pain were terrible. I don't want to be in the position of feeling that again, of having to take care of someone. I'd rather be alone.''

"I'm not asking you to take care of me or Nia."

"No, but love automatically carries that responsibility."

"Of *helping,* yes, of being a *partner* and a *friend,* but don't you understand that you're supposed to get as much out of a relationship as you give to it?"

"Of course."

"From what you've said, I'm not so sure you do. Was Andrew there when you needed him? Did he understand your pain and help you, or make life more difficult?"

"The break-up wasn't entirely his fault."

"You're not answering me."

"Okay, he wasn't much help. Is that what you want to hear? Having to worry about his feelings on top of everything else put more strain on me. Frankly, he was selfish. He never tried to understand how difficult my life was or to ease my burden.''

"I thought so. And your mother drained you, too.''

She pulled away. "Now, wait. That was a totally different situation. She was seriously ill and she didn't have anyone else. She was terrified of having to go into a nursing home and being cared for by strangers. I owed it to her to help any way I could.''

''I'm not criticizing you for it, only pointing out that the strong relationships you've had in recent years have both been one-sided, and that's forced you to close off your emotions.'' He pulled her back into his arms and rested his chin on the top of her head. ''I'd like the chance to prove to you that letting someone in doesn't have to be painful, but I can't do that if you're not here. Stay awhile. No pressure, I promise. If you decide you're unhappy and want to leave, I won't make it hard on you.''

''Ryan, you're trying to get me to give up my newfound freedom.''

''No, I'm not, but I know you've been happy here. All I ask is that you be honest about that and consider staying. Think about it some more and don't make a hasty decision.''

''All right.''

Nia came over then and showed him a pretty rock she'd found under the snow. ''Do you think the Little People left it for me?''

''They might have.''

''We need to give them somethin' back.''

He reached in his pocket and got a quarter. ''They like shiny things. Leave this where you found the rock.''

She went back, gingerly placed it on the ground and began looking for more rocks.

"I hope you have a lot of quarters," Susannah said.

AS THEY DROVE down into the valley, she asked him about the various places and how they got their names. Ryan didn't mind. He liked talking about his home and the history of his area.

"Why Snowbird?"

"The old ones say a giant snowbird used to live on top of the tallest mountain," he said. "That's how the range got its name. We call our single mountain Snowbird because we have so many of the birds every winter, but it's only a nickname."

"And why is the community called Sitting Dog?"

"Have you noticed the big outcropping of rock above the house and to the left? Up close it looks like a sitting dog. I'll take you there one day this week. It's only a short walk. I also want to show you something else, near the rock."

They drove to Robbinsville so Nia could see the Christmas lights strung across the streets and those in the store windows.

"We should be getting ours out and putting them up," he told her. "Did you tell Susannah that you're an elf in your ballet recital?"

"I forgot!" Excitedly she gave Susannah every

little detail of her performance. "I wanted to be a deer," she finished, "but Miss Cummings said I had to be an elf. That's what she calls them. They're really Little People, though."

"Oh, that sounds wonderful. Do you get to wear a costume?"

"Uh-huh. A green one. Will you make it for me?"

"Nia, Gran already said she'd do it," Ryan told her.

"But I want Susannah to."

He glanced across the truck at her. "You don't have to, Susannah. My mother already volunteered."

"I don't mind. Actually, I love to sew. I used to do it all the time, but I sold my sewing machine when I sold the house because I didn't think I'd have any use for it."

"You'll probably regret taking on this project."

"Oh, don't spoil my fun." She turned to Nia in the back seat. "Tell you what. I'll make your costume if you'll help me make decorations to hang in the cabin."

"I can do that!"

"Your daddy was telling me how your family celebrates with natural and handmade decorations. We can make colored rings and popcorn balls and stars out of aluminum foil. Stars are okay, aren't they, Ryan?"

"Stars are fine." Ryan smiled to himself. She was enjoying this as much as Nia.

"And we can get pinecones from the woods. Let's see what else. Oh, we can dry orange slices and sprinkle them with sugar."

"Can we eat them?" Nia asked.

"Eat my decorations?" She gasped. "Certainly not. Well, maybe a few of them."

Ryan told her it was fine to collect berries, seed pods, discarded nests, nuts and whatever else she needed from the property but to be careful not to stray too far from the house.

"When? When?" Nia asked. "Today?"

"Mm, *if* we get back in time. But next Saturday would be better because we'd have all day to gather what we're going to use. And first we'll have to make a list of other things we need, like glue and paper and ribbon. Did your ballet teacher give you any instructions about your costume? We could get the fabric at the same time."

"Nia brought home a sheet saying when the recital is and what they need," Ryan said. "I'll show it to you when we get home."

THEY VISITED Helen and Maggie at the hospital, then drove home; it was already dark when they arrived.

"You're coming in, aren't you?" Ryan asked.

Susannah decided she wouldn't. He'd want to talk about her staying, and she didn't want to discuss it anymore. What was the point?

"I think I'll take a bath, maybe read a while and go to bed early. And you should spend some time with Nia for a change—without me always hanging around."

He didn't argue. She couldn't tell from his expression what he was thinking or feeling. "I'll see you in the morning then," was his only response.

She told them both good-night and walked over to the cabin with a heavy heart. Why did everything always have to be so complicated?

She'd come here with a simple goal—to take lessons—and now Ryan was asking her to change their entire arrangement. And for what? The *chance* that they *might* be able to build a lasting relationship. No, thanks. She'd been through that once and she never intended to open herself up to that kind of pain again.

Even if she did stay and things worked out, he had a sick daughter who needed special attention and—fond as she was of Nia—Susannah had spent nearly a third of her life in the role of caregiver. She didn't need, didn't want, that responsibility again.

Once inside, she turned up the heat, filled the tub and had a long, leisurely soak. The warm water soothed her body but not her troubled mind.

She looked around the cabin at all the little improvements she'd made—the throw rug, the pillows for the couch, the Kiss the Cook spoon holder for the kitchen—and realized she'd turned it into a home, a foolish thing to do.

And why on earth had she asked Nia to help her decorate when she wouldn't even be here for Christmas? She'd be on the road somewhere between North Carolina and New York.

She'd gotten caught up in the idea of having a true Christmas again, been reminded of her own childhood when she and her mother had decorated the house. But she *wasn't* Nia's mother. Best to remember that for the child's sake and her own.

A hard knock sounded. She grabbed her towel.

"Who is it?"

"It's me," Ryan said.

"Are you alone?"

"Yes."

Susannah relaxed and tossed the towel onto the floor. "Come in."

He opened the door, then stopped abruptly and stared.

"Well, come in or get out, for goodness' sake.

I'm freezing to death!'' She settled back and sponged bubbles over her arm.

He closed the door and walked toward her.

"Where's Nia?" she asked.

"I took her to Mother's for a little while."

"Why?"

"Because I wanted to be with you."

"You've been with me all day. Go home, Ryan. I'm taking a bath."

"You seem to be having a good time."

"I'm having a wonderful time."

He bent over and pulled off one boot, then the second one. He started on his shirt.

"What are you *doing?*"

"What does it look like I'm doing? I'm getting in there with you."

"Oh, no, you're not. Ryan!" She giggled as he hastily stripped down to nothing. He got in, sloshing water everywhere. "Look at the mess you've made all over the floor."

"I'll mop it up."

"And you've soaked my cast."

"It's about to come off anyway."

His big body had displaced so much water it was still spilling over the rim.

He grabbed her around the waist and pulled her forward, maneuvering them both until she was sitting between his legs.

"Growing up, I once asked my father why mother had insisted on having such a big bathtub in here and he just grinned. Now I know why." He took her sponge away and began using it to wash her shoulders and breasts.

"You felt bad when he didn't call on Thanksgiving, didn't you? I overheard you saying something to your mother."

"He could at least have bothered to pick up the phone."

"Has it been hard for you, being the oldest and feeling responsible for everyone? I know you're paying Anita's tuition and I've seen you slip money to Joe more than once."

"Sometimes it's hard. But being a part of this family means I have obligations, and not only financial ones. But it's the same with each of us. My brothers and sister, Mom, Nana—they've been my strength. I hope, in return, I've been theirs."

"You're a nice man. Do you know that?"

"I know," he teased. "I'm special."

Susannah laughed. "And modest."

"I also have some very selective skills."

"Oh? And tell me, what might those be?"

He picked her up and sat her down on his lap so that her legs hooked behind him and their most intimate places touched. "I'd rather show you."

CHAPTER TEN

THE FOLLOWING Tuesday Susannah went with Ryan to the community center to begin assembling the mosaic. Joe came to help and brought a digital video camera.

"Nice equipment," Susannah said, admiring it. Very high-end. Expensive. She looked through the viewfinder and tinkered with all the controls. "Brand-new?"

"Yep."

"Hooks into a TV or computer?"

"Right."

"I'm so jealous. Must've cost you a fortune."

"Hey, not me. Ryan paid for it."

Ryan jumped in and said he wanted to have a video record of the mural.

"What a great idea," Susannah told him. "You should do that with all your commissions, start to finish. Video the work while it's in progress and the final product and make a compact disc. You'd have a terrific sales tool, much better than the still photographs we've been mailing out."

"Pretty much what I had in mind *if* I can learn to work the stupid thing."

Joe had used a friend's before, so he spent five minutes showing them both what to do.

"Simple," he said, finishing. "Not too different from Susannah's camera."

"Looks pretty simple," Ryan agreed, "even for me."

They began installing the panels, putting in both a water-resistant and a soundproof membrane and then attaching the cement backerboard to the wall studs. At intervals, Joe took video of Ryan at work with Susannah helping.

Because this room would be used primarily for a day care center and the walls would take a lot of abuse, Ryan had used vitreous tile fired for thirty-plus hours at twenty-two hundred degrees.

Joints cleverly hidden in the design would allow the materials to expand and contract without damage.

Vitreous, impervious...Susannah had picked up the terminology and actually understood what it meant. She knew the difference between an edging and a margin trowel. The array of adhesives still confused her, but she was pleased with what she'd learned.

Ryan looked around and said they were making

excellent progress. Completing the work wouldn't take many more days.

He'd finished tiling every panel, with the exception of the one that held the caricatures of his own family. That one he'd been working on after hours and hadn't brought down from the workshop.

"When are you going to let me have a peek?" Susannah asked.

"I'm not."

"How come?"

"Because the only reward I get from a donated project like this is people's reaction. If you or Joe or anybody else knows what it all looks like, you won't be surprised. That spoils it for me. So I'm holding something back. You'll have to wait for the dedication."

"Makes sense," Joe said.

She pinched him on the arm.

"Ouch!"

"You're supposed to side with me, you traitor."

"Joe's going to help me install the panel because it's too heavy to do alone. Once it's up, I'll lay in the tile on the missing part. Then we'll be ready for the unveiling."

"How have you portrayed your mother and grandmother?"

"You'll have to wait and see."

"No hints even?"

"All I'll tell you is that your birds are going in there."

She smiled delightedly. One day he'd supervised as she'd created a pair of snowbirds out of the tiniest tiles, but she'd assumed the piece was only for practice and not of any importance.

"Oh, Ryan, seriously? You're going to use my birds?"

When he nodded, she was so excited, she kissed both him and Joe, then danced around.

Joe grabbed the video camera and recorded her craziness.

She didn't care. She had created something artistic and beautiful! *Her!* Susannah Pelton. And for years and years people would enjoy her work.

This was so much better than just assisting with the background pieces. She'd only been following Ryan's design and pattern then. The birds were *her* idea, her creation. Even Ryan had said she'd done a great job.

"Where are they going exactly?" she asked.

"I'm not telling."

She begged for details, but he wouldn't give in. If Joe hadn't been there, she probably could have convinced him to tell, but she had to behave. Joe was already suspicious of them. He'd been sending them sly grins all afternoon.

Ryan had gently patted her bottom when she

kissed him and the intimacy of that hadn't escaped Joe's notice. He'd winked at her over Ryan's shoulder.

She had a hard time settling down. Twice Ryan told her to stop singing because it was driving him crazy.

"Okay, Mr. Grinch."

Late in the afternoon, Ryan looked at his watch and commented that it was nearly time for Nia's bus to arrive.

"How about picking her up and staying through her ballet lesson?" he asked Susannah. "You can watch the kids practice for their recital. Joe and I can handle things here."

"Yeah, get lost," Joe suggested. "We need some peace and quiet."

"I get the impression you don't like my singing."

"That's putting it mildly," Ryan said, making Joe snicker.

She said she'd go. She needed to talk to Nia's teacher, anyway, about her costume for the dance.

On her way out, she launched into a loud chorus of "Respect." Joe got it all on video, including Ryan covering his ears.

RYAN WAITED until he was certain Susannah had left the room, then asked Joe if he thought she'd suspected.

"Didn't seem to."

"I appreciate your helping me pull this off. You sure you can find someone to put together what I want?"

"Positive. All we have to do is get enough video of her to have a good selection. I know a guy who can do the editing."

"Perfect. What about the other? Did you have any problems getting Sandy to agree?"

"No, she's glad to do it."

"More likely glad to do *you* a favor."

"Things aren't like that between us."

"You've never dated her? I thought you had. She's had a crush on you since first grade."

"Nah, she's a good kid. I like her too much. I don't date women I like."

"Run that by me again."

"I date for fun and for, you know…"

"To get laid."

"Yeah, but once I've been in a woman's bed a few times, she starts getting clingy and I have to break it off. If it's someone I like or I've grown up with, it wrecks the friendship."

"You have a strange way of handling women."

"Look who's talking! You say you care about Susannah and want her to stay, yet you're helping her fulfill her fantasies and go off without you. I don't get it."

"Do you remember the story about eagle and mouse? One of the elders told it last summer at the powwow."

"No, I sneaked off to swap body fluids with Willow Silverfox."

"I should've guessed. Anyway…the point of the story was that sometimes the best way to hold on is to let go."

"Damn, Ryan, I swear half the time I don't understand you. You're sounding more like Nana Sipsey every day."

"I'll take that as a great compliment, brother."

SHE LOVED WATCHING the girls dance. A couple of times Susannah had picked Nia up on Tuesday and come early enough to sit through class.

The dance performance was about the mother spirit of earth who gives presents to good children. Afterward, small boxes of sugar cookies would be handed out by the girls to each family.

In a way, it was the Santa Claus legend, but the young teacher had wisely incorporated the beliefs of the Cherokee. Both whites and Indians should enjoy the performance.

Nia and her friends Iva and Mary were elves, or rather Little People. The other five girls would be sacred deer or reindeer, however you wanted to look at it.

Nia seemed to love her class. Susannah suspected it was because this was one of the few times she saw her friends outside of school.

She'd only go to Mary's or Iva's if Ryan stayed with her, and that had become a problem. The girls had noticed Nia's reluctance to be separated from her father. They'd begun to tease her.

"My shoes, please," she said from the metal chair beside her. She stuck her tiny feet in Susannah's lap for help in putting on her ballet slippers.

"How did things go today?" Susannah asked.

Nia obviously knew what she meant: had the girls said anything hurtful?

"Mary called me a name."

"What did she say?"

"She's not gonna invite me to her house anymore. She said I don't come 'cause I'm a baby."

"And what did you tell her?"

"That I didn't want to go to her stupid house, anyway."

Nia glanced over at the girls, sitting on the floor putting on their ballet shoes. Mary looked at Nia and whispered something to Iva. They both giggled.

"They don't like me anymore," Nia said, crestfallen.

"Oh, I'm sure that's not true. Go over there and talk to them. Act like nothing's happened."

"Can I wear your magic ring? Please, please? I promise I'll give it back after class."

"You understand, don't you, that this ring isn't really magic? What makes it special is that it was given to me by someone who loved me very much. Her *love*—not the ring—is what gave me the courage not to be afraid."

"Okay, but can I please wear it?"

Susannah wasn't sure her lecture had made an impact. Nia was six and scared. Like every child, she craved belief in a protector, even if it came in the form of a magic ring.

"All right, this one time, but be very careful. My mother gave it to me when I was six or seven, I've kept it all these years." Susannah took the ring from the chain. "Don't lose it."

"I won't." Nia slipped it on her finger.

She hopped down and kissed her, then scurried off to face her friends.

The sweet gesture touched Susannah. Tears formed, but she quickly got herself under control. Crying here in public would be embarrassing. Several of the mothers had stayed to watch their daughters rehearse.

Sandy Cummings, the young teacher, waved at her from across the room and walked over.

"I'm glad to see you here today. I wanted to ask a favor."

"Sure."

"I was wondering if you'd consider being our mother spirit for the recital. I'm doing the narration, so I'd planned to ask one of the parents to play the role."

"Sandy, I'm not Nia's parent, only a friend of the family."

"I know, but that doesn't matter. You've shown an interest in the class, and you're about my size so we could easily make you a costume from one of my old leotards."

She leaned over and whispered that some of the mothers were a bit too hefty to consider putting into stretch fabric.

"I'm not sure about this," Susannah said.

"The dance you'd do isn't hard. A few twirls. Some basic movements. I could teach you in thirty minutes if you could stay after class."

"You mean I'd actually dance? I thought you wanted me to pass out gift boxes to the elves or something."

"Well, of course you'd dance. Please, Susannah. You'd be perfect."

Imagining the mothers and fathers staring at her made gooseflesh appear on her arms. How silly she'd look out there on the floor, flitting around with the kids.

But so what? Dancing in a ballet *was* on her list.

"I'll do it."

"AND RIGHT HERE I jump and make a turn." Susannah demonstrated for them in the living room of his mother's house. "And then I bow gracefully."

"Yay!" Nia cheered.

"Lovely, Susannah!" his mother said.

Nana clapped and said it was wonderful. *"Do yu yo go os da!"*

Ryan put down the video camera and clapped, too. "You'll do a great job."

"I hope so. I wouldn't want to mess up and ruin the performance."

"I doubt you could do that. Sa Sa, your turn. Dance for Gran and Nana and I'll record it."

Like Susannah, she got up and went through her part.

"Now you and Susannah together."

They dipped and glided, a couple of times nearly bumping into each other, making everyone laugh.

"We're good, aren't we, Daddy?" Nia asked.

"You sure are. I've never seen anything prettier."

"Of course we don't have our music," Susannah

pointed out. "We'd be much better, wouldn't we, Nia?"

"Uh-huh. A hundred times better."

"I'm not sure I could stand you being any better," Ryan told them.

They wanted to show him a second time. After both had gone through their routines, Susannah hooked the camera to the TV and they watched the replay.

"Show it again," Nia said.

"No, that's enough for one night. Time for us to head home."

"Not yet. Please?"

"'Dexter's Laboratory' comes on in twenty minutes. You don't want to miss that."

"Can't I watch it here?"

"No, we need to go. Daddy wants to work later tonight."

Susannah said she could bring her home after the TV show was over, that she wanted to stay a little longer, too, and visit with his mother and grandmother.

"Why don't you let Nia spend the night with me at the cabin?" she said. "I can take her to school in the morning, since I've got to go to town anyway and have my cast removed. Nia, would you like to come home with me? We could make popcorn and play Go Fish.''

"Our own sleep-over?" she asked. Ryan could tell by her voice she was interested but hesitant.

"That's right. Except that your daddy would be close by, just across the driveway.''

Nia bit her lip and thought about it.

Ryan pulled Susannah aside. He wasn't sure this was a good idea and he told her so. "I've explained what can happen.''

"Ryan, this is a perfect chance for her to be away from you, but not so far that she gets upset. She does okay when she stays here with your mother, doesn't she?''

"Most of the time. Sometimes she cries and wants to come home, but not very often. She's used to Mom and Nana. But that doesn't mean she *won't* have an anxiety attack and they're scary as hell.''

"Give me your cell phone. That way I can reach you, and she'll be able to call if she feels homesick or afraid.''

"She'd probably end up not staying the night.''

"If she doesn't, that's okay. Let her try.''

"I worry she'll get sick.''

"Ryan, her friends are starting to make fun of her. Do you realize that?''

"She told you they have?''

"I've seen them. And she's miserable because of it. They don't want to invite her over anymore and they've stopped coming here. Do you want her to become even more isolated than she already is?"

"No."

"Then let her spend the night with me."

He had reservations, but hell, she was right. Nia had to learn that she could be separated from him and nothing bad would happen. Susannah was trustworthy. And he'd be two minutes away if they needed him.

"She has to *want* to go," he stipulated.

"Help me convince her."

THE WOMEN had moved to the kitchen for a cup of tea, but they could see Nia through the doorway watching her program. Ryan had left to work for a few hours.

"Do you think she'll come?" Susannah asked Ryan's mother.

"If not this night, then another."

"I don't have too many more nights left here. I hate to leave Sitting Dog not knowing if she's going to be okay."

"Then stay," Annie suggested. "You're welcome to live in the cabin as long as you'd like."

"I appreciate that, but I've already made plans to drive to New York around Christmas."

"Plans can be changed. Is what's in New York so important?"

"Yes. Well, no. It's hard to explain."

Granted, the event itself wasn't that important. They'd been dropping the ball on New Year's Eve for years and would probably continue to do it for many more. But being able to see it represented the freedom Susannah had gained upon her mother's death, the freedom she wanted to protect.

Maybe that was being shallow and self-serving, but she feared the outcome if she changed her plans. That one concession might lead to another, then another, and pretty soon she'd be right back where she'd been originally, catering to the needs and desires of someone else.

"My leaving doesn't mean I don't care about Nia's welfare," she told Annie. "Please understand that."

"I do. Don't fret about it. Ryan explained about your mother and your role in looking after her."

"Nia means a great deal to me, and I'm worried about her."

Nana Sipsey nodded and said something in Cherokee mixed with English. Susannah only understood a little bit. *Heart* was one of the words. And something about many children.

"I didn't get all of that. What about children?"

"She says you worry because the child is already in your heart," Ryan's mother said. "But there's no need for concern. Nia will be happy again. Nana has burned the sacred tobacco. In the smoke she's seen the child surrounded by many others she'll call brother and sister, including two little ones with identical faces."

"She has visions?"

"Glimpses of what will come. I've never known her to be wrong."

Susannah swallowed hard. She wanted Nia to be well, but she hated imagining Ryan married and creating lots of babies with some other woman.

"No disrespect to Nana, but I'm not sure I believe in such things."

"You're young. In time, the truth will find you."

NIA DECIDED she *would* spend the night. They stopped by the barn, packed a suitcase with clothes and everything else she thought she'd need, which turned out to be enough that Ryan had to drive them over in the truck.

Dolls, toys, books... She even insisted on taking the cat, which meant they also had to make sure they brought her food and rigged up a temporary litter box.

Ryan found a discarded plant tray that would do if he taped over the drainage holes in the bottom.

They got everything inside the cabin and an area for Abigail squared away. Susannah warned him not to linger or make a fuss.

"Act like this is no big deal and Nia will, too."

"I'll try."

"'Night, you two," he called out. "Have fun."

"We will," Susannah said cheerily.

Nia was busy unpacking the ten million games she'd brought. She stopped and turned. "Daddy?"

Susannah held her breath. Beside her, Ryan had stiffened.

"Yes, goosey?"

"You forgot my kiss."

They both exhaled.

"You're right, I did. Come here."

She ran to him and he kissed her on the forehead.

"Now give one to Susannah."

Ryan gave Susannah a kiss on the forehead, too. His look said he'd like to give her a much better one and on the mouth.

"Rain check," she murmured.

He left quickly as promised. Susannah, deter-

mined to make this work, suggested she and Nia first
take their baths and get into their pajamas.

"Then we won't have to worry about doing that
when we're sleepy and ready to go to bed."

Nia took her bath, then Susannah. They had a tea
party with apple juice and popcorn and played some
of the child's favorite games.

As her bedtime approached, Nia got more restless.
Twice she went to the window and looked across to
the barn.

"Will Daddy be unhappy without me?" she
asked.

"He'll be fine. He's not far. See his light? If he's
feeling sad, he can walk over."

"And I can walk over there?"

"You could, but it would be such a nice present
if we left him alone to work. He very much wants
to finish the mosaic he's doing for the center."

"But if I get scared I can call him?"

"Of course you can. We'll put the phone right
here—" she set it on the corner of the table
"—where you can see it from the bed. And we'll
leave a light on. Okay?"

"Are you gonna sleep with me?"

"I sure am. I'm really tired." She wasn't, but if
her lying down made Nia feel better, she would.

They brushed their teeth and used the bathroom.

Nia said her prayers; noticeably absent was any mention of her mother, which Susannah thought strange.

They climbed into bed. Abigail immediately jumped up and settled at Susannah's feet. Cooper the bear lay tucked between them.

"Was Mary nicer to you at ballet? I saw all you girls giggling over something."

"She called me a baby. I told her she was an old poop head."

"That's one way to handle it."

"Iva laughed and then I did and then Mary did."

"Sounds like you're friends again. Sometimes kids say mean things to each other, but it's best to make up and not let it bother you."

"Did kids call you names when you was little?"

"Sometimes. One little boy used to call me 'carrot head' all the time."

"Did you get mad?"

"A little bit, but he was silly and I told him so."

She thought Nia would close her eyes then and go to sleep, but she wanted to talk a while. She told her about the other kids at school, the ones she liked and didn't and about one named Woody who put a snail on her milk carton.

"Boys are weird."

Susannah had to agree.

Nia yawned and rolled in her direction, resting her head on Susannah's shoulder. Once during the night she cried out, but didn't wake. Susannah held her close and rubbed her back.

Nana was right. This child was in her heart. And she would miss her terribly.

CHAPTER ELEVEN

RYAN PUT THE FOOD in his backpack and added two bottles of water. What else did they need? The video camera. He hurried to get it.

Susannah saw the bath towels he'd laid out and wrinkled her nose. "Why are we taking these?"

"So we can dry off at the pool."

"*Dry off?* Ryan, it's thirty-five degrees outside! We can't go swimming in this cold!"

"Where we're going it's warm."

"In the middle of the woods?"

"Yep." He wriggled his eyebrows. "And bathing suits are optional."

"This place isn't too far, is it?"

"Only forty-five minutes or so."

"Couldn't we do something a little less...outdoorsy?"

"You'll love this. I promise."

"A picnic in the snow and a dip in a pond in December?"

"That's right."

"Okay." She threw up her hands. "If you're willing, so am I."

Climbing the mountain, she kept up better than he'd thought she would and didn't complain. Not too much, anyway. A couple of times he stopped and took video of the scenery, always careful to include her.

"I understand why you're in such good shape," she said, resting a moment with her hands on her waist. "This kind of activity definitely keeps you slim."

"We're lucky the snow's almost melted. Let me know when you need a break and we'll stop."

"I'm fine. Don't get too far ahead, though. I have no idea where we are."

A while later he called a halt and they shared some of the water. He pulled her woolen cap down further on her ears.

"We're almost there."

They were playing hooky today, celebrating three things: Nia's staying at the cabin all night, Ryan's finishing the last of the tiling for the mosaic and Susannah's getting the cast off her wrist.

Nia was in school, and that meant he and Susannah could be alone for a little while. He also wanted to show her several places that were special to him.

First they went to the outcropping of rock that had given the community its name.

"Oh, gosh, it *does* look like a sitting dog," Susannah said. "And from below I never would've guessed how big it is."

"Estimating size is hard in the woods. What looks ten feet tall from far away can be a hundred feet when you get close. Same with distance. You can think you're a mile from something and you're really twenty miles."

"How tall would you guess the dog is? Sixty feet?"

"She's that easily."

"She? Rocks are females?"

"Grandfather said when he was a little boy *his* grandfather told him the legend of this place. Want to hear it?"

"You know I do."

"A wild dog—a wolf—disappeared during a hunt. His mate sat here waiting for him to return, but days and nights passed, then more days and nights. Obviously he'd been killed, but she wouldn't accept it. She said he'd only lost his way and she'd guide him home with her voice. Her long, forlorn howls could be heard with each rising of the moon. She died, looking out across the mountains, still waiting for the one she loved to come back to her. The spirit of the wind was so impressed with her devotion that it turned her into a large stone. Now she's a guide to all who might lose their way and the wind still carries her nightly cries."

"That's one of your sadder stories."

"I don't make them up. I only tell them."

She breathed in the air. "This is a lovely place. So quiet."

"Grandfather bought it years ago to preserve where his ancestors hid out during the removal. When he died, he left this part of the mountain to me. He said I was the only one in the family who truly appreciated it as much as he did."

"Your grandmother didn't mind?"

"No, she says we're all simply guests of the land, anyway."

They climbed out onto one of the rock's ledges and ate the cheese and bread he'd brought. After, he took her to the cave, a ten-minute hike. He crawled inside and helped her through the passage.

"Wait a minute while I get us some light." He struck a match and lit a kerosene lamp, then the torches in the wall holders.

"Oh!" Susannah walked around in amazement.

"My ancestors lived here for more than two years. I still have pieces of some of the skins they used and the arrow points. Come see this." He showed her the crudely drawn pictures and the handprints. "Here's the one for *Numma hi tsune ga*. His father's. My grandfather's. My father's. This is mine.''

"*Siquutsets,*" she read below it.

"My Indian name. Possum. Grandfather said as a baby I'd eat anything that didn't try to eat me first."

That made her chuckle. "I can believe that. I've seen you eat."

"He was of the *Ani Wahwa,* the wolf clan, once known as the warriors of the tribe. Long ago, members of a clan were like families and forbidden to marry each other. Most Cherokee don't know their clan affiliations today, but Grandfather still believed in the old ways. And even though he loved a girl, he wouldn't marry her because she was *Ani Wahwa.* He made a match with a stranger, a girl of the *Ani Wodi.* Her ancestors had made the red paint for war and religious ceremonies. They were also known for their ability to heal."

"So he and your grandmother didn't love each other when they got married?"

"No, but they came to in time."

"I'm glad about that. I'd hate to think Nana had a loveless marriage."

He took down the jar of dried ground clay and dipped his fingers in the dust.

"She says red is the color of a woman's power. Her ability to create life makes her superior to a man."

"I doubt many men would agree. Do you? Are women superior because they can give birth?"

"I believe a woman's ability to conceive makes her *special*. Neither sex is superior."

"A diplomatic answer."

"No, I'm being honest. Men and women have different strengths. Where one is weak, the other is strong. We were created that way on purpose. Conception may be a miracle, but the act that brings it about is commonplace, so I'd argue that the willingness to raise a child after its birth is more important than either conception or delivery."

"I agree with that."

He showed her the rest of the cave, the back room, the little basin of water suitable for washing utensils but not to drink.

"I keep a few supplies and wood for a fire," he explained. "I come here when I need to clear my head."

"You spend the night?"

"Sometimes. As a boy I spent a lot of nights here."

"Alone?" She shivered as if she had a chill. "I don't think I'd be brave enough for that."

"I always believed the souls of my ancestors watched over me."

Her eyes widened, and she glanced about with trepidation.

"They aren't here right now, are they?"

He laughed loudly, his voice echoing off the rock.

THE CREEK was high due to runoff from all the snowfall, and Susannah seemed nervous at crossing the narrow log bridge.

"I should admit I don't swim well, hardly at all. If I fall in, don't expect me to be able to save myself."

Ryan took her hand. "We'll cross together. I only see one icy patch. Step over it."

Despite her uneasiness, she went ahead, and they made it to the other side without incident. Upstream they climbed through rocks pushed to the surface by recent volcanic activity, "recent" meaning a few hundred thousand years ago.

The hot springs was another of his secret places, thirty minutes from the cave. Not even his siblings knew about this spot. Susannah laughed with delight when she saw the series of pools, steam rising from their surfaces.

"We can go in? The water isn't too hot?"

"The temperature's usually perfect, but since the water's heated by vents in the earth and they can be unpredictable, I'm careful to check first before I go in."

"Which should we try?"

"That one has the best depth for sitting and relaxing. The thermometer on the post over here tells me it's safe.''

They stayed in the pool for more than an hour, splashing, soaking, making love.

''Do you suppose your great-great-whatever-grandparents played like this?'' she asked, settling against his side.

''Probably.''

''I feel like I'm in our own little Garden of Eden.''

''Isn't this better than Paris?''

''Mm...different.'' She rubbed her hand across his naked chest and down his stomach to his groin. He inhaled as she teased him with her fingers.

''What has Paris got that my mountain doesn't?''

''The Eiffel Tower, cafés that serve real French onion soup, the River Seine...''

''Are those things really so important?''

''They are if you've never experienced them. I want to see and do everything I can while I'm still young enough.''

''So you keep reminding me.''

He climbed out of the pool, his joy in the day tarnished.

''Ryan?''

''Time to leave.''

''Are you mad at me?''

''Not mad. Disappointed.'' He grabbed a towel

and hastily began to dry off before the cold air chilled him.

She followed him out and sought her own towel.

"I don't understand why you're hell-bent on running all over the world when the best it has to offer you is right here," he said. "It's crazy."

"That's not fair! You've seen this world you say isn't as special as your mountain. I haven't. You get to fly places and visit clients all the time."

"Not anymore."

"But you used to before Nia got sick, and you will again when she's well. Plus, you've been to other countries. All I've ever done is drive through a few states."

They quickly hopped into their clothes.

"That's a minor problem. I could take you with me when I travel on business and we'll plan vacations anywhere you want to go."

"That sounds very much like a commitment."

"Maybe it is."

"Only a few days ago you weren't ready for one."

"Things can change in a few days."

"We hardly know each other."

"I know enough about you to be certain I don't want you walking out of my life in three weeks." He took a breath and tried to calm down. "Stay longer. Give us…six months. If you're not happy at the end of it and still want to go, I'll help you pack.''

"Ryan, I…'' She shook her head. ''I'm not ready for this. It's too soon.''

He clasped her by the shoulders. ''You're scared. I understand that. The last few years have been tough for you. But you can't keep running away from life.''

"I'm not. I'm *embracing* life.''

"Are you? How? By jumping off bridges? Susannah, real life isn't an adrenaline rush. It's ballet lessons…and playing the tooth fairy… It's sitting up with your spouse after the kids have gone to bed to talk about each other's day. Don't you want that? Don't you want to be part of a family again, to love and be loved?''

"Yes, someday. Maybe.''

He let his hands drop. ''Maybe?''

"The pain of Andrew's desertion and the memories of what I had to endure during my mother's illness are still too fresh for me to know what I want. That's my whole reason for traveling and seeing new things. Until my mother died I'd hardly ever been out of Georgia. My only experience living on my own had been the year away at college, and that was in the next state. You have a strong sense of who you are and what your place is on this planet. Who am I? What's my place?''

"I can't answer that for you."

"Which is my point. You're asking me to choose a life that might not be the right one for me."

"You won't know if it's right until you give it a fair chance."

"I won't know it's right until I see what else is out there."

"Do you hear yourself? You're talking about love by default, of settling for it only if you can't find something more exciting. Well, sorry, sweetheart, that's not the way it works. And I don't buy your flimsy excuse for running off. If you're really free, then you can decide to stay just as much as you can decide to go. You're letting that stupid list dictate what you do, and that's worse than being confused about what you want and who you are."

Fully dressed, he jerked up the backpack and headed out. She fell in behind him.

"I'm sorry," she said. "I don't want to hurt you."

"You're too damn late."

THEY WORKED in near silence the rest of the afternoon. Susannah felt miserable. Ryan would hardly look at her. He only spoke when she asked him a question.

She tried to apologize again, but he refused to discuss the issue anymore.

"I have work to do in back," he finally said, picking up a hammer and leaving.

Susannah slumped in the chair. What had started out as a lovely day was ruined and she didn't know how to fix it. She didn't want Ryan mad at her, but she also wasn't going to lie to him. Why did he have to push so hard? He was asking too much of her.

Clearly it would be best for both of them if she simply left, but how could she when she'd made promises she couldn't break?

Ryan expected her to join the family for the Winter Solstice celebration on December 22. Then there was the center dedication and community party on Christmas Eve when he'd unveil the mosaic. She didn't want to miss that.

Nia would be heartbroken if she didn't attend the ballet recital on the eighteenth or sew that costume. And Sandy Cummings was counting on her participation.

She also had to complete the basket she'd volunteered to make for the arts cooperative. And she couldn't leave without first making Christmas presents for the family.

Okay, she'd have to stick it out until the morning of December 25. Picking up the calendar, she counted the days. Twenty-one. Christmas was just three weeks from today.

She'd take the advice she'd given Nia yesterday

and act as if nothing had happened. Ryan couldn't stay mad at her forever.

He banged away with his hammer all afternoon, occasionally coming in to pick up tiles but not speaking even once.

When it was time to leave, Susannah walked to the door and poked her head inside. He was pounding at a stack of tile he'd wrapped in a sheet, breaking them into random pieces.

He noticed her and took off his safety glasses.

"What?"

"Nia wanted me to get her today so we could buy the material for her costume. Is that okay with you?"

"Fine."

"Are the three of us still going over to Bass and Helen's later?" Helen had come home from the hospital the day before with baby Maggie, and Nia wanted to see her. She'd been too young to go upstairs the night they'd driven to the hospital.

"If you still want to," Ryan said.

"I do. How about if I pick up some chicken on the way back? We can take it with us. I'll get enough for Helen and Bass."

"That's fine." He put down his hammer and reached for his wallet.

"I'll pay for it."

"No, you won't." He came to the door and tried to hand her several bills.

"I said I'll get it."

"Take the money."

"No, I've got money."

They argued back and forth until he shook his head. "Damn, you can be downright stubborn at times," he said, a hint of a smile on his lips.

"No more than you."

"Will you take the damn money?"

"Only if you give me a kiss and tell me you don't hate me."

"You know I don't hate you, Susannah. I wouldn't be so pissed off if I hated you. That's my problem."

"Ryan, please don't be mad. We have so little time left together. I can't bear the thought of us spending it arguing."

He sighed deeply and nodded. "You're right. I'm sorry I lost my temper."

"And I'm sorry I made you lose it. Can we please not fight about this?"

"Come here." He took hold of her shirt and pulled her into his arms. He kissed her deeply and lovingly. "I want you to be happy. Go wherever you feel you have to. See all those places you've dreamed about. I promise I won't try to make you stay."

''Thank you.''

She should've been glad, but for some reason she felt even more miserable than before.

THE BABY WAS as cute as Susannah remembered and Helen seemed to be recovering well.

Nia found the infant fascinating. She'd been warned by her daddy not to touch it, but that didn't stop her from standing by the bassinet and gazing at Maggie with wonder while she slept.

She drove Helen crazy asking questions. What did she eat? Why were her fingernails so little? Why did she have a bandage on her belly button? Did she have a boo boo?

Bass teased her and said they'd found Maggie growing in a pumpkin patch. The place on her stomach was where she'd been attached to the plant.

As if she'd been slapped, Nia burst into tears and ran to Ryan, crawling into his lap for consolation.

''Hey, what is it?'' Nia didn't answer, only sobbed harder. Susannah tried to comfort her. She pushed her hand away.

''Honestly, Bass,'' Helen scolded. ''Did you have to upset the child?''

''What did I say?''

Their voices and Nia's crying woke the baby. Helen picked her up and walked about, trying to soothe her.

"Nia, honey," she said gently, pacing back and forth, "Uncle Bass was only teasing. Maggie didn't grow on a pumpkin. You remember me showing you my big tummy and telling you the baby was inside?"

Her cries dwindled to sniffles.

"You put your hand there and felt the baby moving around. Remember?"

Nia nodded hesitantly.

"Hey, kiddo, I'm sorry," Bass told her. "I didn't mean to make you cry. I was only playing with you. We didn't find Maggie. Helen and I made her."

"How?" Nia wanted to know.

"Uh, with sugar and spice and everything nice."

"Will she melt?" Her bottom lip trembled.

"Oh, Bass," Helen said, clearly exasperated. She told Nia, "With love, honey. Bass and I made Maggie with love. And that means she'll always be here."

The baby finally stopped crying and immediately began rooting for a nipple.

"She's hungry," Helen said. "Let me go feed her and put her to bed."

Susannah and Ryan stayed another hour and then came home and put Nia to bed, as well. She'd been strangely subdued since her crying spell.

"That was all a bit unnerving," Susannah said when she'd fallen asleep and Ryan had returned to the den. "Why would Bass's joke have gotten her so upset?"

"She told me it wasn't right for people to take babies away. I think she believed they'd found Maggie and decided to keep her."

"I guess when you're six, childbirth is a confusing concept."

"No kidding. You should've heard her asking me questions about how Bass and Helen made the baby."

"What did you tell her?"

"I more or less repeated what Helen said, that sometimes a man and woman can love each other so much that a baby is the result."

"That satisfied her?"

"Yeah, except she turned around and asked me if I'd loved her mother, which threw me for a loop. I didn't know what to say. I'd just told her babies were conceived with love so I didn't want her to think she *wasn't*."

"How did you handle it?"

"I told her I loved her mother in my own way."

"You did the right thing. She was looking for reassurance and you gave it to her, but you didn't lie."

"When she's older, she'll understand my relationship with Carla better. Hell, when I'm older maybe I will, too."

"What do you mean?"

"Nothing. I'm tired and talking crazy. I worked too late last night."

He stretched out on the couch on his stomach and laid his head on her thigh. She rubbed his back while he talked to her, telling about the first time he'd seen Nia.

"She was ugly as sin. Blotchy red. No hair whatsoever."

"And you loved her on sight."

"Yeah, I did. Amazing, isn't it, how something so tiny can have so much power over you? Until I brought Nia home, I didn't realize how much I could love someone. I mean, I love my mother and my family, but when it's your kid... Hell, listen to me. I sound like some old sap."

"I don't think so. There's something incredibly sexy about a man who can have so much devotion to a child."

She ran her fingers through his luxurious hair.

"Mm, that feels good." He yawned twice in rapid succession.

A few minutes later, his breathing deepened and he dropped off to sleep. Susannah didn't disturb him but continued to touch his back and head, enjoying the intimacy of it.

This was what he'd meant by "real" life, a man and woman talking at the end of the day, taking comfort in being with each other, sharing both the good and bad. She had to admit it was nice.

She looked up. Nia stood in the doorway.

"I wet my bed," she said.

Susannah sighed to herself.

This, too, was real life.

CHAPTER TWELVE

IF TIME WAS a constant thing, Susannah wondered why it suddenly seemed to move so swiftly.

When she was a child, the days leading up to Christmas had passed with excruciating slowness. She'd counted them off and dreamed of Santa coming and what he'd leave under the tree. But now they raced by. Two weeks felt like two days.

The flurry of activity was one reason. She hardly had time to breathe. The Whitepaths went all out in celebrating Christmas and the Winter Solstice.

Decorations, entertaining friends, preparing their handmade presents—every moment brought something else to do, including many unusual things she'd never experienced before.

She enjoyed creating the "wishing tree" with its bits of paper in the shape of leaves on which everyone wrote their wishes. *Peace,* she'd written on her leaf, but secretly she'd been more selfish and wished for happiness.

One night the community held a giveaway, where

each family brought a gift and people competed for them with songs, dances and games.

Susannah had never been much of a baker. The best she could do was a store-bought brownie mix now and then. So she didn't volunteer to help with the numerous cakes, breads and desserts the women prepared, but she did have a knack for creating something out of nothing.

With Nia's eager assistance, she gathered fir boughs and other plant materials, attached plaid ribbons and pinecones. They decorated the house, barn and cabin, inside and out. Electric candles and colored lights gave everything a warm old-fashioned look.

Ryan said the idea was to make it seem as if they were outdoors, and Susannah felt she'd accomplished that.

Before she could believe it, the night of the dance recital arrived. Nervous to her toes, she nonetheless went out on the floor, determined to enjoy herself.

When she'd dreamed of dancing in a ballet, she'd had much higher aspirations than this, but she couldn't imagine a professional ballerina having more fun than she did that night.

"I wish we got to dance again," Nia said the next morning.

"So do I. But you'll have other recitals."

"I had the prettiest costume. Everybody said so."

"Did they?" The comment made Susannah proud. She'd worked hard to put it together.

"Whatcha doin'?"

"Sending out some invoices for your daddy."

"Huh?"

"Business things. Making sure everybody pays what they owe your daddy for the work he's done."

"Can I play on the computer?"

"No, not right now. I'm using it."

Out of school for the holidays, Nia had nothing to keep her occupied, so she'd come down to the workshop to be with her and Ryan.

She'd been chattering all morning and Susannah was her captive audience. Ryan had left a while ago to finish grouting the last of the tiles for the center dedication.

"Why don't you go outside and play? The sun's shining, and with your gloves and cap on you'll be warm enough."

"I want to stay in here with you."

"Okay, it was just a thought. Why don't you watch a video or play with your dolls?"

"You said you'd help me wrap my present for Daddy."

"I'll help you later. Right now I need to do this."

She put Nia at one of the tables with crayons and paper and told her to draw, but that didn't last. Her attention span today was only fifteen minutes.

"Will you play a game with me?"

"No, honey, I can't. Not right now. I have things I need to get done so your daddy won't have to worry about them after…"

After I'm gone. She couldn't say it out loud, not just because it upset Nia to be reminded that she was going away, but because Susannah's heart ached so badly whenever she thought about it.

The pain would pass; she was certain of it. Once she got to New York amid all the New Year's Eve revelers, she'd be her old self. She'd drop all this useless sentimentality.

And Nia would be fine, too. She probably wouldn't even remember her in a couple of months.

"I wanna wrap Daddy's present."

Susannah blew out a breath and rubbed her temples, where a headache had started to pound. The child was bored. She couldn't fault her for being a little irritating this morning but wished she'd find some way to entertain herself.

"Let me print out the rest of these statements and then I'll stop and help you wrap your gift. But you have to promise to sit there and draw quietly for ten minutes. Can you do it?"

"How long is that?"

Susannah got the timer Ryan sometimes used when he dipped tiles in a chemical bath.

"When the time is up, it makes a noise." She

demonstrated for Nia how it worked, showing her the big hand moving around the dial and counting off one minute.

Nia put her hands over her ears when the buzzer sounded. "That was loud."

"Now I'm going to set it for ten minutes. That's ten times as long as before, so don't get antsy. Think you can be quiet and work on your picture that long?" Nia nodded. "Okay, here we go. No talking or bumping the table or anything until you hear the noise."

Susannah was able to finish the printing before the timer wound down.

"I did it!" Nia yelled.

Susannah took her upstairs and told her to get the gift while she found wrapping paper, tape and scissors.

Nia was excited about the little flannel pouch filled with rocks she planned to give Ryan. She'd collected them a couple of weeks ago during their excursion for fir branches and decorating materials. Ryan sometimes used pebbles and broken china in his mosaics. Nia thought her rocks would be a perfect present.

Susannah had made the pouch out of leftover felt from Nia's costume and a cord drawstring.

"Susannah!" She ran into the den. "I can't find them."

"Look in the drawer of your bedside table. That's where we put them."

"I did."

"They have to be there."

But they weren't. They weren't anywhere. Susannah looked in every conceivable spot in the child's room—the drawers, the closet, under the bed, through her toy chest. She didn't find them in her backpack or under the tree with the rest of the gifts.

"I don't understand it. They didn't grow legs and walk out of here. Did you take them to school or to Gran's?"

"Uh-uh." She looked like she was going to cry. "Now I don't got a present for Daddy."

"Oh, now, don't worry. We'll find them."

Susannah searched every crook and cranny in the loft and still came up empty-handed. One day, months from now, the rocks would probably show up in the pocket of a jumper, but for now they weren't anywhere to be found.

"I was bad," Nia said, letting out the first pitiful sob. "The Little People came and got my rocks 'cause I forgot to leave them somethin'."

"I'm sure that's not it."

But Nia persisted and couldn't be consoled.

Susannah felt so sorry for her, she was almost in tears herself. She held her. "Stop crying, okay?

We'll go find some more pretty rocks for your daddy.''

"Now?"

"Yes, now. We'll do it before he gets back. Go wash your face and blow your nose."

Susannah got their coats. She put a ten in the petty cash box and took out a roll of quarters. These were going to be some expensive rocks.

When they'd bundled up with extra sweaters, scarves, caps, gloves and boots, they set out. Last time, during their excursion into the woods, they'd gone down the driveway. This time they headed the other way, taking a horizontal line from the house.

"There's some over here," Nia said. "I've seen them." She picked up a few, but wasn't happy with them. "I want pretty ones."

"Those looked nice to me."

"Over this way."

"Wait. We can't go too far."

"I know a good place. Daddy and I go sometimes to get blackberries in the summer."

They took what appeared to be a trail, climbing for a short spell and then going downhill again.

"How far is it?"

"Up there."

The terrain got steeper. "Nia, honey, this doesn't look safe. Take my hand and let's go back. We can find plenty of rocks closer to the house."

They backtracked, following their footprints until they came to a spot where the trees were so thick the snow covered the ground only in patches. Here there were no footprints to follow.

"This way," Nia said, pulling her to the left.

"Are you sure? I thought we came up by that big oak."

They walked for a few minutes, until Susannah stopped. "This doesn't look right," she said, but she wasn't sure. It *could* be.

"Are you positive this is the way we came?" she asked Nia.

"Mm, maybe it's that way."

Great.

They backtracked again, but she couldn't find the oak. Were they above the house or below it? It was impossible to tell. The hardwood trees were leafless, but the pines and other evergreens formed a canopy. Through them, the only thing Susannah could see was a patch of sky.

A rustling in the bushes startled them both. Whatever was out there was big.

"Nia, honey, come with me. Quietly now. This way."

Hurriedly they went in the other direction. The animal might only have been a deer, but Susannah wasn't taking any chances.

"Are we lost?" Nia asked.

"Oh, no, we're not lost. We simply got turned around. I think I know the way now."

"What about getting my rocks?"

"I see a pretty one over there."

Nia picked it up, decided it would do and asked Susannah to leave one of the quarters.

"Let's see what's over here," Susannah told her once the quarter had been carefully placed on the ground. She decided to head downhill. If they missed the house they'd eventually run into the road. Wouldn't they?

They started, but soon found themselves climbing. The problem was that you had to take a circuitous path to get anywhere. You couldn't go straight up or straight down because of boulders and stands of trees too thick to pass through. Sometimes when it seemed you were going downhill, it turned out only to be the side of a ravine.

Nia selected another rock, and then another. Susannah dutifully left a quarter for each.

After an hour, she stopped so Nia could rest.

She tried to remain calm for the child's sake, but they were in trouble. She checked her watch. After two o'clock. They'd been gone more than three hours. Nia was tired and cold.

Why hadn't she told Annie where they were going? Or called Ryan before they left? Stupid, stupid, stupid! He'd warned her about straying too far from the house. She'd been irresponsible and put both Nia's life and her own in danger.

She tried to figure out what to do. Bass had told her a story the other night about two hikers getting lost in the isolated Snowbird backcountry. They'd used their cell phone to guide the rescue helicopter.

But she didn't have a cell phone. And Ryan had taken his to the center. Those lost hikers had been wise enough to carry supplies. She didn't have matches or even water.

"I'm hungry," Nia said. "And thirsty."

Susannah didn't have anything in her pockets but rocks and a handful of quarters.

"I'm sorry, baby, but we'll be home soon." She took off a glove and scooped up some snow. "Put a little of this in your mouth and let it melt."

If this was summer, she'd stay put and wait. Their chances of surviving until help came would've been good. But night would fall by about four-thirty. And Ryan might not even miss them until much later than that. She had no idea how long he planned to work.

They had to keep moving, to somehow find their way home.

She coaxed Nia into getting up. A sound drew her forward, but she couldn't be certain she was moving toward it or hearing an echo. Rushing water. She saw it now through the trees, a creek and a small waterfall.

She didn't know if it was the same creek she and Ryan had crossed during their hike two weeks ago. Anyway, that information wouldn't help her. She still didn't know which way to go to find the house.

"Can I drink the water?" Nia asked as they approached it.

"No, we'd better not. Sometimes water in the woods has bacteria in it and can make you sick."

"But I'm thirsty," she whined, growing more impatient.

"I know. I am, too. We'll eat more snow."

As before, she knelt, took off her glove and began raking down to a cleaner layer.

"Susannah, I see a pretty gold rock."

"Okay, honey."

If she only had something to scoop with, Nia could crunch the snow as if she were eating it from a cone. She pulled a piece of bark from a nearby tree and found it worked pretty well.

"Try this." Holding the bark piled with snow, she stood and looked up—and lost her breath. Nia had walked out onto rocks in the stream and was bent over the water, reaching for something. "Oh, Nia, no!" She tried to keep panic out of her voice. "Don't move!"

As quickly as she could, Susannah ran toward her.

"But I've almost got it...." Nia said, leaning farther.

"No, don't. You'll—"

Nia's scream as she fell into the water was like a knife in Susannah's heart. She plunged in after her. The shock of the cold was nearly unbearable.

The water was swift. Nia couldn't stand up and was being pulled downstream.

With every ounce of strength Susannah had, she raced after Nia, twice going under before she struggled back to the surface.

Nia grabbed hold of a thin branch hanging over the water and held on, but Susannah knew she couldn't do it for long. Even now, her own limbs and hands were numb with cold.

Finally, she reached her. She crawled onto the bank, dragging Nia behind her by the back of her coat. Violent tremors shook them both. With no shelter and no dry clothes, they had little chance of survival.

"Oh, God!" Susannah cried. "Please let me save this child."

"Sus-ann-ah." Nia tried to say more but had trouble getting it out through her chattering teeth. Susannah realized she was trying to tell her she was sorry.

"Oh, baby, it wasn't your fault," she sobbed. "I'm to blame."

She refused to let this child she loved die. She had to get her bearings and find the house. If only she could see above the trees.

"Lie still and don't move. I'll be right back."

Twice she tried to climb a tree, but her legs didn't want to cooperate. She railed at the heavens, asking for help. On the third attempt, she had better success. The twenty feet she shimmied up the branches didn't allow her to see much, but it was enough.

She'd spotted the sitting dog. And it wasn't too far above them.

SHE CARRIED Nia, forcing her legs to keep moving. The cave, she remembered, was a short walk from the rock. Ryan had matches there and firewood. If she could find it, they'd be all right.

Each step was agonizing. She felt herself drifting off, wanting to stop and rest, but fear, guilt—and love—kept her going.

She found the boards and the brush Ryan had placed over the hidden entrance and threw them aside. She ended up dragging Nia in behind her; the child was too limp to stand.

Nia's trembling had stopped and that scared Susannah. Her body had gone beyond trying to shake off the cold. She had to get the fire started and Nia out of her wet clothes.

The lantern lit easily. She didn't waste time on

the torches, but worked feverishly to get the fire going, every minute that passed feeling like an eternity.

The wood caught fire and began to burn. She stripped Nia of everything and covered her with a blanket she found in Ryan's cache of supplies.

"Come on, baby, stay awake. Nia?" The girl's eyes blinked open. "That's it. Don't go to sleep."

She stripped out of her own clothes and wrapped herself in a second blanket. Kneeling at Nia's legs, she began to rub them briskly with her palms, trying to warm the skin and bring back the circulation.

Every few minutes she'd add more wood to the fire, then rush back and begin rubbing Nia's chilled body again.

Susannah lay down next to her and used what was left of her own body heat to try to warm her.

"Are we gonna die?" Nia whispered, her voice so hoarse she could barely speak.

"No," Susannah told her. "Your ancestors will watch over us."

"SUSANNAH? NIA?"

They weren't in the workshop or upstairs. Ryan went over to the cabin, and although Susannah's truck was there, he didn't get an answer at the door.

He walked back to the barn and dialed the house. His mother hadn't seen them.

"Did they leave a note?" she asked.

"No, I didn't find one. And they've apparently been gone all afternoon because I've called three or four times and left messages. Susannah never returned the calls."

"Maybe they caught a ride over to Helen's."

Unlikely, but he tried anyway. Helen hadn't heard from them.

He called everyone Susannah knew—the ladies from the arts cooperative, John and Bitsy Taylor, Sandy Cummings, Nia's friends. No one had seen either of them.

"Joe." Maybe he'd come by and taken them to town. He caught his brother at his shop.

"Sorry, I haven't seen them since last night."

"I don't like this. Susannah's truck is here. Unless they went off with someone, that leaves only one possibility. And it's nearly dark."

"Get in touch with Bass. I'm on my way."

SUSANNAH WILLED herself not to fall asleep, but it was hard. The drowsiness was like a shroud that kept wanting to wrap her in a warm embrace.

"Must stay awake," she chanted to herself over and over. She stoked the fire again and felt Nia's arms and legs. The color had returned to them and she seemed warmer.

She lit the torches so she could see Ryan's supplies. No food, but she found a small metal boiler and a tin cup.

Nia needed hot liquid. Susannah could use the boiler to melt snow.

She couldn't put on her clothes again until they dried and she couldn't risk getting the blanket wet. She crawled through the opening naked, hastily raked snow into the pan and crawled back inside.

When the liquid was hot, she tested it and poured it in the cup. Propping Nia up, she helped her take tiny sips.

"This will make you feel better. That's right. Drink it all down. Are you feeling warmer?"

"Uh-huh."

Thank God she'd been able to get them here so quickly. Had the cave been another ten minutes away—well, she didn't want to think about that.

She took some of the firewood, stacked it on the other side of the fire and laid their clothes on top to dry. She unbraided Nia's hair so it, too, would dry.

Three more times, Susannah crawled out and got snow to heat. She made Nia drink every drop of the hot liquid.

"How do your toes feel? Wriggle them for me. And your fingers?" They seemed to be working okay.

"I wanna go home."

"I do, too, sweetheart, but we can't yet. We don't

have any warm clothes and it's going to be dark soon.''

That had been the wrong thing to say. The dark scared her. She cried for her daddy, for her grandmother and Nana. Susannah rocked her in her arms.

''We'll be fine. I promise. Daddy will find us.''

Nia's breathing became more erratic, escalating until she began to gasp. She seemed on the verge of a panic attack and Susannah had no way of getting help.

Tears streamed down both their faces. She tried to calm the child by rocking her and talking to her gently.

''Nia, put on my magic ring.'' She slipped it off the chain. ''Remember, it gives you courage. Nothing can hurt you as long as you're wearing it.''

She told her stories, about how the redbird got its color, about bat and mouse and why possum had no hair on its tail. Slowly, Nia's breathing eased.

''Do you know that Possum is your daddy's Indian name? Has he ever brought you to this place? Did you know about it?''

Nia shook her head.

Susannah told her the story of her ancestors, about the little boy named Whitepath who had been born in this cave and had lived here with his mother and father.

''His handprint is on the wall over here, along

with your daddy's, his daddy's and even his grand-daddy's. Would you like to see? Keep your blanket wrapped tightly around you.''

Susannah brought the lantern and held it up to the wall. The flames of the fire cast dancing shadows on the pictures.

"See, here's the little boy's. And here's your daddy's.''

"It's too small.''

"That's because he put it here when he was a little boy. One day your handprint will be here, too.''

"No, it won't," she said.

"Yes, it will. Every time a child is born in your family they get to put their handprint on the wall. Uncle Joe and Uncle Charlie's are here and Aunt Anita's. You're next.''

She hung her head. "I bet Daddy won't let me," she whispered.

"Why on earth would you think that?''

She looked up at Susannah with the most devastated expression she'd ever seen on a child.

"Because I'm not really his little girl.''

CHAPTER THIRTEEN

BASS QUICKLY brought in search parties of deputies, rescue squad members and volunteers, but darkness fell before they could get organized. He wouldn't let anyone go out.

Ryan went ballistic. He ranted and cursed him.

"Dammit, Bass! We can't leave them overnight in this weather! They'll die!"

"I've got a helicopter in the air with spotlights and as soon as they see something, we'll make a rescue, but I'm not sending people out to stumble around in the dark. You know that's not the way. Now, calm down."

"If it was your wife and daughter out there—"

"I wouldn't do a damn thing differently and you know it."

Joe pulled him back. "Ryan, come on. He'll move heaven and earth to find them."

Ryan felt shamed by his actions. Bascombe Miller had been his best friend all his life. He loved Nia like his own.

He nearly broke down. "I'm sorry, Bass. I just feel so useless. If anything happens to them…"

Bass put one hand on his shoulder. "The best thing you can do right now is help me do my job. You know this mountain better than anyone. When the helo spots them, we have to be ready to move. We need you to lead us. Stay strong."

Ryan steeled his courage and nodded.

"We'll find them," Joe said. "Now help me calm Mom and Nana. They're insane with worry."

"Nia, I don't understand what you're saying."

"I'm not his little girl."

Susannah knelt and took her by the arms. "Honey, what makes you think that?"

"I heard Mommy tell the man in the black dress. He came to help her go to heaven."

A man in a…? The priest. Carla had wanted to die at home in her own bed, according to Ryan. She must have asked for the priest to hear her confession.

"I wasn't supposed to be in there," Nia said, "but I forgot Cooper. I sneaked in her room to get him."

"What did you hear your mother tell the man in the black dress?"

"She said Daddy wasn't my real daddy, but he'd be good to me."

Oh, Lord! For months this poor child had gone through the anguish of believing she didn't belong to the one person she cared for the most.

Could she be right? And if so, did Ryan know?

"Don't tell him I'm not *Tsalagi*," Nia pleaded.

Now Susannah understood fully. Nia reasoned that if she wasn't Ryan's child, she wasn't Cherokee. And if he found that out, he might not want her.

How tragic that Ryan's strong pride in his heritage had caused such pain for his daughter.

"Nia, come over here and sit down. I want to talk to you." They crossed back to the fire. "Cover up. That's good. Not too long ago, your daddy told me a story. He said the first time he saw you he thought you were the most special thing on earth. He knew he'd love you forever and ever."

"Like Uncle Bass loves Maggie?"

"Exactly like that."

"But she's his real little girl. He has to."

"Well, daddies do love their real little girls. That's true. But they can also love little girls who aren't theirs. Uncle Bass and Aunt Helen are going to adopt a child. Do you know what adopt means?"

"A little boy or girl don't got a mommy or daddy?"

"Mm, that's close enough. Bass and Helen will be the mommy and daddy. And they'll love that child just as much as Maggie. You don't have to be people's real little girl for them to love you.''

''Daddy loves me.''

''Yes, he does and he will, no matter what. You see, love doesn't depend on whether you're born to someone or not, or even if you're *Tsalagi* or white. Love is just the way you feel.''

Sometimes, Susannah realized, it could even happen when it was the last thing you were looking for.

''Now, let's lie down and try to rest.'' She covered Nia and lay with one arm around her.

''Susannah?''

''Yes, baby?''

''I love *you.*''

She stroked Nia's head and shed silent tears. ''I love you, too.''

THROUGHOUT THE NIGHT, more and more people arrived as word spread, neighbors wanting to join the search party, women bringing hot coffee and food for the searchers.

Using the house as the center, the helicopter made an ever widening circle, but hour after hour passed with no news. Expressions turned grim. Ryan started hearing words like *hopeless* and *impossible*.

Helen had come over with the baby and was holding vigil with his mother and grandmother at the house. He was thankful for that. He couldn't deal with them right now, couldn't pretend everything was going to be okay.

He thought about calling Anita, but she was supposed to be home tomorrow anyway. No use getting her up in the middle of the night.

Charlie, Barbara and the kids were scheduled to arrive the day after and stay through Christmas. If the news was bad, he'd call them tomorrow.

But he couldn't think about that now. He couldn't allow his faith to waver. Like Bass said, he had to stay strong.

A MOURNFUL HOWL startled Susannah in the night. She wondered if she'd dreamed it. Or perhaps the sitting dog was calling for her mate.

Again she heard it. Low, sorrowful.

She put more wood on the fire and checked to make sure the barrier she'd erected over the entry was secure. The dark she could handle, but wild animals were something else.

Nia had finally fallen asleep. Susannah hoped she'd stay that way until morning.

She had no idea of the time. Her watch had gotten water in it and stopped. But their clothes had dried, with the exception of their coats, and being able to dress again had made them both feel safer, somehow.

The cave was warm. The ground was hard, difficult to sleep on, but she could stand it. Before dark, she'd gathered enough snow and melted drinking water in case they needed it during the night.

Nothing would stop the growl of hunger in her belly, but help would surely come in the morning. It *had* to come. The wood was running out. They didn't have enough for another night.

She could chance finding her way down the mountain tomorrow. Or she might have to risk their remaining wood on an outside fire where searchers would be more likely to see the smoke.

How many days, she wondered, could they survive here without food?

She lay down, exhausted and afraid, at Nia's back and pulled the blanket over the child's shoulders. The smoke curled upward and out the hole in the rock above and she watched its lazy journey until her lids began to get heavy.

Ryan had told her once that fire was a messenger and that smoke carried your prayers where they were supposed to go.

She wanted to believe it. Right now she *needed* to believe it.

"If you're listening up there," she whispered, "this is Susannah. And I have a favor to ask...."

DAWN BROKE. Search teams of men from Sitting Dog and Robbinsville started a grid-by-grid search of the mountain. John Taylor from the store, accompanied by ten men, headed east. Joe and his group took the area from the house down to the road. Bass and his party headed for the slope to the west.

Ryan felt it unlikely Susannah and Nia had gone up the mountain, but he couldn't be sure. He knew the top reaches better than anyone, so he led a group of five men and made a quick sweep above the house.

Bass told them that if they didn't find signs they should break up and join the searchers to the east and west.

They were twenty minutes out when one of the sheriff's deputies called to him from his right.

"Mr. Whitepath?"

"Yeah?"

"What do you make of this?"

Ryan rushed over. The man handed him a quarter. "I found it here by this rock. And look, there's another one. And a third."

"Paying the Little People," Ryan muttered.

"Who?"

"My daughter," he said, getting excited. "She's been here."

"SUSANNAH!" The voice called from far away.

"I'm coming, Mama."

She sat up, rubbing the sleep from her eyes and fighting the fog that clouded her mind.

For a moment she thought she was home, back in her old room and the call of her name had come from the adjoining bedroom.

"Susannah!"

There it was again. This time she shot up straight. The woods. The water. The cave. She realized where she was.

"Susannah!"

That voice! That gloriously wonderful voice.

"Ryan! Ryan, in here!" Hurriedly, she put on her boots and began clawing at the timbers blocking the passage. "We're in here!"

"Susannah?"

"Yes, yes, we're here. Oh, Ryan!"

He was working as frantically from the other side as she was from hers. Nia woke. She began echoing Susannah's cries, calling out for her daddy.

Ryan pushed through the barrier and took Susannah into his arms. Nia ran to him and he bent and scooped her up.

"Are you all right? Are you hurt?"

Susannah was so overwhelmed she burst into tears. Words came pouring out. "We were looking for rocks and we got lost, and I thought we were going the right way, but we weren't and there was a bear or something so we ran away and then Nia fell into the water and got wet and I didn't know what else to do and I remembered the sitting dog and thank God I found the cave or we would have died and—''

"Hush, you're safe now. You're both safe."

"Ryan?" Bass called from outside. "I've got a paramedic team here."

Ryan crawled out first and led Nia. Susannah followed. Someone threw a shiny blanket around her shoulders and began taking her pulse and asking her questions.

"I'm okay. Take care of Nia."

"She's in good hands. Don't worry."

Looking past the man's shoulder, she saw the child held in the safety of her father's arms.

"Yes, you're right about that."

ASIDE FROM a few cuts and bruises, Susannah was fine.

Nia didn't seem to have suffered any ill effects from her night on the mountain, but the hospital in Andrews wanted to keep her a few hours for observation and to bring her body temperature up a few degrees, back to normal.

She was still in the emergency room, having an X ray made of her chest.

"Let me have Joe drive you home," Ryan told

Susannah as they waited in the hall. "You look beat."

"I want to stay."

He took her hand and held on tightly. "Okay."

"Did you call your mother? She'll be worried."

"When I got your coffee and sandwich."

She thought about her harrowing experience and wanted to cry all over again. But mostly, she wanted to cry for Ryan, for the thing she had to tell him.

"People know about your cave now," she said. "Will that be a problem?"

"I don't think so. Except for Bass, they thought it was a bear cave. And not even he's been inside."

"Why not? I thought that as boys the two of you probably spent a lot of time there."

"No, only me. The cave is for our family."

"But you took *me* there."

"And why do you think I did that?"

"I don't know. Until this moment, I didn't realize I was so privileged."

"Maybe you should give it some thought."

"I will, but right now I have something…I need to tell you some things. They're important."

"I'm listening."

"First, I'm sorry. My irresponsibility nearly got Nia killed. I should never have taken her into the woods."

"Beating yourself up over it now won't help."

"I don't understand why you aren't angry."

"I guess I should be, but I'm so relieved you're both okay that being angry seems counterproductive. Besides, Nia told me what you did for her, how she fell in the water and you jumped in after her. I know you don't swim well."

"That never crossed my mind. All I could think of was that she'd drown if I didn't get to her."

"I know how well you took care of her at the cave, too. She said you heated water for her and kept her warm. The walking around naked part tickled her a bit. I'd like to have seen that myself."

Across the corridor on the other bench, Joe overheard and laughed.

"Could you find a nurse to flirt with while your brother and I have a private chat?" Susannah asked him.

"Yeah, I can do that." He got up and started to walk away.

"Hey, Joe," she called after him. He turned. "Ryan said you stayed with him all night and led a search party to look for us this morning. Thank you."

"No problem. Glad you're okay." He ambled off.

"What was I saying? Oh, at the time, being naked wasn't very funny. I heard the sitting dog, I think. I heard *something* howl. I thought it might try to come into the cave."

"A red wolf maybe. Once they were nearly hunted to extinction, but they've been reintroduced into the mountains in recent years. It's unusual to hear one, though."

"The whole night was unusual. I asked the fire to send my prayers to the sky."

"And it was the smoke that led me to you."

"You saw it?"

"No, the haze obscured it, but I smelled it on the wind. I knew that if you had fire you could only be in one place."

She couldn't believe it.

"I hoped you'd think to look for us there."

He told her about finding her quarters and knowing he was heading in the right direction. "But I was afraid you might be hurt. The woods are full of wild Russian boar and they can be aggressive."

"Physically, I was fine, but emotionally I wasn't doing too well. I never want to go through another night like that."

"Nia said you told her stories about the animals to keep her from being afraid. You've learned well, *To tsu hwa*. You make a good Cherokee."

"A redheaded, white-skinned, freckle-faced, blue-eyed Cherokee. Now, that's one for the record books."

"What makes you Cherokee isn't here." He rubbed his fingers across the pale skin of her palm.

"What makes you Cherokee is in here." He placed her palm against her heart.

"Is that really true?"

"Yes. It's not the blood that makes you *Tsalagi* but the practice of the ways of our tribe."

"Your daughter needs to understand that."

"She does understand."

"No, she doesn't. Let's step outside where we won't be overheard. There's something you should know, and it may be the hardest thing you ever have to hear."

RYAN SANK DOWN on the concrete wall as Susannah delivered her news, his legs unable to support him.

"Do you know for certain she's your biological daughter?" Susannah asked.

"She's not."

She, too, sat down. "I wasn't sure if it was true, and whether or not you knew. I've been in agony all night, wondering how I was going to break the news to you."

"I've known almost from the beginning. But it never mattered. In every way that counts, she's my child."

"Does your family know?"

"No, well…" He hesitated. "Not Mom or my brothers and sister. Nana I'm not sure about. I've never come out and told her, but she has an uncanny way of knowing things."

"I'm catching on to that."

"My arrangement with Carla was that I'd raise Nia as my own, but she could never tell anyone the truth. I felt it was better not to mention it to my own family, in case they let something slip to Nia."

"The father? Who is he?"

"He was her lover before me, an English businessman she met through her job at the gallery. He already had a wife and three children. When she called him and said she was pregnant, that the child might be his, he told her to get rid of it and not bother him again. But she was Catholic. And she couldn't be sure which of us was the father until Nia was born."

"You had blood tests after her birth?"

"Yes, but by then I no longer cared about the results. Carla said she'd put the baby up for adoption, but I couldn't let her. I'd been abandoned in a way by my own father. I wasn't a child at the time, but I remembered the hurt of knowing he didn't want to be with us."

"I know that pain is still with you."

"That little baby deserved better. I had Carla list me as the father on the birth certificate and I agreed to raise her."

"Nia's hurting. She's been afraid you'd find out

she's not your blood child, not *Tsalagi*, and wouldn't want her.''

"Had I known this was causing her problems... Not once in all these months did it occur to me that she might have learned the truth.''

"She never would have if she hadn't overheard Carla's confession.''

"What should I do?''

"I don't know. You should talk to Dr. Thompson about this.''

"I will, but Nia opened up to you, not the therapist. In fact, her doctor was so far off base, I'm not sure I trust her advice.''

"That's unfair. Dr. Thompson's done the best she could with the information she had. If *you* didn't suspect what the problem was with Nia, how can you blame the therapist?''

"I guess I want someone to blame other than myself.''

"I don't see a reason to blame anyone. Be thankful you finally know what's been hurting her.''

"Which brings me back to the question of what I should do.''

"Ryan, I...all right. If I were Nia...I'd want to know that *you* know the truth and have always loved me anyway.''

"So, you're saying I should be honest with her.''

"I would, about that part. The rest, I'm not at all

sure what to tell you. She'll probably ask where her real father is and you need to be prepared to answer that. But should you tell her the truth now? If you do, could she be hurt at knowing *he* didn't want her? She might. But she might also be relieved to know he'll never come to take her away from you."

"What do you think?"

"The latter. That she'll be relieved. But I can't be certain of that."

"This is so damn confusing. I don't really know how to handle it."

"Just remember, whatever you do, that she won't always be six. Sooner or later she'll be old enough to ask questions and get information from sources other than you."

"Meaning if I lie to her now, she could find out twenty years from now and hate me for it."

"Possibly. I'm wondering if there's a way to be both honest with her about her biological father, yet give her the reassurance she needs. Try to reach her doctor before you talk to her."

"I will."

"Oh!" She sucked in a breath.

"What?"

"I have an idea. I think I know a way to help her accept that she's truly part of your family."

CHAPTER FOURTEEN

HAD ANYONE TOLD Ryan he'd be taking Nia back up the mountain two days later, he wouldn't have believed it.

"Here, Sa Sa. Ride on my back a while and rest your legs."

She put her arms around his neck and he picked her up.

"Why didn't Susannah come?" she asked as they continued to climb.

"Because what we're about to do is special. She felt we needed to be alone."

"I don't have to spend the night, do I?"

"No, don't worry. We'll only stay a few minutes. We'll be back in time to begin our celebration of the Winter Solstice."

"We'll light the big fire and the tree outside."

"Yes, and as dawn comes, we'll welcome the return of the sun. That's why we celebrate. Do you understand?"

"Mmm. It's Christmas?"

"Nearly. We honor the rhythms of the earth and

the sun because they make our seasons—winter when everything's cold and the animals rest; spring when the seeds begin to push their heads up through Nana's garden; summer when there's plenty of light and the animals are at play; and fall when the earth gets sleepy and the animals store their food."

"I like summer 'cause we get to eat Nana's tomatoes."

"Me, too," he said with a chuckle. "Do you know what season this is?"

"Winter."

"Right. And today is what we call *midwinter,* the shortest day of the year. Night will come early. Little by little, ever since summer, the days have been getting shorter. But after tonight the days will begin to get longer again."

"And that's good 'cause we can play outside."

"Absolutely. That's the best reason of all."

They reached the cave. Nia was a bit reluctant to go inside until he reminded her of what they were here to do.

He went first and helped her through the opening.

"I should've brought you here before," he said, lighting the torches so they could see.

Ryan had told his family the truth. And he'd told Nia. Her biological father, like her mother, hadn't been in a position to keep her, he'd explained, but Ryan had wanted her very much as *his* little girl.

His words had been enough for her—for now. Later, as she grew older and could understand adult relationships better, he'd answer whatever questions she asked.

He took the tin of paint and mixed some with water in the wooden bowl. He helped her dip her hand in the paint and press it against the wall next to his own.

"Spirits of my ancestors, see this little one and know she belongs to me and to our family. *Aquetsi.*" *My child.*

With the small brush he'd brought, they printed her Indian name under her handprint.

"I'm a Whitepath now, Daddy?"

"Yes, Sa Sa, you're a Whitepath."

SUSANNAH FELT the bedsprings dip and the warm body slide in next to her under the covers.

"Nap time's over," Ryan whispered in her ear, nipping at her earlobe. He reached under her T-shirt and rubbed her back, then slipped his hand down into her panties. "Time to get up."

"Leave me alone. I'm tired."

"You've slept half the day."

"Because you kept me up all night."

"I thought you liked our celebration."

"I loved it, but you wouldn't let me go to bed

until we greeted the sun. A girl's got to get her beauty rest."

"You're beautiful enough."

"Ha! What time is it?"

"One."

"Uh. Too early. Go away. Come back in a couple of hours."

"You can't lounge around in bed all day."

"I can try. Where's Nia?"

"At my mom's eating lunch with the family."

"Everyone's up already?"

"Everyone but you. They sent me to get you."

"Agh!"

She'd truly enjoyed last night's Solstice rituals, but she didn't operate well on five hours' sleep.

He reached around and stroked her breasts. "Not fair," she mumbled. His hand moved between her legs. Against her will they opened for him, letting him dip into her moisture. "Really, really not fair."

She rolled over onto her back and let him touch wherever he wanted with his hands and mouth, until she was so aroused she couldn't get him out of his clothes fast enough.

"Did they tell you to wake me up this way?" she asked breathlessly.

He slipped on a condom, hooked her legs around him and slid into her. "No, this was my own idea."

Moving together furiously, too impatient for finesse, they rocked the old bed until it sounded like a rocket ship about to blast into orbit.

"I need to oil this thing."

"You or the bed?" she joked.

"Hell, not me!"

She raked her nails along his back, exciting him more, as she knew it would. They were both nearly at the edge.

"This is better than an alarm clock anyday," she said.

"I'm glad you think so. I'll wake you up like this every morning from now on."

She stilled beneath him, but she was so close to her orgasm that it surged through her anyway, sending her arching off the bed. With a roar he climaxed a moment later.

She'd never felt so physically wonderful and so emotionally miserable at the same instant.

He collapsed on top of her. She was afraid to move, afraid to speak.

"What happened there at the end?" he asked when he'd recovered. "Why did you stop?"

"Let me up so I can go to the bathroom." She kept her head turned away, but he made her look at him.

"Is something wrong? Hey, are you crying?"

"Ryan, let me up, please."

"No, tell me what's wrong."

"Ryan, please let me up!"

He did.

She ran to the bathroom and stayed a long time. Hiding was more like it. Being a coward. While she was in the shower, she heard him come in and clean up at the sink, but he said nothing.

Wrapped in a towel, she finally emerged. Ryan sat on the couch with his back to her, already dressed. She quickly pulled on her clothes.

"You're still planning to leave the day after tomorrow, aren't you?" he said, without turning.

She couldn't speak. Her voice wouldn't come out of her throat. But she didn't need to give an answer. He already knew.

He got up and faced her, his expression stony. "I thought...I hoped you'd changed your mind."

"No, I haven't."

He grabbed his jacket and stalked toward the door.

"Ryan, wait! Don't be angry. We have to talk about this."

"Talk? Hell, Susannah! You already know how I feel about you. I've asked you to stay with me. What else do you want me to say? That I'm in love with you? I am. That I want to marry you and spend our lives together raising our daughter? I do. But if you don't love me, I can't force you to. Things are as simple as that."

As he went out, he slammed the door. Susannah sank down on her knees and wept.

RYAN AVOIDED HER the rest of the day. If she went to the workshop, he went to the house. If she went to the house, he found something to do in the workshop.

The tension between them was so obvious that even Nia noticed it.

"Are you and Daddy mad?" she asked.

Everyone in the room stopped talking and turned to look at her.

"No, honey, not really. He's a bit sad because I'm leaving. Remember I told you it's nearly time for me to go away? We talked about this. You promised me you'd be really brave."

"Nana Sipsey says you won't go. You're the redbird with the broken wing. The spirits sent you to help me."

Susannah cocked her head questioningly at Nana. The old woman nodded.

"You're wrong this time," she told her.

"Hmph," she said, her expression smug.

"You aren't really going away, are you, Susannah?" Nia asked.

"Yes, sweetheart, I am."

Nia's little face fell. She pulled off the ring Susannah had let her wear the night in the cave. "I better give this back. You might need the magic."

"No, I want you to keep it. My mother gave it to me with love. I gave it to you the same way."

"Will you ever come back?"

She wanted to say she would, but she refused to make a promise she couldn't keep.

"I hope so, Nia. But if I don't, you have my name on Cooper and my ring. And I saved my cast with your name on it. I'll never throw it away."

"Promise?"

"I promise."

LATER THAT EVENING she decided she couldn't bear staying here two more days. Dragging out her good-byes when it was painful for everyone was stupid. Better to make a quick, clean break and get a head start on her holiday plans than spend the next forty-eight hours in misery. She'd leave in the morning.

Willing herself not to cry, she pulled out her suitcase and began packing. This was the right thing to do, wasn't it? Her grief was still too new and her feelings too tender to make a permanent commitment, and remaining would only confuse Nia and prevent Ryan from finding someone else to share his life.

Someone else.

"Don't think about it," she warned herself. She couldn't afford tears right now, and focusing on who might come along to take her place in Ryan's heart would only produce them.

Wrapping her remaining Christmas gifts for the family, she loaded them in the truck and drove back to the house. For Nia she had a new jumper and blouse. For Nana a lovely hat for church.

She'd blown up some of the photographs she'd taken at Thanksgiving and had them matted. Annie was going to love the family portrait. Charlie had his own shot with Barbara and the kids. Anita's photo was a pose of her with her mother and grandmother.

Joe had been a problem. Borrowing Annie's sewing machine, she'd made him a quilted jacket, sleeveless like he preferred to wear. And Ryan. His gift had stumped her. Nothing she could imagine making him was good enough, so she'd cheated. She'd wrapped an eight-by-ten photograph of him and Nia that she'd taken, but also bought him an expensive set of grinding tools he'd admired in a catalog.

Joe came out and helped her get everything into the house and under the tree. Ryan had emerged from his workshop several hours ago, but then taken off in the truck.

"I'll be leaving in the morning," she announced. "I want to tell you all while I have the chance that I appreciate your hospitality. Thank you for letting me be a part of your family for these last two months.''

"Susannah, please don't," Annie appealed to her. "Wait until Christmas. You'll miss the dedication of Ryan's mosaic tomorrow night and you've worked so hard on that. And Christmas—you have to stay and open presents with us.''

"I think it's best if I go. I have a long way to drive over the next week and it'll be easier if I get an early start.''

"Does Ryan know?''

"No, I haven't spoken with him," she said, trying not to cry. "I'll be leaving very early, so I won't see you again." She kissed them all.

"You've become like my own daughter," Ryan's mother told her. "Remember you always have a home with us.''

"Thank you, Annie. That means a great deal to me.''

Annie suggested they open presents that night so Susannah could enjoy hers. Susannah said they shouldn't; she told them to go ahead with their normal plans.

"At least take the ones we made you," Annie said. "Save them for Christmas morning and think of us.''

"I will.'' Joe brought them down to the cabin for her.

A while later, while she was packing, Ryan knocked softly. "Susannah?"

Her face was tearstained, but she no longer cared. She opened the door and they stared at each other.

"Hi," he said.

"Hi. Um, would you like to come in?"

"No, I'd better not. I see you're packing."

"I was going to come over and talk to you, but I didn't know you were home yet."

"Mother called me on my cell phone and said you'd decided to leave in the morning."

"Yes, I think it's best for both of us if I do."

"You don't have to, Susannah. I know I've been a bastard today, but being near you..."

"That's okay, Ryan. Being near you has been hard for me, too."

"You don't have to go. Stay for the dedication. Don't you want to see the mural?"

"I'm sure it's beautiful. You're the most talented man I've ever met."

"Please stay."

"I can't. It would be too hard."

He nodded slowly. "I understand."

"How does Nia feel about my leaving?"

"She's upset, but don't worry. She'll be fine."

"I hope this won't cause a setback in her progress."

"No, the doctor says she has some distance to go

before she gets well, but she's made a strong start. The two of them have talked a couple of times by phone and Nia's finally willing to discuss her mother. This morning I noticed she'd taken her mother's photographs out and put them in her room.''

''That's good, Ryan. I'm happy for her and for you.''

''She wanted to be sure I brought these over.'' He handed her a shopping bag. ''Gifts from the two of us.''

''Thank you. I left yours at the house.'' She remembered something. ''Oh, just a minute.'' She ran inside and came back with a package of photographs. ''I'd be grateful if you'd give this to Helen and Bass for me. Tell them…tell them I wish them all the happiness in the world and that I hope the adoption comes through soon.''

''I will.''

''Strange, isn't it, this world we live in? Nia wanted to be Cherokee because she thought that was the only way she'd be accepted by her Cherokee father. And little Maggie will probably one day wish she was white so her white grandparents will accept *her*.''

''Not strange. Sad that we can't see past the color of each other's skin.'' He stared at her again for a minute in silence. "Well," he said finally. "I'd better go."

"Thank you, Ryan. For everything. For what you've taught me. For…being you." She began to cry and couldn't go on.

He leaned in and kissed her. They clung to each other for a moment. "Be happy, Susannah. I hope you find what you're looking for."

And then he turned and was gone.

THE DINER next to the motel was nearly deserted. A couple occupied the booth next to the front window and a truck driver was working on his third cup of black coffee at the counter two seats over.

The man and woman were headed north to Virginia to spend Christmas with their son, Susannah had heard them tell the waitress. The driver was hauling pipe the other way, south to Florida.

"Anything else?" the waitress asked her.

"No, thank you." She opened her wallet and handed her a ten.

"Ah, what a cute little girl. Yours?"

"No, a friend's."

"What's her name?"

"Sa Sa." She touched the photo and felt an overwhelming longing.

"Strange name for a kid."

"It's a nickname. In Cherokee it means goose or swan."

"She's a real doll."

"Yes, she is."

She gave Susannah her change. "Merry Christmas. Hope you have a good one with your family."

"Yes, I will. Same to you."

Back in her room, there was nothing on TV worth watching and she didn't have a book. The motel had a selection of movies, any of which you could rent and have delivered to the room, but nothing appealed to her.

Where, she wondered, was the enthusiasm she'd expected to feel?

She was on the road again and should be bursting with excitement at what lay ahead. Instead, her thoughts turned not to what was in front of her but what she'd left behind, a man and a child she'd come to love.

The clock by the bed said eight. The dedication would be over by now. The Whitepaths were probably gathered around the kitchen table eating supper.

Nana would be fussing about people not eating enough. Nia and her cousins would be getting anxious about Santa's visit in a few hours.

And Ryan. What would he be doing? Thinking of her the way she was thinking of him?

She went out to the truck and got the shopping

bag containing his and Nia's presents and the other gifts from the family. She'd be traveling tomorrow. The thought of waking up in a motel room on Christmas morning and opening presents by herself was pretty depressing. She'd have her own little Christmas party tonight and avoid the morning blues, thank you very much.

She laid everything on the bed and opened the packages one by one. Ryan's mother had woven a beautiful basket for her. Nana had embroidered a hand towel.

Anita had fashioned her earrings from beautiful shells. Joe had carved a deer out of wood.

Even Charlie, whom she'd hardly gotten to know, had made her something. He'd built and painted her a whimsical whirligig in the shape of a duck.

If she only had a yard, she'd have a place to put it.

She opened Nia's present next. The drawing was of a house with a mommy, daddy and little girl. "I love you," she'd printed across the top.

Susannah wiped her eyes.

Ryan had put two presents in the sack, a rectangular box and an envelope. "Open me first," a note on the box said.

Inside was a videotape. She put it into the VCR on the top of the TV and pushed the "play" button on the remote.

Opening credits began to roll. *Christmas on Snowbird Mountain,* they read. *Starring Susannah Pelton.*

She let out a squeal. How had he done this?

She watched the movie with delight. It was hilarious and included a commentary by someone whose voice she didn't recognize.

There she was singing while they worked on the mural. And they'd taken video of her performing in the recital!

All those times Joe and Ryan had pulled out the camera and she hadn't suspected this was what they were doing. The "movie" showed her climbing the mountain that day on the way to the hot springs. And, oh God, here she was with Nia, reading a bedtime story, playing Chutes and Ladders and making their decorations!

How precious this was. "Oh, Ryan."

She opened the envelope. Inside was a note in his handwriting that said:

Susannah,

I hope you enjoyed being the star of your own movie. You can mark that one off your list. I didn't know how to go about getting you on a cruise down the Amazon, but if you'll call the number below, a round-trip airline ticket has been reserved in your name to use whenever you want. I understand Paris is beautiful in April.

Love forever,
Ryan

CHAPTER FIFTEEN

RYAN TRIED to stay upbeat and not put a damper on everyone's Christmas morning, but it was tough when he was hurting so much inside.

The children, at least, were having fun. They squealed as they played with their toys and ran through the house. Wrapping paper lay discarded everywhere.

He'd given Nia the stroller she wanted and the doll she'd been begging for that went with it, the baby that wet and cried. Now, he could see, he'd live to regret it. She'd forced him to bottle feed and diaper the thing ten times already.

"The baby's hungry, Daddy," she said again.

"The baby's going to get sick if you keep making me feed it."

"Uh-uh, she tee tees it out."

"So I noticed." The diapers weren't completely waterproof. He had a big wet spot on his shirt.

She pushed its stomach and it cried again to be fed.

Nana Sipsey, sitting next to him on the couch,

patted his leg and told him she'd take over nursery duty. He might want to go out on the porch and get some air.

"Thanks. I could use it."

He handed over all the doll paraphernalia. Grabbing his jacket, he went out and sat on the top step. A few minutes later, Joe joined him.

"Too much noise for me," his brother told him. "I don't see how Charlie and Barb stand it. That little one is a real terror. How come if he can't talk he can scream so loud?"

"Wait until you have four of five of your own running around. You'll think their voices are music."

"No way. Kids are too loud and too sticky."

"They don't always smell good, either, but I promise it won't matter when you get ready to settle down."

"I'll never be ready for that. Give me wine, women and more women."

"You're hopeless. You know that?"

"Yeah, but having a hell of a good time."

They both looked off down the drive at the sound of a vehicle. Ryan stood as a familiar gray truck came closer. He wanted to fly from the porch and meet it, but pride wouldn't let him.

"Well, I'll be," Joe said, getting up. "Look who decided to come back. Wonder why?" He grinned and slapped Ryan on the back. "I think I'll go in and let you two have a private reunion."

So many cars and trucks were in the yard, she had to park down the driveway a bit. She got out, walked to the house and stopped at the bottom of the steps.

His heart felt like a lead weight inside his chest. What was she doing here? He was afraid to be happy, afraid she'd simply forgotten something or wanted to tell him off in person for his plane ticket gift.

"I thought you'd be halfway to New York City by now," he said.

"So did I."

"Why aren't you?"

"Because I finally realized what an idiot I am. I've been searching for something that's been in front of me all this time."

He didn't dare breathe. "And what's that?"

"Real life."

"Real life isn't very exciting."

"Isn't it? Oh, I don't know." She walked up the steps and faced him. "I can't think of anything that will give me more of an adrenaline rush than playing the tooth fairy, taking my little girl to ballet lessons or winding down at the end of the day by talking to the man I love."

"Susannah, be sure."

"I am sure. I love you, Ryan. I love Nia. I love

your mother and Nana and Joe. I'm certain I'll come to love Anita and Charlie when I know them better.''

''And what happens in three months or six months when you get the itch to go ramble or jump off a bridge?''

''Why would I want to go anywhere when the best place on earth is this mountain? I've created something beautiful, had sex with a handsome stranger and starred in my very own movie. That should be enough to satisfy any person for a lifetime. Oh, and I've danced in a ballet. You had something to do with that last one, too, didn't you?''

''I might have.''

''I suspected it when I watched the movie, which I loved by the way. The movie was on my list and so was the ballet. I figured if you had a hand in the first, you probably did with the second.''

''I got Joe to ask Sandy to find you a part in the recital. I wanted you to be happy. And if dancing and being in a movie got you a step closer to that goal, then I felt I had to try and give them to you.''

''You were wrong. I was wrong, too. I don't need anything to be happy but you…and Nia.''

''What about Paris?''

''When I held your note in my hand and realized I could fulfill that dream, I didn't want it. I really don't care about the Eiffel Tower. I have Snowbird.

Eating French onion soup in a sidewalk café can't compare to cheese and bread on a rock that looks like a sitting dog.''

He reached out and touched her face. "I love you so much. When you left, I died inside a little bit.''

"I'm sorry I hurt you. I believed I was past my grief, but I wasn't. I ran from what we have because it hurt to care for someone and to have someone care for me. But I'll never run again. I promise you.'' She stepped closer and put her arms around his waist. "Will you forgive me for being such a fool?''

"Every day for the rest of my life.''

He kissed her and a cheer went up from inside the house. They laughed at the faces in the windows, everyone pressed to the glass watching them.

"We have an audience,'' he said. "And I warn you, they can be a rowdy bunch.''

"Then let's really give them something to hoot about.''

"My pleasure.''

"NANA WAS RIGHT!'' Nia shouted, throwing herself into Susannah's arms. "You're here! You're here.''

Susannah laughed and twirled her around. "I missed you, too.''

"Nana said if I wrote what I wanted on my leaf for the tree, it would come true. See?''

She took her by the hand and pulled her over to the little wishing tree. Susannah looked at the leaf with Nia's name on the front. Someone had helped her print her wish in Cherokee. "What does it say?"

"That I wish you'd come and live with me and Daddy."

She glanced up at Ryan and he winked. "Sounds like a great idea to me," he told his daughter. "But maybe we should marry her first."

"Really? We're gonna get married? All three of us?"

"All three of us," Susannah assured her. "I can't walk down the aisle without you."

"Yippee!" Nia started jumping up and down. "We're getting married!" she told her grandmother.

Susannah was hugged and kissed and crushed all over again by every person in the room.

"Can you handle all this attention?" Ryan asked. "This family tends to be a bit demonstrative."

"Are you kidding? I love it! I never thought I'd ever be part of a family again."

"Come with me." He pulled her away and out the front door. "I want you all to myself."

"Do you still have the key to the center? Take me there and show me your mosaic."

"Right now? I had something else in mind."

"Please?"

"Whatever you want."

He drove them over and unlocked the front door. When they got to the extension, he told her to close her eyes. She heard him flip on the lights. He guided her inside and around the tables and chairs that had been set up for last night's dedication of the room and the mural.

"Okay, ready? Open your eyes."

She stood and stared, taking it all in. She'd seen most of it, of course, but the effect of the whole piece was glorious. And the vignette of the White-paths on the last panel...

"Oh, Ryan!"

He had them around the kitchen table in a scene that was so familiar. Nana sat peeling potatoes into a pan. His mother and siblings had gathered around like they often did when they helped prepare a meal.

The scene represented home and family.

And she was there with them, standing next to Ryan. They both had their hands on Nia's shoulders. He'd even managed to work in her snowbirds by showing part of the outdoors through the kitchen window.

She walked over and touched the tiles, the faces of her soon-to-be family. The nearby plaque said the mosaic had been designed and created by Ryan Whitepath...with help from Susannah Pelton.

"It's wonderful. But you shouldn't have given me any credit."

"I couldn't have done it without you. We created something beautiful, and like you said, people will appreciate it for years to come."

"But why did you include me with your family? You couldn't have known I'd come back."

"You were part of us from the very beginning, even if you didn't realize it. Our own little redbird with a broken wing who came to our mountain one day and changed all our lives."

"Nana Sipsey and her vision."

"She told you?"

"Nia did. But I didn't understand all of it."

"Nana said you'd heal Nia of her grief and pain. And that you'd heal yourself…"

"She was right. I do feel as if I've finally put the past behind me. I loved my mother, and I miss her more than I can ever express, but it's time to move beyond her illness and what it did to both our lives. She wouldn't want me to continue to suffer."

"No, she wouldn't."

"And Andrew…God! He *was* a jerk. I can't imagine why I've been stupid enough to grieve over what he did. I'm glad he left me. Otherwise, I never would've met you. I finally understood last night, how lucky I am to get a second chance at happiness. I wondered what on earth I was doing, sitting alone in a motel room on Christmas Eve when I could be with the man and the child I love. Nothing can compare with Christmas on this mountain.''

''Not even April in Paris?''

''Especially not that.''

''I'll take you to Paris on our honeymoon, if you want.''

''No, my traveling days are over. The last two months have been some of the best of my life. Now I'd rather stay on Snowbird with you and Nia and spend every Christmas as we've done this year.''

''That suits me just fine.''

''We should get back. Your family won't eat without us, and I don't want to spoil their dinner.''

''*Our* family,'' he corrected her.

She smiled with joy. ''Yes, our family. They're probably waiting for us.''

They locked the center and drove home. As they got out, she could hear laughter from inside Annie's. She halted at the bottom of the steps.

''Something wrong?'' Ryan asked.

''No, something's very right. I'm imagining all the wonderful Christmases we'll have together. Nia helping me decorate the barn. The family gathered at the table for dinner. Yesterday, I was desolate. Today, I have so much to look forward to.''

''We both do.''

''Nana Sipsey predicted I'd find a place for myself here. I think she always knew we'd end up together. Do you believe she really does have second sight?''

''I never did until now.''

''I wonder if all her prophesies come true.''

''My mother says so.''

Susannah thought about another of Nana's visions—Nia surrounded by many brothers and sisters, two with identical faces.

''Do twins run in your family?''

''Yeah, my mother's a twin. Aunt Eileen lives in Texas.''

''How do you feel about having more children? Lots and lots of children?''

His eyebrows lifted. ''Fine...I guess.''

She slipped her arm in his and smiled. ''Maybe you should start getting used to the idea.''

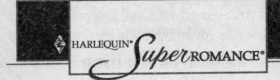

If you enjoyed what you just read,
then we've got an offer you can't resist!

Take 2 bestselling love stories FREE!

Plus get a FREE surprise gift!

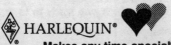

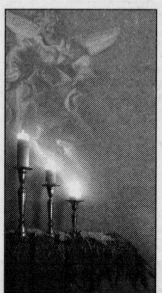

Free book offer!

During the month of November, send us 4 proofs of purchase from any 4 Harlequin Supperromance® books and receive TWO FREE BOOKS by bestselling authors Tara Taylor Quinn and Judith Arnold!

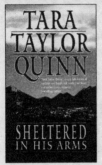 

All you have to do is send 4 proofs of purchase to:

In the U.S.:	In Canada:
Harlequin Books	Harlequin Books
P.O. Box 9057	P.O. Box 622
Buffalo, NY	Fort Erie, Ontario
14269-9057	L2A 5X3

Name (PLEASE PRINT)

Address   Apt. #

City   State/Prov.   Zip/Postal Code

098 KJO DNDR

To receive your 2 FREE books (retail value for the two books is $11.98 U.S./$13.98 CAN.), complete the above form. Mail it to us with 4 proofs of purchase (found in all November 2002 Harlequin Supperromance® books), one of which can be found in the right-hand corner of this page. Requests must be postmarked no later than December 30, 2002. Please enclose $2.00 (checks made payable to Harlequin Books) for shipping and handling and allow 4-6 weeks for receipt of order. New York State residents must add applicable sales tax on shipping and handling charge, and Canadian residents please add 7% G.S.T. Offer valid in Canada and the U.S. only, while quantities last. Offer limited to one per household.

© 2002 Harlequin Enterprises Limited

Visit us at www.eHarlequin.com

HSRPOPN03

HARLEQUIN® *Super*ROMANCE®

presents a compelling family drama—
an exciting new trilogy
by popular author Debra Salonen

THOSE SULLIVAN SISTERS

Jenny, Andrea and Kristin Sullivan are much more
than sisters—*they're triplets!* Growing up as one of
a threesome meant life was never lonely...or dull.

Now they're adults—with separate lives, loves,
dreams and secrets. But underneath everything that
keeps them apart is the bond that holds them together.

MY HUSBAND, MY BABIES
(Jenny's story)
available December 2002

WITHOUT A PAST
(Andi's story)
available January 2003

THE COMEBACK GIRL
(Kristin's story)
available February 2003

HARLEQUIN®

Makes any time special ®